Th

Producer & International Distributor
eBookPro Publishing
www.ebook-pro.com

THE WAR TWINS OF LONDON
Deb Stratas

Website: debstratas.com

ISBN 9798865215875

The War Twins *of* London

A WWII Historical Fiction Novel

Deb Stratas

The War Twins of London is dedicated
to my Aunt **Shirley**, who passed away in 2021.
She was a second mother to me
after my own mum died many years ago.
You were always so supportive and loving.
I miss you.

Glossary

- **Ack-ack guns** – British World War II jargon for anti-aircraft guns.
- **AFS** – Auxiliary Fire Service.
- **Aga** – a range cooker or stove unit.
- **Anderson shelter** – a temporary air raid shelter erected outside UK households during World War II.
- **Angel on horseback** – a canapé made with oysters wrapped in bacon.
- **ARP** – Air Raid Precautions, organizations dedicated to protecting civilians from air raids.
- **Barrage balloon** – a large, tethered balloon used to defend ground targets against aircraft attacks.
- **Biscuit** – unlike an American biscuit, a British biscuit is a hard or crisp cookie.
- **Buck House** – Buckingham Palace (shortened).
- **Cardie** – cardigan (shortened).
- **Chit** – memo.
- **Chuffed** – pleased or proud.
- **Chum** – friend.
- **Clotted cream** – a thick, heavy cream usually served on cakes and desserts such as English scones.
- **Cuppa** – a cup of tea (shortened).
- **Fire watching** – patrolling roofs and buildings to watch for incendiary bombs or outbreaks of fires.
- **Firemen** – firefighters.
- **Gobsmacked** – utterly astounded.
- **Golly** – an exclamation used to express surprise.
- **HE** – high-order explosive.
- **Jerry** – an Allied nickname given to Germans and Germany.
- **Kip** – sleep or rest.
- **LAAS** – London Auxiliary Ambulance Service.
- **Lippy** – lipstick (shortened).
- **Lorry** – truck.
- **NAAFI** – Navy, Army, and Air Force Institutes.
- **Natter** – chat, talk conversationally.
- **Nippy** – a waitress who worked for the J. Lyons & Co tea shops and cafés in London.
- **Post** – mail.
- **Pudding** – refers to any kind of dessert.
- **Queue** – line.
- **RAF** – Royal Air Force, the British air force.
- **The Great War** – WWI.

CHAPTER ONE

"Come on, Tillie. We're going to be late," Maggie called up the staircase. Silence. "We were meant to leave at ten past." Impatience crept into her voice.

Heels clattered down the stairs.

"Keep your hair on. We won't be late. Sorry, ducks. My stocking laddered, so I had to open a new pair." Tillie gave her sister an apologetic hug as she pulled on her raincoat. "Is it still wet outside?"

"Yes, it's teeming at the moment. I've got the umbrellas. Let's get on, Tillie!" Maggie pulled her sister towards the front door as she adjusted her hat. "Ta ra, Mum. We'll be home for tea after our shift."

"Wait, girls," their mother called as she emerged from the long hallway. She was a middle-aged woman with brown hair and a ready smile. As she hugged both girls, she pressed small waxed-paper-wrapped packages into their hands.

"Just a couple of cheese and pickle sandwiches for your dinner break," she smiled at them.

"Mum, you know we can have whatever we fancy at Lyons when we're on shift," Tillie protested as she hugged her mother back.

"But thanks all the same. I'm sure they are tasty. Tillie, let's go! Alfie will have our guts for garters if we're late. And the tube will be packed with the rain."

Two blond-haired, brown-eyed young women dashed out the door, linking arms and laughing.

Alice Kingston shut the door thoughtfully as silence filled the townhouse. What did the future hold for her oldest girls if war came? What would happen to their youth? Their hopes and dreams? At forty-four, Alice remembered all too well the depravations and horrors of the Great War, and felt sick to her stomach to think her family might face this again. She longed to rush out the door and gather her girls close to her, to protect them from what was to come. But events were in play, and she could only hope with all her heart that Hitler would honor the Munich Agreement, and peace would prevail.

It was May 1939 and war talk pervaded every household, every conversation, and indeed, almost every mind across Britain. Most carried on as usual but underneath the hustle and bustle of daily life, an undercurrent of fear and anxiety underlined bright and cheerful outward appearances.

"Mum, the toast is burning," called Kenny from the downstairs kitchen. Alice sighed and rushed down the stairs towards her son.

* * *

"Whew, what a crush," exclaimed Tillie as the sisters found a seat on the tube. Umbrellas down, they shook out their wet hair. The underground was buzzing with Londoners on their way to work.

"Too right. So, what is this meeting about then?" Maggie gazed at her sister, creasing her brow.

The girls were the objects of strangers' stares, but they were oblivious to them, or, more precisely, they were used to it.

Mathilda and Margaret Kingston were identical twins. And beautiful. Honey-blond hair curled loosely on their shoulders, and their large chocolate-brown eyes startled most people with their wide expressions. Their skin was a tone darker than the pale English rose complexion, but suited their overall coloring, and their lips were currently sporting pale pink lipstick.

Tillie and Maggie had inherited their height from their father, and were slim and lithe, at almost five and a half feet tall.

The twins turned heads wherever they went, with strangers literally doing double takes as the identical beauties strolled by.

They both hated this unwanted attention, and did their best to ignore it. To them, being twins was normal and they didn't think their looks were anything special.

"Do you reckon there are new girls coming in?" Asked Tillie.

"I don't imagine Alfie would call a special meeting for that, would he?" Maggie countered. "Perhaps they are switching us around again to different stations?"

"Maybe." Tillie shrugged. "Or important guests are coming for a special event?"

"I suppose there is only one way to find out. Let's not be late, at least."

The girls chattered as they sat in the muggy compartment and hurried out at the Piccadilly Circus station, moving with the throng along Coventry Street. Thankfully the rain had stopped.

They halted in front of Lyons Corner House, which occupied five floors on the corner of Coventry and Rupert Streets. It was an imposing corner building, white brick facade, decorated pillars and center dome.

Noticing none of this, the twins hurried in, through a side door and up the back stairs to the dressing room, right into the hectic pace that would continue throughout the day.

"Hello, Lila. Dorothy, how was your date with Nigel?" Tillie called out to the girls. The room was bustling with young women in various states of undress. Tillie quickly stripped out of her street clothes and put on her work uniform, with Maggie doing the same.

The famous Nippy uniform included a black bombazine frock with what seemed like a hundred tiny white buttons with red thread up the front, and a smart white collar and matching cuffs. It was topped with a white apron, and set off with a distinctive white cap trimmed with black ribbon. They completed the outfit with black stockings and polished black shoes with a medium heel, easier for the constant running they had to do all day long.

"It were awright," answered Dorothy with a grimace. "Nigel were all 'ands in the cinema. I like 'im, but bloody hell, it's a sport trying to keep 'im off 'o me."

Laughter erupted in the dressing room as calls of 'too right' and 'poor you' surrounded Dot.

Lila put the finishing touches on her cap to secure it to her hair, making sure the embroidered "L" was properly centered, as she turned to the twins.

"I wonder what Alfie has to tell us? I hope I'm not in trouble." Lila was a trifle shorter and rounder than the twins, with rosy cheeks and a beaming smile.

The clock struck nine, and the Nippies quickly finished dressing, and rushed into the huge restaurant, which was still empty of customers.

The vast room was opulent and glamorous with high ceilings, extravagant chandeliers, velvet curtains, and beautiful paintings on the walls. It was filled with rows of tables, which would soon be filled with hungry Londoners wanting their elevenses or dinner. The band warmed up on the corner stage, getting ready to serenade the customers and give them the Lyons Corner House experience they expected.

The J. Lyons and Company was set up in 1894 as a partnership between an artist, Joseph Lyons, and his two brothers-in-law. They opened a teashop in Piccadilly, London, which expanded into a chain. The Lyons Corner Houses were London fixtures, with their large corner storefronts, huge restaurants and the friendly Nippies who served thousands of reasonably priced meals a day. Some locations even offered hairdressing and the company launched a range of teas, biscuits and cakes that were sold in grocery stores around the world.

Tillie and Maggie had fallen in love with the warm and welcoming environment, and begged their father to let them apply as Nippies. At first, Walter Kington was dismayed and rather disappointed that his older girls weren't keen on the office jobs he had provided for them in his accounting business. He thought the job was a bit common for their sheltered upbringing. But once they turned twenty-one, he couldn't hold them back. They had both applied to and been accepted at the Corner House. This happened just over a year ago and the twins were thriving in their chosen job.

Passing their daily inspection, the group of thirty Nippies chatted, awaiting Alfie, the restaurant manager.

They didn't have to wait long. Alfie's booming voice and large presence filled the room almost before he strode in.

"Never mind cats and dogs. It's raining chickens and ducks this morning. Fowl weather." He beamed, and the Nippies laughed in response. They were well used to Alfie's puns and jokes.

At six feet two, Alfie Williamson was an imposing figure. In his mid-fifties, with a full head of greying hair and a stocky physique, he towered over most of the staff. His large frame could have been intimidating and he commanded respect, yet his bluff demeanor hid a genuine care and concern for his Nippies. He protected them as fiercely as he did his own daughters.

"Well, then," he boomed. "I expect you are all wondering about this morning's announcement. Let's get right to it. Their Majesties, the King and Queen, are hosting a royal garden party at Buckingham Palace in two weeks. They have asked the J. Lyons Company to set up an afternoon tea for thousands of guests on the back lawn. Who better to serve royal guests than our own Nippies?" He looked at each girl, proud of the honor bestowed on Lyons. This was an annual event, but you never knew if the Nippies were up to standard and would be asked back next year.

A collective gasp burst from the group. A royal garden party! Serving the guests of King George VI and Queen Elizabeth! How glamourous!

"Of course, all of you can't be spared, but we are providing quite a number of Nippies, here from this restaurant, as well as from the other floors. You'll be expected to arrive at noon on May 23, looking smart, where you will receive your orders. You'll be serving a full tea in the large white tents on the lawn – one for the guests of their Majesties, one for military attendees, and of course, the royal tent. Service will end at four o'clock when the guests depart." He took a deep breath.

"All of you are worthy of this honor, but we've selected the Nippies who most embody our motto 'Happy to Help You' here at Corner House."

Maggie and Tillie gave each other a thumb up, smiling hopefully. What an honor it would be to serve at such an important event. Tillie crossed her fingers behind her back and Maggie held her breath. Would they be chosen?

Alfie began reading from a list.

"Mavis Bolton, Gertrude Cork, Lila Foster, Betty Gains, June Harper, Iris Jones." He cleared his throat. "Margaret Kingston, Mathilda Kingston, Ann Morris..."

Tillie and Maggie stopped listening. They'd been selected! The twins clutched each other's hands as Alfie read off the remaining names.

"And that's the lot. I know you'll do J. Lyons and Company right. Right, then." He clapped his hands. "Stations please. The doors are about to open."

Maggie and Tillie weren't allowed to chat until their break. Once the doors opened and the patrons spilled in, they were run off their feet as always.

"Good morning," Maggie greeted a young family at one of her tables. Clearly awed by their surroundings, the husband and wife tried not to gape as their two little girls sat quietly. "Has the rain stopped? You don't look too soaked," She told them as she handed out menus. "I'm sure a cuppa wouldn't go amiss." She stood holding her notebook and pencil, a warm smile on her face.

"My, what a busy place," exclaimed the young mother. "Tea would be lovely and milk for the girls. Perhaps a cake?" She looked tentatively at her husband.

"This is our first time at a Corner House," he explained, as he scanned the menu, worriedly noting the prices.

"We'll take right good care of you, Sir. Perhaps a selection of cakes to share? That will be 1s 2d. Reasonable, and I'm sure a fairy cake would go down a treat." She winked at the two girls.

"Splendid," responded the man, as he handed back the menu with obvious relief. "We can just about manage that. Thank you."

"My pleasure, Sir, Madam. I'll be back in a jiffy with your order."

Maggie returned in what seemed like moments, carrying the order on her tray and skillfully placed their order on the table.

On the other side of the restaurant, Tillie was equally busy serving five tables in her block including an elderly couple who couldn't decide what to order. They eventually settled on two poached eggs on toast, tea, and assorted cakes for dessert. Tillie served them efficiently, pocketed the small but kindly offered tip, and met up with Maggie for their own break.

"Golly, what a busy dinner hour," sighed Maggie, as she slipped gratefully into a chair in the staff canteen. "You'd think the rain would have kept them away."

"Nothing keeps them away," chirped Tillie, as she bit into Mum's cheese and pickle sarnie. "Just as well, ducks. It keeps us busy."

Maggie nodded and took a large gulp of tea. "Not as busy as a royal garden party though, Tillie! Can you believe we were both chosen? How lucky we are."

"Shhh. Let's not gloat in front of the others," Tillie motioned to another table of Nippies, looking slightly morose. "But it is wonderful. Imagine, us meeting the King and Queen!"

"Oh, I hope so," replied her sister. "Do you think we might serve in the royal tent?" Maggie's brown eyes glistened with excitement.

Tillie shrugged. "It doesn't matter to me. Just seeing Buckingham Palace and the royal family on the terrace is enough for me. I wonder if the princesses will be there."

"I expect not," Maggie argued. "Princess Elizabeth has not yet had her thirteenth birthday and Princess Margaret is just eight years old."

"I suppose you are right but it will be brilliant, no matter what. I can't wait to tell Mum. She'll be that pleased to hear it."

Maggie giggled. "I'm sure she'll remind us again of the King and Queen's coronation. What a spectacle that was!"

"Too right, sis. Well, let's get back to it before Alfie comes looking for us." The twins cheerfully tidied up the remains of their meal and sped back to the floor to finish their shifts.

The rain was pouring as they left the Corner House a few hours later, but it didn't dampen the spirits of the Kingston twins. They were buzzing with talk of the upcoming royal garden party.

"It's too bad we can't dress up like everyone else," sighed Tillie. "But let's ensure our uniforms are perfect."

"Maybe a hair trim? And a manicure," suggested Maggie as they jostled for a seat on the tube.

"Just so, and let's use our nail trick to avoid confusion on the day."

As identical twins, it was almost impossible to tell the girls apart. Maggie was a bit taller, but it was almost imperceptible. She had a small smattering of cute sandy-colored freckles across her nose, which she usually powdered to cover them up. Tillie was the more outgoing of the two, but aside from that, most people couldn't tell them apart. At work, Tillie always wore red nail polish, and Maggie pink, so at a glance, the other Nippies and managers could tell them apart by their hands.

Maggie nodded. "That will help. Now, let's tell Mum and Katie about the garden party. Katie will be green with envy."

The girls sprinted from the station to their Longridge Road townhouse, ignoring the rain.

CHAPTER TWO

"Mum, we're home. And we have news." Maggie and Tillie skipped up the front stairs of the elegant townhouse and pushed open the door.

"I'm in the morning room, girls. Come through," called a cheery voice from the back of the house.

The girls took off their coats and hats, and hung them on the coat rack in the spacious front hall. They propped their umbrellas against it, half-open to dry out.

Mum was knitting in the sunny morning room, past the dining room and just a few steps down the hallway. The spacious room was decorated with heavy Victorian furniture, lamps, and drapes. She loved knick knacks, and every surface was covered with ceramic animal figurines, wooden boxes, and glass candy dishes.

The five-story townhouse had been home since the twins were little. It was narrow but roomy. The warm kitchen, pantry, and exit to the back garden could be found in the basement. At the front on the street level was the dining room and a sunny morning room down the hall. On the first floor were the large drawing room and the library. Upstairs were the master bedroom, the twins' room, and the family bathroom. Up the last set of stairs, Kenny and Katie's rooms were located, along with a couple of rooms currently used for storage. Everyone had their space, with ample room for family time at Number 40 Longridge Road.

The girls excitedly kissed their Mum on the cheek and sat down on the sofa, their words spilling on top of each other.

"We were chosen by Alfie..."

"Buckingham Palace..."

"Meet the King and Queen, I hope..."

"We are so lucky..."

"Whoa," laughed Alice. "One at a time, please. Tillie, you start," she said putting down her knitting.

"Right, then. We were selected to serve at a royal garden party hosted by Their Majesties. Several Nippies will serve a full tea in tents on the back lawn." Tillie's cheeks were rosy and her eyes sparkled.

"There will be three tents and thousands of guests. Perhaps we'll be serving Their Majesties, the King and Queen in the royal tent," sighed Maggie.

"How splendid, girls! They must think highly of your work to be chosen for such an important event." She clapped her hands. "I think we should celebrate. Sherry anyone?"

"Yes, please, Mum. Shall I pour?" Asked Maggie, rising up from the sofa.

"I'm having none of that," admonished Alice with a smile. "You two have been on your feet all day. I'll serve."

"Ta, Mum," smiled Tillie. "Just a small one for me. Colin is taking me to the cinema later so I want to be fresh for him." Tillie was not a big drinker and felt sleepy after just one glass of wine.

Alice nodded and poured three small Sherries.

"Cheers, girls, and congratulations," she lifted her small glass. "I'm proper proud of you. And your father will be so pleased. I wonder if you will meet the King and Queen. Do you remember the coronation? What a wonderful day that was." She took a sip of sherry and sat back in her comfortable chair.

The twins smiled at each other as they each took a sip.

"Yes, Mum," they replied in unison. "It was a marvelous day," added Tillie.

At five feet four inches, Alice Kingston was an older, slightly plumper version of her daughters. Her brown hair was pulled back in a small bun. Her big brown eyes mirrored Tillie and Maggie's, and she had passed on her freckles to Maggie. She wasn't as striking as her daughters, but she smiled easily and doted on her family.

"Seeing the new King and Queen on the Buckingham Palace balcony

– the jewels and crowns sparkled all the way down on us like diamonds," sighed Alice. "The crowns were so loaded with jewels and the ermine! Not only on the crowns themselves but the King's mantle. I suppose all those beautiful pieces will be locked away again for many years now."

"For me, it was the gowns," put in Maggie. "The little princesses were so adorable with their pretty dresses and miniature crowns. And the Queen. She looked so regal with her Norman Hartnell white satin gown. With gold and silver embroidery, even. She almost looked like a bride. And she was smiling so much. You'd never know they are reluctant monarchs," she added ruefully.

"All courtesy of that ninny of a brother of his," snorted Alice. Like many Britons, she had nothing but disdain for the disgraced, ex-King Edward VIII, who had abdicated his throne for a twice-divorced American woman—Wallis Simpson. "He's made his bed, now he can lie in it – with *that woman*."

"That was shameful, Mum," agreed Tillie, shaking her head. "I think the Duke of Windsor was beyond shocked that none of the royal family attended his makeshift wedding in France. But he surely couldn't expect to have his new wife greeted with open arms, could he? I can't imagine how distraught his poor mother was – Queen Mary is the epitome of English duty and honor."

"Well, it will all go to pot, mark my words," Alice replied ominously.

"In the event, the new King and Queen are ideally suited for their roles. And perhaps we'll see them at the garden party. Although without their crowns I expect," Tillie brought them back to the present.

"You're right, love. Let's not dwell on that bounder. The Kingston twins take on Buckingham Palace," she held up her glass and took another sip.

"What about Buck House?" chirped Katie Kingston as she entered the morning room. "Hello, Mum, girls," she nodded to her sisters as she kissed her mother on the cheek.

Katie Kingston was the twins' younger sister. At eighteen, she resembled Tillie and Maggie but without their glamorous looks. She lacked their height, being short like their mother with the same brown wavy hair also falling to her shoulders. She had inherited more of the

Kingston freckles than Maggie had as well as having a perky personality that matched her cute appearance.

"The girls have been selected to serve at a royal garden party. Isn't that marvelous?"

Katie squealed, "How brilliant. When?" She perched on the edge of Alice's wingback.

"In about two weeks' time," Maggie piped in. "Lyons is providing Nippies for the tea in the tents. We were chosen from a group from our Corner House. We're both right chuffed," she smiled.

"I'm jealous, I won't lie," Katie grimaced. "Maybe I should quit at Pop's too and join you at Lyons."

"You're welcome anytime! We've got Pops all warmed up. It should be easier to convince him now – we've got royal connections, don't you know?" Tillie pulled off Katie's hat and pretended it was a crown.

Alice briefly shut her eyes, knowing her husband cherished the notion of his children working at Kingston and Knight and even taking it over someday. At least Kenny was still there, she breathed a sigh of relief.

Katie shrugged. "Just joking, girls. I don't fancy being run off my feet all day serving all those ungrateful customers. But do try to nick me a slice of royal cake, will you?" She grinned at her sisters.

"We'll see what we can do, right Mags?" Tillie nudged her sister.

"Speaking of food, any chance of tea tonight?" asked Katie. "Or at least a cuppa?"

"I'll put the kettle on," replied Alice as she jumped to her feet. "And Faye left us lamb chops with mint sauce, mashed potatoes and runner beans."

"Sounds grand, Mum. Let's get out of these wet things, and we'll give you a hand in the kitchen," Tillie offered.

"Ta, love," smiled Alice.

* * *

"I think we should mentally prepare ourselves for the inevitable." Walter said seriously at the dinner table. "I believe war is coming. And sooner than we may think."

"Oh no, dear. I just don't believe it. After the last time...we never imagined we could be facing this again," Alice burst out.

Looking around the table, Alice feared the worst for her family. Walter sat at the head, a tall man with greying blond hair and blue eyes. On one side of the long mahogany table, Maggie and Tillie both paused with their forks to their mouths. On the other side, Katie quietly wiped her mouth with her cloth napkin, while her brother Kenny looked up eagerly at his father. Thankfully he was only sixteen so would not be called up. But what of the girls? Could they be called up for some kind of war work? Her heart sank.

"Do you really think so, Pops? I noticed the zigzag trenches being built in the parks. Will people really shelter there in case of bombing?" Kenny spoke loudly, in deference to his father being deaf in one ear, a remnant of his World War I service and injury.

Alice held her breath.

"I'm afraid so, son. We are expecting this war to be fought in the air. And London will be a major target." He glanced at his wife who had turned white. "I'm sorry, Alice."

"We've seen the sandbags piling up all around London," added Tillie seriously. "And Lila mentioned we might have to be fitted for gas masks. Is that true, Pops?" She turned her brown eyes to her father.

He nodded his head slowly. "Yes, it's true. We will all have to be measured for them. I've been talking to Thomas about obtaining Anderson shelters for the back gardens." He paused for a moment as five pairs of eyes were riveted to him. "I think evacuation is inevitable. Tens of thousands of schoolchildren, if not more, will be sent to the country for their safety."

Kenny whistled. "Wow, Pops. That sounds serious."

"Will we send Kenny to your brother in Wiltshire?" Alice asked tentatively. She couldn't bear to part from her son but his safety was paramount.

"I'm not a child," protested Kenny with a scowl. He was the male version of his older sisters with a shock of wheat-colored, blond hair and large brown eyes. He was growing taller by the day although still hadn't filled out his five-foot, ten-inch frame. "I'm ready to serve my country, as a man – not be shipped off to my uncle's farm like a baby."

"I agree you are too old for evacuation – for now, Kenneth." He held up his hand. "But neither are you old enough for active service, chap. There will be plenty of jobs for those left behind like you and I." As an accountant, Walter was in a reserved occupation.

Kenny slumped in his seat trying to hide his disappointment. At least I won't be sent off like a child, he thought sulkily.

"Anderson shelters?" Alice tilted her head to one side. "Shirley never mentioned that to me."

Shirley Fowler was Alice's sister. She and Thomas lived just two streets away. Thomas was a civil servant with a position so senior that no one even knew his title. He was obviously in the know about the war efforts underway – seen and unseen by the British public.

"Yes, dear. We've put in our orders. We'll each get a metal structure to place in our back gardens. Apparently, they need to be dug into the ground for further protection. And covered with dirt. The government is urging us to plant vegetables on the roof, as food will become scarce once the Germans attack our ships. Thomas assures me the shelters will withstand air attacks. I won't sugarcoat this for you all. This is a very grave situation." He pushed back from the table. Supper ended. "How is everyone feeling about this? Let's start with you, Tillie."

This was a family ritual. Pops always wanted to hear everyone's opinion on important matters.

"If I'm honest, I don't really believe it's all going to happen, Pops," Tillie replied forcefully. "Hitler will back down."

"What about Czechoslovakia?" Walter probed gently. "Hitler moved into Czech lands in March. And he won't stop there."

"What about the Munich Agreement, Pops? Didn't Prime Minister Chamberlain get Hitler's signature saying there would no longer be any further territorial problems for Germany in Europe?" Tillie leaned forward so her father could hear her.

"My poppet, Hitler violated that agreement with his invasion of Czechoslovakia. We can't stand for this. Britain mustn't tolerate this dangerous man. War is all but assured." Walter's voice was soft but firm.

"I have to agree with you, Pops," echoed Maggie in a wobbly voice. "We must stand strong. The Kingston family must do whatever it takes to fight with England." Her voice rose, and then cracked. Tillie quickly grabbed her hand.

"Me too, Pops," jumped in Kenny. "We'll have to do our part no matter how tough it gets, right, sis?" He elbowed Katie.

She stuck her chin out stubbornly. "Hitler will never breach our shores. Our men are the bravest fighters in the world. So, we must be strong too."

"I guess we are united then," Alice said quietly. "We don't know what the future will bring but we are in it together. Our fortitude is our family." She gazed at her husband with pride and fear – but mostly pride.

"Well said, my dear. We are going to need all the strength and determination we can muster over the next few months. Let's help each other wherever we can." He took a deep breath as he saw his family nodding their heads soberly. "Now, on to a more pleasant subject." He turned to the twins. "You have a birthday coming up if I recollect rightly. Next month. I'd like to propose a family outing to Brighton Beach for the day. How does that sound?"

Twin squeals greeted his announcement.

"Pops, that would be brilliant. We'll have to get the day off work, right Maggie?" Tillie spoke first.

"Too right, sis. And thank you, Pops. Will anyone else join us?" Maggie chimed in with a big smile.

"I think this is your department, dear," Walter turned to Alice.

"We did want to make rather a day of it, Maggie. Uncle Thomas, Aunt Shirley, with Geoffrey, of course. I also thought to invite our dear neighbors, the Goldbachs. And Tillie, would you like to ask Colin? Oh, and you two can each bring a chum along," she nodded towards Kenny and Katie. "We'll have a proper party for your twenty-third birthdays."

"I'd love to bring Colin, ta Mum," replied Tillie with a slight blush spreading up her cheeks. "I'll ask him tonight. We're off to the cinema."

"Well, that's just fine, then," boomed Walter. "Alice, did Faye leave us a pudding I wonder?"

* * *

"What do you reckon about all this war talk, Tillie?" asked Maggie, as the pair made their way up to their second-floor bedroom. They could have had separate rooms, one floor above, but insisted on being together. Maggie slumped on her bed as Tillie changed into a dress for her date with Colin. She selected a navy-blue shirtwaist frock with a white collar and cuffs.

"Pops scared me; I must admit. I've been hiding my head in the sand hoping against hope it was all old folks' talk. Now, I'm starting to believe war really is coming. It's all Colin talks about anyway," she finished ruefully as she tightened the matching belt around her slender waist.

"It makes me feel gloomy, all of it," Maggie picked at a loose thread on the coverlet.

"Chin up, ducks." Tillie gave her sister a quick smile. "At least we'll have a day in Brighton before it all starts." She turned to the mirror, and applied bright red lipstick. "And you and Micah can moon about together on the beach," she teased.

"Micah and I are just friends, Tillie. You know that." It was Maggie's turn to blush. Micah Goldbach was the neighbor's son, and a mate of Maggie's. The two loved long walks together. Talking about who-knew-what, Tillie thought with a giggle.

"Whatever you say, Mags. How do I look? Will I do?" Tillie twirled, as she pinned on her hat.

"Smashing, Tillie. Oh – there's the door. Best not to keep the handsome Colin waiting." Maggie handed her twin her bag.

"It won't hurt him to wait a few minutes," Tillie laughed. "I'll see you later tonight, darling. I'll let you know if *Dark Victory* is as good as they say. Ta ra." Tillie skipped down the stairs. The room felt suddenly empty without her, but Maggie picked up a book

CHAPTER THREE

"I'm sorry I got a smidge weepy back there, Colin. When Bette Davis went slowly up to her bedroom, I knew it was the end for her. She was so brave, finding her way blindly knowing it was the last time she would be with her beloved husband." Tillie sniffed as they waited for the bus after the cinema.

Colin shrugged. "I thought the acting was pretty good, but don't you think a little dramatic, Tillie?" He gazed at her lovely face with her eyes brimming with tears and hugged her. "It's alright, sweetheart. It was just a film."

"I know," replied Tillie softly, wiping her cheek. "I just got lost in the story. Silly me." She mustered up a watery smile.

"Your tender heart is one of the reasons I fancy you, Tillie. You're just an old softie." He gently elbowed her

The bus pulled up, and the couple jumped aboard, paid the fare, and settled into a seat.

"Fancy a drink at the Prince of Teck before I walk you home, sweetheart?" Colin pulled her hand into his own. "Let's make a night of it." He gave her a lopsided grin.

"Well, perhaps just a fast shandy, Colin. We both have to work tomorrow." She held his hand a little tighter.

Tillie met Colin Redwood at Kingston and Knight two years ago. He was a junior banker at her father's firm and the two had hit it off immediately. Colin was confident and bright with a promising career ahead of him. A few inches taller than her with curly brown hair and green eyes, he wasn't classically handsome but had even features and a ready smile. If his ears protruded just a bit, well, that just made him more adorable.

Pops liked him, so that was a bonus!

A few minutes later Tillie sat at a corner table in the Prince of Teck pub as Colin made his way to the bar for drinks.

He placed Tillie's shandy in front of her as he sipped a pint of Fuller's ale.

"I have something rather serious to tell you, Tils," he began with his typical directness.

Tillie took a large gulp of her drink and tried to quell her churning stomach. Was Colin going to break things off with her? She thought they'd been getting on so well.

"I've been talking it over with my mates and I've decided I'm joining up before I get my call-up papers. I want to choose where I fight in this war." He studied her face for a reaction, as he reached again for her hand.

Tillie gasped gaping at him in alarm. "Colin, no. You mustn't. There isn't even a war yet, there might not be, and even if there is, it's far too soon to consider joining up." Her throat constricted, and she felt dizzy. She couldn't lose Colin. She loved him so much.

"Sweetheart, shhh now. Don't get ahead of yourself. Of course, I must enlist. War is coming, darling. Surely, you must know that. Don't you see we must crush Hitler? He has his eyes on all of Europe, if not more. Britain must stand up – sooner rather than later." His confidence was intense. "You do see that, Tillie, don't you?" His green eyes bored into her soft doe eyes.

"I just don't know, Colin," she whispered. "I don't want to believe war is coming but the signs are all around us. Pops seems certain, as well." She didn't look convinced herself, not one bit. "But why must you enlist now? You're needed at Pop's firm. Why not wait until war is official?" A note of desperation crept into her voice.

"I told you, Tillie. I'm set on joining the RAF. They need men as pilots. This war will be fought in the air. Mark my words," he retorted, a trifle impatiently.

Tillie gulped. Colin had talked endlessly about the Royal Air Force and his desire to fly, but Tillie had never imagined he meant to sign up straight away. Her Colin fighting German bombers in the air. She felt cold again and hugged herself.

"I don't know what to say, Colin. I stand with Britain, of course, but I don't want to lose you." She looked deep into his eyes, trying to show her support rather than fear.

Colin finished his pint in one long gulp. "Bollocks. Don't you have any faith in me? Once we're in this thing, we'll pummel the Huns by Christmas. Then, you and I shall plan our future properly," he finished with the smugness of youth.

Tillie smiled wanly, pushing down her feelings. "Of course, love," she put in. "And you'll be a smashing pilot. I just don't want any of it to happen is all."

"Come on, Tils. Let's get you home. Tomorrow morning will come early enough." He helped her with her coat as she nodded.

During the short walk home, Colin chattered on about spitfires and the enemy, while Tillie listened with only half an ear. The war had suddenly become very personal.

"Give us a proper kiss, Tillie," he cajoled, on the front steps of the townhouse. He took her into his arms and bent to kiss her soft lips. "Mmm, you are so lovely, sweetheart." He tightened his grip and deepened the kiss.

Tillie felt the familiar warmth creeping throughout her body as Colin masterfully took charge of the embrace. She kissed him back eagerly, feeling close to him in this intimate moment. He was so solid and reliable, so sure of himself, that she melted into the delicious feelings flooding her insides.

Colin reluctantly pulled away.

"I'd best get away, sweetheart. Much as I'd love to stay and explore more of your tempting lips. I daresay your Pops wouldn't take kindly to me ravishing his daughter outside his front door.

She smiled up at him.

"No, he wouldn't. Thank you for a lovely evening, Colin." She said straightening her dress.

"Goodnight, sweetheart. I'll see you in a few days." He kissed the tip of her nose.

As she thoughtfully let herself into the house, she heard him whistling down the street.

* * *

Tillie resolutely put her conversation with Colin out of her mind, determined not to get too upset. She confided Colin's plans to Maggie and the two quietly talked over the implications late into the night. Maggie worried for her sister as the unknowns crept over their day-to-day lives. But they both resolved to put their best foot forward, watch and wait.

Suddenly, the day of the Buckingham Palace Royal Garden Party was upon them. The twins took extra time over their toilettes, brushing their hair until it shone and ensuring their makeup was perfect. They'd given each other fresh manicures the previous night – Tillie with her signature red, and Maggie with her rosy pink nail polish.

"I dreamt last night that the King and Queen invited us for tea at the royal table, sis," Tillie said ruefully. Maggie just snorted as the girls bounded down the stairs, along the hallway to the back kitchen.

"Good morning, Mum, Faye. What a lovely day," greeted Tillie, as she slipped into a chair.

"Just tea and toast for me, please, Faye," Maggie turned to the housekeeper. "I couldn't keep anything down today. My stomach is turning somersaults." She smiled at her Mum as she sat next to her sister and placed a napkin on her lap.

"As you wish, Maggie," Faye replied from her usual place at the aga. She turned with a smile, spatula in hand, familiar pink and white striped apron tightly wrapped around her solid frame. "And for you, Tillie?"

Faye was the family's long-serving housekeeper. The kitchen was her domain, which was a good thing, as Alice was a disaster whenever she tried her hand at cooking. Faye oversaw the planning, shopping, cleaning, and overall household management. Jessie, a local girl who came in for heavy cleaning, laundry, and seasonal tasks, helped her three days a week.

At thirty-seven, Faye was a handsome woman, a bit on the stocky side, with prematurely grey hair. When no one was looking at her, her face turned sad. As soon as someone engaged her in conversation, the sadness disappeared into a smile. She had lost her fiancé in the Great War and had never looked at another man since. She had thrown herself into domestic work to support herself and the Kingstons considered her a valued family member and a treasure.

"The same for me, Faye. My stomach is in knots."

Faye nodded and carried on with breakfast. The rest of the family had eaten earlier and left for the office.

"Excited about the garden party, girls?" asked Alice, as she sipped her tea. "I'd give anything to tag along. You must remember *everything* and tell me later. What the Queen wore, the music, the guests, just everything," she sighed. What she wouldn't give to slip into a Nippy uniform and be in the presence of Their Majesties!

"Yes, Mum, we'll try to remember everything," Maggie assured her mother. "Bear in mind, we will be rather busy, though?"

"Of course, darling, just do your best. I'm so proud of you both."

The hall clock struck the hour. As one, the twins stuffed a last bite of toast and jam in their mouths, gulped their tea, and jumped off their chairs.

"We're off then," Tillie said in a rush. "It won't do to be late today of all days."

The girls kissed their mother, waved at Faye, and hurried up the stairs for their hats and handbags. They needed to get a move on to catch the tube to get their newly cleaned and pressed uniforms, pass inspection, and get some basic instructions before heading as a group to Buckingham Palace.

For once, Alfie was serious, no jokes.

"Lyons is proud to serve Their Majesties and their guests. You have been hand-picked for your high standards, excellent service, and exemplary attitudes. Give the King and Queen your absolute best today. We are relying on you to do Lyons proud."

The Nippies stood a little taller after his pep talk, bursting with the responsibility and honor bestowed upon them.

"You'll see Mrs. Sims at Buck House. She and her team will provide further orders for the day. That's all," he finished. "Oh, and have a good look round. This is a special occasion."

As it was such a bright May morning, the girls decided to walk the twenty minutes to the palace. It was quite a sight – a group of black-clad

Nippies walking briskly down Coventry Street, chatting all together at once.

At the palace, the Nippies were let in a side entrance and whisked to the back garden. Two large white tents stood on the pristine lawn that spread out from the wide palace steps.

Tillie and Maggie tried to look nonchalant as they listened to the instructions dispatched by the efficient Mrs. Sims.

"The guests will enter at three o'clock. They will be guided through the Bow Room from the front gates. We are expecting 13,000 today – I believe that's a palace record. You'll be on duty immediately. Those of you in the main tent will serve buffet-style. You'll be in teams of five or six behind each table. The guests will queue before you in a series of organized lines. Each guest should be offered his or her choice of Earl Grey tea or iced coffee. As it's a warm day, the iced coffee should be popular. Then, you'll offer them a choice of sandwiches – egg, cucumber, and chicken–as well as scones, jam and clotted cream. Finally, there is an assortment of cakes and pastries on offer. You'll serve on a small rectangular plate that holds the cup and remaining tea things. Guests can return as often as they like but must queue up again," she paused. "Most do."

The girls giggled.

"It's important to move quickly to serve all the guests without making them feel rushed in any way. They will take their tea to the tables dotted here around the tent, albeit there is not sufficient seating for all the company so many will mill around. They'll come back for ice cream and perhaps another cup of tea. We aim for first class service – for each and every guest. Any questions?"

Most of the Nippies were too awed to utter a word. Rosie Coombs raised a tentative hand.

"What if we run out of any items, Mrs. Sims?"

Mrs. Sims gave her a stern look.

"We never run out, Miss. Just look for the manageresses in white if you need anything at all. Anything," she emphasized.

"Thank you, Mrs. Sims," Rosie replied with flaming cheeks.

"At precisely four o'clock, the band will strike up *God Save the King* as the royal family stands on the terrace. Then, they will stroll down the lawn in separate lanes to greet as many guests as possible. Small groups of specially chosen guests will greet Their Majesties, and receive personal attention. Then, the royal party will meet up down there." Mrs. Sims pointed to the smaller tent facing the terrace at the bottom of the lawn.

"For those of you serving in the main tent, this will give you a slight break as the guests will be absorbed in the procession of the royal family. You can enjoy the band playing throughout the afternoon as well. For those of you serving in the royal tea tent, you will serve Their Majesties, The King and Queen, and about one hundred VIP guests. They will be served at tables, of course and the menu is the same with just a few added items."

She glanced at her clipboard.

"Once the royals have entered the royal tea tent, the rest of the guests will tour the beautiful gardens and may meet up with some of the royal family once they've had their own tea. At six p.m., Their Majesties and the rest of the royal family will return up the lanes smiling and waving to their guests. The musicians will play *God Save the King* again before the family retreats into the palace. At that point, the guests will be ushered back through the Bow Room, and out the gates. Then it will be time for cleanup. Once the tents are spotless, you may have your own tea as a thank you for your service. Now, as to the assignments for the royal tea tent," she continued, looking at her clipboard again. "If I read your name, please nip smartly down to the tent for further instructions from the Lord Chamberlain."

Tillie and Maggie held hands, hoping for this plum assignment.

"Miss Ivy Ackland, Miss Ruby Harris, Miss Elizabeth Holmes, Miss Mathilda Kingston..."

Tillie smiled, and the girls held their breath, hoping against hope that they would both be called.

"Miss Susan Payne, Miss Gertrude Stewart..." Mrs. Sims droned on, but the twins stopped listening.

"You can take my place," whispered Tillie at Maggie's crestfallen face. "They'll never know the difference."

"Not a chance," whispered Maggie, clutching her sister's hand. "I'm fine, really. You can tell me all about it later."

Tillie nodded uncertainly. "Are you sure?"

There was no time to respond.

Mrs. Sims clapped her hands.

"That's it then. Off you go to your posts. Good luck and do Lyons proud," she echoed Alfie's earlier words.

Tillie was hurried along with the other royal tea tent Nippies down the lawn to get ready. She waved at her sister who was walking with the other set of Nippies to the main tent.

Everyone did their part to get ready for the onslaught of royal guests. At three o'clock, the brightly dressed ladies in their best finery and hats were escorted by smiling men in uniform or suits, some with top hats. The air was festive and expectant. The sun shone down brightly with a slight breeze.

Maggie and the public tent Nippies were kept on their toes, serving tea, sandwiches, and delectable-looking cakes to the buzzing crowds. She lost count of the number of cups of tea she served (no spills!), and asking if guests wanted it white or black.

At four p.m., the national anthem played at the corner of the lawn where the royal family entered. Maggie snuck a glance at the family as they stood at attention.

King George VI was dressed in a formal grey suit, with no top hat. Queen Elizabeth was breathtaking in a violet silk dress with matching overcoat, long white gloves, and a fantastic broad-brimmed hat.

Joining the royal couple were Princesses Elizabeth and Margaret – identical in matching yellow organza dresses, white gloves and straw hats with yellow bands.

Queen Mary was resplendent in an ivory high-necked dress, decorated with her trademark ropes of pearls. She towered over everyone, including her son, with her tall hat adorned with spring flowers. She carried a matching ivory parasol.

They were joined by other members of the royal family, whom Maggie did not recognize. She hoped some of the other Nippies could fill her in.

It was going to be an exciting afternoon!

CHAPTER FOUR

Maggie was pulled back to the job at hand as guests queued again for second and third helpings. For most, this was likely the best afternoon tea they would ever have. Maggie's mouth watered staring at the delicious sandwiches and cakes, but she continued her work. She had been switched to serving ice cream and she happily served the waiting guests from large tubs of vanilla and strawberry ice cream.

Meanwhile, Tillie was trying to maintain a professional Nippy image whilst being totally star-struck in the royal presence. She hadn't been chosen to serve the King and Queen at their table, but it didn't matter. Their royalty glittered and mesmerized everyone in the tent.

Queen Elizabeth was more beautiful in person than her photos in the newspapers. She was tiny and trim breathtakingly glamourous. Jewels sparkled from her ears, throat, wrist, and even her hat. She smiled so constantly that Tillie marveled that her cheeks didn't hurt. She had quite a formal air about her but was charming to everyone she met.

The King was relaxed but you could tell he was quite shy. He was polite but not comfortable with small talk. He looked at his wife adoringly and appeared grateful that she could graciously chatter with the important guests around them.

The princesses were certainly well trained in social matters. They sat ramrod straight, their gloves spotless, as they daintily chewed sandwiches. Princess Elizabeth spoke in a low voice to the man seated next to her. Tillie thought she heard them talking about the princess' dog, Dookie. Margaret listened but said nothing.

Queen Mary was assertive, barking out commands for her tea. She chatted easily with two of her children – the Duke of Kent with his wife,

Marina, and Mary, the Princess Royal, with her husband, the 6th Earl of Harewood.

Tillie tried not to stare as she carried loaded trays of tea, sandwiches, scones, and cakes to guests in military uniform, elegant daywear, and their best family furs and jewelry.

A rather stout woman, wearing a fox stole over a heavily brocaded blue dress, sat watching the royal couple spellbound. She helped herself freely to the champagne and wiped her damp brow constantly. The warm day and crowds in the tent were plainly getting to her.

As guests finished their tea, the King and Queen got up, and started circulating to the tables to speak with them. As the Queen approached her table, the Fox Lady was almost apoplectic.

"Sir Arthur Danvers and Lady Martha Danvers," intoned the Lord Chamberlain in introduction. The Queen smiled as both rose. The husband bowed, and Fox Lady quickly got up to curtsey. She leaned over, almost losing her balance as she steadied herself on the table's edge. The Queen looked on in horror as Lady Danvers tried to put down her champagne glass but only succeeded in crushing it in her hand, as she miscalculated and slammed it down too hastily.

The sound of breaking glass split the silence that had taken over the tent, as Lady Danvers looked at the blood streaming down her hand and shrieked.

Queen Elizabeth automatically took a step backwards, turning to her husband.

Lord Chamberlain tried to approach the unfortunate woman but Tillie was faster. She put down her tray and rushed to Lady Danvers' side.

"It's alright now, Ma'am," she soothed. "Let's just sit down and have a look at that hand. I think you may have cut yourself rather badly."

She eased the woman into her seat, completely ignoring the horrified Queen standing inches away. Tillie grabbed a cloth napkin and wrapped it around Lady Danvers' hand, putting pressure on the thumb from where most of the blood seemed to spurt.

She quietly murmured soothing words as she grabbed a nearby water glass and held it to the woman's lips.

"Please take a sip, Ma'am. It will help to settle you."

Tillie peeked at Lady Danvers' face and observed the clammy complexion, dilated pupils, and white pallor. This poor woman is in shock, she thought sympathetically. She turned to find Lord Chamberlain at her elbow.

"Sir, I fear this lady needs medical attention. Is there a doctor or nurse at hand?" Tillie knew she did the best she could muster of her first aid abilities.

"Quite so, Miss. We have a medical tent and staff just up the lawn." He turned towards the serving end of the tent and nodded to two young men in white. "James, Rory, please assist Lady Danvers."

Tillie stood up, relinquishing the woman's hand.

"Don't leave me, Miss. Please," Lady Danvers called out in alarm, her eyes wide.

Tillie glanced at Lord Chamberlain, who nodded.

Between them and Lord Danvers, they brought the woman to the medical tent, grumbling all the while. She was quickly examined, stitched, bandaged, and served a cup of tea.

"That wine glass was pure rubbish. It should not have come apart in my hand," she fussed loudly.

Tillie realized she was no longer needed and left. She sensed rather than heard a commotion behind her, and holding her breath, she couldn't help but notice, right behind her, the Queen!

"How are you getting on, Lady Danvers? Have they seen to you properly? I'm so terribly sorry for the ordeal you've suffered. I do hope you can accept my apology?"

The Queen had entered the tent alone, save for a lady-in-waiting. She looked kindly at the astonished Lady Danvers who rose to curtsey. Her Majesty really does have a very sweet smile, thought Tillie.

"Yes Ma'am, they have looked after me quite well indeed." She held up her bandaged hand. "And please accept my apologies for disrupting your lovely garden party," Lady Danvers simpered.

"Not at all, Lady Danvers. And where is that clever Nippy who leaped to your aid?" The Queen cast her gaze around the small medical tent.

Tillie shrunk near the doorway. She couldn't greet Her Majesty like this. Her pristine white apron was smeared with blood, as were her hands. Her cap was askew and she could only imagine the state of her face. Good thing too, as she had a trace of blood across one cheek.

Just then, Maggie appeared through the tent door. She immediately spotted her sister and gasped.

"What happened, love? My goodness, have you been injured?"

"My goodness indeed. Are there two of you then or am I seeing double?" The Queen had made her way towards Tillie, who hung back in embarrassment.

Both girls curtseyed.

"Yes, we are twins, Your Majesty," Tillie spoke first. Maggie was gob-smacked. "This is my sister, Maggie, er… Margaret."

The Queen nodded politely.

"I just wanted to give you my thanks, young lady. You reacted so quickly. Are you a nurse? And what is your name?"

Tillie bobbed again. "I'm Tillie, Ma'am. Mathilda Kingston. And no, I'm not a nurse. I have had some first aid training though, Ma'am," she added again. She was more than nervous.

"Well, you should consider a post in nursing or perhaps the ambulance service. With a war coming, we will need competent young women like you to minister to our wounded. We are most grateful."

With another kind smile, she swept out of the tent in a whiff of expensive perfume.

Tillie and Maggie clutched each other's hands. Had they just met Queen Elizabeth? How thrilling.

Everybody in the tent grew silent for a moment, star-struck as well. Then, everyone smiled happily and hurried back to work.

"Miss, are you in need of any assistance?" A tall young man had just entered the tent. He had on rubber boots, trousers, waterproof leggings and a steel helmet.

"I'm with the AFS, Miss. Do you have any injuries that need seeing to?" He asked with concern.

"No, thank you," Tillie replied. This firefighter was too good-looking for comfort. Tall with black hair and piercing blue eyes, he looked like a film star. "I've just been helping an injured lady. This is her blood, not mine," she stammered.

"Oh, that's all right, then. I can show you where to wash up, if you like, Miss...?" He left his sentence hanging.

"I'm Tillie Kingston. And thank you, that would be most kind," she smiled at him.

Maggie stared on in dismay. What was Tillie doing fluttering her eyes at this man when she was all but spoken for by Colin?

"Right this way, Miss Kingston. Trevor Drummond, at your service," he took her off to a washing corner, where he left her with a small bow. "You'll excuse me if I don't shake your hand. It's rather a mess at the moment."

Tillie nodded her head and concentrated on cleaning herself.

"Of course. Thanks ever so much. I'm fine from here."

* * *

"Tillie, I can only hope that the shock of your incident has rattled you. Otherwise, I can't think why you were making up to that firefighter," Maggie scolded as the pair sat on the tube a short while later, on their way home.

"Sod off, Mags," retorted Tillie. "I was just being polite. I spoke to him for all of three minutes."

"With that silly smile on your face the whole time? Hah!" Maggie teased.

As usual, the twins received all kinds of stares on the tube. They'd removed their caps but had just thrown coats over their uniforms, choosing to bypass a trip back to Lyons for their street clothes. They'd pick them up at their next shift.

"He was just being nice, that's all, Mags. But did you see that dimple? He was handsome, I'll give you that."

"Well, he was rather kind. You're right about that," Maggie conceded.

"But what about Her Majesty actually speaking to me? That's what I want to talk about." Tillie's eyes sparkled.

"Too right. Now tell me exactly what happened," Maggie replied, leaning forward. "Word for word. Mum just won't believe it."

* * *

"And what did the Queen say to you, again, Tillie?" Alice sat enthralled over the dining room table. "I can scarcely imagine it."

"Mum, I already told you," Tillie replied, her mouth full of parsnips. "She thanked me for helping Lady Danvers, met Maggie, and then left with her attendants. It was all quite brief."

"That's not all, Tillie. You're forgetting the bit where she thought you should be a nurse," Maggie added, as she passed the scones around the table.

"Oh yes, that or an ambulance worker. If war comes," confirmed Tillie. "I'm not sure about nursing, but I could fancy driving an ambulance. Only if the time comes," she amended, as she saw the fearful look on her mother's face. "I should like helping people in trouble."

"What a thing for Her Majesty to say," Alice enthused. "But it sounds awfully dangerous."

"We will all have to do our part," Walter spoke from the end of the table, giving his wife a piercing look. "And both the girls have learned how to drive the Flying 16, so driving an ambulance is an interesting idea."

"Do you think I really might, Pops?" asked Tillie curiously. "I'm not really that good at driving," she thought of the confusing clutch, brake, and steering."

"Nonsense, you're perfectly able, as is Maggie," reassured her father.

"Oh no, not me," Maggie made a face. "Besides, aren't those ambulances enormous beasts? I'm quite sure I couldn't manage."

"Enough of this war and ambulance talk," interjected Alice with a frown. "I thought we were talking about the garden party and Their Majesties."

"Dear, you can put your head in the sand but the war is coming. You'll have to get used to the idea, in your own time," Walter added gently. "In fact, I've asked Faye to order blackout material for the windows. Sunday next, we'll have to make the curtains for every window. We'll not give the Germans any light to serve as targets."

Alice turned pale.

"So soon, darling? Is it really that bad?"

He nodded slowly.

"Many preparations are underway. Thomas and I have both joined the Local Defence Volunteers. Even if we are too old to join up, we will protect our families at home from advance German parachutes." He held up a hand amidst cries of protest from the women. "We must all do our bit. Girls, I expect you to join the WVS working along with your mother and Aunt Shirley. Kenny, there will doubtless be war work for you as well – thankfully you are too young to be called up. The Kingston family will do our duty proudly – I know I can count on each of you."

Alice looked around the table at her four children, each with a mix of fear, uncertainty, and curiosity on their faces. God help them. They shouldn't have to go through what we had. But she knew her husband wanted her to put on a strong face for their sake.

"Of course, you are right, Walter," she said simply. "Surely, the WVS services will be in great demand. We will all pitch in. And I'll speak to Faye about the material and a pattern. We'll have Shirley join us – she's a marvel at sewing. Girls, you'll all help too."

Tillie, Maggie, and Katie all nodded soberly.

"Very good. Now, before I have my pipe, I wanted to remind you all of our outing to Brighton for Maggie and Tillie's birthday in two weeks' time. Have a think about what to pack for our picnic, type of birthday cake, and so on. Something cheerful to plan," he pushed back from the table, signaling the end of the meal. "And Tillie, I'm right proud of how you handled yourself today. Surely, a day to remember."

Tillie beamed.

The girls rose to help Faye with the clearing up. As usual, Kenny left quickly to meet a mate.

"Your father is right. Let's do think about the picnic. With Thomas, Shirley, and Geoffrey, plus the Goldbachs –we'll be thirteen. Then, there's Colin, and chums for Katie and Kenny. My goodness, that's sixteen – quite a party."

"Let's have sandwiches – chicken, cucumber, maybe ham?" asked Tillie. "Oh, and scotch eggs."

"I fancy sausage rolls, please," added Maggie.

"Sounds lovely, girls. And what about a birthday cake? Can you agree on one to share?" She asked with a smile as she stacked the last of the plates in the small scullery next to the kitchen. "Let's go to the sitting room and have a natter."

"Just a brief one, Mum. Colin will be here soon," Tillie said. "I need to fix my face before he comes."

"And we're off for a walk," Katie added. Maggie nodded.

"I think I'd like a lemon drizzle cake," Maggie said.

"I was thinking either that or a Victoria sponge. But I'm quite content with a lemon drizzle. Any cake that Faye makes will be delicious," Tillie agreed.

"Brilliant. I will speak to her. And perhaps Shirley can bring some of her famous meat pies. I'm sure Ruth Goldbach will be happy to contribute as well. Leave it to me girls, I'll organize everything. You'll just have to help carry the lot. With our crowd, it will be quite the adventure."

"Ta, Mum, and see you later. I'm off to get ready for Colin." Tillie gave her mother a kiss on the cheek.

Alice kissed her back.

"And I'm dead proud of you too, Tillie. Both of you," she glanced at Maggie. "The Kingstons were well represented today at Buckingham Palace."

Alice sat down with her knitting as her three daughters raced up the stairs giggling.

CHAPTER FIVE

Tillie took some good-natured teasing over the next several shifts, her friends calling her *Queenie* and *Your Majesty*. She laughed it off, secretly thrilled about her royal encounter.

"What do you call a pancake that marries an aristocratic lady?" asked Alfie at the next inspection. "*Sir Up*," he chortled.

The girls groaned, familiar with Alfie's constant puns.

Maggie wasn't working today but Tillie was run off her feet as usual. She loved meeting new people and her shift flew by. She was looking forward to meeting Colin for supper. He was taking her to the nearby *Frascati Restaurant*. She wondered why did he choose such a fancy place for their date, but was too busy to contemplate it further.

With three quarters of an hour remaining before Colin was to pick her up, Tillie tried not to look at the clock as she served her last few tables. What looked like a mother and son were seated in her section and she greeted them with her characteristic smile.

"Welcome to Lyons Corner House," she passed out the menus, and paused. It was him. The firefighter from the Buck House Garden party.

"Well, hello, Miss Kingston, isn't it?" He asked smoothly. Damn, he didn't look at all surprised to see her. Had he tracked her to her place of work?

"Yes, it is. Mr. Drummond. How nice to see you." Tillie felt a blush creep up her neck. "And welcome to you, too, Ma'am," she turned to the older woman, who bore more than a passing resemblance to the fire-fighter – Trevor, was it? She had the same twinkling blue eyes, but with greying-blond hair, not black.

"This is my mother, Isla Drummond," he introduced. "I have just been out to the shops with her and she fancied a cup of tea." Why was he grinning at her like that? The blush was now seeping up to the roots of her blond hair.

"Nice to meet you, Mrs. Drummond. Would you like a cup of tea and something to eat as well?" She turned to her, hoping to calm her pounding heart.

"I'll have the cream tea, dear, with Earl Grey. Darling?" She turned to her son.

"I'll have tea with a cake or two if that's alright, Miss Kingston."

"Certainly, I'll bring you a selection straight away," she picked up the menus and headed to the kitchen. Goodness, what was happening to her? She was about to meet the love of her life for a romantic dinner. Why was she getting flustered over this man she barely knew?

She was back with their orders in no time, and served them without any further small talk.

When she brought the bill, Trevor took it and looked straight at her.

"You've certainly smartened up since the last time I saw you. None the worse for wear, then?" He flashed his dimple.

"I'm just fine, thanks. Nice to meet you, Mrs. Drummond. The Lyons Corner House thanks you for your custom." What was she blabbering about? What was wrong with her? "I hope to see you again sometime, Mrs. Drummond, Mr. Drummond." She turned away.

"Goodbye, Miss Kingston. Perhaps we'll meet around London sometime soon."

Tillie left without a backwards glance and finished serving her last two tables. She gladly ended her shift, changed into her street clothes, and freshened up her makeup.

Meet her around London, indeed. Not unless he was stalking her. Which she fervently hoped he wasn't. He had left a generous tip, though. However, she had a certain green-eyed, curly-haired young man waiting to pick her up. She resolutely put Trevor Drummond out of her mind.

"Darling," she greeted Colin fifteen minutes later with a fervent kiss.

"Well, not sure how I deserve that welcome, but I'll take it," he kissed her back, and put his hand on her elbow as they walked towards

Oxford Street.

"I'm just glad to see you, that's all," she replied. "Can't a girl be happy to see her chap?" She'd shaken out her hair and the long blond loose curls framed her lovely face.

"Glad to see you too, sweetheart. Are you hungry?"

"Hungry for something that's not Lyons Food," she replied as they navigated the busy streets. It was a warm June day and Tillie lifted her face up. "It's lovely to feel the sun after being cooped up all day."

They soon reached Frascati's and entered the elegant restaurant. The entrance hall was covered in thick red carpets with futuristic patterns, and the lounge was dotted with brightly colored brocade settees and curtains, and large gilt chandeliers. Tillie took little notice of her surroundings, being immune to the opulence at the Corner House.

They passed the live trout tank and took a table in an alcove corner. She'd hoped to sit in the beautiful Winter Garden under the dome but Colin had wanted a more private spot.

"Shall we have a bottle of wine, sweetheart?" Colin inquired politely as the waiter hovered.

"Just a glass for me, Colin. I don't want to have a head tomorrow," she looked at his dear face, grateful to be out and alone with him.

He looked slightly cross but ordered two glasses of white wine.

"Are we celebrating something, Colin?" She asked as the waiter deftly served the wine. She gave him a grateful smile. She always treated anyone that served the public with respect and grace. And always left a big tip. She knew how hard the work was.

"Maybe," he answered enigmatically. "Shall I order for us?"

"I was thinking maybe the fish?" Tillie perused the menu.

"No, let's go all out." He ordered chilled pea soup, followed by beef bordelaise, and a knickerbocker glory for afters for both of them.

Tillie mentally shrugged her shoulders. What he had chosen for them sounded delicious and for once, she didn't have to serve it.

She took a sip of wine and gazed at Colin.

"You seem fit to bursting. What's your news, then?"

He took a big gulp.

"I've done it, Tillie. I've signed up for the RAF. I went to the recruiting office this morning. I should get my papers and find out about basic training in a fortnight or so."

He held up his glass.

Tillie went cold and put her glass down. What she had dreaded had happened. Oh no, her poor Colin. At war. Suddenly, he looked quite young.

"I don't know what to say, Colin. I know how badly you want to go but I don't want to lose you." She reached for his hand.

"Your hand is freezing, sweetheart." He rubbed it within his own two. "Don't look so downhearted. Won't you be right proud of me, shooting down Germans in my own Spitfire?"

She tried to look supportive.

"Yes, but I can't bear the thought of you in danger. They'll be shooting at you too." Tillie could just picture it – Colin in his little plane, with German bombers all around – with no hope for his survival.

"Have a little faith, Tillie. We must all be brave – those fighting and you at home. Where's my girl now with her beautiful smile? We are celebrating, remember?"

Tillie nodded and tried to swallow another sip of wine. She picked away at the tasty meal, trying not to make Colin cross with her.

"Shall we walk around the square before going home?" He suggested as they sipped their tea. Tillie's ice cream sundae sat almost untouched in front of her.

"All right," she tried to muster a smile. Colin helped her into her coat and they walked out into the warm June evening.

Colin chattered excitedly about his plans as they walked around Soho square.

"You are hardly paying attention, Tillie. I might as well take you home," he finished irritably.

"I'm sorry, Colin," she began lamely. She had no words to cheer him up, only gloom enveloped her. This bloody war that hadn't even happened yet.

He didn't answer, hurt and sullen.

They sat quietly on the bus ride back to Earl's Court and the Longridge Road townhouse.

"Sweetheart, all will be well I promise," he breathed into her neck as he embraced her at the door. He kissed her. She tried to get enthused, but her heart just wasn't in it. And Colin knew it.

"All right then, Tillie. A waste of a proper supper then, wasn't it? Stop looking at me with those big brown eyes looking so sad."

Tillie pressed her lips to his.

"I'm sorry, Colin. Just give me some time to adjust to your news. You did rather spring it on me."

"Goodnight, Tillie. I'll see you Saturday morning at Waterloo Station."

"Colin, wait!" She called after him, but he'd already run down the steps, and was lost in the night.

Tears pricked her eyelids and she wiped them away angrily. Nothing was going to be settled tonight.

* * *

"It's alright, Tillie. Just cry it out," Maggie held her sobbing sister. Tillie had rushed up to their room and thrown herself into her twin's arms. Between the sobs, Maggie made out that Colin had enlisted in the RAF and would leave for basic training in a matter of weeks.

"I just don't want him to go. RAF pilots get shot down. They are sitting ducks in the sky. I can't lose him," Tillie tried but failed to regain her composure.

"Shh, shh, now, love. Our pilots shoot down the enemy, too, you know. And war isn't even declared yet. He may go through training or maneuvers or whatever they are called, and never get into active service. Or they may post him somewhere here in England in a defense role or training other pilots. The truth is – you just don't know, Tillie."

Tillie looked at her with a blotchy face and puffy eyes. She sniffed, and Maggie silently handed her a handkerchief.

"I suppose you're right. My heart just feels so heavy about this, Mags." She blew her nose and hiccupped.

"You are a sorry mess, that's for certain," Maggie tried to cheer her sister up.

"Too right, sis. Thanks for the shoulder to cry on…. literally. I suppose needs must these days. I should just take it one day at a time. What else is there to do really?"

"That's the only way, Tillie."

"Can I sleep in your bed tonight, Mags?" asked Tillie, as she picked up her sponge bag.

"Of course, love," Maggie murmured. "I'll bring us up a nice cup of cocoa, shall I?"

* * *

The day of the twins' twenty-third birthday dawned warm but cloudy. They exchanged small gifts in the morning and Faye cooked the girls a full English breakfast.

The family quickly prepared for their Brighton outing, with Alice and Faye packing the oversized hamper, while the girls fought over the bathroom.

The large party convened at Waterloo station. It was a festive group as family and friends reconnected. Everyone was determined to have a fun day at the beach celebrating the twins' birthday and ignore the war clouds gathering over their heads. Sisters Alice and Shirley commiserated with Ruth Goldbach over the blackout curtains, having each spent hours in their respective homes sparring with the heavy black material to cover dozens of windows. Shirley was the elder of the two sisters and slightly taller.

Her husband Thomas sat with Walter and Samuel Goldbach, looking serious during the inevitable war talk. Samuel's son Micah chatted with Maggie, and Tillie and Colin shared a seat. The rest of the young people scattered in small groups.

Once they arrived at the beach, the sun peaked out from time to time from behind the clouds as the party picked their way along the pebbled beach, each with a blanket or food item of some sort. They found a spot and the men tried to stake large umbrellas into the rocky ground to provide some shade.

Everyone was starving so the picnic was laid out straightaway. Faye had outdone herself with everything on the request list, and loads more. Shirley and Ruth had also contributed large food baskets. No one went hungry with all the sandwiches, pies, cheeses, pickles, eggs, homemade breads and preserves, and even pancakes. There was a cold boiled beef cut, a honeyed ham, and plenty of drinks, including ginger beer, lemonade and tea. Before the birthday cake was cut, fruit pastries, steamed pudding dessert, and jam pastry puffs were produced from the various households.

To the off-key song of Happy Birthday, Alice brought out the lemon drizzle cake. Because of the wind there were only two candles and the twins blew them out together. Maggie wished things would stay as they were, and Tillie wished with all her heart that Colin would return home safely by Christmas.

As the cake was cut, Colin stood and cleared his throat. Here it comes, thought Tillie, as her stomach lurched. He's going to tell them about the RAF.

"Folks, thank you for inviting me to this splendid outing. The food is delicious and the company smashing. I'd like to make an announcement if I may. I've signed up for the RAF and I'm proud to serve my country in this capacity. I'll be getting my orders shortly. I am determined to do my bit to make Britain safe again."

Amidst cries of *congratulations,* and *well done you,* Colin puffed up with pride. Tillie tried to smile, but it felt stilted.

Colin pulled her up and put an arm around her.

"Tillie is not exactly ecstatic about this decision, but she understands and will support me. She's my girl," he hugged her close. "My number one girl, in fact. And I can't live without her. So, in front of all these witnesses..." He knelt on the hard pebbled beach, took a small, square blue velvet box from his pocket, and held it up to a startled Tillie. "Life is uncertain at the moment. But I am sure of my love for you. I want to go away and fight, knowing you are here waiting for me. Tillie Kingston, will you do me the great honor of becoming my wife?" He opened the box and revealed a slim gold band with a twinkling diamond flower in the middle.

Tillie's mind swirled from emotion to emotion – shock, delight, embarrassment, fear, love, uncertainty, and finally, happiness. Her hand flew to her neck, which was turning pink in its habitual and maddening way. She struggled to get the words out as she felt the breeze off the English Channel on her face, and heard the cry of the gulls overhead.

Everyone waited expectantly for her answer, none more eagerly than Colin. He stood up, took the ring out of the box, and reached for Tillie's left hand.

"Tillie?" He squeaked.

"Yes, Colin. Yes, I will marry you," she gave him her broadest smile as he placed the ring on her finger. He kissed her heartily and turned to present the pair of them as a couple to the waiting family and friends.

"Happy Birthday, sweetheart," he whispered to her amongst the well wishes, hugs, kisses, and handshakes that followed.

Tillie smiled brightly at him – her fiancé – as she obediently showed off the ring to her sisters and mother. At that moment nothing seemed real and she felt herself smiling and answering questions almost outside of her own body.

She loved Colin, she knew she did, yet this proposal was utterly unexpected. Two major shocks in a matter of days caught her unaware.

She. A married woman. With a husband. Colin. She looked from his smiling face to those of her dear family around her. Her throat tightened with that familiar sense of unworthiness. Did she deserve Colin? Could she even marry? Was she meant to be truly happy? And was it the right time to marry? On the cusp of war? With all the apprehension and disquietude facing them all? Should she become Mrs. Colin Redwood? Could she?

CHAPTER SIX

Maggie was the first to hug her twin.

"Darling, congratulations! How wonderful. Did you suspect anything?"

"Nothing," whispered Tillie, clutching her sister tightly.

"Darling, I'm chuffed to bits. Colin is a wonderful man." Mum kissed her on both cheeks, flushed and proud.

"Let's have a look at the ring, Tillie." Katie was next. She oohed over the pretty setting while Tillie examined it for the first time. It was a small diamond, surrounded by eight diamond chips as a flower. She thought it was beautiful. "It's brilliant, sis. So different."

Colin lifted Tillie's hand possessively and gazed at the ring.

"I hope you like it, sweetheart. I thought it was so unique and would suit you. And it does. You are my beautiful flower," he kissed her hand, and then her cheek.

"Congratulations, young man. Well done," Walter shook Colin's hand, and leaned over to kiss his daughter. "And for the record Colin did ask my permission to marry you at the office last week. And I gave him my blessing, most unreservedly."

"Colin, you devil. How long have you been planning this?" Tillie gently elbowed him.

"Quite some time, sweetheart. I couldn't let you get away. Especially with a war coming." He pulled her close again. "And I don't believe in long engagements," he added meaningfully.

The rest of the party surrounded the couple with bright smiles, hugs, asking to see the ring.

Once the celebration subsided, everyone wanted to enjoy the afternoon. The lovely day was not to be wasted.

The youngest of the crowd – Kenny, Katie, and their friends made a beeline for the Palace Pier jutting out enticingly from the beach. They were intent on visiting the *Stop Me and Buy One* cart for ice creams and exploring the funfair. Geoffrey was persuaded to accompany them to ensure they didn't get into trouble.

Alice, Shirley, and Ruth went for a walk along the beach and stopped to collect headscarves and cardies. The men went in search of a pint, presumably at the Grand Hotel on the beachfront.

"Just one, mind," admonished Alice. "We're set for the 4:09 train back to London, remember?" Walter smiled at his wife while Thomas and Samuel tried to keep their balance across the pebbly beach.

"Mind you have to muddle across the stones to get back here," teased Shirley. "We don't want to carry you lads if you can't see straight."

"Don't be cheeky, dear. We are respectable blokes. Enjoy your walk," Thomas called over his shoulder.

Tillie, Colin, Maggie, and Micah braved the water for a swim. After changing into their swimming things, they waded into the cool water.

"Crikey, this water is cold," Colin howled. "Come here, love and warm us." He reached for Tillie, hovering on the beach and pulled her in.

"Let's you and I take our time. I don't fancy a cold dunking all at once," Maggie urged Micah, who was cautiously wading into the water.

"I'm with you, Maggie," he said with a shy smile. Micah was tall and lean, with sandy brown hair, and kind brown eyes that twinkled behind his glasses when he laughed. He was quiet and very smart. He often loaned poetry books to Maggie.

Maggie grinned, trying to warm up the goosebumps on her arms.

"Come on, the pair of you. You're doing it the painful way. Just go under. The water is wonderful," teased Colin, as he splashed in their direction.

"Leave off, Col," chided Tillie, as she bravely dove in. "Brrr," she gasped coming up for air.

"I'll warm you, Tillie," Colin swam over and put his arms around her, then promptly pushed her down under the water.

"Stop, Colin!" She sputtered, as she bubbled to the surface. "What a way to treat your future bride." She hovered between amusement and annoyance.

"Sorry sweetheart. Is this a better way to treat my fiancé?" He planted a firm kiss on her cold lips. She kissed him back before playfully pushing him away.

"Leave off, Colin. Mum and the others are watching."

Colin splashed her again. "We're respectable now, Tils. No one will mind." He reached for her again.

"I'll race you to the shore. I fancy an ice cream," she replied, as she took off with a head start.

"You're on, Tils," he plunged his powerful arms into the water, and quickly overtook her, both of them laughing. He easily beat her and pulled her out towards their picnic spot to dry off.

Micah and Maggie watched from the shallows.

"Don't you dare try to dunk me under, Micah," Maggie pleaded as she clutched his arm. "I'm not as strong a swimmer as my sister."

The two had carefully made their way to about waist-deep.

"Don't worry, Maggie," Micah replied in his quiet voice. "I'd never do that to you," he gave her his kind smile.

"I know, Micah." Maggie smiled in return, as they waded in a little deeper.

"Was the engagement truly a surprise? Tillie certainly looked taken aback," Micah asked. "I don't know Colin all that well, but they seem a good match."

"I think she truly was. I should think it's about time. Tillie really cares deeply for him. But, with everything so uncertain with the war coming, is now the time to rush into marriage?" Maggie's eyebrows furrowed.

Micah shrugged.

"In the coming months I should think you'll see people doing all kinds of things they never would have done before the war," he replied. "Life will become awfully precious, and many will want to make the most of it whilst they can."

"You're scaring me, Micah," Maggie shivered, as he rubbed her shoulders to warm her.

"I'm sorry, Maggie, but we must be realistic." He looked up at the sunny sky, paused, and turned to face her.

"I wanted to speak to you about something serious myself, Maggie," he continued and they both turned back to the beach.

She said nothing, looking up at him with alarm in her big, brown eyes.

"You know my grandfather started our jewelry business in France. My father and mother emigrated here before Hannah and I were born. Grandfather has written to my father. His health is poorly, he has a weak heart, and he wants us to move back to Paris to take over the business permanently. So, Father has put up our business for sale and the house will be sold soon."

By now, the couple had reached the picnic spot, collected their towels, and continued walking along the beach, hand-in-hand.

Maggie stopped short.

"You're leaving London? For Paris? When?" She was dismayed, but tried to hide her fear and panic.

"We have no choice, Maggie. We must help Grandfather," he shrugged. "I'm not sure exactly when, but things are moving swiftly. I expect within a few weeks."

The sun disappeared behind the clouds again, and it turned chilly. Maggie was glad of the cardigans they'd picked up before the walk. They strolled past the pier and all she could hear was loud music coming from the fair and the sound of people laughing. She smelled popcorn. All her senses seemed heightened except for one. She struggled to find her voice. Tears sprang to her eyes.

"I understand, of course, but well, I will miss you," she whispered.

They had known each other since childhood and were firm friends. Maggie admired his intellect and calm and had slowly developed deeper feelings for him, which she had never voiced.

Micah stopped. He seemed lost for words as well.

"I'll miss you too, Maggie," he said softly, as he looked into her eyes.

"Would you consider writing to me? I'd be glad to see your letters in the post reminding me of home."

Maggie turned slightly pale. Where her sister flushed with potent emotions, she whitened.

"I would consider it an honor, Micah. I don't want to lose touch with you." She thought of Paris, so much closer to Germany than London. "But what of the call up? Won't you have to serve?"

"I'm not sure about that, Maggie. I suppose I'll deal with that when it comes. Perhaps I'll be more needed on the continent with my fluent French? Or they may call me back to England. I'll just have to wait and see." He bent to kiss her softly on the lips. "Thank you for agreeing to write to me. You don't know how much it means to me."

Maggie nodded. He'd never kissed her before! She tried to look nonchalant, but her heart was racing. Maybe Micah cared more for her than she thought.

"For now, please say nothing. Mother is upset about the move and leaving all her friends in London. I'm sure Father will make an announcement when all the arrangements have been organized."

Maggie nodded again and the couple slowly walked back to the picnic spot, each lost in their own thoughts.

Miraculously, the entire group had convened at about the same time. The picnic was packed up, last tea drunk from the flasks, and blankets shook out, sending small pebbles tumbling.

A tired, contented, and slightly sunburned little group made its way back to the station, caught trains back to London, and dispersed to their respective homes.

Two weeks later, on July 2, 1939, Brighton's beaches were officially closed. Within a frighteningly short time, the beaches were lined with barbed wire, and sections of the Palace Pier were removed to prevent the enemy from landing and invading the town.

* * *

"Ready, girls? Let's not waste the day." Alice called up the stairs. It was a steamy July morning and shopping followed by dinner was the plan for the day.

"Do I need a cardie?" Katie piped up from her room as the twins appeared on the landing.

"No, love, it's a hot day," replied Alice as she picked up her handbag and gloves. She was dressed in a pink-flowered summer dress and matching hat. "You look very smart, girls," she smiled approvingly at her three daughters.

The twins wore similar flowery dresses with matching belts and accessories. Maggie tilted her white hat in a jaunty angle as Tillie collected her grey beret. Katie looked fetching in a frilly white blouse and green skirt.

"Mum, I really need some new gloves. And a handbag. This old thing was worn when Tillie passed it to me." She grimaced at the battered leather bag.

"Stockings for me, Mum," laughed Tillie as the three crowded out the front door. "And I'm desperate for a new hat."

"And you, Maggie? What's on your Selfridges list?" Mum smiled as the three briskly left for the underground.

"I don't need much, Mum," Maggie replied. "Perhaps a new blouse? And some stationery. I'm all out."

"Well, let's get a move on then. Now is the time to stock up before rationing starts. Who knows what we'll be able to put our hands on then?" Alice said.

Tillie and Maggie exchanged a worried glance. If Mum was resigned to the war coming – well, that was serious.

"Let's not talk of war today. It's a beautiful sunny day and the Kingston girls are shopping." Katie shook her brown curls, skipping along the pavement.

After a short tube ride, they emerged to the busy Oxford Street for their shopping expedition. Several lively shopping hours later, they reappeared from Selfridges, bags in hand, thirsty for a cup of tea and hungry for a celebration dinner.

"We have a one o'clock reservation at *Quaglinos*, so our timing is perfect. Everyone happy with your lot?" Alice beamed a weary smile at her girls. They never tired of shopping but her feet were sore and she was perspiring from the heat.

"Quite, Mum. Thanks ever so much." Tillie held half a dozen bags. "I never expected to find an autumn coat but I just love the camel color. And the matching hat is brilliant."

"Me too, thank you," echoed Maggie. She had only needed a few things but Mum had talked her into a new fountain pen along with the stationery, and she was excited to put them both to use.

"And I'm chuffed about my new handbag. And the shoes were a complete surprise. You are the best, Mum," Katie gave her Mum a hug.

"I hope your father likes the new shirts – they were on sale. And the bits and bobs I collected for Kenny. It was rather busy, wasn't it?" Alice felt good about buying only what they needed. She knew some of her WVS friends had been stockpiling food for weeks – despite strict orders from the Ministry of Food not to do so. Alice and Faye had planned and bought ahead a small quantity of produce complying with the government regulations. Still, she was happy to get this lot. Who knew when they'd have another chance to go shopping again?

"We're here," announced Tillie in relief. "I'm gasping for a cup of tea. The food here is always so delicious."

They were seated in no time and ordered tea and a light meal. After gratefully gulping down their first cup, the girls sat back, looking around the restaurant, waiting for their dinner to arrive.

"Girls, whilst we are waiting, I would like to talk to you about helping more at the WVS as your father suggested. With war expected to break out at any moment, we are all needed. Shirley and I have already upped our weekly shifts to three times per week."

The Women's Volunteer Service was set up in 1938, already looking ahead to a possible war. Hundreds of thousands of women had joined with numbers swelling daily. They recruited for ARP (Air Raid Precautions) services, and had a primary role in assisting with children's evacuations to the countryside, and much more.

"What can we do, Mum?" asked Maggie.

"There is loads you can do, Maggie. Starting with our knitting nights to help knit socks and caps for our soldiers overseas. They are also looking for volunteers to help with canteens at the railway stations – I thought that might just fit you two," she looked at the twins. "And once the bombs fall," she took a deep breath regaining her courage, "there will be field kitchens, rest centers, and helping people who have lost their homes. And probably so much more that they haven't even conceived yet."

"Count me in, Mum. The canteen sounds just the ticket with our Lyons experience," offered Maggie straightaway.

"I'll do whatever I can, Mum," seconded Katie. "Even if I'm younger, I can help with the knitting or making cups of tea."

"I'll be glad to help too, Mum," said Tillie slowly. "Albeit I have also been thinking about what the Queen said about the volunteer ambulance service. I might give that a go." She raised her brown eyes to her mother's.

"My goodness, wouldn't that be something?" Alice burst out. "Well, I'm so relieved to hear you girls are so willing to do your bit. Our next knitting night is Tuesday so I'll count all of you in."

Three heads bobbed quietly.

"And about the ambulance, Tillie. Let's see what your father has to say about that. It sounds proper dangerous."

"But, Mum – all of London will be in danger. The entire country, in fact. Surely they will need drivers to transport the injured whilst the men are away fighting?" Tillie made her case.

Alice sighed. "True enough, my love. True enough."

CHAPTER SEVEN

"Do you really fancy a job with the ambulance, Tils?" asked Maggie in the privacy of their room. "Or were you just having Mum on?"

"Of course, I meant it, Maggie." She applied Pond's Cold Cream to her face, whilst Maggie pinned up her sister's hair in their nightly pin curl ritual. Somehow, it didn't feel like such a chore when they did each other's hair. They both loved the same off the forehead style, with honey-blond tresses in loose demi-curls falling just above their shoulders. "If Her Majesty thinks I have what it takes, that means a lot to me. Everything, in fact. And after listening to Mum today, I'm even more sure. I can keep my post at the Corner House, and volunteer nights and weekends whilst Colin is away. Goodness knows I'll be at a loose end." She gazed down morosely at the sparkling ring on her left hand.

"Well, sis, I think you are proper brave. For me, serving tea to displaced Londoners seems daunting enough. I can't imagine driving an ambulance through the streets with bombs dropping all over and people being gassed." She shuddered, trying to imagine London during air attacks.

"We'll all have to be brave, ducks. And much better to be busy and helping, than sitting home worrying about Colin in danger." She sighed, as Maggie put the last touches on her pin curls and looped the hairnet into place.

"There, you're done." Maggie gave her sister an impulsive hug. "You really are bothered, I understand. I'm here, and we'll get through this together. Like we always do."

"I don't know how I'm going to say goodbye to him. I really don't,

Mags." She stood up from their shared dressing table and plopped onto her bed. "He's leaving the day before his birthday – for RAF training at Anderby Creek in Lincolnshire."

"Oh, Tillie. That's so soon!" Maggie exclaimed.

"Don't I know it?" replied Tillie miserably. "And Maggie, he's pouring on the pressure for a quick wedding. He's given up on a date before his training, but is insisting on a ceremony when he's home on his first leave. He's keen as mustard. I'm just not ready, Mags. It's too fast."

Maggie hugged her sister again, then sat back cross-legged on the bed.

"Oh my, that is a pickle." Maggie picked at a loose thread. "When do you want to get married, then?"

"After the war," Tillie replied promptly. "Everyone is saying it will all be over by Christmas, so why not just wait till 1940? We'll have time to plan a proper spring wedding, and then I'll have my husband with me. We can buy a small house for ourselves and start our new life. Doesn't that sound smashing?" Brown eyes met brown.

"It does sound brilliant, sis. But will he wait?"

Tillie shrugged.

"I surely hope so. I do love him, and I'm so afraid he won't come back. And what if we start a baby? Then I'll be all on my own. He just has to see the sense of it. He will, won't he, Mags?" She sounded bright, almost too much so.

"Of course, he will love. He'll be so busy with training, and learning how to fly, the time will pass quickly." She hesitated. "I think I'm going to miss Micah just as much," she said shyly. "It's for certain they are going back to France."

"Oh, Maggie. Here's me whingeing on about something that hasn't even happened yet, and you are about to say goodbye to your true love," exclaimed Tillie guiltily.

"Give over, he's not my true love," protested Maggie, looking down. "At least not yet."

"Tell me about it, sis," said Tillie quietly. Maggie was always so close-lipped about her relationship with Micah, so she trod carefully.

Maggie chewed her bottom lip.

"You know we've been good friends ever since his family moved into the neighborhood. We've talked, played music together, and walked for miles. But he's never said he wants to be more than just mates."

"Bollocks, Mags. Anyone can see he has feelings for you. His eyes follow you everywhere around the room, and he has that cute, awkward manner that speaks to how much he cares for you," Tillie was quick to reassure her twin.

"Oh, I'm not sure." Maggie couldn't quite see it. "He's never said as much, and certainly hasn't even tried to – well, you know," she finished uncomfortably.

"Kiss you, you mean?" Tillie teased. "Well, he's a slow mover. For that matter, so are you. I should think he's afraid you'll rebuff him?"

"Well, I wouldn't," Maggie jutted her chin out. "I'd welcome it. He did give me a kiss on our birthdays, but it was just a peck, not a proper kiss."

"I should knock your two heads together," Tillie replied. "In the event, it will be years before either of you makes a move."

"I will not make a move, Tillie!" Maggie cried, her face turning pale. "That's up to the chap."

"You're right, of course. But I wish it didn't have to be that way. When are they leaving for France?"

"In just a few weeks. He's my best friend, Tillie. Besides you, of course. At least he's asked me to write to him."

"Sis, you never said! That's brilliant. You know he must be serious. Blokes don't ask just anyone to write to them. How long do you think they'll be in Paris? What a time to go, with war around the corner."

Maggie sighed.

"Too right, Tils. Who knows? Right now, he's saying they will be there indefinitely, taking over the grandfather's jewelry business. I fear it may be permanent. They have rented their house here, so that's a positive sign they may come back. Who knows?"

Tillie hugged her sister.

"What a pair we are," Tillie said. "Twenty-three years old, with our chaps going away, and not knowing when they'll return. We'll just have to be here for each other, alright?"

"Absolutely, Tillie. What else can we do?" She yawned. "I'm going to turn in. I'm exhausted."

"Goodnight, love. Sleep well and dream of your fine young man."

The pair hugged one last time and turned into their beds.

The grandfather clock in the front hallway tolled eleven o'clock, and Tillie was still awake. She couldn't stop thinking of Colin and their coming separation. He'd been pressing her on all fronts – not just to set a wedding date, but also to progress their physical relationship. He wanted something to remember her by, he kept insisting, as their kisses became more heated. He'd begun by unbuttoning her blouse and touching her over her bra. Now, he was constantly trying to further undress her. Just last night, she'd had to stop him from dipping his head to taste her breasts. He'd been breathing hard and was not pleased when she stopped him. At the cinema, his hands crawled all over her, and he'd even taken her hand and placed it over the bulge in his trousers. She'd immediately snatched her hand back in shock, and he'd glared at her irritably.

What was wrong with her? She loved this man dearly, but his hot embraces and probing lips left her cold. Where were the tingling and excitement that she longed for?

She tossed over and over, too restless to sleep.

Was it that same old guilt holding her back? She fought to keep the memories away but to no avail. They came pressing in.

She'd been five years old when Kenny was born, six weeks prematurely, and it was her fault that he almost died. All her fault. She'd caused Mum to go into early labor, and Kenny had been born underweight and frail. As much as she'd tried to make it up to him, Mum, and everyone else, there was a part deep inside her that couldn't let go. She simply couldn't feel worthy of being loved just for herself.

Now she was a grown woman, and had put off ever getting into a serious relationship until she met Colin. He was so confident, so sure, and so in love with her that he'd swept her along with him. But she was holding him back.

Tillie flipped on her back and willed her body to relax. She would show Colin how much she loved him, and set a wedding date for early spring. She'd prove how much she believed in him and their love. She started counting backwards from one hundred until she dropped off into a restless sleep.

In the matching twin bed next to her, Maggie slept, unaware of the torturous thoughts of her sister, dreaming of Micah smiling at her.

* * *

The following weekend found most of the Kingston family in the back garden, dressed in sturdy footwear, trousers, and casual shirts. The girls wore kerchiefs to protect their hair, and Walter had provided cotton gloves for everyone. Thomas and Geoffrey Fowler had joined the party as well as Colin.

"I saw the barrage balloons going up today in Hyde Park. I understand they'll be flying over all the open spaces in London, and around the country – especially the ports and harbors." Colin was eager to spread the war news.

"What do they do?" Asked Katie as she slipped on her gloves.

"They keep the enemy planes from landing or getting too low on easy landing strips. They'll get tangled in the wire cables. It will force them to fly higher, making it harder to get close to their targets."

"We had them in the Great War," Thomas Fowler said. "By the end, we had barrage nets that stretched something like fifty miles. The German pilots hated them. I'm glad to see them up again."

Walter nodded in agreement.

It was a sunny August day, with a light breeze providing relief from what was proving to be a hot day.

"So how much did the shelter cost, Pops?" asked Kenny eagerly.

"£7 and a good bargain at that," replied Walter as he handed spades to the men.

"Why is it called an Anderson Shelter, Pops?" asked Katie curiously.

"I believe it was named after Sir John Anderson – the Lord Privy Seal who has been responsible for the air-raid precautions. All right, men, let's get to it. The council has come and marked out the best spot for it here in the back corner. We need to dig a hole to sink it in four feet deep, build it in, and then we'll need to pile about eighteen inches of soil on the roof and sides when we're done. I understand it's the done thing to plant flowers or vegetables in that soil. It seems the most prudent option to plant vegetables – to be sure they'll be needed in the coming months." Nodding faces gazed at him seriously.

"Righto then, girls, whilst we're digging, can you organize the corrugated steel panels? There should be six curved ones that bolt together at the top – that's the main body. And some straight panels for each end – one has the door. There's a leaflet with instructions. Once we've got ours sorted, we'll come to yours Thomas, tomorrow, and build one for your family too."

"Let's get stuck in, then," called Tillie gaily, as she headed for the pile of materials.

Within a few hours, they had built the rather ordinary-looking grey curved structure.

Walter tried not to look concerned at the size of the finished product – just six feet high, four and a half feet wide, and six and a half feet long. How would his entire family of six fit in this shelter?

"So, we'll all be okay in here, Pops?" Asked Maggie tentatively.

"It's built for six people, and we'll manage just fine. It will be a squash if we're all in with Faye, but we'll make do. I've ordered bunks, which should arrive next week. I'm sure Mum will make it cozy for the whole family," Walter said.

"And the bombs won't get us, Pops?" Tillie asked the question which was on all their minds. She had a smudge of dirt on her cheek that just enhanced her natural beauty. Maggie had somehow managed a similar patch of dirt on her face, and his twins had never looked more beautiful.

Walter looked at his family somberly. His greying hair was mussed up, and his forehead glistened with all the heavy work.

"This curved design will make it more difficult for the bombs to land or make a direct hit. It should perform well under blast and ground shock because of the steel. And being dug in deep with the soil on top will not make an easy target for the Germans. I can't promise it will always be comfortable or easy, but I should think we will be safe."

The little group was silent, surveying the tiny shed-like structure that was meant to shelter and protect all of them.

"So, who's for lemonade, then?" Alice appeared just then with a tray with a pitcher and glasses. She stopped short in front of the solemn party.

"Oh my, you are finished already. Well, doesn't that look splendid. Aren't you all so clever?"

"Just in time, my dear. And the refreshments are welcome. We've all worked up rather a sweat this morning. Thank you for the lemonade."

"I've brought a plate of biscuits as well – Faye just took them out of the oven. Come and help yourselves. I, for one, would like to take a look inside."

She placed the tray on an outside table and walked up to the shelter. Kenny had beat her to it, and was inside testing the strength of the curved beams, and swinging the door.

Determined to set a good example, Alice gave the structure and its builders, high marks.

"Mum, there's a leaflet here suggesting items to stock in the shelter – torches, blankets, and so on. I'd be happy to help you gather what we need, and get it sorted after dinner," offered Tillie helpfully.

"Brilliant, Tils. And whatever we don't have, we can buy at the shops. Let's do our best to make it as cozy and homely as possible," Alice inadvertently mimicked her husband's sentiment earlier. He smiled encouragingly, both of them looking for their children to feel safe and snug. It was all rather scary, given the circumstances.

"I can make a start on a list of veg for the top of the shelter, Mum," piped in Maggie. "Let's make sure we plant our favorites, in the event."

"No swedes, please," begged Kenny. "And loads of carrots," he added.

At just-turned sixteen, he was starting to look like his father. Still slender, he was more man than boy.

Thank goodness he's too young to be called up, Alice thought for the thousandth time. Hoping it would stay that way for the duration of this war.

"Mum, I forgot. This leaflet was pushed through the post today." He pulled a crumpled sheet of paper from his pocket and handed it to his mother.

"It's from the Ministry of Information," read Alice with surprise. She quickly scanned it, stood up tall and bravely read it out loud.

"WHAT DO I DO when I hear guns, explosions, air-raid warnings?

I keep a cool head. I take cover.

I gather my family, with gas masks, and go quietly to my shelter or refuge room.

I do NOT try to 'have a look.'

I do NOT rush about alarming people.

I remember that a lot of the noise is GOOD noise – our guns firing at the enemy.

And I remember the odds are thousands to one against my being hurt."

Silence descended on the group. The enormity of the upcoming war suddenly becoming a reality.

Walter was the first to speak.

"I think that should be the first posting on the wall in our new shelter. Kenny, fetch the Sellotape."

"Well, that was a morning's work," Alice jumped in. "Faye has prepared a hearty dinner for all of you, so clear away this mess, get washed up, and come and join us. Thomas, Geoffrey, Colin – there's more than plenty for all of you too. We so appreciate you helping us build our shelter."

"And we'll return the favor tomorrow, Thomas," Walter reminded, as the family picked up the remnants of the building project.

"Let's get a move on. I'm hungry," wailed Kenny. Everyone laughed.

* * *

After a hearty dinner, the group scattered. Thomas and Geoffrey went home. After a quick wash-up, Colin and Tillie went for a walk around Philbeach Gardens. Maggie and Katie washed their hair, and Kenny loped off for an afternoon with his friends.

Walter and Alice sat with their tea in the sitting room.

"My dear, you handled that brilliantly. I know you are afraid, but the children see you being strong. We'll have to keep each other resolute."

Alice smiled faintly as she patted her husband's hand.

"I'm trying, darling. We have such a large brood, and such a long road ahead of us." She sighed. "Are you sure we shouldn't evacuate Kenny to your brother in Wiltshire? Thousands of children are leaving the country by the day. The train stations are filled with them. But how awful for the parents. What a wrench to send your children to strangers."

"It's necessary though, my dear. We must keep them safe. But I should think Kenny is too old. They are recommending pregnant mothers and young children for the evacuation. And I'm quite sure he would put up a fuss about leaving London now. He's not a child, you know."

"He's not a man, either," Alice was quick to add. "And too young to fight."

Walter nodded.

"We'll keep him home. I'm sure he'll be of great use to us here." He took a sip of his tea. "And this week, we'll get fitted for our gas masks. Preparation is key. We want to be as ready as we can."

Alice nodded and was thankful yet again that none of her children would have to fight in the war. It would be hard enough in the coming months.

CHAPTER EIGHT

September 1939

"This is London.

I am speaking to you from the cabinet room at 10 Downing Street. This morning the British ambassador in Berlin handed the German government a final note stating that unless we heard from them by eleven o'clock that they were prepared at once to withdraw their troops from Poland, a state of war would exist between us. I have to tell you now that no such undertaking has been received, and that consequently, this country is at war with Germany...

The Government have made plans under which it will be possible to carry on the work of the nation in the days of stress and strain that may be ahead. But these plans need your help. You may be taking your part in the fighting services or as a volunteer in one of the branches of Civil Defense. If so, you will report for duty in accordance with the instructions you have received. You may be engaged in work essential to the prosecution of war for the maintenance of the life of the people – in factories, in transport, in public utility concerns, or in the supply of other necessaries of life. If so, it is of vital importance that you should carry on with your jobs..."

Prime Minister Neville Chamberlain continued his speech. It was a quarter past eleven on September 3, 1939.

"Now may God bless you all. May He defend the right. It is the evil things that we shall be fighting against – brute force, bad faith, injustice, oppression and persecution – and against them I am certain that the right will prevail."

The Kingston family gathered around the wireless in their first-floor drawing room. They looked at each other in a mixture of dismay, fear, resignation, and anxiety.

The National Anthem played and as one, they stood in respect. Walter placed his hand over his heart.

Then, the instructions to the public began.

"No cinemas, no sports, no large gatherings of any manner. The sounds of air raid warnings, and the all-clear. Rattles to warn of poison gas. Schools closed for at least a week. Keep off the streets as much as possible. Carry your gas mask with you always. Tube stations are not available as air raid shelters."

Everyone was stunned, despite it being expected.

Walter knew, as the head of the family, that he must say something.

"Well, there it is then. We are at war. As much as we can, we have prepared. The rest we will leave to the government, the goodness of our fellow man, and fate itself.

Maggie and Tillie – you will be responsible for the blackout at night – thirty minutes after sunset. Faye can see to the morning opening when she arrives for work. Kenny, let's reinforce the windows tonight with tape – to protect us and our belongings from flying glass. You and I will represent the Kingstons in civil defense. After supper, let's collect spades and other implements we could use to defend the family, if needed."

Kenny stood up a little taller. "Yes, Pops. Let's not forget knives as well."

Walter gave his son a small smile and continued.

"Mum, I'd like you to prepare a shelter kit – what we will need to take with us at a moment's notice. Please prepare a tick list, with a name next to each item. It will be that person's responsibility to bring the item to the shelter, replace it by the back door after the all-clear has sounded, and replenish it as needed – flasks for example."

Alice nodded.

"I'll lend a hand with the list, Mum," Katie offered. Alice smiled gratefully.

"Splendid," replied Walter. "As for movements outside our home, I'd like us to keep these to a minimum. Work, of course, and war duties. Shopping, errands, and the like. And at least for the time being, I'd like us all to be home before the blackout each night. The streets are going to be treacherous and difficult to navigate.

We need to keep an eye out for each other. I'd prefer us to travel in pairs as much as possible. Tillie and Maggie, you can stick together – especially if your Lyons House shifts align. Katie and Kenny, you can also be a pair. Mum–you and I will look out for each other. When we hear the sound of the air raid alarm, find your partner and get yourselves to the shelter as quickly as possible. No stopping for lipstick or a snack. Time is of the essence. Just your gas mask. And, it goes without saying that no one may leave the shelter for any reason until the all-clear. I know this is loads to take on board. These measures are necessary for our safety, and I know I can count on each of you to do your part. Does anyone have a question?"

"What about seeing our friends, Uncle Thomas and Aunt Shirley? Colin?" Tillie asked nervously. She had never seen her father more serious.

"We will have to sort that, Tillie. We don't want to make this any harder on you than it already will be, but I want to be cautious. We'll find a way to stay in touch with family and close neighbors. We will need each other in the coming months. But to answer your real question – yes, you can still see Colin. He's shortly leaving for training. But please be careful."

"We will, Pops. I promise," Tillie said gratefully.

"There are many unknowns at the moment. We have our ration books, but it's unclear what foods will be on the ration and when. Because of his government position, Uncle Thomas may be able to tell us as soon as he learns. We will have to pay close attention to the news on the wireless and comply accordingly. Now, about the blackout..." Walter's voice trailed off, as suddenly, the air raid alarm sounded, eerie and penetrating.

Everyone jumped up and looked at each other in panic.

"Jerry is wasting no time," Walter said grimly. "Everyone, calmly file down the stairs and out the library door to the shelter. Collect your gas masks. Kenny, lead the way."

Within moments, the entire family had made their way to the shelter, including Faye. Each of them tentatively eyed the sky on the way out, certain to see it black with German bombers. But none were spotted.

Two bunks had been ordered and installed along one side, with a bench facing them. It was definitely a tight squeeze with all of them in there. And the gas masks smelled of rubber and disinfectant – definitely not comfortable.

"I hope we won't have to do this very often," Tillie spoke for all of them, her voice nasal in her mask. "Hours in here won't be much fun."

"At least we are safe," Katie countered. "Maybe we should add a deck of cards to our list, Mum?"

"Brilliant," Alice answered. "I suppose this is a fair test. I welcome any other ideas to increase our comfort that won't take up much room."

They sat in an uncomfortable silence. Any attempts at small talk fell flat. They were all terrified, straining their ears for the sound of approaching aircraft dropping bombs.

Tillie tormented herself thinking of Colin. Had he made it safely to a shelter? He was meant to be on his way over to her house. Where was he? Was he safe?

Likewise, Maggie's thoughts turned to Micah. He was working with his father at their jewelry shop today. She hoped they had both found a nearby shelter.

Alice thought of her sister and brother-in-law, and assumed they were safe in their own shelter with their son, Geoffrey.

Just a few minutes later, the all-clear sounded. The Kingston family heaved a collective sigh of relief and slowly came out to the September sunshine.

"My dear, I think a glass of brandy before our Sunday dinner wouldn't go amiss, I shouldn't think," announced Walter shakily, as they all trooped into the house.

"I heartily agree, Walter. Well done, all of you. Faye, let's get this dinner sorted quickly. I'm not sure of everyone's appetite, but I want us to enjoy this fine meal that you have cooked for us." Alice spoke quickly to cover her anxiety. "Katie, please set the table. Maggie and Tillie – can you pop by Aunt Shirley's to make certain they are all right? And

Micah's family, too." She knew her older girls would be anxious about their young men.

"We'll be back directly, Mum," answered Maggie, as she and Tillie put on their hats and slung their gas masks over their shoulders.

"I'll keep a watch out for Colin, too. He should be here anytime," Tillie responded with a worried frown.

"He'll be alright, love," assured Alice. "That was such a brief alarm, and we heard no planes overhead."

Tillie opened the front door and literally fell into Colin's arms. She hugged him madly, raining kisses on his face and neck. She let out a breath she didn't even know she was holding.

"I ducked into an outdoor shelter when I heard the alarm on my way here," he told her. "Whoa – what a start to this war!" He looked flushed – and excited even.

"Mum, Colin is here and he's safe," Maggie called, before turning back and closing the door. "It's good to see you, Colin. Let's go, Tillie."

Having ensured the safety of family and friends, the Kingston family and Colin sat down to a much-delayed Sunday dinner.

Tillie could hardly eat a bite; she was such a bundle of nerves.

"Pops, is it alright if Colin and I go for a walk? We promise to stay close by."

Walter and Alice exchanged a look. Was it safe?

"We must continue to live our lives," Walter replied steadily. "According to the wireless report, that was just a false alarm. So yes, you can walk with your young man, Tillie. Colin, I know you'll take good care of her. We mustn't let the enemy scare us out of our everyday activities."

Colin nodded.

"Thank you, Pops," Tillie added, as the two stood up.

As they walked the quiet streets of Earl's Court, Colin and Tillie clung together.

"I'll come with you to the train, when you leave for Lincolnshire next week," she said through teary eyes. "How long is the training?"

Colin put his arm around his fiancé.

"Shh, sweetheart. I know you're scared, but it's going to be alright. My training is in three parts – three months each of primary, basic, and advanced training. I need something like one hundred and fifty flying hours to get my wings. I will get some leave after each part. And that's if I qualify. So, it will be some months sadly, before I can get up in the air and give those Germans what they deserve."

Tillie struggled to get herself under control.

"I understand, Colin. And that makes me feel a tad better. I'm sorry we won't be able to celebrate your birthday before you leave. I do have a gift for you – I'll wrap it up and give it to you at the train."

"That sounds smashing, Tillie. It seems strange that we'll have to go to work tomorrow, as usual. The world seems to have changed forever, in just one day."

"Too right, darling. I don't fancy offering tea and cakes at Lyons. It doesn't seem right, somehow."

"Well, as your father said – we can't let the enemy destroy our British way of life. And aside from the present, they can't take away our future. What do you say, Tillie? Stop holding me back. Let's set a date for a small wedding after my first leave. Maybe even a Christmas celebration?"

Tillie stopped and looked into the hopeful eyes of her love. He had never looked cuter – his brown curly hair, green eyes, even his too-large ears were all so endearing after such an anxious day.

She gave him a quick kiss.

"Maybe, darling. Today has been too much of a strain to make such an important decision on the spot. Let's see how you get on with your training. You will write every day?" She clutched his arm.

"I suppose I'll have to settle for that. For the moment. But I will not stop pressing, Tils. This war is real. Let's take whatever happiness we can." He took her arm and kept walking, in obvious irritation.

"And I'll write as often as I can," he promised, softening just a little. "Let's try to enjoy this last week together whilst we can."

Tillie gave him a sweet smile.

* * *

At six p.m., the family gathered again by the wireless for the King's first wartime speech.

"In this grave hour, perhaps the most fateful in our history, I send to every household of my peoples, both at home and overseas, this message, spoken with the same depth of feeling for each one of you as if I were able to cross your threshold and speak to you myself.

For the second time in the lives of most of us we are at war.

Over and over again, we have tried to find a peaceful way out of the differences between ourselves and those who are now our enemies. But it has been in vain. We have been forced into a conflict. For we are called, with our allies, to meet the challenge of a principle which, if it were to prevail, would be fatal to any civilized order in the world... It is to this high purpose that I now call my people at home and my peoples across the seas, who will make our cause their own. I ask them to stand calm and firm and united in this time of trial. The task will be hard. There may be dark days ahead, and war can no longer be confined to the battlefield. But we can only do the right as we see the right, and reverently commit our cause to God.

If one and all we keep resolutely faithful to it, ready for whatever service or sacrifice it may demand, then, with God's help, we shall prevail.

May He bless and keep us all."

Kenny switched off the wireless.

"What a moving speech," praised Alice, wiping away a tear. "He sounded so statesman's-like. He is the best King to lead us through these troubled times."

"I agree, my dear. Quite reassuring."

"Who is for a cuppa, then? You know what they say – when in doubt, brew up. It's been quite a day." Alice turned to her treasured family, hoping against hope to keep them all safe in the trying times ahead.

After England declared war, France followed six hours later, quickly followed by Australia, Canada, New Zealand, and South Africa.

* * *

A week later, a tearful Tillie saw Colin off at the train station. The Paddington station was jammed with what seemed liked thousands of military personnel being seen off by loved ones. Some women were in tears, all tried to put on a brave face.

"You look so handsome in your uniform," Tillie straightened Colin's tie.

Colin took out his cigarette pack and lit up an Old Gold.

"Wait, darling," Tillie pulled out a brightly colored package from her handbag and handed it to him.

Colin quickly unwrapped to reveal a silver lighter.

"This is smashing, sweetheart. And even my initials." Colin turned it over in his hand before lighting his cigarette.

"You can think of me every time you have a smoke, Colin," she said with a shaky smile.

"I'll think of you more often than that, Tils. Thanks ever so much."

The train whistle blew.

"I must go. I'll write as soon as I can. And I'll be home for Christmas, I promise." Colin gave her a hug, a quick hard kiss, and picked up his kit bag.

"Goodbye, darling." Tillie tried to smile brightly.

Colin waved and turned to board the train. He watched his lovely young fiancé from the window – her blond hair blowing in the breeze, her camel-colored hat set at a jaunty angle, her brown eyes filled with tears.

Tillie waited until she couldn't see even a speck of the retreating train. She took out a handkerchief from her handbag and wiped her tears.

Maggie was working at the WVS canteen that day, so Tillie headed in search of her sister, a cup of tea, and a friendly face on that sad day.

CHAPTER NINE

Tillie tried to shake off her despondency.

"I'll have a cup of tea, please," she ordered at the green WVS canteen lorry.

An identical face appeared at the counter.

"Tillie, you're here. Was it awful?" Maggie asked with concern. She looked smart in her new WVS uniform – green overcoat and felt hat, which was warm for that September day. She handed her sister a cup of tea through the open window in the mobile canteen.

Tillie took the cup gratefully and nodded.

"Worse," she said gloomily. "I tried not to cry, but I got that bloody lump in my throat and could hardly speak."

Maggie turned to an other volunteer.

"Lois, can I have my break now? It's not busy at the moment."

"Sure, love. Be back by half-past," called a voice from inside the van.

As usual, the twins drew curious looks and double takes for their identical looks.

"Let's just sit here on this bench, Tils," Maggie pulled her sister into a space left by a departing couple. "I don't have much time."

"Thanks, sis," Tillie sat and took another gulp of tea. "I didn't think I'd feel so empty – at least not so soon. Is any of this real?" She stared at her twin.

"Too real, Tils. I've served probably five hundred cups of tea today to departing soldiers. And every one of them seemed to have a weepy wife, girl, mother, or sister seeing them off. Did Colin fancy the lighter?"

"He did. I hope it brings him luck. It makes my heart lift – just a bit –

to picture him in training, lighting up his cigarettes and thinking of me. Does that sound rubbish?"

"Not at all, Tils. It's understandable to hang onto memories or thoughts that make us feel close to those we love."

Tillie gazed down at her ring and nodded.

"I appreciate the pep talk, Mags," she brightened a little. "You always make me feel better. Now, I'd best leave you to work. I promised Mum I'd stop at the shops for her on my way home, so I'll be on my way."

The girls hugged and said their goodbyes.

* * *

"Pops, Mum, come quickly! Katie's been hurt."

Kenny burst through the door later that night.

Walter and Alice were listening to Sandy McPherson play organ music on the wireless in the drawing room. They, jumped up alarmed and hurried down the stairs to the front hall, Alice dropping her knitting on the way.

"Slow down, Kenny. Take a breath. What's happened?" Walter laid his arm on his son's shoulders.

"You must come straightaway. Katie fell in the blackout. I think she's hurt her foot badly."

"Where is she?" Asked Alice frantically, as she slipped on her coat.

"Somewhere on Templeton," Kenny called, as they all felt their way down the outdoor stair rail in the pitch black.

"What happened?" Alice gasped, as she clutched Walter's arm.

"I was picking her up from her friend Marjorie's house. You know they evacuated her little sister Vera to the country, and the whole family has been in pieces. Katie went to cheer her up and stayed a bit too long. When I got there, it was already after the blackout . You can't see a thing out here, especially with no moon."

The trio had been carefully picking their way down Longridge Street, towards the neighboring road. All was quiet.

"As we were walking home, we heard a car coming down the street, but we couldn't see it. We tried to huddle together to avoid it, but at the last second, it came up on the pavement, and knocked Katie down."

Alice gasped and stumbled. Walter steadied her as they hurried along.

"She's all alone? My poor girl," Alice struggled to stay strong.

"No, the man who drove the car stopped, and he's waiting with her. Okay, we're almost there."

"Katie, can you hear us? It's Mum and Pops."

"Mum? I'm here," a faint voice called, a few hundred yards away.

"Katie! Are you alright, darling? Keep talking to us so we can find you."

"I think I'm okay, Mum. It's just my ankle. I tried but I just can't stand." Alice could hear the pain in her daughter's voice.

"I'm here also," a masculine voice was heard. "My name is Clive Turner. Over here."

The Kingstons rushed to the accident site, almost tripping over Katie, who was sitting propped up against someone's staircase, on the sidewalk.

"Is that you, love?" Alice felt around until her arms landed on her daughter's shoulders. She hugged her gingerly and felt the tears on Katie's face. "Are you alright? How is your ankle?"

"I'm so sorry I wasn't home before the blackout, Mum," Katie's voice shook. "Marjorie was so distraught. The whole family is suffering without little Vera. And then, they had to put down their dog today because of the war. I just couldn't leave her. It hurts, Mum," she cried in earnest now that she didn't have to be brave anymore.

"It's going to be alright, now," Pops added soothingly.

"I'm so sorry, Sir, for this mishap. I was driving so slowly, but we can't see anything in this damn blackout. I think my car is undamaged. May I please drive you and the young lady to the nearest hospital?" He sounded contrite.

Walter hesitated.

"I'll drive extremely slowly, I promise. And with the extra pairs of eyes, we should just about be able to manage."

"The Princess Beatrice Hospital is not far from here – on Finborough Road," offered Alice. "I think that's the best plan, Walter. Otherwise, how will we get her looked after?"

She felt rather than saw her husband nod as he made a decision.

"Righto, then. Kenny, help me lift your sister into the back seat. Mr. Turner, is it? Can you open the door, please?"

They eased Katie into the back seat. By now, she was moaning. Alice and Kenny sat next to her, as Walter slipped into the front seat next to Turner.

"Let's creep as slowly as possible. Any signposts or markers, kindly call them out," Turner said, obviously nervous.

A tense ten minutes later, they reached the hospital, which was also in total darkness. Walter and Kenny lifted Katie out, and Alice ran ahead to alert the nurses.

Turner accompanied them to just inside the door. Alice was surprised to see he was a young man, in his late twenties. Bright red hair and blue eyes made him quite memorable.

Again, he apologized for the mishap.

"I'm so sorry, Sir. If there's anything I can do, I'll leave my information at the nurses' station. I really hope your daughter will be just fine. I'm so very sorry," he repeated.

"Don't bother about it, Mr. Turner. It was an accident. A horrible misfortune caused by this war. At this rate, the blackout is going to be more dangerous than the enemy is. Thank you for your care of my daughter. And for the drive here to the hospital." Walter shook his hand.

"Thank you, Sir. Now I suppose I must brave the blackout to find my way home. Goodbye."

"Goodbye, Mr. Turner, and good luck."

Katie's ankle was broken, but luckily didn't require surgery. They placed her foot in a cast, and wanted to keep her for a week or so with her foot elevated, to avoid putting any weight on it. Then, she'd be sent home with crutches for four-to-six weeks of convalescing.

"I hate to leave you, darling," Alice whispered, as she held Katie's hand. "I'll be back first thing in the morning, I promise." Alice didn't notice the sounds and smells of the busy hospital. She sat in a chair, close to the still figure in the bed.

"It's alright, Mum. I just really want to sleep," Katie mumbled. She'd been given pain tablets, and was having trouble keeping her eyes open.

"I'm eighteen years old, after all," her voice drifted off.

"I think we'd best leave her, dear," Walter spoke quietly from behind his wife's chair. "She's in fine hands here. Thank you, Nurse," he nodded to the hovering attendant, waiting to see them out. "We'll see you tomorrow, Katie. Sleep well, brave girl."

"I'll bring along some of your bits and pieces tomorrow, darling." Alice kissed her daughter gently on the forehead. "And I know your sisters will be here, too," she reassured her, but Katie had already dropped off.

A rota started the next morning, and for the rest of her stay at Princess Beatrice Hospital, Katie was scarcely alone. During the first few days, she was in a lot of pain. Her sisters, brother, parents, and other family members tried to brighten up her hospital room with flowers, magazines, fruit, and other comforts from home.

Tillie took the lead in spending time with her sister, reading to her, brushing her hair, feeding her tasty treats, and distracting her with stories of funny and annoying Lyons customers. She barely slept, rushing to the hospital any spare moment she could between her Nippy shifts.

A week later, Katie was released, eager to come home with a pair of crutches under her arms. They had set up a temporary bed in the morning room so Katie wouldn't have to manage the stairs.

She was one of the lucky ones. During September 1939, road accidents increased dramatically, with 1,130 deaths –double that of the previous September – all caused by the new blackout regulations.

"It feels so good to be out of there," Katie breathed in the crisp, autumn air. "They took proper good care of me but I couldn't wait to get home. And look how well I'm managing on my crutches." She demonstrated a few wobbly steps on the road. "Tillie has been helping me so much," she smiled at her sister.

"You're doing smashing, darling," Tillie replied, ignoring the compliment. "We're all going to help you, little one." She gave her sister a gentle hug.

"Let's get you home, love," encouraged Alice. "Look, here's Pops with the car. He took it out of the garage especially for you today. And you're home just in time for Micah's farewell party."

A short while later, Katie was settled into a comfortable chair with her leg on a footstool in the drawing room. The room was colorfully decorated with streamers and a Welcome Home sign made by Tillie.

"I barely recognized our townhouse, Maggie, with the wrought-iron railing taken down. Everything looks so bare on the street," she sipped a cup of tea her sister brought her.

"It's happening all over London, Britain, in fact. It is rather unnerving. They are collecting all the railings and gates for scrap metal for munitions in our factories. We must all do our bit. I expect we'll see more of this as time goes on," advised Walter.

"Enough of this war talk, dear. We're having a double celebration this afternoon – welcoming home our dear Katie, whilst seeing off young Micah. Maggie dear, can you help me bring out the punch and food trays?"

"Can Tillie do it, Mum? I want to wait for Micah and his family by the door." Maggie pleaded.

"I'll do it." Tillie jumped up from the sofa. "You go, love," she pushed her sister out of the doorway and down the hall. "I want to nick a sausage roll or angel on horseback."

Micah and his family arrived at almost the same time as the Fowlers. They all crowded into the drawing room, greeting each other affectionately.

Tillie and Alice carried in trays of hot and cold food. Walter served sherry, wine, and lemon refresher.

"How is your father doing, Samuel?" Asked Shirley Fowler kindly.

"His heart is weakening, I'm afraid," Samuel replied shaking his head. "He should have retired long ago, but he loves the shop and his customers. I know I'll have a job on my hands to get him to slow down. But with Micah and I willing and able to take on the business, I hope he can take care and let go."

"Will you live with him over the shop?" Shirley asked, sipping her sherry. "I'm sure he will appreciate your help – in the business and at home."

"Yes," replied Ruth. "That's our plan. I can imagine Papa hasn't had too many home-cooked meals lately."

"Do you know much of the conditions in Paris?" Alice asked. "Are they on the ration yet?"

"I'm not quite sure," answered Ruth truthfully. "It scares me how much closer we are to Germany on the continent. Especially now that Warsaw has capitulated to German troops. Where is Hitler going next?" Ruth was clearly worried.

"Now, my dear. Have faith. Let's keep a positive sentiment," her husband gently chided.

Geoffrey Fowler broke the awkward silence.

"I have news. I've received my call-up papers," he announced eagerly. "I've joined the army, The British Expeditionary Forces – the BEF Rifle Brigade. I start my training in Winchester in a fortnight." He suddenly looked younger than his twenty-two years. His eyes were bright with excitement.

Alice immediately turned to her sister. Shirley nodded. She'd known about this, of course, but hearing it out loud made it that real.

Alice knew this would be a bitter pill for her sister to swallow. Thomas and Shirley only had one child – Geoffrey – despite trying for many years to add to their family. Shirley had lost two babies, one before and one after Geoffrey. He was cherished, actually overprotected. She could only imagine what Shirley was feeling. She sent her a sympathetic glance across the room.

Everyone was congratulating Geoffrey, clapping him on the back and saying *well done you*. Another young man off to fight the war.

Toasts were raised to wish the Goldbachs well, Geoffrey's success in the army, and Katie's good health.

After the cake was served, Micah and Maggie slipped off. They wandered the streets with no particular destination in mind, contented just to be together. After the bustle of the party, they both needed some quiet time.

After a while, Micah broke the silence.

"I'll write to you once we're settled, Maggie. I'm not sure when but it will be soon. I promise."

She smiled at him.

"And I'll write back directly once I hear from you. It will be quiet without you, lonely even," she added shyly.

Micah ran a hand through his light brown hair, pushed his glasses back to his nose, and sighed.

"Maggie, we've never really spoken about the future, our future. It doesn't feel right with everything so precarious. It's impossible to make any concrete plans. I don't know when I'll be back, if I'll be back. But you must know how I feel about you," he gazed at her intently.

Maggie took a deep breath, her heart pumping wildly.

"Actually, I don't know, Micah. How *do* you feel about me?" She whispered.

Micah noticed a bench and pulled Maggie to sit next to him.

"I care about you a lot, Maggie. More than just friends. I can't imagine a future without you. I can't ask you to wait for me – it wouldn't be fair. I just don't know how long it will be..." His voice trailed off as he bit his lip.

Maggie placed her hand on his.

"I will wait for you, Micah. I care a lot about you, too. I think about you all the time. I don't see a future without you either." She gave him a shaky smile.

"Really?" He broke into a broad grin. "I didn't know, I mean, I couldn't imagine, well..." he stumbled over his words. "The poets say it so much better than I can."

He leaned over and placed a soft kiss on her lips. Maggie closed her eyes.

"More," she breathed in a husky voice.

He kissed her again, deeper this time.

"I have something for you," Micah broke away, and reached into his pocket.

Maggie's heart felt like a jackhammer in her chest.

Micah pulled out a small black velvet box and handed it to her.

"Micah, what in the world?" She turned her dark brown eyes to his lighter ones. She opened the box to reveal a stunning ruby necklace. The pendant stone was oval-shaped and hung on a delicate gold chain.

"It's beautiful," she breathed. "I'm so surprised. This means so much, Micah. Will you put it on me?"

Micah took the necklace out from its case, undid the clasp, and placed it around Maggie's neck. She lifted her hair and he quickly fastened it.

He touched the stone and Maggie felt her skin burning.

"I wanted to give you something to remember me by. I can't give you more than this right now. You understand, don't you, my sweet?" His eyes pleaded for her to know what he meant.

Maggie nodded.

"I want only this, Micah. This necklace is perfect. And I will keep it on every day until I see you again. The rest we can work out together. Thank you so much. This will make it easier to say goodbye. Well, a little easier," she said shakily.

"I'll be able to come back a few times to settle up some business for the next few months. At least as long as I'm able. I'm very much hoping to be back in December," he finished with a lopsided smile.

They walked back to the house hand-in-hand.

The Goldbachs left the next morning.

CHAPTER TEN

December 1939

The war had been underway since September, but nothing seemed to happen. Their men were gone, sandbags piled up all over London, the blackout caused continual havoc, children tearfully evacuated to the country; yet life strangely went on as usual.

The bombing of London, that had been expected, had yet to happen, and although every single Londoner was grateful for this, they also wondered if they were really at war.

Of course, there were signs of military action outside of England. *HMS Courageous* had been sunk by German U-boats in the waters, patrolling Ireland, killing 519 of her crew, including the captain.

On the same day, working together with Hitler, Soviet leader Joseph Stalin ordered the invasion of Poland, securing a share of Polish territory.

And on December 13th, British cruisers defeated a German battleship at the Battle of the River Plate, the first major naval battle of the war.

The Kingston family carried on.

There had been a few more air raids, but none brought bombs. The family grew used to huddling together in the Anderson shelter until the all-clear, and Alice had made it as homely as possible.

Walter had unsuccessfully tried to enlist, but was refused because of the severe hearing loss he'd suffered in the Great War. He had told no one he'd attempted to join the Army. After they refused him, he'd been quiet and distant for a few days, seeking comfort in Philbeach Gardens allotment.

After coming to terms with the rejection, he threw himself into his ARP Warden duties with passion.

Alice and Shirley stepped up their WVS duties, co-hosting their knitting evenings at least once a week. Shirley was helping set up Rest Centers – shelters for bomb evacuees and refugees where they were given clothes and new ration books. She worried endlessly about Geoffrey, though he wrote home regularly which somewhat lifted up her spirits. Alice helped with taking in clothes donations and sorting.

Katie had happily bid goodbye to her cast and crutches, and walked around unaided, having fully recovered.

Kenny kept up with his work at his father's firm, but was impatient to do his bit for the war effort. He longed for some action and was annoyed by the wartime restrictions.

Tillie and Maggie were going strong with their Nippy posts at Lyons, but helped with the WVS most nights. They both lived for letters from their boys away from home, and raced to collect the post when they heard it drop through the door slot.

"Oh, thank heavens, a letter from Colin. And look, Maggie – here's one for you from Micah." The girls beamed as they each grabbed the letters hungrily.

"I'm going to take a little walk to read mine, Tils," said Maggie. "I want to savor every word to myself – even with the censor's bloody black marks through every other sentence."

"Brilliant, darling. I'm going to take mine up to our room. See you in a while." Tillie bounded up the stairs and ripped open her letter.

"Dearest Sweetheart,

I hope this letter finds you well. I can just picture you sitting on your bed, reading with a lovely smile on your beautiful face. How I miss that face!

It's hard going here. I won't lie. The basic training was difficult enough, I suppose. Although we must all learn to march, and obey orders without thinking, so it's all for the good. We've had lectures, kitting out, kit layout, inoculations and vaccinations, marching at 140 paces per minute, and saluting, amongst other maneuvers.

The flying is much harder than I expected. There are even more lectures, as well as getting in my hours in the air. But nothing can beat that glorious feeling of freedom as you soar through the clouds on a sunny day. I long to take you up in a bird someday, Tillie. You would love to see it – the ground so small beneath you.

We've gotten word that our second set of training may be shortened to just ten weeks. It will be hard to manage all the bookwork, plus flying hours, but I suppose we are needed flying Spitfires as soon as we qualify.

I've saved my best news for last. I'm due five days' leave, and I'll be home on the eighteenth! More's the pity I'll have to return to camp before Christmas, but let's make the best of it, shall we, Tils? We can have our own holiday celebrations a tad early is all.

I can't wait to see you, sweetheart. I've missed you so, and stare at your picture all the time. My mates all agree that I've been damned lucky to land a looker like you, and how can I argue with that? I can't wait until I have you in my arms again.

I'll write again soon, my love with my train times. Although I wager you'll have to wait for me. I understand there are interminable delays, because of the system being overloaded with servicemen.

All my love, Colin xx

P.S. Your lighter is my lucky charm, darling. I never fly without it."

Tillie read it straight through three times. She then traced her finger over the closing signature, sighed, and clutched the thin papers to her heart.

Five days with Colin! And just a week away. How marvelous. She rushed down the stairs to share the news with Mum.

Maggie, too, pored over her letter from Micah, as she sat on a cold bench, huddled in her coat.

"My dear Maggie,
I think often of our last time together. Your brown eyes looked up at mine so trustingly, and I take that faith in me seriously.

Life is very different here in France. The war is much closer. There is much fear in Paris. And frighteningly, the anti-Semitic feelings run high. Grandfather was so relieved to see us. His health is worse than he told us. Besides his heart, his mind wanders and he is more than a little forgetful.

His business affairs are rather in a muddle, and Papa and I are having a proper time of trying to sort it. But despite the parting from you, it was the right decision to come. He really needs us.

I will come back on the thirteenth to settle some of our British affairs and can stay a week. Isn't that splendid news? At least, I hope you think so. The Fowlers have kindly offered for me to stay in their home, so we shall see loads of each other.

I'll sign off for now. I do miss you, and look forward to seeing you soon. I'll leave you with some of Keat's finest poetry.

Hither hither, love—
'Tis a shady mead—
Hither, hither, love!
Let us feed and feed!

Hither, hither, sweet—
'Tis a cowslip bed—
Hither, hither, sweet!
'Tis with dew bespread!

Hither, hither, dear
By the breath of life,
Hither, hither, dear!—
Be the summer's wife!

Though one moment's pleasure
In one moment flies—

Though the passion's treasure
In one moment dies;—

Yet it has not passed—
Think how near, how near!—
And while it doth last,
Think how dear, how dear!

Hither, hither, hither
Love its boon has sent—
If I die and wither
I shall die content!

Take care of yourself, my dear.
Fondly, Micah"

A poem from Keats. It was as close to an admission of love as Micah had ever expressed. Maggie, too, clutched the letter to her heart. She memorized each word, and re-read it as her sister had done. She, however, would keep the cherished letter to herself. And Micah was coming home for a visit. What a lovely Christmas 1939 would be!

* * *

"Shall we plan a welcome home party, Mags?" Tillie asked the next morning, as the two prepared for work. "We can invite all the families. Even though Colin and Micah won't be able to be home for Christmas, we want a proper celebration with them." Tillie applied her red lipstick, as Maggie smoothed some petroleum jelly on her eyebrows.

"What a marvelous idea. Let's have a fitting do. How lucky they are both arriving the same day. And I'm at the canteen so I hope to meet Micah." Maggie was glowing at the thought.

"I'm going to ask Alfie for the day off. He must give it to me, he must, Mags," exclaimed Tillie. "I've missed Colin so."

Maggie gave her sister a reassuring smile.

"It's not long now, darling. And I'm certain Alfie will give you the time. Or you can swap shifts." Maggie paused to gaze at her twin. "And that red lippy suits you. I'm not sure I have the nerve to wear it."

Tillie smiled wickedly.

"Didn't you hear Hitler hates red lipstick on women? Now, it's our patriotic duty to wear it. It's called Victory Red. Would you like to try it?" She offered it to Maggie.

"No, thanks all the same. I'll stick with my pink rose for now." She glanced at her watch. "Goodness, let's get a move on."

"So, Alfie. I need the afternoon of December 13th off. Colin's train is due to arrive at half-one, but he warned me of serious delays. So, I may be there for a few hours. Please say it's alright."

Dressed for her shift in her black and white Nippy uniform, Tillie turned pleading eyes to her supervisor.

Alfie took in her pleading brown eyes the clenched hands, and hunched shoulders. These poor girls, he thought to himself. Holding on tightly to these men off at war, desperately trying to plan futures in quicksand. Well, far be it for him to stand in the way of true love.

"Take the whole day, Tillie. I know you girls need time to do your hair, and put on your face or some such. You can make up the time after his leave is over." He patted her awkwardly on the shoulder.

Surprising them both, Tillie burst into tears.

"Thank you so much, Alfie. This means the world to me. I'm sorry, I don't know what's gotten into me." She tried to regain control. "I suppose I really miss Colin," she added shakily.

"Only natural, young lady," Alfie tried to comfort her, whilst looking around the room for someone to rescue him. "Hey, why did the aeroplane get sent to his room?" He punned.

"Tell me why, Alfie," Tillie said obediently.

"Bad altitude," Alfie chuckled.

"Thanks, Alfie," Tillie smiled in return. "For everything." She leaned over and kissed him on his cheek.

"Nonsense, just helping our flying men. Now, off to your shift. And put on that Lyons smile," Alfie shooed her off.

Tillie nodded, adjusted her cap, and headed to the floor, determined to show Alfie she was the best Nippy at Lyons Corner House.

The days crawled by until the thirteenth. It was cloudy and cold. Maggie donned her WVS uniform, whilst Tillie admired herself in a new blue dress.

"Are my seams straight, Mags? I'm so nervous, my hands are shaking."

Maggie glanced at the back of Tillie's legs.

"Perfect, darling. You look wonderful. And just take a breath. It's the same Colin you know and love. Is he still expected at half-one?"

Tillie nodded, as she placed a matching blue cloche hat on her blonde hair.

"What about Micah? When is his Paris train due?" Tillie asked. "I'm so sorry you couldn't sort your canteen shift today, love." Tillie clucked. What a shame that Micah would have to wait at the station for Maggie to finish her shift.

"He's due at noon, but my shift isn't over till half-past. I'm hoping to slip away early, fingers crossed, Tils."

Tillie paused, thinking. They were both going to be at the same railway station – Paddington. There must be a way. She snapped her fingers.

"I just thought of a means for you to be in two places at once, darling. I'll come to the station a tad early – if I'm honest, I was planning on it anyway. I can cover for you, for the time you take to meet Micah's train till the end of your shift. We'll pull our old twin trick. We can switch clothes in the bathroom. You meet Micah, then we can switch back and I'll wait for Colin. It should work a treat." Tillie smiled from ear to ear.

Maggie thought quickly.

"You know, it just might work. The canteen work will be a breeze for you, and if Micah's train is on time, then I should return in time to swap clothes. If our luck holds, no one will be the wiser. Tils, what a smashing idea!"

She grabbed Tillie's hands and the girls spun each other around the bedroom.

The plan seemed foolproof. The girls giggled on the way to the tube, and parted before arriving at the station's WVS canteen. They agreed to meet in the bathroom in a couple of hours. In the meantime, Tillie would run an errand or two, buy some treats for Colin, have a cup of tea, and wait.

They met up promptly at 11:30, swapped outfits, down to the jewelry and shoes, and examined each other carefully. Tillie had reluctantly handed over her engagement ring, knowing it was crucial to the subterfuge.

"You look good Mags, very fashionable. How do I look?" Tillie gave a quick spin in the green WVS uniform.

"Smashing, darling. The real deal. Just remember, I'm not as loud as you so be a little quieter. The two other girls on shift are Marion and Winnie. They are both loads of fun and know their stuff. Just follow what they are doing, and stay out of trouble."

Tillie gave her sister a smart salute.

"Yes, ma'am. I'll do my best. Now let's get a move on. We'll meet at the Praed Street entrance to switch back after my shift, then I'll wait for Colin's train. Good luck, darling, and give my best to Micah."

Tillie handled the canteen beautifully. She served tea, cocoa, coffee, sandwiches, soup, rolls, and cakes to a stream of departing soldiers with tearful mothers, wives, and loved ones. She turned on her natural Nippy charm and efficiency, and was certain she was pulling it off. After all, wasn't Maggie a Nippy too? She kept checking her watch scanning the crowd, looking for Micah and Maggie.

Finally, her shift (or rather Maggie's) ended at half-past twelve. She waved goodbye gaily to her fellow WVS workers and started towards the entrance.

On the other side of the station, Maggie's eyes were fixed on the Arrivals and Departures board. Micah's train was delayed, and she waited impatiently, her eyes glued to the ever-shifting timetable.

"How is my girl? I've missed you, sweetheart," a man's husky voice greeted her from behind, nuzzling her neck. Before Maggie could take a breath, he had spun her around and planted a hearty kiss on her lips.

Maggie broke away and stepped back.

"Colin, what are you doing? You're not meant to arrive for at least an hour," she sputtered.

"What kind of greeting is that for your fiancé who you haven't seen in three months?" Colin said angry and confused.

"Oh dear, Colin. It's not Tillie. It's me, Maggie. She's taken my WVS shift so I can wait for Micah." Her words spilled over each other. "She has my uniform," she finished lamely.

Colin threw back his head and laughed.

"Well, that's a relief. I thought you – I mean Tillie – had gone cold on me. Where is she?" His eyes searched the busy waiting area. A blur of brown, blue, and khaki was all he could see.

Maggie started laughing too.

"Come on, I'll take you to her. Then I'll have to rush back for Micah."

Colin gallantly offered his arm. Maggie took it, and they made their way to find Tillie.

CHAPTER ELEVEN

"Tillie, look who turned up..." Maggie began as she spotted her sister. But it was unnecessary. Colin was one step ahead of her, sweeping Tillie into his arms, raining kisses all over her face and neck.

"Colin," squealed Tillie, when she could take a breath. "What in the world? You aren't meant to arrive till this afternoon."

Tillie looked at her fiancé, feeling breathless. It was the same dear Colin but somehow strange. They cut his hair quite short, which made his ears stick out a little more, and he was growing a small pencil mustache! He also looked a little tired, which was to be expected.

"My CO put some of us on an earlier train but I had no way to let you know."

"I'm so happy he did, Colin. It's marvelous to see you." She looked up at him with a mixture of relief and awkwardness. "You look so smart in your uniform," she added.

"Not to be rude, Colin but I need to find Micah. His train should be in anytime now." Maggie hated to interrupt but was anxious to find her own man.

"Of course, Maggie, please shoo. Thank you for bringing me to Tillie. We'll catch up later." Colin smiled.

"Ta ra, then. See you at home, Tillie. I guess we'll swap clothes then? For now, take care of my uniform."

Tillie laughed.

"Certainly, love. Give our best to Micah and I hope you don't have to wait too long. See you at supper." Tillie gave her sister a push.

As it happened, Maggie had a rather long wait – three hours in fact. She actually regretted the twin swap – it would have taken her mind off things to actually keep serving at the WVS canteen, but she couldn't show up without her uniform, and wasn't about to confess. She paced restlessly, had a watery cup of tea in the station café, and watched couples being separated or reunited.

Finally, the train from Paris pulled in. As the passengers disembarked, Maggie scanned the open windows and doorways, looking for Micah. Suddenly she saw him, just behind a young family that was struggling with an abundance of cases. He helped them alight, looking round the station for Maggie.

When their eyes met, they moved as one towards each other.

"Micah," called Maggie, waving wildly, rushing to him.

And there he stood in front of her.

"Maggie," he gave her his wide smile. "I'm so sorry I'm late. The trains," he shrugged.

Maggie drank in the sight of him. He looked a little tired but otherwise the same. Tall, lean, with his sandy brown hair and eyes peering through his round spectacles that never left her face.

He hesitated and then pulled her into a tight embrace.

"May I kiss you?" He asked shyly.

Maggie nodded, and he dipped his head for a brief, soft kiss.

"I'm so glad to see you, Micah. It seems an age since you left."

They started moving with the throng, Micah holding his leather case in one hand, whilst steering Maggie's elbow towards the exit with the other.

He looked around at the sea of military colors swarming the station.

"London seems the same, yet there's a hum here that I didn't notice before," he said.

"Perhaps it's a note of impatience, Micah," Maggie replied. "You know they are calling it a Phoney War now? All the bombing and devastation that was expected straightaway hasn't happened. People are bringing home their evacuated children from the country. And, as you can see, loads of folks aren't even carrying their gas masks anymore. We're not quite sure what to do."

Micah stopped.

"Oh no," he replied. "That is a dangerous way to think. Hitler has his eyes all over Europe. We mustn't let our guard down for a second."

Maggie nodded.

"Let's get home, Micah," she said softly. "We have somewhat of a knees-up planned for you and Colin for tonight. Can we try to just spend time together and forget about the war this evening?" She pleaded with her big, brown eyes.

"Surely we can, my dear," replied Micah in his serious voice, knowing that the war would crowd in on them again soon.

* * *

"So, Colin, how are you getting on with the RAF? Training hard, I expect?" Walter questioned over dinner.

Faye had outdone herself with a large beef joint, Yorkshire pudding, plenty of vegetables, and wine the Fowlers brought over.

The large group was crammed into the second-floor dining room. Along with the entire Kingston family, Thomas and Shirley had joined them, trying to keep up a cheerful face without Geoffrey who was not yet due leave. Of course, Micah was the only Goldbach present, but Colin had brought along his parents, Henry and Audrey, who couldn't let their son out of their sight.

"Very well, Sir, that is to say," Colin looked flustered, and stared at his plate. Tillie put down her fork, not knowing what was on his mind.

"That is," he cleared his throat, his neck and ear tips turning red. "As it turns out, they have re-assigned me as a tail gunner. It seems more are needed." He took a sip of wine, embarrassed.

"Does that mean you won't be flying bombers, then?" Kenny asked.

"No, in fact, a rear gunner plays a very important role," interjected Walter in his measured voice. "He acts as a lookout for attacking enemy fighters, especially upon British bombers operating at nighttime. I imagine it's rather difficult."

"I'll still be flying, mate, just at the back, not the front," Colin smiled at the young man, trying to break the somber atmosphere.

"That sounds brilliant," Kenny replied, awestruck. "I can't wait for my turn to sign up. Nothing is happening here. Except for more false alarms." His tone was morose.

"Kenneth, we'll have no talk of you signing up. You're far too young. This war will be over before anything like that happens to sixteen-year-olds." Alice jumped in. She knew her son was restless at home, but was grateful every night that he was still there.

"I've signed on as a bicycle messenger but it's been slow going so far." Kenny broke apart his Yorkshire pudding into a dozen pieces in frustration.

"1940 is going to bring many changes, not all of them good ones. We should be thankful for the quiet now," Thomas Fowler spoke. "More rationing is coming in early January I expect," he added. In his role in the civil service, he was privy to information that was unavailable to the public. His lips were sealed on several subjects, but he tried to keep the families informed as much as he could.

"What will be on the ration, Uncle Thomas?" asked Tillie, in between spoonfuls of Brussel sprouts. "We've already had to manage with petrol rationing – Pops hasn't had the car out in weeks. What's next?"

"The car is perfectly safe at the garage, Tillie. We can all do without that luxury," Walter interjected.

"I can't say for certain, Tillie. But you can be fairly sure that bacon, butter, and sugar will all be on the ration shortly. The government has undertaken to create new recipes to help housewives manage with less of these items in tasty new ways, so I'm told." Thomas shared what he could.

"Sugar!" cried Katie. "With my sweet tooth, that will be a real hardship. We all have our ration books but how will it work, exactly?" She asked around the table at no one in particular.

Walter and Thomas exchanged looks before Thomas spoke.

"All the wives will have to register at specific local shops. You can only buy the rationed food there, to avoid people trying to get more of their ration at different places. Each family can pool their ration books together, so all the butter, for example, can be purchased at one time," Thomas advised. "I fear there may be long queues at times," he finished as he gazed at the three women who would lead this effort for their families. Alice and Shirley clucked under their breaths, as Audrey Redwood nodded.

"A shortage of butter is going to make the weekly baking difficult," said Shirley, grimacing. "But we all have to do our bit," she added as Thomas raised an eyebrow in her direction.

"How much bacon will we get a week?" Kenny asked. "I love bacon," he added, smacking his lips.

This broke the tension and everyone laughed.

"I can't say for certain, Kenny, but I expect it will be far fewer rashers than you're accustomed to. You'll need to get used to oatmeal for breakfast before long," Thomas added with a smile.

"Ugh, oatmeal," both Katie and Kenny replied in unison.

"Fresh fruit will be in short supply, I expect," added Thomas thoughtfully. "But I don't believe vegetables will be rationed, which is why it's more important than ever that we all cultivate our shelter gardens."

"We saw loads of *Dig for Victory* posters today at the railway station," Maggie put in.

"Just so," said Walter. "Well, let's not spend too much time speculating until we know what we are dealing with. Now, we've been rude to our other guest. Micah, how are things in France? How is your grandfather? How are your parents getting on?" He asked.

All eyes turned to Micah, who looked uncomfortable with the attention.

"My grandfather is holding his own, but his heart is definitely weakening. Papa and I have had our hands full, sorting through the business – particularly the paperwork side of things. It's rather a mess, I'm afraid," he said wryly.

"Well, I'm sure your grandfather is grateful for your help," sympathized Alice. "How is the mood in Paris?"

"Uneasy, but everyone is going on as usual. A number of people are leaving, some for Canada and America."

"Oh my," exclaimed Shirley. "Are they as afraid as all of that of Hitler invading?"

"Yes," replied Micah shortly. "Especially the Jewish families. Anti-Semitic feelings are all round. Many are emigrating to their extended families to start a new life in a safer place."

"And your family?" Walter gently asked the question on everyone's mind. Maggie held her breath.

"We are not going anywhere," Micah replied, looking directly at Maggie. "Grandfather is going to need us for some while yet. And I still harbor thoughts of returning to London in the future, albeit I don't know when."

"Well, that's good then, isn't it?" Alice said brightly. "Can we please stop this gloomy talk? This is meant to be a celebration tonight." She gestured to Tillie, who slipped into the adjoining morning room.

She returned with a cake aglow with candles.

"Happy Birthday to you, Happy Birthday to you," she began singing. The others joined in, looking around the table expectantly, not quite sure whose birthday it was.

Tillie placed the cake in front of Micah, shock spreading across his face.

"But my birthday isn't until the twenty-ninth," he objected as the voices died down.

"Well, you won't be here then, so we're celebrating now. Are you surprised?" Maggie beamed from ear to ear, clearly the mastermind of this entire operation. "Now, make a wish, Micah," she encouraged. "Before we burn the house down."

Micah closed his eyes, paused, and then blew out the candles in one go. Everyone believed he was wishing for a speedy end to the war, or peace in 1940. But of course, no one knew what was in his heart or what he truly wished for.

"Let's have our cake and coffee in the drawing room. Perhaps we can convince Micah to play the piano and the girls to sing," suggested Alice hopefully. Everyone thought this was a smashing idea, and in no time, Micah was at the piano with the twins standing nearby.

They began with some Noel Coward favorites, including *Don't Put Your Daughter on the Stage, Mrs. Worthington,* and his new one, *A Marvellous Party.* Shirley requested some Glenn Miller tunes: *Moonlight Serenade* and *In the Mood.* Micah was an accomplished pianist who had been classically trained since childhood. He played effortlessly, and the twins sang along. Tillie had a clear voice that rang out confidently.

Maggie was shyer and preferred to harmonize and let Tillie take the lead.

It was a scene that had been repeated many times before. It was particularly poignant tonight, with all the unpredictability in everyone's future. Shirley fought back tears, missing Geoffrey, who would typically join the small musical group with his violin. He had been sent to northern France, and she was in a constant state of worry. So far, he'd not seen active service for which she was thankful.

"I think the boys are getting tired from their travel day. Perhaps we should call it a night," suggested Thomas from his corner chair.

"Just one more," begged Katie. "How about *There'll Always be an England?*"

It seemed a fitting end to the evening, and the trio sang of England's country lanes, cottages, and marching feet. By the time they got to the chorus, everyone joined in:

There'll always be an England,
And England shall be free.
If England means as much to you,
As England means to me.

As Micah tinkled the last few notes and laid his hands in his lap, the room fell silent.

"I think that's a perfect ending to this evening. Thank you, Micah, girls. Thank you all for coming," Walter stood up and the party was officially over.

* * *

The boys' leaves raced by faster than they could have imagined. Micah returned first, promising Maggie to return as soon as possible in the new year. Maggie sent small gifts for his parents, grandfather, and sister and Alice added some home-baked goods.

Micah and Maggie parted at the train station.

"It won't be long before we meet again, dear Maggie," Micah stroked her cheek. She struggled to maintain her composure. "We'll keep writing to each other and take things day by day." He kissed her and stroked her hair. "All will be well, little one."

Maggie gulped, an achy lump forming in her throat.

"Goodbye, Micah. Please be safe. And write soon." She hugged him.

He picked up his case and headed to the platform. As he boarded the train, he turned and waved, giving Maggie an encouraging smile.

She waved back, hearing nothing of the whistles and train wheels screeching around her, smelling none of the brake dust or creosote, seeing none of the hellos and goodbyes.

After a time, she turned and walked out of the station, bound for the Corner House and her afternoon shift.

A similar scene played out two days later with Colin and Tillie. They had enjoyed their time together, but there had been the usual tensions. Colin continually pushed the limits of their physical relationship, which made Tillie uncomfortable. Even at twenty-three, she wanted to wait until the sanctity of marriage to truly give herself to her husband – no matter how much she loved Colin.

He still wanted an early wedding, and now that he was on a different path with the RAF, he would qualify sooner as a rear gunner. He wanted a wedding on his last leave before starting his rear gunner service in the spring. Tillie hesitated and tried to put him off.

He reluctantly accepted her choice but had spoiled more than one evening with his sullen moods. Tillie found herself trying to cheer him up to salvage their time together, which was exhausting her. She found herself slightly relieved to see him off, which, in turn, made her feel extremely guilty.

"Write to me soon, darling, and let me know how you are getting on with your training. I know you'll do brilliantly on the airfield."

"I'll do my best, Tils. And I'll write soon – I'm not the poet that Micah is, but I can tell you how much I miss you."

He enveloped her in a tight hug and kissed her deeply.

Tillie kissed him back, willing him to stay safe.

"Goodbye, darling. Be safe."

Colin saluted smartly and raced down the platform to catch his departing train.

* * *

Christmas was a quiet affair, partially out of respect for the older girls and the Fowlers – all missing their men away from home. They exchanged small gifts, enjoyed a modest Christmas feast, and gathered to listen to the King's speech.

"The festival which we all know as Christmas is, above all, the festival of peace, and of the home. Among all free peoples, the love of peace is profound, for this alone gives security to the home. But true peace is in the hearts of men, and it is the tragedy of this time that there are powerful countries whose whole direction and policy are based on aggression and the suppression of all that we hold dear for mankind.

And to all who are preparing themselves to serve their country on sea, on land, or in the air, I send my greeting at this time...

A new year is at hand. We cannot tell which it will bring. If it brings peace how thankful we shall all be. If it brings continued struggle, we shall remain undaunted.

I said to the man who stood at the gate of the year. 'Give me a light that I may tread safely into the unknown.' And he replied. 'Go out into the darkness and put your hand into the hand of God. That shall be to you better than light and safer than a known way.'

May that Almighty hand guide and uphold us all."

CHAPTER TWELVE

May 1940

"On Friday evening last, I received His Majesty's commission to form a new administration...
I have nothing to offer but blood, toil, tears and sweat...

You ask, what is our aim? I can answer in one word: It is victory; victory at all costs; victory in spite of all terror; victory, however long and hard the road may be. For without victory, there is no survival...

Come then, let us go forward together with our united strength."

Walter got up from his comfortable chair to turn off the wireless.

"So, what do you think of our new Prime Minister then?" He gazed around the drawing room at his family.

"I think that was smashing," Kenny said enthusiastically. "If Mr. Churchill had been in charge, we wouldn't have let the Germans attack Norway last month. He'll be tough on the Huns, just watch." Kenny followed the military progress of war most carefully.

After eight months of war, Neville Chamberlain had been forced to resign. Hitler had invaded Denmark and Norway on April 8, and on May 10, he conquered Belgium, Luxembourg, the Netherlands and France. The same day, Chamberlain formally lost the confidence of the House of Commons. Churchill had formed an all-party coalition and quickly won the support of the British people.

"Mr. Chamberlain was in over his head, I fear," said Alice with regret. "He was so proud of the Munich agreement, even if Hitler never intended to honor it."

"What did he mean, Pops, when he said 'victory in spite of all terror?'" Asked Katie with a worried frown.

"I suppose that the war is about to get serious now and more deadly. Our allies must join us in this fight against Hitler and the Nazis. With united strength, as Churchill says," responded Walter. He lit his pipe thoughtfully.

Maggie and Tillie put down their knitting and turned to their father.

"Does that mean bombs over London?" Maggie asked.

"I don't know for sure, love, but I expect so. All of this practice we have had in this Phoney War is going to be needed now. Courage and perseverance."

Tillie just nodded, thinking of Colin. He had written that he would soon be going overseas. He didn't say where, but he was due a forty-eight-hour pass sometimes in the next few weeks. I wonder if he'll be dispatched to Belgium or even further. She shuddered.

The mood in London and around the country had been tense in the past few months. Without exception, all Londoners peered fearfully at the sky whenever outdoors, searching for the dreaded Luftwaffe bombers. The blackout was still a dreadful inconvenience, causing pedestrian and vehicle accidents, and making it difficult for everyone to get around the city. Sadly, the lowest of society were taking advantage. With the cloak of pure blackness,

looting, theft, burglary, fraud, gang-related activities, and even rape and murder had been on the rise. London didn't feel safe anymore.

As a result, most people worked, stood in long lines for rationed food, and hurried home each night before the blackout. They were annoyed at the restraints and restrictions, and tempers were frayed, with almost everyone sorely missing a husband, lover, son, or brother.

Luckily, the cinemas had opened up about a month after war had been declared, which offered some needed distraction for the bored public. Albeit the British newsreels, shown before the double features, showed grim war images.

Almost half the evacuated children had returned home by January, which was a huge relief to thousands of frantic parents. Although some schools had reopened, many had been requisitioned for military purposes, so classes were overcrowded. Some children were taught at home, and many didn't return at all. Life was nothing like it had been before the war, even if it still seemed like a *Phoney War*.

So, news of the war stepping up was almost a relief. Now, citizens could take action, needed action, welcome action, as did the Kingston family.

"Kenny and I have signed up for fire watching. That will be at least two nights a week each. Our initial training is this weekend," Walter spoke softly.

"Can you tell us what is involved with fire watching, dear? I understand we all may have to take shifts." Mum looked down at a lost stitch and fixed it.

"From what I know so far, we'll be posted to higher elevation spots – tops of buildings, fire escapes, and so on – to watch for incendiaries dropped by German planes. Unless quickly extinguished, these can start fierce fires." Walter reported proudly.

"How will you put them out?" Tillie asked intently.

"Using stirrup pumps," he answered. "We keep a full bucket of water at the ready. It's a two-man job. One person places one end into the water and hand pumps, whilst the other uses the hose and nozzle to spray the incendiary bomb to extinguish it." He stopped for a moment. "At least that's how it's supposed to work in theory. I suppose we'll see in practice soon enough, righto Kenny?"

"You bet, Pops," Kenny agreed, a little too eagerly.

"I should think you girls will get involved as the bombing gets heavier. It's imperative that we get those small fires under control quickly. The enemy will be looking for any fires on the ground, and use them as targets to create larger ones. If Londoners can do their part to extinguish these small fires, our Fire Brigade can focus on the bigger blazes."

They all nodded soberly.

"We'll do our part, Pops," said Maggie. "I can take on more WVS canteen shifts. I should imagine now with more men shipping out, the station canteens will be that much busier. And I know the WVS has many more tasks that need doing. I've been thinking about giving up my Nippy post to volunteer full-time for the WVS. I feel I'm more needed there. As long as my salary is not necessary here at home?" She turned to her parents.

"We can absolutely manage without your pay package, Maggie," Walter looked at his daughter. "We'll need to sort a small allowance for your pocket money in the meantime. I'm proud of you, dear. We both are."

"Thank you, Pops, Mum. I'll speak to Alfie about putting in my notice."

"And you are spot-on about the WVS, Maggie. Our rest centers will be busier than ever. Clothing drives, field kitchens, salvage, child evacuation escorts, and so much more. The Women's Voluntary Service has more work than we can handle. I'm proud of you, too, love," she beamed at Maggie.

"I can step up my WVS work as well, Mum," chimed in Katie. "Now that my ankle is good as new, I can do more."

Mum gazed at her gratefully.

"That's brilliant, Katie. We can use every pair of hands. And one more thing. Between Faye and us girls – queuing will need to be shared. It's not glamorous but necessary."

"Definitely not glamorous," said Katie glumly. "But we will do our bit." No one liked spending hours waiting in long lines, listening to others moan, just to be disappointed when the shopkeeper was out of pretty much everything.

Tillie nodded and looked around the room.

"I will do my share of queuing at the shops, I promise. But my plans are a tad different. I've been talking about this for months, but it's time to stop dithering. I'm going to see if the British Red Cross will take me on as an ambulance driver. Pops, do you think you could take the car out of the garage for a practice turn or two with me?"

Silence greeted her surprise announcement.

"Tillie, are you quite certain about this? Driving an ambulance will be rather dangerous," Walter gently asked.

"Yes, Pops. I know. Not as dangerous as flying planes, surely? Or dropping bombs on the enemy. Or sinking U-boats. Or marching into enemy territory, terrified. With Colin about to be shipped who-knows-where, and Geoffrey almost finished his basic training and soon in danger, I feel I must do more." She tossed her blonde curls in defiance.

"Won't you be terribly frightened, Tils?" Katie asked nervously.

"Bloody terrified, Katie. But that won't stop me. Isn't everyone scared?"

"True enough, my dear," assured Walter. "And to answer your question, Tillie – even with the petrol rationing, I should just about be able to manage taking you out for a spin or two to bone up on your driving skills. As I recall, the clutch gave you particular anguish at times." He sounded solemn but his eyes twinkled.

"Too right, Pops, but you needn't rub it in. I'll need to brush up my form – those ambulances will be bigger beasts than I'm used to," she gave a rueful smile in return.

"It's all well and good for you lot. Me, I'm stuck fire watching and delivering a few messages on my bicycle each day. I wish I were eighteen and could sign up properly."

Kenny stood, raked his hand through his blonde hair, and paced the drawing room.

Fear gripped Alice and she studiously worked on her knitting. Kenny had just turned seventeen in February and was dangerously close to being called up. Please, please let this war be over and peace restored before he turns eighteen. She knew how tortured her sister was with Geoffrey away. She consoled her sister almost daily and was selfishly grateful that her own son was still too young to enlist or be called up.

"Son, those are both necessary and important roles to play in this fight for peace and democracy. You can count on the messaging getting busier – and more urgent. Telegrams will come fast and furious now, I'm afraid. And doubtless, other opportunities to serve will be forthcoming. With every man between the ages of eighteen and forty-one called up, the work left behind will be momentous. We need to count on you, my boy," he stopped Kenny in his pacing and placed a hand on his shoulder.

"I'm going to my room." Kenny strode down the hallway and bounded up the two flights of stairs to his bedroom. Tillie stood up to go after him.

"Leave him be, love," called Alice. "He needs to spend a little time alone to sort his feelings."

Tillie sat back down.

"Is anyone else hungry? Now that we've listened to the wireless and gone the rounds here, I'm fairly starving," Maggie interjected to change the subject.

Katie jumped in.

"Me too, although I shudder to think what's on the supper table now that meat's been rationed too."

"Now, now, Katie. Faye does the best she can with the ration. Tonight, it's vegetable soup, fish pie, and rhubarb crumble. Pops picked the rhubarb himself from the allotment. Now, go and wash up and I'll check on the supper. I can fair smell the fish pie from here. Thank goodness fish is not on the ration." Alice scurried from the room, glad to turn her thoughts away from the vision of Kenny in a soldier's uniform, and to the more tangible, yet somehow inadequate role she could play in feeding her family.

After supper, Maggie and Tillie went to their room for a twin talk.

"Are you really going to put in your notice, Maggie? That's so brave of you." Tillie sat at their dressing table, examining imagined frown lines and smoothing on some Pond's cream.

Maggie kicked off her shoes and sat cross-legged on the floor.

"I've thought about it long and hard, and I'm sure it's the right decision. After all, I'm serving tea and cakes all day at Lyons. It's not much different with the WVS – except it's for departing soldiers, so it seems more like war work. And I should think we'll be called to serve homeless people in no time – those families bombed out of their houses. If Pops is right, that is. And that is a bigger contribution than just staving off flirting men as a Nippy."

"I know, love. You have thought about this – listed the pros and cons and so forth. But I will proper miss you at work. We've been together since we both started." Tillie said with a touch of regret.

"I know, Tills, but you'll be doing fewer shifts once you start with the ambulance. Speaking of being brave – golly, you'll be driving around bombed streets, picking up the injured and the – dead. Have you thought of that?"

"You know I have ducks, and it's important work. You heard Pops – men between eighteen and forty-one will be scarce as hens' teeth in no time. I'm young, strong, and know how to drive. So, I reckon I'm fair qualified."

Maggie jumped up and hugged her sister.

"I hate change and this bloody war is already coming between us. Promise things won't change any more, Tillie, please?" Maggie choked up.

Tillie shook her head slowly.

"I can't promise that, love, but I will pledge that we'll always look out for each other, no matter what." They clung together.

There was too much emotion in the room and Maggie was the first to break it.

"Will you come to the Lyons dance with me next week? After Colin's leave, I would think you'll be in need of cheering up."

Tillie frowned.

"I'm not sure Colin would approve of me going to a dance without him. We are engaged, after all."

"Rubbish," Maggie snapped. "Engaged girls go to these dances all the time. As well you know. And with men being in such short supply, we'll all be dancing with each other anyway. And besides, it will be my last dance as an official Nippy, so you must come. You can talk to Colin about it tomorrow. He's sure to agree."

Tillie looked doubtful.

"Well, I will ask but I'm not at all certain he'll agree. Oh, Mags, only forty-eight hours, and then he's being deployed to missions over in Europe somewhere. How can I make these two days last and last?"

Maggie took her turn at the dressing table, removing her bracelet and earrings. The necklace from Micah she only took off at work.

"You must not think about the future and all the what-ifs that might happen. You always do that, and then forget to enjoy the moment. Just enjoy every second you can with Colin, Tils. Show him a bright face. Give him loads of happy memories to take with him."

"You're right, sis. That's exactly what I'll do. Heaven knows when I'll see him again..." She paused as Maggie held up a hand in protest. "Alright, just live for the moment. That's all any of us can do with this bloody war."

Maggie smiled and started brushing her hair.

* * *

Tillie had begged Alfie for the two days off, which he had grudgingly granted her understanding that Colin was about to leave for overseas. She prepared carefully to meet him at the train station. She had washed her hair last night, and Maggie had carefully set it with pin curls. She had brushed it out into soft, shining waves that cascaded almost to her shoulders. Aside from her Victory Red lipstick, her makeup was light. She put on a grey suit, tucked in at the waist, with large shoulder pads. The skirt was slim-fitting and a blue chiffon blouse gave her some needed color. She put on a matching grey turban hat, adorned with a blue feather. Foregoing gloves, she picked up a small black handbag that matched her pumps.

Twisting in front of the dressing table mirror to ensure her stocking seams were straight, she then carefully dabbed some *Evening in Paris* perfume on her wrists and behind her ears.

She glanced at herself one more time in the mirror, practiced a bright smile, and swept out of the room.

It was a beautiful May morning. Tillie determined to imprint every minute of the next two days in her memory. She breathed in the fresh air, listened to the chirping of robins and goldfinches, and ignored the sandbags and fenceless front gardens that looked like toothless mouths, as she made her way to the tube. The lingering musky and earthy scent of the worms left by this morning's rain reminded her it was truly spring. She touched soft yellow daffodils growing on the edges of several townhouses on her street. If it had been raining, she would have stuck out her tongue to taste the drops. She took in the day with all her senses.

The tube was crowded with the working people of London and uniformed men, presumably on their way to the train and bus stations. Sweat mingled with perfume and soap and Tillie was lucky enough to grab a seat so she sat in relative comfort amongst the throng.

She shortly found herself back at the railway station, although Maggie wasn't working at the WVS canteen today. She went to the bathroom to refresh her lipstick, dab some powder on her nose, and re-adjust her hat and tuck in a stray blonde hair from her forehead. Her stomach was churning but she was determined to overcome her trepidation.

Satisfied with her appearance, she sat on a bench near the tracks where Colin was expected to get in. As always, she was early and tapped her foot impatiently as she scanned each incoming train. Pigeons flew in from the rafters and fed on rubbish under the benches.

Tillie waited for a few minutes, which for her seemed like hours.

A train whistled, pulled in slowly, and finally stopped. She heard the grind of the metal wheels on the track as it came to a halt. Men in all kinds of uniforms spilled onto the platform, met by tearful loved ones.

Suddenly, she saw a smiling face jump off the train. Dressed in his blue RAF uniform, with his kitbag slung over his shoulder, Colin hurried towards her.

He was here!

CHAPTER THIRTEEN

"Tillie! Sweetheart!" Colin dropped his kitbag, picked up his fiancé, and spun her around. He kissed her until she was breathless and finally put her down.

"Colin. Stop. Everyone is looking." Tillie felt her neck flush.

"No one is looking, Tillie. Every soldier here has his own girl," he laughed as he picked up his bag.

"How was your journey?" Tillie asked, feeling a bit shy. Come on girl, this is your fiancé. You've been longing to see him. Pull yourself up! She gave him her biggest smile.

"It was fine, but long. With all the city and town markings taken down, you never know where you are and how long it will be to London. But that's finished, and I'm here. God, you're beautiful."

"I missed you so, darling. I have loads of fun things planned for us so we'll be laughing and gay the whole time." Tillie felt herself looking forward to their time together.

"Sounds brilliant, sweetheart. Let's swing by my parents to say hello and drop my kit. Are they still coming to yours for supper tonight?"

"Yes, everyone is coming. The usual gang, you know?" She added sheepishly.

"Smashing. I love a good family party. And your Faye is a cracking cook."

"Well, don't expect much, darling. With the ration, it's bound to be something tasteless and in short supply. But Mum will have combined coupons with Aunt Shirley, so they'll have made the best of it."

"It can't be worse than what the slop jockey serves up in the canteen," Colin said cheerfully.

"Slop jockey? What's that when it's at home?" Tillie asked, as they left the station.

"The canteen cook. He could use a lesson or two from Faye. Everything tastes the same – stew and more stew – with unidentified meat, if any. But enough of that. I agree with you – let's just focus on fun. What's on tap after supper?"

"I thought we could take in the new film, *Gone With the Wind,* at the Leicester Square cinema. It's pretty long with an interval in the middle but it's supposed to be marvellous. I just love Vivien Leigh."

"Brilliant, sweetheart. More time to cuddle in the back row," Colin leered at her.

"Stop, Colin," Tillie elbowed him. "I've invited Maggie and her friend Marjorie along."

"That's fine. But they can sit near the front. I only have a short time with you, sweetheart. I don't want to waste a minute."

Colin's parents were waiting eagerly to greet their son. Henry and Audrey had obviously been standing by, perhaps even peeking through the curtains. Although the Redwood's house wasn't as grand as the Kingston's, it was spotless and Audrey clearly took pride in keeping a neat and tidy home.

"Colin!" She cried as the couple came through the front door. She hugged him tightly through her tears.

"Mum, Mum, it's alright. I'm fine," he reassured her, slightly embarrassed.

Henry shook Colin's hand.

"It's good to see you, son. You're looking fit," he added. He was an older version of Colin, big ears and all.

"Come through. Tillie, it's lovely to see you, dear. I've made you a coffee and walnut cake, Colin. We've had to save our butter and sugar rations, but it's your favorite, dear. I'll just put on the kettle," Audrey fussed.

"How is the training going, son?"

"Better now, Dad. Now that I'm not drowning in figures and calculations, I've rather enjoyed it. I've made some smashing mates, and the camaraderie amongst the chaps makes you feel good. We all have each other's backs. Even though I won't be a glamour boy, I'll still be up in a kite. My job is an important one and I'm keen to do my bit."

"I'm so proud of you, Colin. Just don't take too many chances. I suppose you can't tell us where your missions are going?" his mother asked, worried. She was short, a little on the stout side with greying hair and a beautiful English rose complexion.

"You know I can't, Mum. Even Tillie doesn't know. Careless talk and all that."

The government had released several posters in a campaign to stop Londoners from gossiping. German spies could be anywhere so messages of *Be Careful What You Say, Zipp It – Careless Talk Costs Lives,* and *Loose Lips Might Sink Ships* were posted all over town.

"Do you know at least when you might have to leave again, dear?" Audrey probed.

"No idea whatsoever, Mum," Colin answered brusquely. "I'll write when I can, but don't expect any details. The censors will make sure of that," he finished grimly.

The government and postal service employed dedicated censors to read all mail during the war. Everyone struggled to make sense of letters with black marker strokes through any words or sentences that could reveal British war plans – even inadvertently. As a result, most British people started self-censoring sensitive information to make sure their letters got through to their loved ones.

The foursome had a pleasant catchup. After three cups of tea, Tillie was floating. Colin gave her a look and stood up.

"Mum, thanks for the cake. It was a treat. Tillie and I must push off now. We'll meet up with you later at the Kingstons for supper."

"Give us your wash, love, and I'll get a start on it whilst you're out," offered his mother.

"Practically my whole kit is full of dirty clothes, Mum, so thanks. Cheers."

His parents chuckled. Tillie powdered her nose in their bathroom as Colin changed into civilian clothes

The two couples said their goodbyes.

"Why the rush, Colin?" Tillie asked, as they took a walk in his neighborhood. "I was enjoying that chat with your parents."

"I need some time with my girl, that's what," he grinned. "And to stretch my legs after that long train ride. Let's take a turn through Battersea Park."

The couple crossed over the Chelsea Bridge and ambled through the grounds. Contented just to be together, they talked of inconsequential things and gazed often at each other.

"Let's pass by the Boating Lake, shall we?" Colin said cheerfully. It was a beautiful sunny May afternoon. "Maybe we can hire a boat and I'll row you round, sweetheart."

Tillie beamed. What a romantic idea, she thought. And it will make such a sweet memory of the day.

They walked to the dock, paid their 10p for an hour's row in a rowing boat, and climbed in. It was a little wobbly but they managed and before long, Colin was rowing them around the small man-made lake.

Tillie trailed her hand in the water, which was a little cool, but refreshing.

"You look a picture, Tillie," commented Colin, as sweat formed on his brow. She had undone a few buttons of her jacket, her blonde hair blowing in the breeze.

She flicked a few droplets of water in Colin's direction. He splashed a paddle at her but she ducked neatly, giggling.

Suddenly, the moaning and menacing sound of the air raid siren pierced the afternoon air.

Colin sprang into action. He rapidly paddled them towards the dock where they jumped out of the boat, and ran towards the nearest shelter, which the dock man had pointed out to them.

With their gas masks swinging against their hips, they held hands and dashed gasping, to one of the park shelters dug last year.

Many walkers had the same idea and the couple crowded in amongst a group of other shelter seekers. They squashed together on a bench in the corner, Tillie practically on Colin's lap.

"How's this for one of your memories then, Tillie?" Colin said shakily in the dim light.

Tillie's heart raced as she tried to catch her breath.

"Not one of my favorites," she muttered. Why was Colin making jokes at a time like this?

They huddled together, ears straining for any whistles, whooshes, crashes, or explosions that would signal a bomb dropping nearby. None came.

"I don't even hear the humming sound of approaching aircraft so I think this must be another false alarm," predicted Colin impatiently.

Sweat trickling down the inside of her blouse, Tillie felt rather faint with the number of people cramped together.

"Are you alright, sweetheart? You're awfully quiet."

"This is my first shelter outside the Anderson in the back garden. I hope everyone is safe there," she whispered.

"I'll take care of you, Tils. And I'm sure our families are safe, as well." He thought of his own parents, hopefully snug in their own Anderson shelter.

A couple of people attempted to start a sing-a-long with limited results. Most everyone was thinking of the sunny May afternoon they had just been enjoying, and longing to get back out.

"Damn that Hitler for spoiling our day," grumbled an older man. Others mumbled their assent.

Tillie was feeling thirsty after their long walk but of course no one had brought any provisions. At least Colin was with her, she tried to comfort herself. She leaned into him even closer.

An hour later, the all-clear sounded. A cheer went up and the shelter emptied quickly.

"I'm parched, Tils. Let's find a pub for a pint."

"I'm thirsty too, but can we make it a quick one? I want to get home to make sure everyone is alright. And it's near suppertime, in the event."

Colin nodded. They found a nearby pub and Tillie snagged a corner table, while Colin put in their order at the bar.

"That's a first, then, isn't it, sweetheart? Our first shelter together?" Colin took a deep gulp of his beer. No one in the pub seemed to know of any bombs landing nearby, so it had likely been another false alarm.

Tillie sipped her lemonade and nodded.

"And with any luck, our last, Colin. It gets no easier. Albeit having you was a comfort." She still looked shaken.

Colin shrugged and Tillie cursed herself. Of course, Colin would be thinking of far greater danger in the sky in the next few months. Being in a safe shelter could not compare to being shot at in a small aeroplane.

"Let's hurry, shall we, darling? I am eager to be home. And I know that Faye and Mum will have pulled out all the stops for this evening's meal."

Colin finished his pint in one long gulp and stood up. Tillie gratefully joined him.

A gloom enveloped Colin's party. Not just the sobering impact of all the guests having spent time in shelters that day, but it had brought home the danger that Colin was flying into in the coming weeks.

"Sorry it's only a stew, Colin – but it's the best way to stretch our meager ration. The butcher put aside a lean bit of beef for us, and the swedes and turnips are from our own allotment," smiled Alice. "We should be soon getting sprouts and cabbage."

"Everything tastes wonderful, Mrs. Kingston," Colin enthused over his mashed potatoes, which were a little more yellow than usual, thanks to the margarine substitute.

"So delicious, and we really appreciate you having us," thanked Audrey Redwood. "I can only see my son for a little while more, so every moment with him is precious."

Everyone nodded and shared shelter stories of the day. After coffee and Aunt Shirley's carrot cake, the young people dispersed for the evening.

Tillie changed into a cooler short-sleeve red and white striped dress with a white collar and matching cuffs. She touched up her makeup and flew down the stairs to meet a waiting Colin.

"Is Marjorie meeting us at the Odeon?" She asked Maggie, as the trio opened the front door.

"Yes, and let's get our skates on. That damn air raid alarm has messed up our day enough."

They met Marjorie in no time, bought tickets and candy, and settled in at the cinema. The girls sat in the orchestra section, while Tillie and Colin made for the upper rows.

"We'll see you at the interval," whispered Tillie, clutching her milk duds. Maggie nodded, already sampling her wine gums.

"What a story!" Exclaimed Marjorie when they all found each other again in the intermission. "That Scarlet O'Hara is a wicked woman!"

"But so beautiful," protested Maggie in the line for drinks. "Vivien Leigh is perfect – and with that Southern accent."

"I don't think my arse can take another two hours of this," complained Colin. "But I do like that Clark Gable character. He's a man's man, he is." He sipped gratefully on a pint.

During the second half of the film, Colin became a little antsy, and his hands roamed all over Tillie – her breasts, lap, and even tried to put them up her dress – all whilst pressing her for kiss after kiss.

"Colin, the film," she kept whispering. "Stop!"

But he wouldn't be dissuaded, and kept up a frontal attack for the rest of the film. Not the least bit aroused, Tillie tried to quiet her irritation. He was just a lad looking for a bit of fun before fighting in the war, wasn't he? But that mustache tickled and she rather wished to see how the film turned out.

"Do you think Scarlett could win Rhett Butler back?" Marjorie asked as they picked their way home through the blackout. They each had small torches now, which had to be pointed downwards. Some streets had painted white lines to aid with visibility, which helped.

"I don't like a film ending like that. After almost four hours, couldn't they have finished it properly? Why leave us guessing?" Colin didn't appreciate the ending of Scarlett saying 'Tomorrow is another day,' after Rhett disappeared into the mist.

"I loved it," mused Tillie gently. "The characters – that poor Melanie! And the Civil War was so cruel."

"Those scenes with all the injured soldiers when Scarlett had to nurse them. It was too much," added Maggie quietly.

They all stayed away from talking about the actual war and fighting. It was just too close to what they were about to face.

They made it home without incident after dropping off Marjorie. Maggie tactfully left Tillie and Colin on the front steps.

"Colin, that was lovely. Thank you so much for the film. And tomorrow is a big day too. I have made dinner reservations at a special restaurant, so you'll have to dress up." Tillie told Colin eagerly.

"Come here, you," he growled as he reached for her. After planting a few ardent kisses, they reluctantly parted.

"Dad has asked me to help with a few things in the morning so I'll swing by after dinner, alright? Since there's nothing much else to do in London these days, I suppose we can go for another walk?"

"That sounds splendid, darling. But do hurry over as soon as you can." He couldn't see her, but Tillie's scent wafted towards him.

Colin kissed her one more time, then ran lightly down the steps and disappeared into the blackness.

The next day flew by. Tillie and Colin only had time for a short walk, then he announced he was meeting some of his mates for beers before their dinner date.

"But Colin, we only have tonight and then you're leaving in the morning. Surely, you can see them at your base?" Tillie was sorely disappointed. She had waited so long to see her love. Why didn't he want to spend every possible moment with her?

"It's just a few pints, sweetheart. I'll collect you at six o'clock just like we said."

Tillie had no option but to agree.

She spent the time carefully getting dressed for their last evening together. She put on a yellow chiffon dress that fell in soft pleats below her knees. Short-sleeved with a V-neck, it was daring, but suited her slim figure perfectly. She pinned her hair up, topped with a soft white beret adorned with yellow flowers. Slipping on white pumps with low heels, she collected her white gloves and handbag. She took a moment to admire her flower engagement ring, noting its sparkle on her left hand. Touching up her red lipstick, she twirled the chiffon fabric to check her seams and bounced out of her room. No making Colin wait for her tonight. Every moment counted.

She had saved from her wages so they could dine at the elite and extravagant Ritz Hotel. The orchestra played beautiful music in the Palm Court, as the waiters served Cornish Lobster Thermidor under silver domes. Colin looked handsome in his grey suit, crisp white shirt and blue tie. They even drank champagne.

"Tillie, I'm overwhelmed," he sputtered, as they lingered over coffee and a lemon raspberry tart. He lit a cigarette nervously.

"You still have my lighter," squealed Tillie in delight.

"I have it with me always, sweetheart – for keeps."

"I wanted tonight to be perfect," she whispered, as she put her left hand on his.

He picked it up, examined the diamond ring and put her hand back down.

"It is perfect, Tils. Only one thing would make it more perfect. Let us set a wedding date, sweetheart. What are we waiting for? We don't know what's going to happen tomorrow. We need to seize every moment of happiness we can. How about it, Mathilda Jean Kingston? Will you marry me on my next leave? Please?"

Tillie looked around the glamorous room, hearing the piano, guests murmuring intimately, and the sound of silver clicking on expensive plates. What was she waiting for? How could she send off this hopeful young man to war without giving him a reason to stay safe, take fewer chances, live?

She turned her most dazzling smile on her fiancé. She had never looked more lovely.

"Yes, Colin. I will marry you on your next leave. I promise."

He jumped up and kissed her in front of the Ritz crowd.

The next morning, he was gone.

CHAPTER FOURTEEN

June 1940

An animal wail greeted Tillie at the door. What on earth? She rushed into the drawing room, where Aunt Shirley was sobbing in her sister's arms.

On the table stood a thin beige piece of paper with POST OFFICE TELEGRAM letterhead, surrounded by a crown. Tillie's heart dropped to her toes.

"Mum?" she asked in an anguished voice. It couldn't be. It couldn't!

"It's Geoffrey," Mum choked out as she stroked Shirley's ravaged face, tears coursing down her own. She nodded at Tillie to read the telegram.

"June 14, 1940

To Mr. and Mrs. Thomas Fowler,
The British Expeditionary Forces deeply regret to inform you that your son, Lance Corporal Geoffrey Fowler, was killed in action at Dunkirk on May 29, 1940.

Regretfully,
Field Marshall Terence Stone"

Tillie carefully placed the paper back on the table and rushed to hug her aunt.

"Oh, Aunt Shirley, I'm so very sorry. I don't even know what to say. Geoffrey, that poor lad," Tillie wept.

For the last fortnight, everyone in Britain had been holding their breaths, hearing about the dramatic operations taking place on the French beach of Dunkirk, from sporadic newspaper reports to carefully curated BBC bulletins on the wireless.

It was both a massive defeat and a tremendous miracle. The French and British troops had been struggling to hold the Maginot Line in northern France. Hitler had invaded Belgium and marched into France. The Allied Forces were out-manned and out-tanked, and ordered to march to Dunkirk beach for evacuation. For days, they withdrew dejectedly to the only possible point of rescue, joined by French refugees who were forced to leave their homes and livelihoods.

Knowing nothing of what was to come, the BEF retreating soldiers obeyed orders to destroy all British tanks, supplies, and ammunition. They left with just their rifles and meager belongings.

Congregating on the open beach with thousands of British and French troops, the soldiers were stranded without food, water, or shelter for days, under constant shelling and bombardment by the German Luftwaffe. Many perished in full view of their comrades. That was a massive defeat.

The miracle came when the British rallied to save their own. The Royal Navy deployed to rescue as many men as possible. However, many of the large destroyers couldn't make it close enough to the beach to rescue the troops.

The British people were called upon to help – by offering the use of or volunteering any and all small crafts to carry the soldiers from the beach to the waiting ships.

This was incredibly dangerous as the Luftwaffe incessantly bombed the beaches and ships, causing the loss of many lives – military and civilian.

In the end, over 300,000 British and 125,000 French troops were saved during this daring rescue, dubbed Operation Dynamo. Sadly, Geoffrey Fowler was not one of them.

The family slowly convened to comfort the inconsolable Shirley. Maggie made tea after her WVS shift and Katie told Faye to hold off on supper.

Walter and Kenny returned from the office and offered their sympathy before quietly withdrawing, leaving the women to grieve.

Thomas was the last to arrive. After being notified at work of the ghastly telegram, he had swiftly approached his Ministry contacts to try and track down the full story about his son.

He entered the drawing-room, looking ten years older than the last time Tillie had seen him. New lines had sprung up over his eyebrows and his complexion was grey.

"Uncle Thomas, I'm so sorry. We are all so sorry about Geoffrey. He is – was the funniest and most kind cousin." Tillie tripped over her words.

Thomas joined his wife on the sofa, silently putting his arm around her. Shirley attempted to gain control but collapsed in fresh tears after seeing her husband.

"Have you found anything more, Thomas?" She asked frantically.

Alice rose.

"Girls, let's leave them alone. Let's help Faye with supper."

"No, no, it's fine," waved Thomas distractedly. "There's not much to report. News is spotty. As best as I can find out, Geoffrey was killed on the beach, waiting with the others to be rescued. The exact date is uncertain, but probably May 29th or 30th. Nothing more is known."

"Will he...his body be coming home for burial?" Shirley asked, her voice breaking.

Thomas shook his head slowly.

"No, my dear. All the men that were lost will stay in France. Perhaps someday there will be a memorial. Now that Hitler has conquered France, there is no way to retrieve them. I'm so sorry, my dear."

She bowed her head.

"Can I get you a brandy, Thomas?" Walter offered as he returned to the room. "I don't think tea will suffice in this circumstance," he offered.

Thomas nodded and Walter crossed to the drinks tray on the sideboard. He poured two large brandies – one each for Thomas and Shirley. They both sipped at the strong liquor, Shirley coughing as it went down.

Without asking he poured one for each of the twins, his wife, and then one for himself. He knew they all needed a remedy for the shock, albeit a short-lived respite.

They sat in silence, no one knowing quite what to say. The downstairs hall clock chimed five o'clock.

"You know, Geoffrey was always quick with a joke and kind. And smart. You just had to look into his brown eyes to see the intelligence behind them," Tillie said softly.

They all conjured up a picture of dear Geoffrey – tall, thin, with curly brown hair and a ready laugh.

"When he hugged you, you knew it," Katie whispered. "Like he hadn't seen you in years and was glad to meet you again. He could hug the breath right out of you," she smiled weakly.

"He would have made a brilliant solicitor," Alice added softly.

They all fought their tears.

"Will you stay to supper?" Alice asked, not sure what else to do.

"I couldn't eat a thing," Shirley whispered. "My poor boy, suffering without food or water, terrified for his life." She wasn't picturing her full-grown son, but him as a baby and young lad, the sweet memories of a mother. She broke down again, burying her head in her hands as great gulping sobs engulfed her.

"He likely didn't suffer, my dear. The Germans are well known for not missing their targets." Thomas' voice was grim as he looked at Alice. "I think I'd best get her home. Thank you for the offer and for all of your warm-hearted words about Geoffrey."

Walter insisted on walking them home, even though they lived just a few blocks away. Alice had pressed a cottage pie into Walter's hands. It was more veg than beef but she hoped Thomas could convince Shirley to have a bite or two later that evening.

"Anything you need, Thomas – day or night. Alice will be over first thing in the morning, but if you need either of us to stay with you, we'll be right over." He clamped a hand on his brother-in-law's shoulder. "He was a good lad, our Geoffrey. He'll be sorely missed."

Thomas nodded, then shepherded his broken wife towards their quiet home.

It was a somber night back at the Kingstons' townhouse. After listening to the evening news, they ate a quiet supper, each one lost in memories of Geoffrey and the senselessness of war. Alice found it hard to keep her composure, her heart breaking for her sister.

Tillie and Maggie retired early, each wanting to process the news together.

"I can't fathom it. Is it really true?" Maggie asked, sitting on her bed, her lower lip quivering.

"I know, love. I can still see him at Brighton Beach last summer, laughing on the pier and eating ice cream. I can't bear to think of him on that French beach, terrified for his life, no place to hide." Tillie cried too.

"As badly as I feel for Uncle Thomas and Aunt Shirley, I'm so fearful for Micah, Tillie," Maggie confided. "I haven't heard from him since early April. And now that France has fallen to the Germans, where is he? What's happened to him? There is so little news from Paris."

"Oh darling, I'm sure he must be safe. The Goldbachs are far, far away from Dunkirk after all."

"Damn this bloody war. And the news that is no news. Does the government think we are daft? They eke out snippets of information that tell us nothing."

Micah had visited London once more in early spring. He and Maggie had cherished a few days together, talking and making hopeful plans for a future that seemed years away. They had kept up their correspondence and Maggie felt the two of them growing closer all the time, despite the distance. She and Tillie still raced each other for the mail each day.

"So, the last time you had a letter was early April?" Tillie asked, her eyes widening.

Maggie pushed her hair out of her face.

"April 16th, to be exact. I've written to him almost every day since then and heard nothing."

"Darling, you know that the post moves as slowly as snails – especially now. I sometimes don't hear from Colin for weeks, then I get a load of letters all at once. And remember darling, he's stationed here in England not over in France where the post is bound to move even more erratically."

"I know," sighed Maggie. "But now that France is occupied, what does that mean for Micah and his family? Especially as they are Jewish. Will they be able to carry on with their business? Or come back to England?" Maggie chewed on a loose fingernail.

"Did he let on anything in his last letter about coming back to London? Would they have been able to convince the grandfather that it's safer here?" Tillie wanted to know all the possibilities.

"He mentioned it in one of his last letters. Let's take a look." Maggie bent under her bed and pulled out the battered chocolate tin where she kept Micah's letters.

She rifled through them.

"We started numbering them so we could keep track when a load came at once. Here's the last one, number twenty-two. She scanned it. "Here it is.

'Mama is getting more frightened to stay in Paris. This is putting Papa in a difficult situation. He doesn't want to pressure Grandfather, but he keeps trying to convince him we'd be safer in London and that he can continue with the business there. Grandfather resists, saying he's too old to leave home. Papa fears the trip may be too much for him, in any case. But he won't leave him here. You do understand, my sweet, that I can't desert them? As much as I long to be at your side, I can't abandon my family. We shall just have to hope that peace comes quickly, or Papa will assure Grandfather he can make the trip, and we'll be better off in London. Be patient, please.'"

Maggie let the fragile papers drop to her lap.

"It doesn't sound too promising, does it, Tils?" She grimaced. "But I understand his loyalty is to his family," she quickly amended.

"What a tough spot. I do hear of many families leaving France. The conditions there for Jewish people are dreadful, I understand." Tillie shook her head in frustration.

Maggie raised her palms helplessly.

"What can I do, Tillie? Just like millions of other women in this war – wait, hope, and pray. As you are doing. I know you worry constantly about Colin. I hear you toss and turn every night."

"I'm sorry, dear sister. Colin has done four successful runs as a rear gunner. He's come back each time. But he hints that they have lost several Spitfires already, including the crew. Young pilots are going up in the air with a shortened training regime. Why did he have to choose such a dangerous branch of the armed forces? I can't lose him."

The twins clung together, crying over their loved ones so far from home, for Geoffrey, for everything really.

"What did Churchill say?" Tillie sniffled. "'We shall go on to the end, we shall fight in France, we shall fight on the seas and oceans, we shall fight with growing confidence and growing strength in the air, we shall defend our island, whatever the cost may be.' If Hitler thinks he's beaten us down, he's wrong by a mile. Dunkirk is just the beginning, and we're more determined than ever."

"You're right, sis. Let's pull ourselves together. Mum needs us now. Shall we make us all a cup of cocoa? To be sure, we need it."

The twins went downstairs arm in arm.

* * *

The WVS rallied around Shirley. After all, she was one of their own. They contrived a rota so that she would never be alone. They joined their coupons and took charge of Shirley's ration book to provide meals for the grieving parents.

Alice spent hours with her sister, listening to stories of Geoffrey's childhood and her lost hopes of his future, a wife, and children. After a while, Alice persuaded Shirley to take up her knitting again, but no one could coax her to leave the house.

Not having a body to bury was the most distressing aspect of the entire tragedy. If they could have put him to rest at St. Luke's, had prayers said over him by the local clergy, and erected a headstone to visit and honor with flowers – that would have gone a long way to the Fowlers accepting Geoffrey's death.

As it was, it seemed unreal. Shirley kept expecting her son to swing through the door, drop his kit bag, and swoop in for one of his trademark bear hugs. But he didn't.

Everyone carried on. What choice did they have? The BEF regrouped and was more determined than ever to prevail over the enemy.

Tillie began her ambulance training with the London Auxiliary Ambulance Service. After her father had used some of his precious petrol coupons to help her brush up on her driving, she was feeling slightly more confident. Her clutching was still a bit wobbly but she thought she'd be able to manage.

She'd been assigned to Station 39 and so far, the crew seemed friendly and helpful. She was one of about ten new recruits, which bolstered her spirit. She wasn't the only novice at the station, and she hoped to make a few friends. From what she understood so far, there would be a fair amount of sitting round waiting for the call-outs.

She was secretly proud of her lancer blue driver's coat with two rows of white metal ARP buttons that fastened to the collar. She'd had to sew her LAAS badge to her dark blue ski cap. Once she was fully trained, she'd be able to wear a smart LAAS pin – a white circle with a navy-blue strip across the middle, and a crown on top. That would truly make her official.

She stopped by her Aunt Shirley's house on her way home from the station. It was a cloudy June day, and as usual, her eyes were drawn to the sky as soon as she left the building. What was Colin doing? Was he preparing for a flying mission tonight? Was he sitting around the NAAFI having a bite to eat and a cigarette? Was he thinking of her?

She shook her head to clear it, mounting the steps to the Fowler's house. She brought some grapes and a magazine for her aunt and crossed her fingers that Aunt Shirley would be feeling brighter today. She spent about an hour with her, having a cup of tea and admiring Geoffrey's pictures (again) in her aunt's photo album.

Poor dear, she thought as she nipped quickly home. She is still suffering so much. Tillie was due to help Faye prepare supper. Mum was at the WVS today and would just about make it home on time.

There was nothing new on the wireless for the six o'clock news as the family trooped upstairs to the dining room. Kenny was late and slipped into his chair as the soup was being served.

"Sorry, Mum, Pops," he leaned over to kiss his mother. "I didn't expect to be home late."

They talked about their day. Tillie shared how her aunt was feeling. Alice tsked and shook her head.

"The best thing for her is to get back to the WVS and get busy again. We desperately need her and I know it would get her back on her feet more quickly."

"I think she just needs a little more time, my dear," said Walter quietly. "It's been an enormous shock. We mustn't rush her."

"You are probably right, Walter. I hate to see her like this."

Kenny looked around the table and seemed near to bursting. He obviously had something to say.

"The reason I'm late is that I've gone and signed up to join the Royal Navy. I was just that impressed with how they rallied to rescue the Dunkirk soldiers. I know I'm only seventeen but I lied. And now it's done." His words came out in a rush.

Alice's fork clattered on her plate as she gasped.

"Oh, Kenny, what have you done?" She whimpered.

CHAPTER FIFTEEN

"You've lied about your age on the application papers?" Walter asked as he stared directly into his son's eyes.

"Yes, Pops. I'm sorry, but I can't just wait eight more months. England needs me now. I'm young, healthy, and I want to serve. What is eight months anyway? We need every able-bodied man fighting in this threatening situation. Britain is hanging by a thread."

"He's not wrong, Alice," Walter said in a halting voice. "What's done is done now. I don't suppose you want Uncle Thomas to pull some strings to try and release you?" He asked, knowing the answer.

"Pops, why would I do that? He's just lost his son. I couldn't ask him. Moreover, I don't want him to. I want to fight for Geoffrey, for all the lads lost on Dunkirk beach."

Walter nodded.

"Children, will you excuse us? Mum and I would like to speak to your brother alone."

The girls collected the half-eaten plates and left the dining room, closing the door without a sound.

An hour later, the threesome emerged. Kenny was cheerful, his parents beaten down. Traces of tears could be seen on Alice's cheeks. But Kenny prevailed.

* * *

A fortnight later Kenny's kitbag sat by the front door. Dressed in naval whites, the new Rating was impatient to get away. Kenny had arranged to go to the train station with his mate Rupert to avoid a tearful public family farewell. The girls had said their goodbyes the night before so just Walter and Alice stood with their son to see him off in the hall. Alice attempted to be stoic, biting her tongue and digging her nails into her palms to fight back tears.

"Darling, we want you to take this with you. It's Pop's gold box from Princess Mary." She held it out to him.

Kenny immediately shook his head no.

"Pops, I couldn't. You received this during the Great War – the first Christmas, right?"

"I did, and it brought me great comfort in the trenches. Your mother and I have filled it with the same treats as I received back in 1914 – cigarettes, sweets, Princess Mary's picture, and a few other bits and pieces. It may well save your life as it did other soldiers and servicemen," Walter said in a halting voice.

Kenny had heard the story before, but wanted to hear it one last time. He accepted the beautiful brass box, with an imprint of the princess's profile, the date, and the initial M for Mary. It was a little dented with age, but still lustered.

"I never saw it in my own unit, but I heard tell that some soldiers who had the box in their breast pocket escaped death as it absorbed a bullet meant for them. We only hope it can bring you the same luck."

The seventeen-year-old Princess Royal (the current King's younger sister) had initiated a 1914 Christmas campaign where she had sent the boxes to "everyone wearing the King's uniform on Christmas Day." By the end of the war, 2.5 million boxes had been sent to troops fighting in all branches of the military.

Walter shook Kenny's hand.

"Take care of yourself, son. Go get the Hun."

Alice gulped a golf ball-sized lump in her throat as she tried to hold on to her youngest child in a vice-like grip.

"Be safe, Kenny. Write often. I love you dearly."

"Thanks Mum, Pops. This means a lot. I'll write soon."

He disentangled himself from his mother, picked up his kit bag, shoved the box into it, and opened the door.

The last Alice saw of him was a carefree smile and wave as he closed the door behind him. She crumpled into her husband's arms as the sob she'd been holding back erupted into the empty hallway.

* * *

"Me leg's broken," wailed the woman lying on the ground. "Please 'elp me, Miss."

Tillie knelt to examine her patient.

"It looks like a bad break, Miss. Let's get you tidied up and over to the nearest hospital. You are going to be just fine."

Tillie wrapped Olive's leg, chattering as she and another trainee picked up the wire mesh stretcher, and loaded her onto it. Ernie backed up and Tillie moved forward towards the open ambulance. It was a modified delivery truck with canvas curtains as back doors. Ernie climbed in and Tillie stepped up, keeping a firm hold on her end of the stretcher. She tripped over the large step, knocking the stretcher into the metal pole frame of the bed.

"Oi, mind how yer go," complained Olive, as her arm bumped into the pole.

"So sorry, Olive," Tillie apologized.

She and Ernie managed to transfer Olive to the lower bed without further incident.

"Passable," grunted Jasper, the station manager. "Your first aid is sound, and keeping the patient calm. Your stretcher steering needs work, Kingston."

Tillie nodded.

"Let me have another go, Jasper. I'll do better, I promise," she squared her shoulders.

"Righto, then, Kingston. Have a go at Daphne then. I believe she is bleeding before your eyes," he added drily.

Jasper Cole knew he needed every driver he could find, borrow, or steal, whether they be men or women. He had faith in these women ambulance drivers but still had trouble coping with the idea of sending young women into danger. He had a daughter himself and couldn't imagine sending her into London streets on fire, with bombs dropping all around. But needs must, and he would do his best to safeguard these girls with as much training and support as possible. But no spoiling, mind, they'd have to toughen up to survive.

Olive Dobbs jumped out of the ambulance, and Tillie bandaged and organized her next patient efficiently into the ambulance.

"The next call-out is yours tonight, Kingston. It's time to test you in a real case. Take Ernie Foster with you as assistant," Jasper barked.

Tillie stood up a little straighter.

"Yes, Sir," she replied. My goodness, could she do this?

Jasper laughed, coughing a bit from his lifelong cigar habit.

"No need to call me Sir, just don't bollocks it up tonight."

Tillie waited nervously for the next few hours, hoping no calls would come through and yet to see if she was up for the job. The common room was sparse but over time, a few comforts had been added. A card table in the corner was always filled with idle staff playing Hearts or Gin Rummy. The concrete floors were scattered with rugs and an oil heater in one corner pumped out very little heat. Old couches and beat-up chairs provided seating.

At half-past eleven, the call came through from the district ARP control.

"One ambulance wanted immediately at 30 Bridle Lane, Mayfair."

"There's your call, Kingston. Buck up, you'll do alright," Jasper encouraged her.

"Let's go then, Ernie," Tillie picked up her cap, placed it on her head, and walked up to the ambulance.

She found it heavy going, driving through the blackout to the site of the fire. More than once, she was grateful not only for Ernie's knowledge of London streets, but also for his eyes and ears during the dark journey. The dimmed and shielded streetlights gave some light though directed to the ground. Newly painted white lines helped guide her on the roads. They crawled at a slow pace which made Tillie all the more eager to reach their destination.

Finally, the fire itself became their signpost. Tillie gave Ernie a grim look and sped up as they saw a corner house aflame, mainly on the first floor.

"Oh, the Fire Brigade is here already. That's a relief," Tillie breathed as they arrived and parked. They both jumped out of the van, ready for action.

Three firefighters were hard at work, using their large hoses to try to douse the first-floor fire. Tillie could feel the searing heat of the blaze and saw multi-colored flames shooting out from the upstairs windows.

"Over there," pointed Ernie to a woman lying on the grass in the front garden.

They ran over, knelt next to her, and began going over the checklist to determine what was wrong with her. She had a pulse, but it was irregular. Through the black streaks on her face, Tillie noted a small gash on her forehead. It was bloody but not deep.

The woman moaned and then started to cough.

She was alive and conscious. Tillie let out the breath she'd been holding.

"Stanley, my husband," the woman whispered as her eyes fluttered. "He's in the house."

"Shh, love, you're going to be alright. Tell me where it hurts." Tillie started feeling the woman's limbs.

"Ow!" cried the patient. "That bloody well hurts."

Tillie stopped at her right arm and slowly explored the injured area. It was so hard to see in the dark with smoke in the air, and only the light of the fire to go by.

"Sorry, love, what's your name?" Tillie asked. The cursory examination didn't seem to detect any other injuries.

"I'm Dorothy," the woman answered. "But please, Stanley is still trapped. You must get him out."

Tillie scanned the house. It seemed that the fire was slowly getting under control but the roof looked none too sturdy. Should she go in and try to save Dorothy's husband?

"Where is he in the house, Dorothy?" she asked as she jumped to her feet.

"In the back in the kitchen. He was sticking on the kettle when we heard a pop or a bang. The fire came on so fast. The smoke filled the front room in no time. I called to Stanley and he told me to run and he would meet me out here. I stumbled out and then I don't know what happened. I suppose I fell and blacked out. I thought he was coming right behind me." She started coughing again.

Tillie only waited to hear the first sentence. Without thinking she ran through the open front door. Smoke was everywhere, making it impossible to see. She pulled a handkerchief from her pocket, covered her face, and ran down the hallway, calling Stanley's name.

She started to feel a bit dizzy but kept going.

"Stanley, it's Tillie Kingston from the ambulance. I'm here to get you out. Where are you?"

She heard moaning down the hall.

Tillie dropped down to her knees and started crawling. She knew that smoke rose up so hoped the air would be slightly fresher down low. It was – but not much. The wooden floor under her hands felt slippery. Linoleum! She was in the kitchen.

She called Stanley again as the moaning grew louder. She felt around, and her hands touched leather. A shoe? It moved. Groping around, she found the other one. Moving upwards, she felt legs in trousers. This was him.

"Stanley, can you hear me? I have to get you out of here."

Inhaling the smoke would be exceedingly dangerous.

He did not respond. She had no choice.

Grabbing the unconscious man by both ankles, she pulled him along the floor towards the hallway door, choking the whole way He was so heavy!

Tillie pulled her shoulders back and redoubled her efforts. She could not fail on her first call-out. She was sweating profusely now and the smoke burned her eyes and throat. She made slow progress pulling him while coughing fits threatened to overtake her, the handkerchief having fallen to the floor.

Suddenly, she felt someone behind her.

"Here, give me one leg," a male voice shouted. Tillie didn't need a second invitation. She let go of one leg and the firefighter grabbed the other. In no time, they pulled him down the hallway to the front door.

The firefighter pushed her out the door and picked up the man, carrying him to safety and placing him on the ground next to his wife.

"Stanley," Dorothy sobbed. "Are you alright, my love?"

Tillie gratefully accepted a wet hankie from Ernie to wipe her face, then bent to examine Stanley. He, too, spluttered into a coughing fit and then regained consciousness. Ernie was already ahead of her. He had bandaged up Dorothy's arm, retrieved the stretcher, and started to assess Stanley.

"The smoke is his biggest problem. I don't feel any other injuries. Let's get them both in the vehicle and to the hospital."

Tillie nodded, her head clearing a little. In no time, they stretchered the couple one by one, and bustled them into the van.

As she turned to get into the driver's side, the firefighter pulled her arm to face him.

"Where are you headquartered?" He asked brusquely.

"Station 39," she answered automatically. "And thank you for your help."

The tall, soot-covered firefighter nodded and ran back to help his mates put out the rest of the fire.

An hour later, Tillie was sitting at the station drinking tea and regaling the rest of the ambulance staff with the story of her first call. The patients had been delivered to the nearest hospital and would fully recover. She was feeling rather proud of herself and after a quick wash-up, was feeling much more clear-headed.

"You should have seen her. She just up and ran into the house, heedless of the fire and the danger." Ernie whistled in admiration.

"Well done you, for rescuing that man but you overstepped your bounds, Kingston. It's not your job to run into burning buildings – that's for the firemen to do with their heavy gear and all." Jasper was a trifle more severe.

"You couldn't be more right, Sir," a voice called from the station door. Everyone turned and Tillie gave an involuntary gasp. Her firefighter was standing at the door looking none too pleased.

"You took an awful chance running in there alone. If I hadn't found you straightaway, I could have had to pull you out along with your patient. That was simply foolish."

Tillie had kept her head down but looked up as he finished. She gasped again. It was Trevor, the firefighter she'd met at Lyons and the garden party before that.

"Trevor, is that you?" She spluttered.

He did a double take.

"Tillie, is it? Bloody hell. I didn't know you were an ambulance driver."

Trevor had removed his helmet to reveal his black hair, covered in soot and dust. Tillie had forgotten how tall he was, and his blue eyes pierced hers with a mixture of surprise, recognition and anger.

"Yes, I've just started volunteering. It was my first call-out. I'm ever so sorry if I caused you any grief or bother," Tillie found herself babbling. "I just followed my instincts."

The rest of the ambulance staff melted away. The couple clearly needed a private moment.

Trevor softened slightly.

"Your first call-out? Then you were quite brave, Tillie. Next time, follow protocol, then instinct. Check in with the Lead firefighter or Chief before rushing into a burning building."

He smiled, showing white teeth in a soot-covered face.

Tillie felt herself reddening. And not just because she was embarrassed. Trevor was deadly handsome.

"Very well," she agreed. "Sorry, Trevor," she apologized again. "Would you like a cup of tea?"

"No, thanks. I've got to get back to the station. I just swung by to chat with you. But I'll probably be seeing more of you. Our fire station is also in this neighborhood."

Tillie nodded.

"Righto. Thanks for stopping by."

Tillie felt disappointed as Trevor left the station. Her old feelings of insecurity welled up. Why was she never good enough? And why was she thinking of this handsome firefighter when her courageous fiancé might be flying a dangerous mission, even now?

* * *

Daily life continued to be challenging. Long lines at the shops were tedious and frustrating. Especially when you got to the front of the line, and the item you needed had just run out. Which happened often.

Everyone was getting used to rationing, but hated it nonetheless. Faye and Alice listened to the BBC each morning for creative new recipes that were short on meat, butter, and eggs. Sadly, many of them were also short on flavor. But they persevered.

For Sale and *To Let* signs could be seen all over London. Removal vans were spotted daily as more families evacuated to the country. Every day the Kingston family heard of a friend, co-worker, or neighbor enlisting or being shipped overseas.

The WVS came door-to-door collecting aluminum pots to melt down and use for making munitions and shells. Faye was left with just a few to make do with in the kitchen.

Jessie, their part-time maid, quit to join the Woman's Land Army.

"I've got to do me part, Mrs. Kingston," she said when handing in her notice. "If I can help one farmer to leave 'is farm in good 'hands, then it's the least I can do, ain't it? I love being outdoors and all. I grew up in the country so I ain't afraid of 'ard work."

"We're very sorry to lose you, Jessie, but so proud of you, too," Alice gave her an impulsive hug. "You will write to us, won't you, and let us know how you are getting on?"

"O course, Mrs. Kingston. I'm just that sorry to leave yer with the extra work, but needs must, as they say."

So, as well as the standing in line, the Kingston women had to add laundry, fireplace cleaning, and floor washing to their to do list.

Walter added Home Guard duties to his ARP role and his day job at the accounting office. He and his fellow neighbors spent hours practicing marching and defense maneuvers with homemade weapons.

Maggie hadn't heard from Micah in months, and worried about him endlessly. She took to listening to the BBC daily for reports of the conditions in France, but news were scarce and censored.

Tillie offered her sister as much support as possible. She started reading Colin's letters in private, to draw attention away from Micah's silence. She was beyond relieved every time she heard from her fiancé, but noted his letters were getting grimmer each time.

"My dearest Tillie,

How are you, sweetheart? How do you fancy driving around London in an ambulance? It's hard for me to picture you in that manly uniform, tending to injured people. The blackout is so unsafe, please be cautious.

Things here are getting very serious, Tils. We're sending Spitfires, Hurricanes, and bombers over the continent almost nightly now. One of my best mates, Simon was forced to bail out but luckily, he was rescued and his Mae West saved him. He landed in the drink close to the coast and was picked up by a local fisherman. His kite was completely destroyed. Aside from a few burns, he's okay so he'll be back up in the air straight away.

Some of the other blokes haven't been so lucky. It's hard cheese when one of our own has bought it. Each of us has our own rituals when going up. We don't make eye contact or wish each other good luck. For me, I flick my lucky lighter three times and hold your picture next to my heart.

I like a night flying meal of bacon, sausage, egg, baked beans, chips, all washed down with a pint of milk before I go up. We all quip that if we are going to buy it tonight, may as well be on a full stomach.

After my last fag, up we go. I unlock the turret and begin the 180-degree square search pattern, which is my task for the next eight hours. I can't say more, Tils, or the censors will just black me out. Suffice to say, it's bloody terrifying yet makes me proud to be an Englishman each time. When I think of all the lads lost at Dunkirk – including your Geoffrey – it gives me all the more reason to do anything I can to shoot down those bandits.

Sweetheart, all leave is canceled at the moment. There's a big operation coming so I won't be able to hold you to your promise to marry me just yet. But I'm counting on you to get planning Tils. You can get a wedding cake from Lyons, right? I don't think coupons will get you a wedding dress, but you will look beautiful in anything – except perhaps your ambulance uniform! We'll likely have to get married at the registry office, and our honeymoon will only be a day or two, but it will be worth it. I can't wait to make you Mrs. Redwood. It keeps me going, Tils, it really does.

Sending love to all your family. Keep writing sweetheart, and I hope to see you soon – maybe for your birthday?

All my love, Colin xxxx"

Tillie put down the letter, peered thoughtfully out the window with its crisscrossed blackout tape view, and sighed. I hate this war and went back to read the letter again and again.

CHAPTER SIXTEEN

August 1940

"Watery tea, no sugar. It's hardly worth the brew," grumbled Alice. She sat in the morning room with Maggie, who had just finished an early shift at the WVS canteen.

"Tea on the ration is ghastly, but it still works a treat after being on your feet all day," Maggie commiserated as she took a sip.

"Biscuit, love? Not homemade, but at least it will take the edge off."

"Ta, Mum. It's been a long day."

"You look knackered, love."

And Maggie did. Purple smudges under her eyes gave away that she wasn't sleeping well. Her eyes were troubled and her overall expression drooped. Even her normally shiny blonde hair looked dull.

"Why don't you have a bath, Maggie? That could cheer you." Alice said impulsively.

"With just five inches of water? Besides, it's not Saturday night yet. How I long for a long, hot soak with bubbles everywhere," Maggie sighed.

"I suppose you're right, love. But at least have a nice wash-up. Take some time for yourself before everyone turns up for supper."

Maggie nodded, but made no move to go.

"Something on your mind, Maggie?" Alice asked gently.

"I just don't know what's happening in France, Mum. With the Germans occupying Paris, I am so fearful for Micah and his family." She picked up the hated knitting, tried a few stitches, and threw it down in frustration.

"Didn't his last letter say they were fleeing to one of the unoccupied zones – Toulouse? Surely, they are safe there?" Alice asked with concern, knitting needles clicking furiously. For Alice, every pair of socks could go to a boy like Kenny, and she spent every spare moment knitting.

"Yes, but the letter was utterly frustrating in the lack of detail, Mum. Apparently, Micah's grandfather was born in Toulouse, and he was hoping to find the small family farm intact. However, Micah's papa is not so sure it's still there. Or that the grandfather can make the trip in his ill health. But they needed to escape the German occupation of Paris. It's not safe for Jews there," Maggie finished raggedly.

Alice jumped up, and squished next to her daughter on the sofa, hugging her tight.

"Oh darling, what a muddle. No wonder you are so jumpy. When was the last letter?" Alice asked concerned for her lovely daughter.

"A fortnight," said Maggie miserably, trying not to cry. "He said he'd write when he could. Mum, even if they make it to Toulouse with the grandfather alright, I don't know how they are going to survive. Micah said they would try to open a small jewelry shop or even offer repairs. If the farm is still there – which is doubtful, perhaps they'll take up farming. It's hard to imagine Micah planting and hoeing," she attempted a joke.

Both women tried – and failed – to picture the lean and sensitive young man out in a field working the land. Or working a tractor. Or tossing hay bales around.

"Needs must, I suppose," Alice put in dubiously. "At least Micah and his father are fit and strong. Oh, what a ghastly situation in France. There's no chance of them escaping back to England? We wouldn't think twice about opening up our home for them."

"Thank you ever so much, Mum but I just don't know," she hugged her mother impulsively.

"Mum," called Katie excitedly from the hall downstairs. "Where are you?"

"Up here, love, in the morning room," Alice called back. "Maggie is with me."

Katie bounded into the room, still in her WVS uniform.

"You won't believe who has turned up." She was breathless.

"Darling, sit and calm down. Who's turned up where?"

"At Aunt Shirley's house. Well, actually he turned up in a letter." She tossed her dark brown curls impatiently.

"Katie, slow down. Start at the beginning."

Katie took a deep breath. She had obviously run all the way home with her news.

"I was visiting Aunt Shirley like always. She sends her best, Mum," Katie started. "Still feeling sad about Geoffrey, but she's getting dressed and putting her face on every day. I even got her to take a short walk around the block."

"That's brilliant, Katie. She has a soft spot for you. You were always like a daughter to her, popping round since you were little," Alice smiled.

"Yes, yes," Katie responded impatiently. "Well, the post came and I collected it from the front door. There was a letter from a chap named Sebastian Cole. He's with the BEF and was a mate of Geoffrey's. He was with him on the Dunkirk beach, and wants to come around for a visit with Aunt Shirley and Uncle Thomas," she finished dramatically.

Maggie gasped.

"My goodness," exclaimed Alice. "How did my sister react?" She half-rose out of her chair as if to rush to Shirley.

"Mum, she's fine, excited even. This Mr. Cole was seriously injured and has been recovering. Now he wants to visit to talk about Geoffrey. Isn't that something?"

"When is he coming?" Maggie asked quietly.

"He asked permission to come in two days-time – Friday. Aunt Shirley is ever so excited and wrote him back straightaway. He's been convalescing here in London." She turned to her mother. "She would like you to be with her, if you can. And she's asked me as well. I suppose she needs some moral support." Katie pushed back a wayward curl from her brow and smiled.

"Of course, I'll come. I'll have to switch my WVS shift. And I'm sure Pops will let you have a couple of hours off work too, Katie. I'm so glad you were there when she got the letter. I must nip over after supper."

"What letter?" Asked Tillie, as she strolled into the morning room, smiling brightly.

Alice and Maggie shared the news that would hopefully bring some peace to the Fowlers.

"That should really help, Mum. I'm glad of it." Tillie paused. "I have something to share, too. A reporter from the *Daily Express* came to the station today. They are doing a series of articles on women in wartime London – including the volunteer ambulance. He spoke to several of us and when I told him that my twin was with the WVS, he asked straightaway if he could take our picture for the paper. I told him yes, Maggie. So, please say yes," she rushed to her sister's side and clutched her hand.

"I'm not sure," Maggie replied uncertainly, biting her lower lip. She preferred to stay in the background.

"Come on then, it's to raise morale and show London what women can do to contribute to the war effort. Besides, it will be fun, Mags." Tillie pleaded. She needed something to cheer her up in these dreary war days.

"Oh, you must," cried Katie as she clapped her hands. "My sisters in the paper. Brilliant!"

"It is for a good cause, Maggie," Alice pressed on. She knew Maggie was reluctant to be in the spotlight.

"What's involved, Tils?" Maggie asked cautiously.

"It will be a breeze, sis. A couple of photos of us together, then one or two each at our work. You serving a cup of tea to a soldier, that sort of thing. Easy peasy," Tillie made it sound so simple.

"Well, I suppose it will be okay. Can I have a think about it?" Maggie said. She hated to be put on the spot.

"Yes, darling. But just till tomorrow. They are starting with me, then want us together on Friday."

Maggie sighed, knowing she'd been beat.

"My goodness, Friday is shaping up to be quite a day," said Alice. "But look, it's near time for the blackout. Girls, let's get on with it and also give Faye a hand with supper. We've sat here nattering long enough." She stuck her knitting needles into the ball of wool, stuffed the works into her bag, and stood up.

"What's for supper, Mum?" Katie asked.

"We're trying a new recipe from the latest *Food Facts* pamphlet. Spam Fritters. It sounds simple."

"Ugh, Spam," frowned Katie. "I'm so sick of it."

"Don't turn your nose up, Miss," admonished Alice. "Plain fare as it is, we have plenty of food. Faye has also made a beetroot soup with some of our allotment veg."

"Anything good for afters?" Tillie asked hopefully. "I'm fair starving. Muscling that large ambulance is hard enough, let alone the weight of those stretchers." She stretched and yawned.

"Carrot cake – and no complaining, chicks. We've an abundance of carrots from our shelter garden. The sultanas will give it added sweetness." With sugar on the ration, finding substitutes for sugary desserts was almost impossible for this family who loved sweets.

The Kingston women trooped to the basement kitchen, greeted Faye at the aga, and got on with the supper preparations.

* * *

Friday arrived. Alice and Katie popped on their hats, collected their handbags, and walked the short distance to Shirley's. Her sister was waiting nervously, while Thomas calmly lit his pipe.

"Whatever will he have to say to us?" Shirley asked for the umpteenth time as she fiddled with the tea things. She'd hardly slept the night before but seemed more animated than she had in weeks. Alice hoped this was a good thing.

"I should think we'll find out soon enough," responded her husband drily. "Sit down, love. Pacing won't bring him any sooner," he added kindly.

Presently, a loud knock was heard at the front door and everyone jumped to their feet. Thomas answered the door, and all that could be heard were male voices before Thomas and the stranger appeared at the sitting room door.

"Mr. and Mrs. Fowler, it's so kind of you to see me. My name is Sebastian Cole – but you already know that," a tall man limped slowly into the room, removed his hat and fiddled with it nervously.

He was a little taller than average, with sandy brown hair and grey eyes. He looked somewhat sad yet determined. His eyes darted around the room and he seemed a bit jumpy.

"Pleased to meet you, Mr. Cole. This is my sister Mrs. Alice Kingston and her daughter, Katie." They all shook hands.

"Please sit, Mr. Cole. I've brewed a fresh pot of tea, and made some scones. I hope you haven't had far to come?" Shirley covered her anxiety with domestic busyness.

"Not too far, Mrs. Fowler. And thank you, a cup of tea wouldn't go amiss." He gingerly sat down, favoring his left leg.

After everyone had been served and small talk exhausted, Sebastian cleared his throat and took a deep breath.

"I'm sure you're wondering why I've come. First, I'm very sorry for your loss. Geoff and I were proper mates. We took to each other straight away. I grew up in nearby Hammersmith, so I reckon we had that in common." He paused.

"You see, Fowler – I mean Geoff and I – made a pact at Dunkirk – that if either of us didn't make it, the other would call on the parents, and share what happened at the end. As you know – he didn't make it, so here I am."

"Can you please tell us about Geoffrey, Mr. Cole? Everything. Please," whispered Shirley. She was sitting on the sofa with Alice and Katie, each holding one of her hands tightly.

"Call me Sebastian, please," he replied, his gaze looking down. "Well, we were in the same division, neither of us knowing what the heck we were doing. Actually, none of us knew what was going on. We'd had scarcely any training, some marching, some rudimentary arms training. If I'm being honest, we were all frightened out of our wits – young lads, homesick, not understanding the language, a mess really.

We tried to hold the Maginot Line, but it was no use. They kept pushing us back and back. We lost so many men." He shook his head. "Boys really, most of them."

He looked up at the little group.

"Then we were ordered to march to Dunkirk. Again, no one knew why. We realized we had failed miserably. We started our retreat – and just as the fighting had started. Jerry had won already."

Thomas spoke up swiftly.

"Sebastian, you didn't fail. You were put in an impossible position. And the retreat was wretchedly handled by all accounts."

Sebastian nodded but appeared unconvinced.

"Thank you, Sir. As I was saying, we all felt demoralized as we marched south. We didn't know why we were ordered to destroy all our military gear and equipment along the way. But we were just soldiers so we obeyed." He turned to Shirley.

"You should have seen your son, Mrs. Fowler. As we marched, we were joined by hundreds, no thousands, of Parisian refugees desperate to escape German occupation. They had nothing but the clothes on their backs and whatever possessions they could carry in farm carts, prams, wagons, the whole lot. Families of all ages and sizes. Grandparents, babies – they all trudged along the dusty roads, hungry, thirsty, and hoping to reach the open territories – Vichy, Lyon, Toulouse – without being attacked by the Germans. It was horrifying and sad all at the same time."

"Toulouse?" interrupted Katie. "Isn't that where Micah and his family were trying to escape to? Maybe you saw them on the road?"

"I don't think so. Surely, Geoff would have recognized the family. But he was ever so kind to the families on the road – especially those with young children. I couldn't even count the number of young ones that he piggybacked for miles when their little legs couldn't carry them anymore. He sang songs, told them little jokes, and helped forage for any fruit or vegetation that was edible. I can still see him in my mind's eye, carrying a young lad during the rain – sharing his soldier's cap for protection. He made many lives easier during that long march, Mrs. Fowler. I wanted you to know that."

Shirley was crying softly, fumbling around for her handkerchief.

"Thank you, Sebastian. And – the end? I need to hear it all."

Sebastian gulped back some tea, clattered the teacup onto the saucer with trembling hands, and straightened his shoulders.

"I can't tell you too much about it. It's still too hard for me, and the nightmares are so vivid that I–I," he covered his face with his hands.

"Take your time, Sebastian, and just tell us what you can," Thomas said. "No, no, this is why I came – to tell you. What happened on that beach is something that no one can possibly imagine who wasn't there. Days of no food, water, and no sense of when we would be rescued, if we would be saved. There didn't seem to be anyone in charge. It was mass chaos. And always, always – the drone of German bombers, gunfire, explosions, and the sound of young men screaming for their mothers as they were hit. There was nowhere to hide, you see. Nowhere to run. The most important thing for you to know is that Geoff hardly suffered. He was hit on the first day. He didn't have to lie there starving and parched like many of us. And it was quick. He felt no pain. I'm sure of it. I hope that brings you some relief."

All three women were weeping.

"Did he leave anything? Anything to give us?" Shirley asked through her tears.

Sebastian shook his head no.

"I'm afraid not, Mrs. Fowler. I'm so sorry."

"Thank you, Sebastian. It was so brave of you to come here. You've eased our minds tremendously. May I ask how you came to be rescued?" Shirley asked gently.

"I was shot in the leg the same day." He patted his left leg. "I couldn't move, so I lay there for who knows how long. My leg got infected and I was in and out of delirium. I don't even know how or when I was rescued. I was suddenly in a London hospital and fighting to keep my leg from being amputated."

Katie gasped.

"As you can see, they were able to save it, but there's still a piece of shrapnel in there. I'll probably always have a limp, but – I'm alive," he finished simply.

"What will you do next?" Katie asked gently. She admired the young man who had been brave on the beach and was showing great courage now.

He patted his leg with a wry grin.

"Once this lot has healed properly, I'm hoping to do my bit with anti-aircraft operations. I don't think I'll be cleared for active service overseas, but with the loss of so much at Dunkirk, we're short on everything, even munitions. Much rests on defending our own ground. If I can help to shoot my share of German bombers out of the sky – even in an administrative role – that will go a little way to make up for all the chaps lost at Dunkirk. Geoff included," he added unnecessarily.

After several more minutes of stilted conversation, there wasn't anything left to say.

Katie walked Sebastian to the door as Alice comforted her sister. Katie pressed a piece of paper into his hand.

"Thank you for coming, Sebastian. I know my aunt and uncle are grateful indeed. Here is my address and the office phone number. If you remember anything else, please let me know."

He nodded, and they shook hands.

Katie walked slowly back into the sitting room.

"Let's go home, Mum."

They left Thomas and Shirley huddled together on the sofa, Shirley's head on her husband's shoulder as he soothed her.

* * *

At the Kingston townhouse, Tillie and Maggie were heroes. *Twins Teach True de-Termination in Tough Times* was the paper's headline. It was accompanied by a eye-catching photo of Tillie in her ambulance uniform holding her tin hat in hand, whilst Maggie held a cup of tea in her WVS uniform. A brief article highlighted their war efforts – although the girls felt it was a trifle sensational for what they really did on a daily basis. Tillie had taken good-natured teasing both at the Corner House and at the ambulance station. Maggie walked around red-faced with embarrassment. It was a storm in a teacup – over in just a few days but Alice carefully cut out the article and photograph, and pasted it into her family scrapbook. Both she and Walter were so very proud of their beautiful and hard-working girls.

CHAPTER SEVENTEEN

September 1940

"So Glamour Girl, are yer available fer the next call-out or will they be making a film of yer life an all?" Olive teased as they cleaned out the back of the ambulance, being sure to replace the bandages, basins, and folded blankets.

"Clear off, Dobbs. I couldn't help what they wrote." Tillie grimaced.

"Well, it's a smashing picture of yer – yer look just like yer sister."

Olive was a plain-looking young woman, but strong and reliable. Tillie knew she could trust her in a real emergency.

"Ta, love. It didn't turn out too rubbish, I suppose," Tillie replied with a cheeky grin. "And yes, we are identical twins," she sighed, having heard it all before.

"Speaking of yer sister, here she is. And with a face like a wet Wednesday," Olive gestured to Maggie, who was standing in the station doorway.

"Maggie. What are you doing here?" Tillie asked, as her heart started beating. She rushed towards her sister. "Is it Kenny?" She asked anxiously.

Maggie was meant to work until half-past four and was still in her WVS uniform. Why was she here, and looking so deadly serious?

Maggie grasped her sister's hands in her own. Both sets were cold and clammy.

"No, it's not Kenny. Tillie, you must be brave now." She exhaled. "It's Colin."

Tillie's throat went dry.

"Colin? What's happened to Colin? I just got a letter from him the other day." She gripped Maggie's hands harder.

"Would you like to use the office?" Jasper appeared out of nowhere.

Maggie nodded and the pair stepped into the small room nearby. She closed the door behind them.

"Just tell me, Maggie. Is he hurt? Missing?" Tillie's voice rose to a shrill.

"Tillie, his parents sent for you. They want you to come to the house. There's no easy way to say this. Colin's been killed. He's dead, love."

Tillie's knees buckled. Maggie caught her before she fell.

"Sit here, darling. It's a dreadful shock."

"How can he be dead?" She asked stupidly.

"It was over France, Tillie. His plane was shot down. There were no survivors."

Jasper knocked gently.

"I've brought you both a cup of tea. That's all." He placed two cups and saucers on the table and swiftly left.

"Take a sip, love, then we'll go to the Redwoods. Tea is always good for a shock," Maggie said shakily as she handed a cup to her sister.

Tillie obediently took a sip of the scalding tea and then put the cup back in the saucer.

"Let's go then. I'm sure they need me."

Maggie had a cab waiting outside, so they reached the Redwoods home in no time.

"Shall I come in with you, Tillie? Or I can wait at the corner café. Just tell me what you need." Maggie was loath to let go of her sister's icy hands but she had no idea how to manage in such a grave situation.

"Oh, please don't leave me, Mags," Tillie replied in a small voice. "Please."

Maggie nodded and knocked on the door.

Henry Redwood answered the door. He looked haggard.

"Come in, come in Tillie, Maggie. Audrey is in the sitting room. Come through." He gave Tillie a long hug. A sob burst from deep inside her.

They heard her before they saw her. A low moan almost as haunting as the air raid alarm filled the room. Audrey sat in a dark blue wing chair, clutching a crumpled telegram. Her face was blotchy and tear-stained, her eyes puffy and red. Her normally coiffed hair was mussed all over.

"Tillie," she cried hoarsely, and held out her arms. Tillie rushed over, fell to her knees and hugged the older woman as tears coursed down her cheeks.

"How? Why? I don't understand," Tillie wept. The two women rocked together.

Wordlessly, Audrey handed her the buff-colored telegram.

Tillie scanned it – "REGRET TO INFORM YOU..." "YOUR SON LANCE CORPORAL COLIN HENRY REDWOOD..." "KILLED IN ACTION OVER FRANCE..." "AUGUST 25th, 1940..." "LETTER TO FOLLOW."

Tillie slowly handed it back to Audrey. It must be true. It can't be true. But it's in black and white so it must be. Her head pounded and felt fuzzy as she tried to absorb the news.

"I'm so sorry, Mrs. Redwood. But it just doesn't feel real. I would *know* if Colin was dead. It just can't be true."

"My boy, my son. He was so brave. Getting shot at by German planes every night. He must have been so frightened."

Tillie didn't even want to imagine how death had taken her dear Colin. They were supposed to be married on his next leave. She was meant to be Mrs. Colin Redwood. She stared down at her flower engagement ring in a blur of tears. Oh, why hadn't she married him sooner when he had begged?

All she wanted to do was run home as fast as she could, throw herself down on her bed, and cry till the tears stopped flowing. But she knew she was needed here.

"Yes, he was very brave. Do you know Mrs. Redwood that Colin wrote in his last letter that he'd completed fourteen missions? He'd shot down enemy planes and helped protect British skies. He is – was – a hero." She started crying again but tried to pull herself together.

"How about I stick on the kettle? A cup of tea is bound to help." Her words sounded hollow, but she thought it was good for the shock.

Maggie had been standing awkwardly by the door.

"I'll do it," she interjected. "And I'm so sorry for your loss, Mr. and Mrs. Redwood. Colin was a fine young man. We were happy to have him in the family." She turned to find the kitchen, tears brimming in her eyes.

"Thank you, Maggie. That's just the thing," replied Henry softly. "I'm sure the letter will give us more information, dear," he soothed his wife. "Perhaps it will be from his Commanding Officer."

This just made Audrey cry harder.

Maggie returned with the tea but it was a subdued group that drank it, in that quiet sitting room, each suffering and lost in thoughts of Colin.

"Mr. and Mrs. Redwood, would you like to come round ours for supper tonight? I'm sure Faye can stretch the rations. You shouldn't be alone," offered Tillie in a halting voice. Her tongue felt thick in her mouth, and she was having trouble making words and sentences in her muddled state.

Colin's parents exchanged a glance and slowly shook their heads no.

"Thanks all the same, Tillie dear, but we want to be on our own. Besides, I couldn't eat a thing," replied Audrey.

The twins took this as a cue to leave the Redwoods alone with their grief.

"Well, I'll pop over after supper to see how you are doing in the event. And you must eat, Mrs. Redwood. You need your strength to cope." Tillie kissed her gently on the cheek and gave Henry a stiff hug.

The girls left the Redwoods sitting on the sofa, re-reading the telegram as if somehow that could change the words.

Leaving the Redwoods, Tillie and Maggie knocked at the neighbors to tell them the tragic news, and asked them to keep an eye on the Redwoods. The girls walked slowly down the street to the bus stop. It seemed cruel that the September sun shone brightly, the light breeze cooled their faces, and people bustled about as usual.

"It's just so final, Maggie," Tillie whispered as they huddled together on a seat at the back of the bus. She couldn't stop quivering and was inexplicably cold. "Killed in action. Stark. Not even a hope that he could be missing, perhaps alive somewhere in France."

Maggie didn't know what to say.

"Hopefully it was sudden like Geoff. At least he's not suffering, darling," she fumbled.

Tillie gulped, trying to hold back her tears. She had a lump as large as a golf ball in her throat.

As soon as they got off the bus, Alice and Katie ran to meet them. They'd obviously been waiting and watching for the twins.

Tillie saw her mother and ran into her arms. Alice hugged her tight and soothed her with words she'd used with her as a child. With her arm tightly squeezed around her waist, Alice led her up the stairs, and up into the drawing room. Walter sat there, solid and steady.

No one knew what to say. They brought out endless cups of tea, hugged Tillie, listened to her sob out her incoherent grief, and echo her disbelief.

After a solemn supper of which Tillie had almost nothing, she insisted on returning to the Redwoods with some fish soup and half a large blackberry jam tart.

"I just need to check on them, especially Mrs. Redwood. She'll need a friendly shoulder and I'm doubtful they've had much to eat." Tillie had dried her red and swollen eyes, rinsed her face, and applied some of her carefully guarded lipstick.

"Love, I don't think that's a sound idea. You're overwrought yourself. You need to rest," Alice put a hand on her arm.

"They need me, Mum. Besides, I promised." Tillie shook off her Mum's hand and slipped on a cardigan.

Walter appeared in the hallway, placing his hat on his head.

"If you're going, I will accompany you." He held up his hand. "No buts. By the time we return, it will be the blackout. You mustn't be alone in the dark tonight."

"Thank you, Pops. I welcome the company." Tillie still felt numb, but at least she was functioning somewhat.

Two hours later, father and daughter returned. The Redwoods had been grateful for the food. Tillie had found Audrey in Colin's room, touching his things, looking into cupboards and drawers, smelling his clothes in search of her son. Tillie helped her fold some of Colin's scattered belongings and put them back in place. She knew Audrey would probably need to spend more time there in the coming weeks.

Tillie's heart felt heavy, like a heavy weight pressing down on her chest. It hurt yet she couldn't feel anything. She was disembodied, distant even from her own self. She thanked her father dully and climbed the stairs to her room which she shared with Maggie.

Her sister sat on her own bed, drawing listlessly in her sketchbook. She put it down as soon as she heard her sister climb up the stairs.

"Darling. How are you holding up? Can I do anything?" She looked at her sister with eyes so sympathetic that Tillie's own welled up again.

"No, Maggie. Thank you, but I just need to sleep. My eyes are burning from so much crying. My head hurts. And look how puffy my face is." She peered at herself in the dressing-table mirror, picked up and then put down the brush, and sank into the chair.

Maggie jumped up, took the brush from her, and started rhythmically brushing her sister's hair. She made soothing sounds as she cared for Tillie. After a while, she fetched her some paracetamol, a cooling cloth, and helped her to undress.

"If you need me at all in the night, just call out, Tils. You're not alone."

"Thanks, love. I will. Goodnight."

Maggie turned off the lamp and the room was enveloped in total darkness.

As often happens, even though Tillie was beyond exhausted, she couldn't sleep. She kept picturing Colin in his bomber aircraft with enemy planes all around, firing at him. What was he feeling when the plane was hit? Did he know he was near death? Did he bail out in his parachute? Was it a fiery death?

Tillie's mind was crowded with horrific thoughts. She hoped, as Maggie said, that it had been quick. Had his last thoughts been of her?

She finally fell into a fitful sleep and woke up feeling exhausted.

Alice was surprised to see her dressed for work.

"Darling, you're not thinking of going into Lyons today? You need a few days, darling. Pops can stop at the call box at the corner and telephone in for you. Surely they'll understand." Alice hadn't slept well either – worrying about Tillie, Colin's parents, and her own Kenny on a ship somewhere.

"Mum, I'm not even his wife. I have no baby to care for. There's no reason I should stay home. Besides, I'd sooner be busy. Otherwise, my mind is just racing imagining him in the plane...and, and I'd really rather just be run off my feet today." Tillie looked pale and drained.

"All right, dear. If you're quite sure?"

Tillie nodded.

"At least have a cup of tea and toast before you leave."

* * *

The next few days were tougher than Tillie could have imagined. Everyone was exceedingly kind to her, almost to the point of treading on eggshells around her. She was happiest helping others, and just wanted to get on with her Nippy shifts, ambulance hours, and checking in on the Redwoods. Through it all, she had the nagging feeling she'd let Colin down by not marrying him when he'd pleaded. It was just one simple thing she could have done to make him happy. Why hadn't she married him months ago? Why?

The Redwoods held a small memorial service for Colin at the local church. The Kingstons and Fowlers attended, as well as two of Colin's friends that happened to be on leave. Audrey cried softly throughout the service. Tillie sat, dry-eyed, beautiful in black, holding Maggie's hand. She felt miserable and deeply guilt-ridden throughout the brief service.

The remorseful thoughts chased endlessly around in her head as she walked home a few days later. She'd worked her Saturday shift and was tired of all the war talk in the Lyons café.

The Air Raid warning sounded. It was half past four p.m. September 7, 1940. Damn. Another false alarm? She looked up at the sky and was shocked to see a v-formation of German planes – Luftwaffe. There were hundreds of planes, headed for London's East End. She started to run and made it home in time to see her father waiting for her at the top of the street. He was dressed in his ARP Warden uniform.

"Hurry, Tillie. The family is all in the shelter. Grab your gas mask and let's go to the back garden."

He didn't have to tell her twice. The sound of approaching engines was so frightening that she barely had time to drop her bag, pick up her gas mask and the flask that Mum had left her, and dash ahead of her father towards the Anderson shelter.

"Thank goodness you are safe, darling," Alice sighed as she made room on the narrow bench, and Maggie gave her a reassuring hug.

"My supper is going to be ruined," grumbled Faye.

"Don't fuss, Faye," Alice said with a hint of a smile. "I'm sure this will be another false alarm, and we'll be inside in no time."

But that wasn't to be. For the next two hours, the family huddled together, hearing the constant drone of planes overhead.

"Is that ours or theirs?" Alice asked fearfully. "It must be the RAF, right?"

"Probably both," Walter answered in a calm voice. He unscrewed the top of his flask and drank some lukewarm tea.

"I saw hundreds of German planes. I think they were headed to the East End," Tillie reported.

"Undoubtedly the docks," said Walter tersely. "They've done enough damage to the RAF bases. Now they want to blow up our ships and God forbid – Londoners."

They heard distant bombing.

"Are those bombs, Pops?"

Walter nodded.

"Let's not waste time whilst we're here. Let's knit, girls. Just think, it could be our Kenny needing these warm socks as the weather cools."

For the next hour or so, the sound of knitting needles clicking interspersed with the droning and distant explosions. It did not sound too close, but it was frightening. The planes just kept coming!

Finally, the all-clear sounded, and the family heaved a collective sigh of relief.

They all gazed upwards as they exited the shelter.

"Look!" cried Maggie, pointing eastward. "The sky is orange. And look at all the black smoke billowing up high. That must have caused a lot of damage for us to see it from such a distance." Luckily, they could see no destruction in their small block of townhouses.

The family filed into the house, freshened up, and had their overdue supper of corned beef hash, late sprouts from the garden, and gold nugget cake for afters.

"I'm on duty tonight at eight o'clock," Walter announced at the end of the makeshift meal. "If you hear the siren again, don't look up – just make for the shelter with our pre-assigned items. Dear, you still have the tick list?"

"Yes, dear. Just be careful out there. Who knows what stray bombs or explosives may land in our own neighborhood?" She shuddered.

"I'll pop by your sister's on the way, Alice. Just to make sure they are getting on alright."

At ten past eight, the alarm sounded again. They'd just finished the washing up and were about to take turns for their Saturday night bath, when the wail went up. Faye had already left for home.

"Oh no, not again," grumbled Tillie. She was already so overwrought with Colin's death that the thought of another night of little or no sleep was horrifying.

"Off we go, girls. Don't forget the torches." Alice rushed them along.

The planes and bombs buzzed and droned for hours. Faint whistling noises could be heard – the precursor to a bomb exploding. They could also hear the distant sound of ack-ack guns as the BEF shot at enemy planes in the black sky.

They didn't know it yet, but the Blitz had begun.

CHAPTER EIGHTEEN

At four-thirty a.m., the all-clear finally sounded. Walter checked on them twice during his ARP shift, assuring the family that their home was safe. In fact, it didn't seem that the area around Earl's Court had sustained any damage.

The weary Kingstons stood up, dead-tired and relieved to leave the cramped shelter. Katie and Maggie managed to doze off for a while, but Alice and Tillie had been awake most of the night, clinging to each other for support. The hurricane lamp had provided some light for knitting and desultory reading, but the grim fear that gripped the women made it hard to concentrate on anything. The tea and sandwiches were long gone and everyone just wanted a couple of hours of sleep in their own beds before heading out to their day jobs.

As they exited the shelter, their eyes were immediately drawn to the sky. The bombers were gone but the sky was orange in the distance, with plumes of black smoke rising above.

"It's definitely the docks, then is it, Walter?" Alice asked tiredly.

He nodded, dead on his feet.

"Yes, the planes kept coming and coming. All headed towards the east end, the Surrey docks. The devastation there is surely unimaginable."

"I'm on early shift tomorrow – I mean today," a sleepy Tillie said, as they trooped into the house. "I expect I'll get more news along with the wounded. I'm for bed. Maggie, are you coming along?"

Maggie smothered a yawn.

"I'm right behind you, Tils."

Alice interrupted them.

"Wouldn't you like a nice cup of tea before bed?" she asked.

"No, I need as much sleep as I can muster, albeit only a couple of hours before I'm due at the WVS canteen. Indeed, there will be thirsty and hungry firemen, heavy and light rescue teams, police, and so on." Maggie yawned again. "Ta, anyway, Mum."

"I'd be glad of a cup of tea, dear," Walter chimed in. It's been a long night for all of London. The cleanup will already be starting. Let's just hope Jerry leaves us alone now for a bit. I'll have a cup, then nip over to Thomas and Shirley's to check on them."

Alice gave her husband a grateful smile.

"I'll have a quick cuppa, too, Mum," Katie added. "I'm not on duty today, but I'll swing by the WVS office to see where I'm needed. After some sleep. Otherwise, I won't be able to see straight."

Alice nodded and slowly stepped towards the basement stairs, touching her precious furniture and knick-knacks as she went. What a relief it had been to see the house standing untouched.

It had been a hectic night at the ambulance station, As Tillie signed in, exhausted crews with dust and soot-covered faces trailed in, booking their last calls. In a raid, staff had to stay on duty past their clock off time until they completed all their calls.

"We were sent to the east end to deal with all the incendiaries and high explosive bombs. The bloody Germans drop the incendiaries to light the way for the other explosives. The stirrup pumps were no match for the bombs that just kept coming and coming," Barbara muttered grimly. She was a fresh recruit and clearly overwhelmed.

"Were there many casualties?" Tillie asked, as she poured cups of tea for the bleary-eyed crews.

"Too many to count yet," replied Donald, an elderly volunteer. "As fast as we could load 'em up and drop 'em at the 'ospital, we'd be called to another burning building to pick up more. Most of 'em never knew what hit 'em. Bless those firemen – time after time goin into those houses, offices, factories – facing raging fires and deadly smoke."

"Shift off, you lot," Jasper said, not unkindly. "You've done your duty and more. Go get some kip and let these fresh crews get on with inspecting the vehicles and supplies for today's calls."

"Are you expecting another siege today?" Tillie asked worriedly. Surely, the Germans wouldn't be coming back so soon.

Jasper shrugged.

"All we can do is prepare for the worst, Kingston. Get to your ambulance and check the mileage, oil, petrol, and water. You'll be with Foster again today – he can inspect the inside to ensure it's clean and restocked with blankets and bandages."

Tillie smiled in assent and set to work on her ambulance.

Someone had stopped at a newsagent and *The Guardian* screamed out these headlines:

BIG AIR BATTLE OVER LONDON

"REPRISAL" FOR ATTACKS ON BERLIN

SIXTY-FIVE RAIDERS SHOT DOWN

98 MINUTES OF FIERCE FIGHTING

FIRES STARTED IN THE EAST END

Tillie was feeling jittery. Every loud noise caused her to jump. It was nerve-wracking just waiting to see if another alert would sound and they'd be called into action.

While civilians headed to the shelters as quickly as possible when an air raid started, the ambulance attendants set to work. As bombs dropped, they'd start their calls, making quick assessments of the wounded – lighter injured would be transported by car to First Aid Posts, while the severely injured were given cursory treatment like bandaging bleeding wounds, or setting simple breaks before being taken to the nearest hospital. Then the ambulance would return to the station to finish the incident report before being called out to the next site.

There's a special kind of bravery attributed to these angels of the night – the ambulance drivers, firefighters, policemen, light and heavy rescuers, and so many more that sprang into action risking their lives during those trying times.

Just after dinner, the first alert sounded. In a sense, Tillie was relieved. Now the interminable waiting was over and she could take action. Her pulse started racing.

"Kingston, Foster – here's your chit. Looks like we'll be supporting the crews in Southwark, Greenwich and Newham again. There's a factory on fire over there so they need several ambulances."

Tillie and Ernie collected their tin hats and gas masks, and raced to their ambulance. They had to dispatch to their call within two minutes of being alerted.

Although Tillie longed to speed towards their destination, she kept to the 16-mph guidelines. With rubber so scarce, the ambulance drivers took care not to puncture their tires with the broken glass and debris on the streets.

As they crawled along to their destination, Tillie and Ernie could hear the buzzing sounds of aircraft overhead. Not daring to look, they stayed focused on their call and getting there as quickly as safely possible.

"So tell me about The Knowledge, Ernie," Tillie chattered to settle her nerves.

He glanced over at her.

"Well, me dad were a London cabbie 'afore me, so I thought I'd be a shoo-in, but they put me straight directly. 'It's not who you know, it's what you know.' I got me green badge back in 1913 – just 'afore the Great War. Book learning was ne'er for me, so memorizing 500 runs around the city, that were a grind." He shook his head. "Those bloody appearances where yer were tested verbally – I shook in my boots every time. I've got thousands of streets, landmarks, and runs in me head. I wonder how many of 'em will still be there when this is all over."

Tillie chanced a quick look at her partner. Ernie was in his mid-sixties, short, bald, with milky blue eyes and ruddy red cheeks.

"The heart of London will still be here, Ernie. We must bank on that." They lapsed into silence.

As they neared the docks, Tillie's jaw dropped as she surveyed the damage from the previous day and night. Entire streets were reduced to rubble. Smoke still filled the air and mingled with the smell of cordite. Large buildings wobbled precariously with two or three sides completely gone. Engineers would come later to fully destroy them to make the area safe. Tillie and Ernie had to make a few detours where streets were so damaged they were impassable.

Finally, they arrived at the factory on East Ferry Road, which was still burning. Firefighters stood in full gear, shooting water from hoses from the nearby red appliance into the tall windows above.

Tillie's teeth were already rattling with the poor suspension of the makeshift ambulance and all the double-clutching needed. An ARP Warden waved her over and she parked as close to the building as she could.

"Can you take four, love?" Asked the bushy-eyed Warden. "They have extensive burns and I think one of 'em has a broken shoulder or collarbone."

"Yes, we can," replied Tillie, as she and Ernie pulled out the stretcher.

"They're right over there," the Warden pointed. At least a dozen men lay on the ground, covered in plaster dust. Some were motionless, others uttered low moans.

Tillie and Ernie began loading the men onto the stretcher and into the ambulance. Reaching over her head to place two grown men on the top bunks was heavy going, but Tillie carried on.

More ambulances pulled up and began loading the rest of the injured men.

As Tillie and Ernie transferred the last patient to the stretcher, she heard a shout.

"Watch out! Bomb!" shouted a loud voice.

Ernie gave Tillie a hearty push, and she landed on her stomach.

A whistling sound preceded the incendiary, which landed where Tillie had been standing seconds before.

Immediately, a nearby firefighter aimed his hose at the bomb, which was reduced to a smoking, wet mess.

"One less target for the Luftwaffe," he mumbled.

"That was close, thanks Ernie," Tillie said shakily, as she pushed back her tin hat to smile at her partner. "Let's get this lot to King's College Hospital."

"Yer welcome, Tillie. It were just luck that I caught a glimpse of it out o' the corner of me eye. Let's go, then."

The rest of the day passed by in a series of calls back and forth between the station, incidents in the east end, and the local hospitals.

With the lack of sleep the night before, and the ongoing tension of raids in progress as they shuffled patients to the hospital, Tillie was thoroughly worn out. But she kept going until the all-clear sounded and her shift was over.

Like the other crews, she returned from her last call sweaty, dirty, bloodstained, and covered in dust and soot. She and Ernie gave the ambulance a final clean before she did her best to tidy up in the bathroom. A face wash didn't do much to clear the grime.

Collapsing onto a chair in the lounge, Tillie gratefully accepted a cup of tea and spam sandwich. She was so worn out that she didn't have the strength to remove her tin hat.

"Oh, that tastes divine," she sighed. "How many patients did we transport today, Ernie?" She asked. Her eyes and throat burned with exhaustion and smoke exposure, but she felt strangely alert, and somewhat proud.

"Twenty-two, Tillie. Well done, us," he replied as he sagged heavily into a chair and gulped his tea.

"But so many lives lost, Ernie," she said. For the many who were saved, there had been rows of dead on the ground, waiting to be taken to the morgue and identified.

"I know, Tillie, but we must carry on. Every life saved is a win for London, ain't it?"

"Too right, Ernie. This just fills me with more determination to protect our people, our streets, our city."

She got up with effort.

"I must get home and check on the family. I'll see you tomorrow, Ernie. Thanks again for pushing me to cover."

"It were nothing, Tillie. Yer would do the same for me."

"Anytime, Ernie. Anytime."

Tillie wearily shed her ambulance coat, brushed it and left it and her tin hat in the cloakroom.

As she sat on the tube mindlessly looking out the window, she noticed people already looking for their places to shelter for the night.

Even though the government discouraged the use of the tube as air-raid shelters, thousands of Londoners hid there whenever they heard the wail of "Moaning Minnie." Many families didn't have a garden for an Anderson Shelter and didn't trust the above-ground shelters scattered around the city.

Therefore, thousands of people trooped nightly to their local tube stations – armed with bedrolls and tea flasks – to camp out until the all-clear or morning came.

Something must be done about this. Tillie shook her head. If Hitler is going to keep bombing London, these locals need better support than these makeshift shelters.

She walked the short distance from Earl's Court to Longridge Road, her feet dragging.

At home, she was met by Maggie, who had just returned from her WVS shift. She hugged her twin tightly.

"How was it, then Sis?" She asked sluggishly as they walked arm-in-arm slowly up the steps to the sitting room.

"Tillie, I still can't believe what my eyes saw. They re-assigned our canteen van down to Canary Wharf to serve the firemen and other rescue workers. Darling, the devastation – the destroyed buildings, the fires, the – the dead people." She burst into tears.

Tillie immediately jumped up to sit by her sister. She pulled her close and laid Maggie's head on her shoulder.

"Shh, love. I know it's a shock to see innocent people like that. They look so strangely peaceful, don't they?"

Maggie shook her head up and down forcefully as more tears flowed.

"I don't know how you can touch them, Tils. And risk yourself to carry them out, all bleeding and burned. Oh, it was so awful," Maggie gasped out between sobs.

"There there, darling. You're exhausted and overwrought. You're helping just as much as I am. It's ghastly to see, to be sure, but we must do our bit. Every bleeding or burnt person on a stretcher is a human, a real person."

"I don't know how you do it," Maggie repeated. "I guess serving countless cups of tea, sarnies, and biscuits to hundreds of firemen, policemen, ARP staff, and so many other Londoners standing tall to save our city just got to me, that's all." Maggie sniffed and wiped her nose.

Faye bustled in with a loaded tea tray, deliberately ignoring the tearful scene in front of her.

"I expect you are both desperate for a cuppa after the days you've had. I've managed some scones too, with one of the last bits of this summer's blackberry jam." Faye swiftly deposited the tray on the round end table, poured two cups of tea, added a drop of milk to each, and handed them to the twins with an encouraging smile.

"You are a dear, Faye. That's just what we need. Will you join us?" Tillie picked up the plate of scones and offered it to Maggie.

"No, thanks, dear. I must do my best to put something tasty on the table. Take your time. Your Mum and Katie should walk in the door anytime." She smiled and left the room with her usual brisk step.

"Sorry about that outburst, Tils. It just all came over me. I fear this is just the beginning. How are we going to cope day after day in this war?" She put a tiny scrape of margarine on her scone, then spread a minuscule amount of jam on top.

"We just carry on, Mags. That's all we can do." She sighed and sipped her tea. "Have you heard from Micah?" She asked gently.

"No," replied Maggie shortly. "And don't say it – I'm sure my exhaustion and misery are making me cross and unsettled. But it's been weeks since I've had any post from him. I'm so worried about him and his whole family." She wrung her hands.

"Steady on, Mags. I'm sure you will hear from him soon. You must stay strong."

Alice walked into the sitting room to see her dirty, tired, sweaty, yet still beautiful daughters, hugging.

"Oh darlings, have you had an awful day? You both look peaky."

Maggie and Tillie burst out in identical peals of laughter.

"Oh Mum, only you can say we look peaky when we actually look like something the cat dragged in." Tillie giggled as she ran her fingers through her messy and dust-covered hair.

"You are too much, Mum," echoed Maggie. "I'm dead on my feet, thanks very much. How was your day?"

"Heartbreaking," said Alice softly as she helped herself to a cup of tea. "We were assigned to a Rest Center, helping bombed-out families get new identity cards and ration books. And giving them clothing. They all had this hollow look – like they couldn't believe they were homeless, and didn't know what to do. These poor families have nothing but the clothes on their backs – and some of them not even that. Can you imagine they had their trousers and shirts blown completely off in the bomb blasts? And now they have to be re-homed. Some are moving in with family members, others are evacuating to the country. It's just so sad, and horrific, and maddening all at the same time. To think that Hitler is deliberately trying to destroy decent civilians just going about their lives. Innocent children, older people – no one is safe."

"I know, Mum. But it just fills me with resolution to do everything I can to beat these damned Germans. Every Londoner counts – and whether it's a cup of tea, a new overcoat, a trip to the hospital – everyone we help is a person not sacrificed. We have to do it for Geoffrey and Colin – and all our boys." Tillie jutted her chin out with determination.

"You're right, Tils. And I'll pull myself together, too." Maggie gave a watery smile, thinking of Micah.

"That's my girls," said Alice, as she patted both their hands. "And you should have seen our Katie today. No one could have been more compassionate and kinder to these displaced families. I'm proud of you all." She bit her lip, thinking of Kenny, fighting who-knew-where. They were all dedicated to someone's honor and bravery – dead or alive.

* * *

For the next two weeks, bombs dropped during daylight hours every day. The Kingston family became accustomed to sheltering near their work locations and carrying on with duties, despite daily attacks. Nerves were frayed as everyday life became harder and harder.

And then the nighttime raids began.

CHAPTER NINETEEN

It was now known as the *Blitzkrieg* – a lightning strike or lightning war. But Londoners just called it the *Blitz*. In retaliation for the Battle of Britain when the RAF bombed Berlin, Hitler was bent on demolishing civilian London. At first, the Luftwaffe made daylight raids. On *Black Saturday* alone, over 400 people were killed with 1,600 badly injured. That was the first night of the Blitz.

After a few weeks, Hitler changed tactics. The RAF was just too powerful in the air during the day, so he switched to the cover of darkness. Since then, every night had seen hundreds of German planes mercilessly bomb London – predominantly, but not limited to the East End. The damage was disastrous – street after street bombed to nothingness. But London carried on. By night, the RAF protected the skies while courageous firefighters, ARP staff, WVS, ambulance, and other civil defense worked tirelessly to put out the fires and save every life they could.

By day, the lorries picked their way through rubble, broken glass, and ongoing fires to carry away the remains of homes, businesses, churches, and other buildings to clear the streets. The engineers carefully inspected and, in some cases, safely removed the precarious remains of unrecognizable structures. City workers repaired broken water pipes and electrical and telephone lines to restore normal service as quickly as possible. Storefronts with blown-out windows propped up perky cardboard signs saying OPEN FOR BUSINESS. Above all, Londoners emerged from cramped shelters, had a cup of tea, and went to work – despite exhaustion, fear, multiple road closures and detours, and a multitude of other obstacles. London would not surrender.

The Kingston and Fowler families were no exception. Since Sebastien had visited Geoffrey's parents, Shirley had found a small measure of inner peace and was again working side-by-side with her sister at the WVS almost every day. Part of her was closed forever but she tried to take it one day at a time.

Colin's parents heard from his squadron leader, who had glowingly reported on Colin's dedication to duty, willingness to volunteer for even the most menial task, and team camaraderie. The Redwoods had taken comfort in the letter and quietly carried on. They had kindly shared it with Tillie who had treasured every word. She had hoped against hope that somehow, his lighter had been recovered, so she'd have a keepsake of her beloved fiancé, but of course, it had gone down with Colin and the aeroplane. She felt a little better but the guilt remained.

The Battle of Britain ended and Tillie was proud of Colin's part in it. The RAF had lost almost 800 aircrafts, compared with Luftwaffe losses of 1,400. It was a significant win for Britain, as Hitler missed his aim of dominating the English skies, thereby making invasion all but impossible. It was an enormous boost for British morale.

Maggie finally heard from Micah after weeks of haunting the front door for the twice-daily post. Everyone was safe – thank goodness – but life was tough in the south of France. Miraculously, the family farm was still standing, but had sustained serious bomb damage, so they were living in just three rooms. Micah and his father went to the local village each day to find any manual jobs they could. His mother tried to keep house as best as possible with limited food and supplies. They took in other refugees when possible, and everyone learned to barter for food and other necessities.

Maggie almost collapsed in relief to read the letter. Micah was alive! She wrote back immediately, asking how her family could help – either with money or other essentials, and began another waiting game.

Kenny wrote on a semi-regular basis. He was posted somewhere in the Mediterranean and seemed to love naval life. He wasn't expected any leave in the near future, which broke Alice's heart. She knew her teenage son was growing into a man and she was missing every moment.

* * *

"Oh, there's the alarm. Right on time. Hitler loves to interrupt our tea time. Let's collect our shelter bits and bobs, Tillie." Alice gritted her teeth, gathered her knitting, and headed for the basement steps. Tillie followed closely behind. Walter was due on ARP duty that night after work, so they wouldn't see him for a few hours. Katie was out fire watching, so she was probably sheltering near work. Maggie was expected after her WVS shift so Alice and Tillie hoped both girls were safely sheltered.

"Faye left us a potato pie. Sadly, she couldn't get any onions at the shops today – despite a long queue. You round up the tea flasks & gas masks, I'll gather the food."

"Righto, Mum. I think my dratted knitting is still there from last time. It's in rather a muddle, so I'm hoping you can help me fix my lost stitches."

Both women were afraid but also somewhat used to the now-nightly routine. There was a common but unspoken belief that keeping up a cheerful face would somehow soothe their fear. It never really worked, but everyone felt they were doing their share to keep up the spirits of their loved ones.

"Of course, love. I keep hoping you'll take to knitting, but somehow you just don't seem to have the knack." Alice's said regretfully.

"Mum, that's not nice!" Tillie retorted. Both women had been speedily assembling their nightly essentials and were already on their way down the back stairs to the shelter. Tillie had already done the blackout so they were able to make it to safety in no time.

Alice did her best to make the shelter cozy. Blankets and pillows made the narrow bunks slightly more comfortable. A hurricane lamp and candle resting between two clay flower pots – one turned upside down – provided scanty light. There was no heat but both women had sweaters to ward off the chill in the October nights. Walter had erected a small wooden bookcase loaded with the families' favorite books. Atop it stood a framed photograph of the King and Queen.

Tillie closed the door and sat on the bench next to her mother.

"I wonder how long they'll be here tonight," she sighed, knowing it would likely be another long, sleepless night.

"Well, let's have a bite to eat whilst it's still a little warm. I won't be able to rest easy until I see Maggie come through that door. And your father and Katie when they are off-shift."

"It's alright, Mum. None of them will take any chances. They'll duck into a local shelter or even the tube."

Under great pressure from the public, the city had capitulated and opened up the public tubes for nighttime sheltering. Those needing a place for the night didn't have to get an underground ticket any longer. Lavatory facilities and drinking water were now being provided. Enterprising businesspeople started selling tea, cocoa, coffee, cakes, biscuits, chocolate, apples, meat pies and even sausage rolls.

Although still crowded, and smelling none too sweet with the accumulated number of bodies, the mood below the streets was generally cheery. Sing-a-longs broke out, and small groups chatted and knitted. After the last trains departed, the lights were turned off and the people would sleep under blankets, rugs, coats, or newspapers.

Early the next morning, these Londoners would pack up their children, belongings, and assorted bits, and pour out of the exits back to their homes ready to get on with their days. This was repeated nightly.

The Anderson shelter was at least private and close to home. Every Kingston was thankful for that.

The two women had the pie the tea as they heard the familiar drone of enemy planes overhead.

"They sound closer tonight," commented Tillie.

Although they kept quiet, both women knew it was a matter of time before bombs were dropped on their neighborhoods – or even on their house.

They heard the whistling sound that preceded a high explosive bomb landing. And waited. The ground shook with the explosion as the bomb hit somewhere nearby. It was followed rapidly by more whistles, bangs and pops. Tillie could smell cordite – familiar now from her ambulance work. They'd given up all pretext of knitting and just clung together.

"Mum, tell me some stories from the past. Something to distract us," Tillie pleaded desperately.

"All right, love. Well, you two were no trouble as youngsters. Once your father and I got over the shock of hearing we were having twins, we couldn't have been more excited. I was as big as a house by the end but then – there you were – two beautiful babies – Mathilda and Margaret."

Another explosion shook the shelter.

Alice spoke faster.

"Then Katie came along and we thought our family was complete. Three lovely little girls. Healthy and thriving. With Katie as dark as you two were fair." Alice smiled a little in remembrance.

"Who was better behaved, Mum? Me or Maggie?" asked Tillie, just to keep the conversation going. The cracks and bangs were coming more frequently now and the shelter shook with each explosion.

"Well, love – Maggie was always better at playing by herself," Alice replied diplomatically.

"Tell me about the time I got into your pancake powder, Mum."

"Oh dear, what a mess. I was changing your sister and left you on the floor in our bedroom with some blocks. I was so dog-tired; I just didn't want to lift the two of you to take you both to the lav. When I returned a few minutes later, you had toddled over to my dressing table, pulled down the powder box, and dumped it all over yourself. You were dust-covered from head to toe. What a mess!"

"And see, twenty-three years later, I'm covered in brick dust almost every night," Tillie attempted a weak laugh as another loud boom split the night.

"Too right, love," Alice hugged her daughter close.

"And then when Kenny came along almost six years later, I thought I was done with babies. But there he was. He started out so tiny, but look at him now," she continued with a catch in her voice, thinking of her only son.

Every muscle in Tillie's body tightened and not from the shaking and thumping. Her mouth went dry. Kenny's birth. Painful memories.

Alice carried on, ignoring Tillie's discomfort.

"Born so early but your father was that chuffed that he was a boy. The whole family was. It was just too bad that we had to stay in hospital for six weeks till his weight came up."

"Mum, I'm so sorry. It was all my fault." Tillie sobbed uncontrollably.

Alice was struck dumb.

"Darling, what is it? What was your fault?"

"Kenny, when Kenny was born," she stumbled incoherently.

"Love, shhh. Calm down. Tell me. What do you think happened?"

Tillie clutched Alice's hands hard.

Another whistle, boom, crash.

"That day, Mum. You asked me to pick up my toys because Aunt Shirley and Uncle Thomas were coming over. There were dolls and blocks on the nursery room floor. I didn't want to do it." She paused and looked at her mother with tear-stained eyes. "And you fell and then the baby came." She broke down afresh, dropping her head into her hands.

"Shh, Tillie. Wait just a minute. So, you think that when I tripped over your toys, that caused the baby to come?"

Tillie nodded miserably.

"Tillie, listen to me. It wasn't your fault. It wasn't. I wasn't meant to have another baby. The doctor warned us that the baby could come early – something to do with me not being able to hold on to a baby full-term." What she didn't confess to her daughter that she'd had two miscarriages after Katie. She'd been ordered on bed rest for the last three months of her pregnancy, but how could she with three little ones at home?

"What? It wasn't because of the fall?" Tillie asked.

"Darling, it was a trip, not a fall. And no, I would have gone into premature labor no matter what."

"Why didn't you ever tell me that, Mum? Here I've been all these years thinking I caused his early birth. And he could have died."

"No, Tillie. He was small, that's all. I'm sure it all seemed bigger and scarier than it actually was to a five-year-old," Alice soothed.

Tillie was shattered. Everything she had ever believed about herself wasn't true. She'd always thought she caused her brother's premature birth, and that he was in deadly danger for weeks. That was the reason she felt unworthy and did not deserve anything good in her life. It had shaped every decision she'd made, every thought she'd had of herself. She'd always put herself and her needs last. By helping others, she'd felt some sense of value before it faded again. And now she realized it was all built on a lie!

"I don't know what to say, Mum. I'm gutted. I really thought it was all my fault. That I'm bad, damaged."

Now Alice was crying.

"Darling, darling, I wish you would have told me this years ago," she breathed. "I never knew you felt that way. You are special, loved, important – just for yourself. You did nothing wrong, nothing."

Amazingly, amidst the sound of bombs dropping all around them, Tillie felt lighter, lighter than she'd felt in years. Was it possible that it wasn't all caused by her? That she'd felt awful about herself for no reason?

"I did nothing wrong," she repeated slowly. "I didn't?" She wiped her tears.

"No, you didn't, you daft girl. How could you be so foolish?" Alice had a sudden thought. "Love, is this why you kept putting Colin off when he wanted to get married?" Alice felt deeply sorry for the misunderstanding. Being a private person, she'd never shared her woman's troubles with her girls. It just wasn't done.

Tillie opened her big brown eyes wide.

"You know what, Mum. I think you may be right. It's all part of this feeling I've always had that I don't deserve to be happy because I almost killed my brother – and you. It's held me back so much."

"Darling, you do understand that you got it all wrong? It's absolutely necessary that you believe this. None of us knows how long we've got in this world, especially now. You must seize every happiness you can lay your hands on. You deserve it." She hugged her daughter again.

"I actually do believe it now, Mum. But it's going to take some time for me to think this through. Thank you for telling me all this. Perhaps Jerry is good for something." This last was punctuated by another loud boom.

Mother and daughter took a sip of the lukewarm tea and held each other's hands in the dimly lit shelter. After a while, they felt a lull. They both tried to stand and stretch their legs when they heard a scuffle at the door. They looked up expectantly.

"What a night," cried Walter as he burst through the door and closed it tightly behind him. "Are you alright?"

"Better now that you're here, dear," answered Alice as she hugged her husband. He smelled of smoke, and gripped her tightly. "But yes, we're fine, aren't we, Tillie?" She turned to her daughter.

"We're okay, Pops. What's going on out there?"

"There's serious damage on Warwick Road. Fires, and houses bombed out. I can only stay a moment – I just wanted to check on you two. I was hoping Maggie would be back by now. I saw Katie fire watching."

"We haven't seen Maggie. She must be safe in a shelter near work," Alice responded emphatically. "What about Shirley? Are she and Thomas safe?"

"Right, well, I'll keep an eye out for Mags. And from last I saw, your sister and her husband's street is still there – for now." Walter adjusted his tin hat, and made for the door. "I must get back."

Just then, the door rattled again and Maggie stepped down into the shelter.

"Hello everyone. Having fun yet?" She quipped.

Tillie noticed her twin was pale.

"We're okay, sis. Was it ghastly getting home?" She took her sister's coat and led her to the bench.

"Pretty much," Maggie replied. She was shaken up. "I was almost home when the alarm sounded. I ducked into a surface shelter, but to be honest, I felt too vulnerable. Those shelters are just easy targets. I dodged and shifted till I got home. Thank goodness I made it," her voice sounded wobbly.

"That was too dangerous, Maggie," scolded Walter. "There are bombs dropping everywhere. You could have been injured or killed."

"I know, Pops and I'm sorry. I waited for a lull and rushed home as quickly as I could. Somehow, I just had to make it. I had an instinct."

They all nodded soberly. People were operating a lot on instinct these days. It made no sense who was bombed and who was safe. Many civilians had adopted a fatalistic attitude, thinking that if a bomb had your name on it, you were done for.

"I wish I had a cup of tea to offer you love, but Tillie and I have drunk it all. There's a bit of potato pie for you both."

"I had tea in the public shelter, Mum. That's okay. I am hungry though."

"I'll eat later, dear," Walter advised as he climbed out of the shelter. "The WVS mobile canteen is taking care of us with tea and biscuits. Stay here, and hopefully I'll be back soon."

But it was hours until Walter and Katie returned after the all-clear sounded. The Kingston family wearily began another tough day in London.

CHAPTER TWENTY

And still the bombs rained down. Throughout October and November there were nightly attacks on all parts of London, but mainly on the East End. Other parts of the country were also targeted including Liverpool, Birmingham, Manchester, Sheffield, and Southampton. It seemed no one was safe from enemy fire. On November 14, a German force of over five hundred bombers destroyed much of the old city of Coventry, killing over five hundred people.

Everyone was weary and angry but no one considered giving up. Despite shortages in almost everything, long daily tedious lines at the shops, disrupted services, and the dread and anxiety of loved ones away fighting or evacuated, the British people just carried on.

On November 9, Sir Neville Chamberlain – former Prime Minister – died of bowel cancer. Although many Britons still blamed him for not being tougher on Hitler to avoid the war, he was still nationally mourned. It was another sad blow to the dispirited and disheartened public.

* * *

"Kingston, you and Foster are on pet round-up this morning. Clock in, do your vehicle check, and off you go," Jasper ordered.

"Yes, Sir," Tillie answered smartly. She almost saluted but caught herself.

It was her day shift, so with the Blitz attacks happening nightly, the daytimes were spent cleaning up and preparation for the busy nights ahead.

Each morning, a crew or two were dispatched to pick up lost and abandoned pets from the previous night's air raids. As people's homes were bombed, cherished dogs, cats, and even birds were left behind as families were rescued from burning or destroyed homes. Many were distraught they couldn't find or bring their pets with them. So, the day after ambulances went around to find and reunite scared pets with their relieved owners.

"Ready, Ernie? Have you checked the board?"

With all the ongoing damage to London's streets, a board was now posted and updated regularly to show which streets were destroyed, off-limits, and where the detours were located.

"Yes, our route is mapped in me head," he answered briskly as he pulled on his coat.

"Ernie, have I told you how much I appreciate you? That you were a cabbie and passed *the Knowledge*, makes you so helpful – especially during the blackout." She beamed a grateful smile at him.

"At yer service, Ma'am," he gave her a mock bow. "It took me near four years to learn all the streets, buildings, and such round London, but once yer know – yer never forget."

"Are you going to stand around all day in a mutual admiration society or are you going to rescue those pets?" Jasper asked drily, as he held out the chit. "More haste, less speed."

"On our way, Jasper. We'll be back once we've collected the animals and taken them to the Animal Rescue Center."

They drove slowly to the first bombed out location. Apparently, there was a cat left there named Percy. As they slowly drove through the ravaged remains of people's lives, Ernie pointed to the young kids rummaging for pieces of enemy shrapnel. These were highly prized as souvenirs and awarded the boys with admiration. It was a testament to the human spirit proving that what caused death and destruction was a cherished treasure to those not directly affected.

They pulled up in front of the debris of a townhouse that stood, rather shakily, in a block where every other home had been destroyed by high explosive bombs the night before. Smoke still rose and everything was soggy and wet from being hosed down with high-powered water. Bricks and mortar piled up dangerously all around the property. Everything smelled of wet plaster, smoke, and burnt rubber. The second and third floors had caved into an enormous pile of rubble, burying the first floor.

"So where is Percy, I wonder?" Tillie asked, as she put her hands on her waist. "Are we going to get lucky and find him wandering around? I don't fancy digging him out of all these bricks."

The two started whistling and calling for the orange cat. A neighbor came by from the local rest center to rummage through the remains to find any possessions that hadn't been destroyed.

"He's usually pretty friendly," she said cheerfully. "I hope you find him."

After calling and searching for about twenty minutes, Ernie spotted Percy behind the residue of an Anderson shelter three houses away. He easily came to Ernie and they put him in the cardboard box they'd brought, and deposited him in the back of the ambulance.

"That wasn't too bad. What's next? Or should I say, who's next?" Tillie asked, as the ambulance engine roared into life.

"Blackie, a dog," Ernie consulted his chit. Tillie nodded.

The tires crunched over debris and broken glass as they made their way to their next stop. Tillie just hoped they wouldn't sustain a puncture.

The next visit wasn't quite so successful. They found Blackie after digging through the rubble under a draper's shop. He had died – presumably of smoke inhalation. He didn't seem to have any broken bones but other than that, it was impossible to precisely pinpoint a cause of death. Tillie wiped away a tear as she and Ernie loaded the large black dog onto the stretcher and into the van.

They drove in silence to the next location.

"Another dog here, Tillie. By the name of Darby."

"Righto, Ernie. Let's find him," she said grimly.

As they pulled onto the bumpy road, Tillie saw two fire trucks still at work putting out a blaze in the upper windows of a small business office. The address for the pet rescue was about halfway down the street so they hoped they wouldn't get in each other's way.

Tillie parked the ambulance and called for Darby. Ernie joined in, whistling and shouting for the missing dog.

Suddenly, Tillie spied a flash of black, white, and grey behind a house that the fire had partially destroyed. She ran after the moving dog, focused on catching him before he got any nearer to the fire, which was still not under control.

"What are you doing back here? Don't you see there's a fire, you foolish – Tillie, is that you?"

Tillie looked up from the piles of brick where she thought the dog had dashed to hide. Trevor!

"Oh my, Trevor. I'm so sorry, am I in the fire zone?" She stood up to face him.

Trevor's irritation vanished. He was more than pleased to see the lovely blonde ambulance driver again.

"Actually, yes, we're still fighting this one. What are you doing back here?" Dressed in full gear, his face was smudged with soot and his suit wet. His trademark dimple flashed when he smiled.

"I'm here to fetch a dog name Darby," Tillie replied. She couldn't help but feel a pull to this handsome firefighter. She felt it each time she'd seen him. "We're on pet rescue," she finished lamely.

"Right, well let's collect him and get you out of here."

Tillie pointed to the brick piles and strode over.

"Come on, fella. Darby, are you under there?" She murmured.

"I'll start pulling off the bricks. You grab him. He's probably scared to death so watch he doesn't bite or worse, run off into the fire."

Trevor methodically pulled bricks off to reveal a small gap. A black and white nose peeked out, then two brown eyes. They heard a whimper. As Trevor removed a few more bricks, he nodded to Tillie who gently reached in to pull out the small dog. He leaped into her arms and immediately snuggled into her. He was sooty but still managed to wag his tail.

Trevor stepped back and immediately pushed Tillie and the dog in the opposite direction.

"Hey, not so rough," Tillie protested.

"You've got to get out of here – NOW," he commanded.

They both started running until they were half a block away from the fire. Tillie hadn't realized how far she had run looking for Darby.

Ernie rushed up to them.

"Found the little nipper, then? Good show." Ernie took the dog, placed him in another box, and walked towards the ambulance to stow him safely away.

"Trevor, I really am sorry. I know better than that. Thank you so much for helping to dig him out." Tillie felt the familiar red rush on her neck and cheeks.

"No harm done, Tillie. But just watch yourself. These fires can shift in an instant. Either you or that dog could have been killed. As much as I admire my new friend here, I really couldn't cope with losing you," he smiled cheekily.

"It won't happen again, I promise," she replied. He couldn't cope with losing her. My goodness, what was he saying? She felt warm all over and not from the fire heat.

"How about you make it up to me over a cup of tea? What time are you off shift today?" Trevor asked, flashing his white teeth.

"Oh, I couldn't, I mean, I don't know," Tillie fumbled. She couldn't possibly date this man. After all she'd only just lost Colin.

"Drummond, are you off duty? Get back here," shouted one of the other firefighters.

Ignoring Tillie's refusal, Trevor strode away with a wink.

"I'll stop by your station one of these days, Tillie. Just you wait," and he was gone.

Tillie smiled thoughtfully as she ran back to the ambulance, utterly embarrassed.

Ernie gently teased her about her new beau as they rounded up another four pets, dropped them off, and returned to the station.

After a light dinner, she and Ernie were sent on the most difficult call that Tillie ever experienced. After a dreadful night of raids and once the fire sites were declared safe, ambulances were dispatched to find, package, and deliver severed limbs to the morgue. It was a top priority to account for every person in a raid, and part of this was literally piecing together body parts to help officials identify the dead from missing lists. It was a gruesome task and one that left many attendants retching and sickened by what they saw and found.

Tillie and Ernie were no exception. Bagging up arms and legs, sometimes with jewelry and shoes still on them, was gut wrenching work. You couldn't help but think of the people that had just recently been attached to them. Because it impacted staff so deeply, the horrible task was rotated amongst them. Tillie didn't throw up today, but fought it the whole time.

Over a cup of tea, she and Ernie spoke of other things because what they had just done was unspeakable. The others left them alone to process.

After a while, Jasper called her into his office.

"Tough shift, Kingston. You held up well. Anything you want to talk about?" He looked down his glasses, which were always perched precariously on his nose.

"No, Jasper," she replied quietly. "It's all part of the job."

"Righto. Kingston, you've come along well these past few weeks. It hasn't been easy for anyone. Is there any chance you can see your way to working here full time? We could really use you in these difficult times."

Tillie brightened slightly.

"Jasper, I appreciate your confidence in me. To be honest, I've been thinking about giving up my work as a Nippy. I find this very fulfilling – well most days," she amended slowly. "And we must all do as much as we can with the Blitz seeming to never end."

"Good," Jasper replied shortly. He was a man of few words. "Give whatever notice you need to, and we'll schedule you on full-time shifts. By the way, the pay is £2 3s a week, with twelve-hour shifts. Any questions?"

"No, Jasper. Thank you. I'll pop by Lyons after work today and hand in my two weeks' notice."

"Kingston, why not go now? It's quiet and your shift is almost over. It's tonight that will be busy, sure as eggs are eggs."

Tillie nodded and left Jasper's office. Despite the horrific day, she was pleased about the direction her life was taking. A few weeks ago, she would have hesitated about becoming a full-time ambulance driver, turning to and her parents first for advice. Now, she felt more confident, and yes – worthy – of the opportunity.

Walking home an hour later, Tillie couldn't have been more pleased with Alfie's reaction to her quitting. He had been gracious and supportive – telling her she only need work out her two remaining shifts that week.

"You are more needed there than here, love," he said gruffly. "More and more young women are leaving every day for the services. I'm sure you noticed a few grey-haired Nippies out on the floor today," he smiled. "You've done us proud, Tillie. Come and see us anytime. Best of luck to both you and Maggie."

Home, Tillie ran lightly up the steps, eager to share her news. For once, all the girls were home. Only Pops was still at the office.

"Hello everyone. Is there a cuppa going?" She called out as she climbed the stairs to the drawing room.

"Up here, dear," Alice answered.

Everybody was there, including her aunt.

"Oh, is this a hen party, then?" She asked as she bent to kiss her mother and Aunt Shirley. She smiled at her sisters.

"Well, with you lot all out on fire watching tonight, Shirley is going to shelter with me."

Tillie nodded. Aunt Shirley had taken to doing this whenever Thomas worked late or had ARP duties himself. The sisters comforted each other in the dark, scary nights in the Anderson.

"Maggie met the Queen today, Tillie," Katie announced dramatically. "She was just telling us."

"Crikey. Do tell, sis," Tillie perched on the edge of a chair.

"She thought I was you, Tils. Can you reckon that?" Maggie reported with excitement.

"Oh my, she never remembered me from the garden party, did she?" Tillie was pleased.

"She did. She asked if you ever joined up as a nurse. I told her you were an ambulance driver. She said that was splendid."

"She must have been shocked when you poured her a cup of tea, then, Mags?" Tillie asked.

"She took a double-take, that's for sure. She was ever so gracious, Tils. She praised us for being so brave during air raids, bringing tea and comfort to front-line servicemen and women. You know she's been visiting bombed-out sites with the King to bring cheer to the homeless. This mobile WVS canteen visit was to help raise morale, too."

"What was she wearing, Maggie?" Katie asked.

"She had on the loveliest pale green chiffon dress with matching coat and hat. She looked like a spring flower. She even took a cup of tea from me. My hands were shaking, I was that afraid of spilling on her."

"I guess she knows what it's like to be bombed. It was such a shame when Buckingham Palace was hit in September," Alice said disapprovingly.

"Yes, someone mentioned how sorry they were about this and Her Majesty just waved her hand. 'Now we can look the East End in the face.' She can relate to all these poor folks now." Maggie was clearly impressed with the Queen.

The women were silent, thinking how much it helped raise spirits when the King and Queen came to visit bombed-out homes, hospitals, factories, and those that worked hard to save them.

"And they've stayed here along with the rest of us. Talk about Blitz spirit," Shirley commented.

"Even the princesses are safe in the country somewhere. The Queen could have taken them to Canada or another safe place. But they are standing alongside us as we fight the enemy together."

The familiar sound of the now-nightly alarm interrupted their patriotic talk.

"Bloody hell," Katie swore. "Not already."

"Katie, language please," Alice admonished as all the women sprang into action.

They quickly headed to the garden shelter, with refreshments, knitting, and books in tow. Faye had left them sausages with mashed potatoes and vegetables for dinner. Shirley had brought a bit of cheese and half a gooseberry pie.

Tillie filled in the family about her ambulance news as they sat in the shelter, waiting for the drone of the planes to start.

"Aren't you the clever one, Tillie!" Maggie said, with a mouthful of what passed for sausage.

"I have been thinking about quitting Lyons but Jasper galvanized me into action. It's rather scary, leaving something I know so well. But I do love the ambulance work. And with a war on, we must all do what we can where we are most needed."

"Tillie, you sound like one of the posters we see plastered all over the city," Katie teased.

Tillie shrugged.

"Say what you will, Katie. We're all doing our best. Now open up that flask. We all need a bracing cup of tea before our fire watching duties tonight."

"Tillie, I'm ever so proud of you," Alice said with a reassuring smile. "You're really stepping up to the mark."

Tillie smiled in the dimly lit shelter.

The three girls left for fire watching before the planes came. Maybe it would be a short night.

But it wasn't. As Tillie sat atop a nearby building with her helmet, armband, stirrup pump with buckets of water, and a sandbag nearby to smother incendiaries, she mused about the ups and downs of her day. She felt confident about her decision to drive ambulance on a full-time basis. She would do everything in her power to thwart Hitler's plan to flatten London. Not on her watch. She owed it to Colin and Geoffrey, and to Kenny fighting so far from home.

Her thoughts drifted to a certain tall, dark firefighter. She was drawn to Trevor. She still missed Colin dreadfully but was having trouble conjuring up his face sometimes. Her guilt was receding, but she was far from ready to look at Trevor in a romantic way. Although a cup of tea with him couldn't do any harm, could it?

CHAPTER TWENTY-ONE

"Mrs. Kingston, may I have a word?"

Faye stood in the doorway of the sitting room. Alice was bent over her knitting as usual. Since Kenny had joined up, she'd spent every spare moment knitting socks, caps, and scarves for the overseas soldiers. Perhaps one of these lovingly knit items would find its way into Kenny's hands. Or at least, take the chill off another hard-working British soldier, sailor or flyer. She looked up, one eyebrow raised.

"Yes, Faye. More shortages at the butcher? Please tell me it's not Woolton Pie again tonight," she teased.

"No, it's a bit more serious, Mrs. Kingston. To get to the point straight away, I've joined up as a nurse. My mum was part of Queen Alexandra's nursing service in the Great War and with this Blitz going on and on, and me being healthy and all, I feel like I should be doing more." She had said more in the last two minutes than Alice had ever heard from her in one go.

Alice took a deep breath and pasted a smile on her face.

"Of course, you must go where you're needed most, Faye. And nurses are sorely called for. But we will miss you dreadfully. You're a part of the family, dear." She gave the housekeeper a cheerful smile.

Faye nodded her head somberly.

"Thank you, Mrs. Kingston. I hate to put the burden of all the shopping and cooking on you and the girls, but I just feel I can play a bigger part than I'm doing here."

With her grey hair and typically serious countenance, you would think Faye was an older woman. In fact, she was only in her late thirties, and would be a tremendous asset as a nurse. No-nonsense, not afraid of hard work, and quite able to learn new skills.

"When will you leave us? I couldn't hope it will be after Christmas?" It was mid-November and Alice couldn't see how the family would cope without her at Christmas.

"I'm afraid not, Mrs. Kingston. I am to report for my physical next week and expect the training to start up shortly after that. I'll try to prepare the house as best as possible. I do appreciate your understanding." She looked pleased with her decision. "More tea?"

Alice laughed. "Might as well do before I haven't the luxury," she added. "And perhaps a cooking lesson or two if you have the time?" Luckily, the twins were good in the kitchen, especially with baking, but Katie was hopeless. She dreaded the thought of trying to make decent meals between the bombing, their jobs, the meager rations, and her own skill level. She just hoped Walter would be patient with her!

The girls took the news cheerfully and reassured their mother that they would do their bit as far as standing in line, meal planning, cooking, and housekeeping. They had already taken up Jesse's cleaning duties, divided them by preference. Katie didn't mind ironing and Maggie took care of the fireplaces and sweeping. Tillie did the dusting and they all shared the washing on Mondays.

"It's lucky neither one of us has a bloke at the moment," Tillie said drily that night as the girls got ready for their evening tasks. Shifts were constantly re-arranged to allow the staff to get as much sleep as possible during the nightly bombings. Accordingly, morning shifts allowed for an extra lie-in and most people hurried to their afternoon duties early, to avoid being caught on the street as the raids started. Most Londoners learned to fall asleep at any chance they had – on the bus, in the shelters, even on a tea break, although some of the more terrified ones sat up shaking and shivering all night.

Maggie nodded, her thoughts on Micah. Technically he wasn't her boyfriend, but she cared for him deeply and thought of him often. What she wouldn't give to be going out on a carefree date with him tonight. However, she was due at the WVS Canteen van in thirty minutes, so she raced around the room collecting her gas mask, hat, and overcoat.

"True that, sis. How one could manage a social life with this war on is unthinkable. Imagine trying to fit in dates between shifts!" She placed her hat on her head and rushed down the stairs. "Be safe tonight, Tillie. There's a moon out, so Jerry will be coming for us early." She gave her twin a bleak smile.

"You too, love. I know you'll be in the thick of it as well. Don't take any more risk than you have to," she admonished sternly. She ran back to give her sister a brief hug, then rushed out of the room.

Tillie was not long after her. Now that she was full time with the ambulance, she was on a steady twelve-hour shift; three days on, two days off, and so on. The evening shifts were the hardest with what seemed like all of London crashing down around them. She was on five-to-five duty tonight and after saying her goodbyes to her mum, she skipped down the front steps, eager to get underground as soon as possible. Many of her colleagues rode scarce but valuable bicycles to work – finding it easier to pick around the rubble and detours than waiting for buses that were inevitably delayed or canceled, depending on what part of London had been bombed the night before. Tillie preferred to walk as quickly as possible to the tube and hope the all-too-common tube delays wouldn't make her late. Jasper was somewhat accepting of the regular tardiness of his staff – after all it wasn't their fault.

She didn't grab a seat today so she swayed back and forth, as the stations blurred through the dark windows. Everyone was still buzzing about what had happened in Coventry. About five hundred German bombers had descended upon the city aiming for its factories and infrastructure, which they did and more.

The first wave had cut off the water, electricity, gas, and telephone lines, crippling the city. High explosive and combustible bombs followed, leveling or severely damaging over half of Coventry's buildings. As always, the London papers were deliberately vague about the number of casualties and injuries – not to alarm the British people and give information to the enemy.

"I 'eard as 'ow many folks left the city and kipped in fields and towns. So, the damage weren't as bad as it coulda ben," one man told the crowd in the tube car. Everybody hung on his every word. One thing about the

Blitz – it had made everyday Londoners more friendly and chatty in public. Tillie smiled to herself.

As she came out of Regent's Park Station, the nightly siren started. She swore under her breath. It was an eight-minute walk to the Weymouth Mews ambulance station. If she ran, could she make it before the bombs started falling? She threw her gas mask over her shoulder and bolted across Marylebone Road. Her eyes kept flitting to the sky as she turned down Harley Street. She heard the not-too-distant hum of the approaching Luftwaffe and darted into a shelter along with other passing pedestrians. When no whistles, bangs, crunches or explosions sounded, she took her chance and ran the last few minutes to the relative safety of the ambulance center.

"Are you barmy, Kingston?" Olive asked drily as Tillie blew in the door, gasping for breath. She'd gotten a stitch in her side running as fast as she could. "You think you can outrun a bomb?"

"Didn't I just?" Tillie smiled, as she prepared for her busy shift ahead.

* * *

Just over three miles away at Victoria Station, Maggie was already hard at work. Sporting her green tweed suit and beret, she staffed the onsite canteen with two other WVS women serving tea and sandwiches to the usual throng of departing military in uniforms in all colors. Besides this familiar sight, there were also the returning wounded men, some with bandages and crutches, and others on stretchers accompanied by medical personnel who were transferring them to London hospitals.

Also new to the scene was an influx of refugees from European countries. It broke Maggie's heart to see the haunted looks in their eyes, as weary families traipsed in with forlorn bags and cases, the sum total of their belongings. Children clutched tightly to their parents' hands looking as if they'd hardly eaten a meal in weeks, which many of them hadn't.

Maggie paid special attention to these needy groups. She handed out cup after cup of hot tea, alongside fish paste sandwiches and biscuits. She listened discreetly for any hint of French accents and upon hearing one, pounced on the unsuspecting owners trying to find out whether they had seen Micah and his family. This was done with a load of gesticulating and Maggie's attempt at French. She was met with either blank stares or sorrowful shakes of the head. It didn't deter her. She would keep asking until Micah appeared. Soon, please, she whispered to herself.

The team kept serving even after the air raid alarm sounded, and they could hear the far-off noise of bombs dropping. Occasionally, the lights flickered and once Maggie was positive the building shook a little, but there were no hits nearby.

About halfway through her shift she received orders to take out a mobile canteen with two other WVS staff to sites, where firefighters and heavy rescuers were hard at work battling ongoing fires, damages, and attempting to rescue civilians.

Maggie didn't have to drive as the van was the domain of Polly, a senior WVS worker. She was quite stout but moved surprisingly fast. She had salt and pepper hair neatly coiled at the back of her head, tucked under her hat. Wearing her WVS pin proudly, she was clearly in charge of tonight's operation.

The third and utterly different member of the team was Clara, a young slip of a girl. She had her brown hair untidily pushed up under her beret and had a rather scatterbrained approach to service. However, she was quick with a ready smile and the men at the site loved her flashing blue eyes and cheeky flirty attitude.

They arrived at the depot to find a fully loaded van ready to go with two tea urns and large trays of sandwiches. Dispatched to Mayfair with an active fire in progress, the trio set off with only a stirrup pump, water and a bucket.

As much as they'd gotten used to the damage and destruction in the streets, it still jarred to see empty spaces where buildings and landmarks had stood. Polly shook her head as they drove past the British Museum, which had sustained significant damage.

"So many books ruined," Maggie commented as they drove past. Hitler was trying to demolish Londoner's spirits in every way.

"If it's your time, nothing you can do," Polly said rather flippantly as she expertly steered through the blackout. White lines had been painted on the roads to help visibility at night, so there had been fewer accidents since. "If a bomb has your name on it, it's your time," she repeated almost cheerfully.

Many Londoners shared her fatalistic attitude. The bombs fell so indiscriminately that there really was no rhyme or reason. On a single block, one house could be bombed to the ground, while a neighbor's was left standing. A family could be obliterated in a direct hit on their Anderson shelter, and the rest of the street walked away completely unhurt.

"You're right but we still have to be as safe as possible and take the right precautions," Maggie chimed in. Too many people had given up their nightly escapes to shelters and just slept in their own beds, prioritizing a good night's sleep over the odds of a bomb hit. And because the predicted gas attacks hadn't happened, gas masks were discarded by many locals.

"That's why I say live life to the fullest whilst we can," piped in Clara. "Have a laugh, a little fun, put on a smile for these lads fighting so hard. I don't even know if I'll make it to my next birthday, so why not enjoy every day whilst I can?"

The same attitude was shared by many people. 'Eat, drink, and be merry, for tomorrow we might die,' was their prevailing chant. There was a widespread frenzy for life, to squeeze every moment of joy and fun out of it. Unfortunately, there had been some lingering consequences to this free-for-all. Departing soldiers pleaded with their girlfriends to 'enjoy the moment,' and some of these women were left pregnant as their men went overseas, some never to return. It was a terrible side effect of this rotten war.

Maggie shook her head at Clara's cavalier beliefs. She liked having fun but her heart was taken. She was a one-man girl.

Her daydream was interrupted by what had to be done. They could tell they were getting close to their destination as the sky was getting brighter. It was lit up in orange and red and yellow – angry at the onslaught coming its way. The heat greeted them as well – a scorching, crackling wall that just kept pushing its way forward.

They saw firefighters everywhere, hoses hissing, water spraying, and ladders propped against swaying buildings. An ARP Warden guided them to a spot next to the major fires on Albemarle Street where thankfully it was a trifle cooler.

The women got to work as soon as Polly parked the van. Maggie opened the window and propped it up. Polly got the tea urns ready, stacking cups for the endless number they'd be pouring out all night. Clara unwrapped the sandwiches and laid them near the counter.

They didn't need an 'Open for Business' sign – the men headed towards the truck almost as soon as the tires stopped turning.

"Yer a sight fer sore eyes, darlins," a sooty firefighter was first in line. "We are parched."

"Happy to serve, lads," quipped Clara as they started pouring and waiting on the growing crowd.

Maggie tried to ignore the whistles and pops as bombs rained down around them. The canteen van itself was good protection from the fires and high explosive bombs, but would not sustain a direct hit. She flinched as shrapnel hit the metal roof like deadly rain.

Time after time, service was halted as a small incendiary dropped near the van and the women rushed to extinguish it with the pump, or smother it with a nearby sandbag. The waiting firefighters helped them and a spirit of camaraderie prevailed.

"Corned beef never tasted so good, love," praised a heavy rescue worker who almost swallowed it whole.

"Have another," urged Maggie as she handed it over. "Lifting all that rubble, digging for survivors – it sure looks like heavy going, chaps." She handed out innumerable sandwiches and cups of tea that Polly poured in a steady rhythm.

"Fancy a night at the cinema, love?" He teased back as he flexed a heavy muscle. "We all need a night off after this."

"Go on with you," Maggie deflected. "Give a man an extra sandwich and he takes a mile."

The man grinned and took off back to the fire site.

Maggie was sweating profusely under her heavy coat. The cool November night was no match for the heat produced by the many fires around her. She wiped her hand over her brow, trying to keep the sweat out of her eyes. She knew the men were working twice as hard as they were in their little van, so she kept a smile on her face and redoubled her efforts.

A gap in the line gave them a moment to breathe. Although deep breaths were impossible. Too much smoke would be inhaled. Maggie's senses were assaulted with the war raging around her. The sound of the ack-ack guns firing at German planes over London in defiance of the bombs whistling and exploding, the red flames painting the sky red and black with smoke, the smell and taste of smoke and cordite, and the feel of wet, slippery hands as soaked firemen took hot cups of tea from her. She was overloaded and overwhelmed but the night was far from over. After gulping a quick cup of tea, Maggie turned back to the crowd of tired firefighters forming again, ARP staff, ambulance workers and more – all waiting for a tiny respite from the firefighting and rescue just down the street.

"Oi, love, there's a massive crater left by Jerry. Did you see it?" A red-haired, freckle-faced firefighter took a sandwich from Clara. "Luckily no one was hurt – they're safe in a nearby shelter."

"That's good news, mate," she answered back. "Cup of tea, then?"

"I wouldn't say no to such a lovely lady," he teased back. "Are you from around here? My name's Sam. What's yours?"

"Ain't you a fast mover, Sam?" She flirted back with a smile.

"Gotta move fast these days. Look at all the competition I've got," he jerked his thumb towards the line of men behind him.

Clara giggled and introduced herself.

"Here you go, Sam. And take care of yourself. Maybe come for a cuppa when your shift is over?"

"We've got a date, Clara. Don't let any of these other blokes talk you out of it." He strode away purposefully.

Clara waved gaily and turned back to her tray of sandwiches.

A loud whistle sounded close by, followed by a loud explosion. The women crouched inside the van.

"That was close," whispered Maggie as the smell of cordite filled the air.

When the smoke cleared, they peered carefully through the window. Not ten feet away, two firefighters were leaning over a comrade who had taken a direct hit.

"Oh no," screamed Clara. "It's Sam."

CHAPTER TWENTY-TWO

Maggie gasped.

Clara threw open the van door and streaked toward the young man lying face down on the filthy street.

The other firefighters were already turning him over, calling his name, and trying to find a pulse that wasn't there. His boots had completely blown off his feet and lay next to one another twenty feet away. He was covered in brick dust and had a large gash across his right eye.

"Sam," Clara moaned brokenly. She tried to wipe the cut clean but the firefighter gently lifted her up.

"We'll take it from here, love," one of them said kindly as a stretcher team appeared from the smoke.

"He was just here, just here," Clara kept repeating dumbly.

Polly recognized the signs of shock and took charge.

"Come along, love, and have a cup of tea. That poor young lad. He was just laughing a moment ago. Come along now and sit for a minute."

Clara allowed herself to be led to the back of the van.

"I didn't know him but yet I feel his loss," she whimpered.

Maggie tried to console her. What a senseless loss. A nice young man struck down before his life had begun. Damn Hitler. Damn him, the Nazis, and the bloody Luftwaffe. The incident just made her angrier and more determined that Britain would never surrender to this evil. Just like Churchill said – never surrender.

"Take as long as you like, dear. Have another cuppa. Maggie and I will manage." Polly nodded to her and Maggie stood up. The line was forming again. This war just didn't stop – for anything or anyone.

They worked until the early hours of the morning. Eventually Clara joined them and worked silently alongside the tired women until the last rescue worker was served. The all-clear sounded just as the sun was rising. It was hard to see it with the smoke and flames still covering the sky overhead, but it was a beacon of a new day, and therefore hope.

They tidied the van, which was near empty of provisions. Polly drove through the grey streets as new wreckage greeted them on the slow journey back to the depot. They were all too bone-weary to make conversation.

A short while later, Maggie put one foot in front of the other as she shuffled down the street on her way home. She allowed herself a tiny moment of relief that there had been no damage to her home or around them. Numb with exhaustion and distress, she used up her last ounce of strength as she mounted the stairs.

She opened the door without making a sound, and was soothed to hear nothing but silence from within. That meant the family had safely made it through the night from their assorted duties and were tucked up in bed, snatching whatever precious sleep they could before plunging into another overcrowded day.

Maggie needed some time to herself to process what happened during the night and wasn't in any shape to share it with her family just yet.

Gazing at the stairs as if they were the enemy, she mustered her last bit of energy to climb to her bed. After a quick wash, she stripped down to her slip and panties, shrugged on a nightdress that Tillie had thoughtfully left at the bottom of her bed, glanced at the almost-comatose twin who snored lightly next to her, climbed into bed pulling the cover to her chin, and promptly dropped off into a dreamless sleep.

Disturbingly, each member of the Kingston family and most Londoners had experienced frightening encounters of their own. Death was becoming all too common and each of them had witnessed gruesome sights that could never be forgotten. Some of them they shared, others they kept tight within themselves, pushing down memories that were too hideous to bring out. They all just trudged on.

* * *

"What a relief to finally have a night without a siren. Who knew sleep was such a luxurious joy?" Tillie stretched her arms over her blonde, tousled head and sat up in bed.

It was November 29th, and only two nights since September 7th had been free of air raid alerts and bombing. By chance, both twins had been off duty, and so had relished a good night's sleep for the first time in weeks.

"Do you think it will last, Tils?" Maggie asked as she mirrored her sister's stretch.

"We can only hope, darling. Let's do the morning blackout and talk to Mum about Christmas."

The girls washed and dressed and met up with their mother in the downstairs kitchen. Alice was bustling around the aga, pulling the kettle off to pour the tea and stirring a lumpy, grey mess in a large pot.

"Good morning, Mum. Did you sleep well?" Tillie looked bright and cheerful in a pair of black trousers and a scarlet top that matched her lipstick. Her hair was loose, with soft curls falling down her shoulders.

"Fantastic, love. And you two? It was lovely, wasn't it? An uninterrupted night in my own bed. Pops and Katie were on top of the world before they set off for work."

"Heaven, Mum," answered Maggie for them both. She had pulled back her hair with kirby grips which accentuated her brown eyes. Wearing a cabled pale blue twin set with a navy skirt, she was fresh and energetic. "But what's in that pot? It smells rather burnt."

Tillie lifted the lid to reveal an unrecognizable, thick grey mound.

Alice sighed.

"It's my attempt at porridge girls. It seemed okay for your dad and sister, but is rather gloppy now."

Tillie tried to pull a heavy wooden spoon out of the pot with no success.

"Mum, did you add any water or milk?" Tillie asked, raising an eyebrow.

"An hour ago, I did," she retorted defensively.

Both girls broke out into giggles.

"Mum, you need some liquid to keep it from getting stuck," Maggie jumped in. "And you have it on too high. You should put it down to notch one." She moved the pot off the heat.

Meanwhile, Tillie was already at the toaster.

Sipping their tea and munching on toast with tiny bits of margarine, the three turned their attention to the upcoming holiday.

"I suppose it will be a quiet Christmas this year," observed Maggie, thinking of the losses they'd suffered in 1940. It would be difficult to celebrate heartily with neither Geoffrey nor Colin at the table, and Kenny far from home.

"Yes, but let's still make it festive," insisted Tillie. She did not want her loss bringing down the family. "Let's start with Christmas dinner. How do you reckon we will manage without Faye?"

"Just fine," replied Alice firmly. "I have my list here." She produced a small piece of paper and a pencil worn to the nub. She began to read. "As far as guests, of course we'll have Shirley and Thomas. They will be at a loose end this year. Tillie, what about inviting Mr. and Mrs. Redwood? Do you know if they have plans?" She looked up from her list.

"I don't know, Mum. I can certainly ask them." Tillie chewed her lower lip. To be honest, it would be a trifle awkward to have them. She dropped in on them from time to time and it was just so sad to see them as shadows of their former selves. Even the house was sorrowful as if still mourning the son who would never come back.

"Whatever you think is best, darling. I just hate to think of them rattling about the house on their own." Alice clucked in sympathy. "Righto, so if they came, that will be..." she started counting on her fingers. "Nine. Oh, my goodness, that's the smallest Christmas gathering we've ever had." Her face crumpled as she burst into tears.

Tillie rushed to comfort her mother.

"Shh, Mum. I know how much you miss Kenny. But didn't you just get a letter from him last week? And wasn't he sounding cheerful?" Tillie tried to cheer her Mum up.

Alice sniffled.

"I'm so sorry, girls. I don't know what came over me. I just miss my boy so much." She wiped her nose. "And you're right, Tillie. So far, he's safe." She paused and gazed at her list again. "Now, as for the food – a turkey or goose if we can get one, or a chicken if not. Maybe two? Roast potatoes and gravy. As far as veg, sprouts and carrots. We have parsnips from the garden as well. What do you think, girls?" She'd regained her composure and didn't want to discuss her emotional outburst.

"Do you think Aunt Shirley can bake her famous mince pies? Those would go down a treat." asked Maggie. She loved mince pies.

"I'm sure she would, love. And her scones are on my list. She told me she's been saving her sugar and flour rations." Like most British people, they longed for even the smallest joy after such a horrendous autumn. Housewives everywhere had been scrimping and saving the rations to make Christmas extra special this year.

"I'm really going to miss Faye's plum pudding. It's rather too late to start one now, not that we could match hers."

"Girls, I'll let you in on a little secret. Faye made the pudding before she left. It's aging in the cold cellar. I wanted to surprise everyone but at least the others won't know about it until Christmas Day."

Maggie and Tillie clapped in unison.

"Smashing," they cried together, looked at each other, and laughed.

They settled on the menu and divided up the chores – the girls taking long shopping waiting lines on, as well as food preparation before and on the day.

"Katie can help with the decorating. No Christmas tree, more's the pity, but we must make do. She can make some paper chains and garlands and hang them about." Alice was doing her best to find alternatives to their usually lavish Christmas festivities.

"It will be brilliant, Mum. Just wait and see. And if Aunt Shirley can come early, she's a splendid cook and will be pleased to get stuck in," Maggie grimaced. "No offense, Mum. Your cooking is getting better, truly," she said loyally.

* * *

Unfortunately, the bombing resumed that night and continued up to Christmas. The family prepared as best they could, although the long lines for food were more than frustrating. They'd managed to get almost everything on Alice's list, but were still waiting for the butcher to come through with at least one chicken.

Three days before Christmas, a large parcel was delivered to the townhouse. Alice undid the string and read the label inside.

"I know you are going to manage just fine without me, but here are a few bits and bobs to make your Christmas even more special. I called in a few favors at the greengrocer and butcher shops. I wish you all a Happy Christmas. Love, Faye. Xx"

"Oh my," Alice felt near tears again.

Katie had already started opening the box.

"Mum, look – a goose! And how on earth did she secure oranges for us all?" She sniffed them appreciatively. "Oh, look, even some chocolates. I wish we could open the tin right now."

Alice slapped her hand playfully.

"Not on your life. We're saving them for the day. How kind of Faye to think of us." She clutched the label to her chest. "I miss her every day but I hope her training is going smoothly."

As it turned out, Christmas was a small but happy affair. They decided to exchange just small gifts, so knitted hats, scarves, and mittens were handed round by Alice. Soap, hard-to-find makeup, and magazines were the sisters' presents, and Walter received tobacco for his pipe and a new garden trowel. Shirley and Walter had contributed the baked goods, and Colin's parents presented a carefully hoarded bottle of brandy, which was ceremonially used to light Faye's delicious plum pudding.

Katie had outdone herself decorating the house with paper chains made from newspapers, holly, and reusing the baubles from prior years.

They all enjoyed the communal dinner and declared it the best ever. No one mentioned the burnt Brussel sprouts for which Alice was supremely grateful.

After a brisk walk around the block, the families gathered to hear the King's Christmas speech on the wireless. They felt emotional listening to his words; "May the New Year carry us towards victory and to happier Christmas days, when everyone will be at home together in the years to come."

They sang Christmas carols and played a few parlor games before saying their goodbyes. Although there was an uneasy ceasefire with Germany, everyone wanted to be tucked in safely at home before the blackout. It had been a lovely, if bittersweet holiday. Everyone thought of those gone or away fighting, and fervently made Christmas wishes it would all be over in 1941.

* * *

January came and the bombing resumed. The families held a quiet joint birthday celebration for Walter and Shirley, but otherwise carried on with the daily frenzy of their daily and nighttime work, ceaseless waiting in line, frigid nights in the shelter, and grim fear.

After being pressed by Trevor, Tillie finally agreed to have a cup of tea with him. They'd met on a mutual day off and Trevor had invited her to the Black Penny Café in Covent Garden. She had dressed carefully, trying to make her precious lipstick last. A black and white belted polka-dot dress accentuated her slender figure. She topped this with her dark grey wool overcoat and matching felt hat. Incredibly nervous, she felt pretty.

She'd insisted on meeting him at the café. After all, this wasn't really a date, was it? When she arrived, he was already there waiting for her outside. It was a chilly January day and after an awkward greeting, they slipped inside to warm up.

"I hope your journey wasn't too bad, Tillie," Trevor smiled at her as they were seated.

"No, just a small stoppage on the line. I'm not late, am I?" She removed her gloves and placed them on the table with her purse.

"No, you're just on time. I was a bit early. Eager and all, you know?" He raked a hand through his thick, black, shiny hair.

A waitress came and took their order. With her Nippy background, Tillie chatted her up in a friendly manner.

"You look lovely, Tillie. I always forget how deep brown your eyes are. I could lose myself in them." His cobalt blue eyes locked with hers. Tillie broke the gaze.

"Go on with you, Trevor. You hardly know me."

"I'm hoping to remedy that fact, starting with today."

They made small talk over tea and cake. They had lapsed into an easy familiarity and Tillie found herself sharing stories of her Nippy days and ambulance shifts. She found him easy to talk to, so she slowly relaxed. She liked that he asked her questions and really listened to the answers. He happily obliged when she pressed him to share more of his life.

"It's just me and Mum. My father died in the Great War, so we've looked after each other ever since. She's worked as a secretary at a bank and also many nights as a cook for the WVS. She's a smashing cook, my Mum." Trevor was obviously proud of her. "With me in a reserved occupation in the London Fire Service and her putting in so many hours at the WVS, neither of us has been called up – yet. I don't know what I would do if I had to leave her all alone." He took a huge bite of his sticky toffee pudding.

"She sounds sweet," Tillie said through a mouthful of Chelsea bun. She could feel an electric current running between them and felt warm even on that wintry day.

"Tillie, I know you are still grieving your fiancé and I understand. But I like you. And with this war on, don't we all deserve a little happiness? We just don't know what tomorrow will bring." He shrugged his shoulders. "Have you heard about the concerts being given at the National Gallery? They've had some talented singers and composers there over the last few months. Michael Tippett is conducting there in a fortnight. Would you fancy going with me?" He looked at her with boyish hope, devastating dimple in full effect.

Tillie's first instinct was to refuse. In fact, she even opened her mouth to say no. But somehow, she found herself saying yes. It had been so long since she'd felt young and carefree, that she embraced the lightness. The block of ice around her heart started to thaw.

Trevor insisted on seeing her home and they hurried to get ahead of the blackout and almost-inevitable nightly Blitz attacks. The underground trip passed by in a blur of talking and laughing and before long, they had arrived home.

"Thank you so much for the tea and cakes, Trevor. And for seeing me home although it was unnecessary. We can all find our way around London – in light or dark – these days."

"I didn't want to let you go," he said in a husky voice. He leaned in.

"I'd invite you in, Trevor – but it's almost the blackout, and we need to get ready for a night in the Andy, and well – you know," she finished lamely. No one in the household knew she'd met up with Trevor and she wasn't quite sure how to explain him.

"I totally understand, Tillie and I must be on my way too. My mother will be looking out for me." He leaned in again and planted a chaste kiss on her cheek. Up close, he smelled marvelous – pear soap, hair pomade and something masculine that she couldn't quite identify. It was a heady combination.

"I'll see you for the concert, Tillie, if not at a fire site in the meantime." He looked deeply into her eyes. "Please take care of yourself, beautiful." He touched her sleeve lightly and sprinted down the steps.

A faint blush spread across her cheeks as Tillie turned to the front door and let herself in.

CHAPTER TWENTY-THREE

The next morning, the twins did their morning chores. The blackout was put away and Maggie cleaned the fire grate in the drawing room, and re-laid it for later today. The family had taken to lighting it early in the afternoon to enjoy the warmth on the cold January afternoons. They banked it before heading to the shelter with hopes of a somewhat warm house when the all-clear sounded.

Tillie ran the hoover over the carpets in the drawing and morning rooms and lightly dusted Alice's knick-knacks and photograph frames.

Katie had made a pot of porridge before she left for work and the smell wafted enticingly up the stairs.

The pair sat in the warm kitchen, drinking tea, and savoring Katie's porridge with a bit of sugar.

"So where did you get to yesterday, Tils? You were gone quite a while but didn't say," Maggie asked her sister. Both dressed casually as they were heading to afternoon shifts later. The winter sun flooded through the basement windows, cheering up the morning.

Tillie cleared her throat and took a sip of tea.

"I had tea with that firefighter, Trevor Drummond, Maggie." She put up her hand. "And before you say anything, it was just tea and cake, nothing more." She sat back, waiting.

"Tillie, you didn't!" Maggie scolded. As expected. "With Colin just gone a few months ago, how could you?" She sputtered.

"Maggie, take that rebuke out of your voice. I did nothing wrong. Besides, Colin would want me to be happy. He wouldn't want me to mourn forever."

"Forever! You couldn't even wait a year. And don't tell me there's a war on. What about respecting the man you say you loved?" Maggie was almost shouting now.

"I did love him, Maggie," Tillie replied quietly. "And believe me, I have enough guilt about not marrying him to last a lifetime. But I can't change that, can I? Nothing will bring Colin back. I must move on with my life. What choice do I have?" Her voice was flat.

Maggie jumped up.

"You can honor the man he was, Tillie. Respect his memory. At least wait a decent amount of time." She slammed down her teacup and fled the room, wiping away tears.

"Thanks for understanding, sis. Just what I needed!" She called angrily after her twin. Silence. Tillie sipped her tea quietly, hating this war even more.

Life went on, fractured as it was. Tillie and Maggie were barely on speaking terms and neither was willing to give an inch.

February came, and with it a bone-cold front that set everyone's nerves on edge. Maggie and Tillie had left for their shifts – Maggie to the WVS mobile canteen and Tillie to her ambulance duties.

Tillie had run into Trevor at a few night fires and was constantly struck with his bravery and bright spirit. She couldn't help but admire his tall, muscular frame and dedication to saving others.

They'd gone to the shilling concert at The National Gallery the previous week. Both had been lost in the moving orchestral music. Tippett had been phenomenal conducting and it had been a special afternoon. They'd had dinner nearby before the concert and Trevor had given her a chaste kiss when he'd deposited her on her doorstep again. She was thinking of him more often as the memory of Colin receded. She felt pangs of guilt in between spurts of joy about the future. Not knowing what to do with these conflicting feelings, she pushed them down to deal with later.

She was reassured that Aunt Shirley was staying with Mum tonight in the Andy shelter. Both women were afraid on their own, and could while away the hours knitting and chatting together as only sisters could. Katie was fire watching, and both Walter and Thomas were hard at work as ARP Wardens.

"Would you like a cup of tea, Shirl?" asked Alice. The alarm had made its nightly appearance, and the two women quickly, if not frantically, collected their shelter kits and walked out to the shelter. Inevitably, Londoners had become somewhat complacent with the night after night sirens, bombs, and sheltering. It was a strange blend of fear and boredom, and it made people anxious.

"I'd love one, sis," smiled Shirley into the semi-darkness. It was much colder now in the shelter. Winter had sunk its icy fingers in and was clinging on tight. The women wore jumpers with two coats each, with hats and gloves that had the fingertips cut off to facilitate knitting. They were also wrapped in blankets and were warm, but barely. They huddled together to keep warmer.

"Jerry came early tonight," commented Shirley as she sipped her tea. It chilled so quickly that it was more like guzzling than dainty swallowing. "And the ack-ack guns are already blaring."

"It's almost a full moon – just how Hitler likes it," Alice said with a grimace.

Whistles followed by booms and crashes shook the shelter.

"I think they're closer tonight, Alice," Shirley whispered. She'd given up the pretense of knitting and clutched her sister's hands.

A loud crash sounded very close. The women looked at each other with terrified eyes.

Suddenly, the door burst open, and Walter almost fell in. "Are you ladies alright?" He was out of breath and fixed his stare on the frightened women huddled together.

"Yes, but what's happening out there? The explosions sound awfully close tonight," Alice jumped up and gave her husband a hasty embrace.

"Earl's Court has been hit," he tried to catch his breath. "North of West Cromwell Road. I only have a minute to check on you. I must ensure all the people in my section are accounted for. I'll look for Thomas to ensure your house is safe, Shirley," he tried to bolster his sister-in-law.

Both women gasped.

"Oh no, Thomas," Alice exclaimed.

"I'm sure he's fine, Shirley. I'll survey the area and come back when I can." He tried to give the women an encouraging smile. "It goes without saying that you should stay put. It's dangerous out there – fires and explosions. You're safest here."

The sisters nodded solemnly as Walter left the shelter and closed the door tightly behind him.

They continued to hear the sickening whine of the planes, long drawn-out whistling wails, vicious bouts of gunfire, and loud explosions that shook the Anderson. The sound of crashing glass and collapsing bricks confirmed that serious damage had been done. To terrify them further, they could smell burning wood, fire, and smoke and cordite – aromas that meant the HEs and incendiaries were landing close by.

"I'm sure if we could look out, we'd see flashes all over the sky and fires blazing everywhere," said Alice to break the bombs' noise.

"Well, we daren't, love. What do you suppose those knocks and hits are on the roof? Shrapnel falling?"

"Maybe. As long as it's not a bomb, that'd be alright, then," answered Alice.

What seemed like an age later, the door rattled again. This time both husbands came through the door, covered in dust and soot.

"Thomas! You're safe," Shirley hugged her husband tightly. "The house? Is it still there? Is it standing?" She searched her husband's dirty face.

"You must be strong, love. Sit down."

"Why must I be strong?" Shirley shrilled. "I have been strong. I've lost my only son. What more must I withstand?"

"The house, dear. It's been hit. By a parachute bomb." He grasped her frozen hands in his. "The house is gone, Shirley. Ours and all the surrounding neighbors. Even the shelter was hit. I'm so sorry, dear. You must be brave."

An animal wail erupted in the awful silence.

"No, no, no. It's too much." Shirley bent over, and for a moment Alice thought she was going to be sick. She straightened back up, tried to stand, and collapsed on the floor. Thomas bent to help her back to the bench.

"Shhh, love. At least no one was in the house. Or the shelter. If you'd been home, or out in the garden..." his voice trailed off.

"I'd be dead, wouldn't I?" She finished bitterly. "I'd rather be dead. I'd rather be dead," she wailed.

Walter and Alice hated to witness this personal tragedy, but there was nowhere to go. Bombs and explosions continued to rain all around them.

After a while, the wailing quieted to steady weeping. Walter stood up, pale and bedraggled.

"I'm sorry, dear, but I must go. We'll be back as soon as the all-clear sounds. Try to get some sleep."

A muffled sob was her only response.

Alice nodded at the men.

"I'll see to her. Go on, then. You're needed out there."

As the long night wore on, Shirley fell into a fitful sleep on her sister's shoulder. Alice couldn't sleep a wink. Devastated for her sister, she couldn't help thinking of Katie atop a nearby building, fire watching right in the line of fire. And the twins – both of them amidst the bombing and fires. Please let them all be safe.

Shirley woke up just before the all-clear sounded about half-past four a.m.

"I'm going round the house as soon as it's over, Alice, and don't try to stop me. I need to see what's happened to our home, to Geoffrey's home."

"Indeed, Shirl. You'll be needing to inspect for yourself. I'll accompany you. We'll need to salvage whatever we can – clothes, furnishings, and other household goods. We can start with the cart, and I'll send Walter for a removal van once we see what's...what's left."

Alice hoped against hope that her sister's home wasn't razed to the ground. That at least some belongings had not been destroyed.

"And of course, you'll both stay here," she went on in what she hoped was a matter-of-fact tone. "We've plenty of room especially with Kenny gone. We'll get you properly settled here today, and then you'll need a good rest."

"Thank you, love," Shirley replied in a shaky voice. "I don't know what we'll do, but the thought of being homeless at a rest center – I just can't face it. Thank you for opening up your home to us."

The women hugged just as the all-clear sounded.

"I know you want to rush to your house but I insist we wait for the men. A hot cup of tea is absolutely what we need first. Come on, then."

The women left the cold, cramped shelter out to the grey pre-dawn morning. The smell of smoke, burnt wood, and rubber, and the wet stench of soaked debris filled the air.

Walter and Thomas returned a short time later, and after a cup of tea all around, prepared to go back to check the house. They loaded up their garden cart with shovels and empty boxes.

As they trudged towards the Fowler's home, the men reported on the evening's incidents.

"Six fatalities – two on Redfield Lane, Shirley. Mr. and Mrs. Moore. They were asleep in their beds and the house just crumbled on top of them. Four others a couple of streets away. Ten injured, although that's a rough number, as people are still being accounted for. Mainly light injuries, except for Mrs. Davies, who's suffering from broken ribs, and a crushed pelvis." Walter laid out the details gently.

"Most of the fires are out and we're not technically supposed to be on active sites, but we need to collect whatever we can before the looters come." Thomas added to the story.

"Oh no, the Moores. They had us over for sherry on Christmas Eve," moaned Shirley. The Moores were an elderly couple who found the Anderson shelter claustrophobic, and had refused to go out since Christmas. Now they were dead.

"Is our house completely gone, Thomas?" Shirley asked in a thin voice.

"The last time I checked, there was still a structure there. The second floor is caved in and some of the kitchen. The first floor looked intact. Not sure about the basement. But let's see, dear."

The four of them were ashen with fatigue as they slowly picked their way carefully through rubble, broken glass, twisted beams, and fallen debris from the bombed buildings.

They reached Redfield Lane and stopped to digest what they saw before them. Chaos prevailed – but everyone had a job to do, and knew how to do it. Bomb disposal teams worked carefully on unexploded bombs. Engineers analyzed hazardous building fragments and advised which to demolish. Firefighters cooled down the fires so no embers remained. Rescue teams looked through rubble, glass, and brick to find and save people and carry them to First Aid posts or waiting ambulances. Air Raid staff checked names against their lists to confirm that every person in their sector was accounted for. Ten townhouses in a row were in various states of ruin. Some looked like gaping wounds with their guts spilling onto the street. Others were just piles of rubble. Remarkably, the Fowler's house still stood – although severely damaged. The front of the house was completely gone, leaving it open for all to see like a woman's negligee agape and in full, disturbing view.

"It looks like Queen Mary's Dolls House – the one at Windsor Castle," Shirley said, her voice rising hysterically.

And, indeed, it did resemble a macabre oversized dollhouse, with random pieces of furniture placed irregularly, shredded curtains swaying in the wind, and odd knick-knacks unbelievably untouched. Cupboards were splintered, shards of glass and crockery littering the floors, and Shirley's prized green ivy wallpaper was ripped off the wall attached to torn pieces of plaster. The pretty yellow paint on the other walls was coated with soot and smoke.

"My mother's lamp," Shirley pointed to the first floor sitting room. And there it was, tottering on the edge of a table with two broken legs. "And why are my kitchen pots all over the street?" She asked curiously.

"The blasts blow in every direction, Shirley," Walter explained. "Let's see what we can salvage."

"Yes, I expect the engineers will be here anytime, and will blow it up. It's not safe anymore," Thomas agreed.

Shirley swallowed a sob, and the little group went systematically through the house trying to find what they could. Thomas wouldn't let the women climb the stairs, which were hanging precariously. Thomas used a neighbor's ladder to retrieve clothes from the bedrooms. The books and photo albums were missing or destroyed, as was most of the furniture.

Alice had left a note for the girls, and one by one they appeared – dead tired – but willing to help their aunt and uncle in any way possible.

Shirley greeted neighbors as they slowly came out of shelters and picked their way through their own belongings. There were tears and angry fisted shouts at Hitler, whilst they all dealt with their massive loss, some wandering around in shock and disbelief.

Alice was so very pleased to see a mobile WVS canteen arrive on the scene. Nothing was better for shock than tea, and the cheerful WVS women knew how to distract trauma victims with everyday solace. The WVS servers knew Alice and Shirley, which brought a small measure of comfort.

Eventually, the Kingstons and Fowlers made their way back home. Four cartloads were all that was left of the Fowlers' house.

When they got home, the men unloaded the carts into Faye's disused housekeeper's room in the basement. The twins made tea and toast, encouraging their aunt and uncle to eat.

"There's much to be sorted, but right now what we all need is a few hours' sleep. Then we'll be able to cope more adequately with all the decisions that need to be made. None of us can think straight at the moment," Walter said in a bleary voice.

To punctuate his statement, Maggie lifted the saltshaker to pour it into her teacup.

"Stop!" Cried her mother, just as Maggie turned over the shaker.

"I see what you mean," Alice said, a trifle sharply.

"Aunt Shirley, Uncle Walter – you can have Maggie and my room," Tillie offered, looking for agreement from her sister. Maggie nodded. They'd been in a silent ceasefire since last night's emergency.

"Absolutely. The beds are made up in our room. We can sleep upstairs. Kenny's room is free, and there are two empty box rooms up there. We can move some beds around and everyone will be snug as bugs in rugs. As Pops says, let's just get some rest and we'll have more energy to deal with it all later."

"That sounds fine, and thanks, Tillie, Maggie. I'm sure we can manage with one of the box rooms upstairs, but for now we're grateful for a clean bed to lay our heads."

They all finished their tea, took turns washing off the grime and dirt of the previous night, and tumbled into beds all over the house. Alice was grateful that her home was big enough to welcome her sister and brother-in-law. They'd likely be there for some time. It was impossible to rebuild quickly in London right now. She and Walter were all the Fowlers had, and she welcomed them with open arms. After all, family was family.

Tillie and Maggie slept in separate rooms for the first time in their lives. Tillie bunked in with Katie, whilst Maggie was on her own in Kenny's room. Neither slept well, not feeling good about their row, but neither one knew how to bridge the rift.

The house fell quiet as its weary and depleted inhabitants surrendered to welcome nothingness.

CHAPTER TWENTY-FOUR

The next few days, in between the continued night bombing, were dedicated to settling the Fowlers and making them feel at home. Tillie and Maggie insisted their aunt and uncle keep their bigger room on the second floor. No one wanted to touch Kenny's room but Katie offered to move into one of the disused box rooms to allow the twins to move back in together into her larger room. There was loads of cleaning, shifting furniture around, and reorganizing, but it kept the Fowlers occupied – particularly Aunt Shirley – and it felt productive for a change. They made several trips back to Redfield Lane for bits and pieces that turned up. And the Fowlers were pathetically pleased that one of their neighbors had rescued a photo album – burnt, charred, and wet – but at least a few precious photos of Geoffrey remained. Shirley cried afresh at all that the war had taken from them.

A few days later, Tillie arranged to visit Alfie and some of her Nippy friends at Lyons. It was an overdue call and she wanted to escape the somber mood at home. She and Maggie were still not really talking. Trevor had asked her out to dinner, and she'd agreed to meet him there after seeing her friends. That was hardly a date, right?

Still, she took care with her appearance. She had on a long-sleeved dark green dress, belted at the waist, with soft pleats below. She'd pulled her hair back into a soft bun, with a black hat perched forward over her forehead. She fastened on small gold rose earrings, and a flower brooch. Of course, she still wore her engagement ring. She didn't know when she'd be ready to take it off.

Shaking her head clear of sad memories, Tillie gathered her personal belongings, put on her coat and winter boots, and called her goodbyes.

"Take an umbrella, love," Alice called from the morning room. "It's foggy out there, rain is doubtless coming."

"Ta, Mum. I will. I'm going straight to work after Lyons. Maybe the fog will keep Hitler's gang home tonight. Be safe and I'll see you tomorrow morning." She kissed her Mum goodbye and went out.

It was foggy. Tillie could hardly see as she walked to Earl's Court underground station. She'd learned how to navigate pretty well in the blackout, but this fog was thick and heavy with sleety drops raining down. Great. A chilly February rain. She stepped up her pace. She had a long afternoon and evening ahead, and she didn't want to start out soaking wet.

By the time she exited Leicester Square, it was pouring. She pushed her umbrella open and jogged to the restaurant. She feared her hair would be a sodden mess.

Everything about Lyons was achingly familiar. Tillie felt a rush of emotion. She'd spent such fun and easy days here before the war. If only they'd known what was ahead, they would have cherished each safe and precious moment. She thought of her sister and wished Maggie were here. She hated quarreling with her twin, and was determined to make up with her the next time they spoke.

"Tillie Kingston. You are looking grand, if a tad damp."

Alfie engulfed her in a bulky hug.

"Oh Alfie, stop. You're going to get soaked."

"I don't mind, Tillie. It's smashing to see you. Come on upstairs. We'll have a cuppa."

Tillie quickly took off her wet coat and had a lovely talk with Alfie in the staff room.

"The girls are looking a bit ... older, shall we say?" Tillie teased. "I didn't recognize any of the Nippies on the floor as we passed through. I was proper looking forward to catching up with the girls."

"They've all been called up, signed up, or registered for factory work. Lila joined up with the WRNS and others are scattered across the British services."

"What about Dot? She was always a laugh."

"Nursing, if you can believe it. Apparently, she thought the uniform was rather smart."

Tillie laughed.

"Sounds like our Dot. I miss her. I miss all of this." She spread her arms wide to encompass the whole Lyons environment. "Are the new girls getting on alright?"

It was Alfie's turn to laugh.

"They are not as quick as you girls, that's for sure. It took a bit of getting used to seeing the grey-haired women bustling about, but they really care about the customers. And they are more than chuffed to be Nippies in their forties and fifties. They tend to mother the customers, particularly the boys."

"Sounds like it's working out just fine then," Tillie sighed.

"You know you and Maggie are welcome back anytime – once this bloody war is over. You two were no trouble, friendly and efficient."

Tillie flashed a brilliant smile at him.

"You're the best, Alfie. Who knows when that will be? But I appreciate the offer, and I know Maggie will as well."

They continued reminiscing about the old days, and Tillie regaled her old supervisor with funny ambulance tales. She turned down the offer of cake but enjoyed two more cups of tea.

"I've got to get on, Alfie. I'm meeting someone for dinner downstairs. This has been brilliant. We must do it again soon." Tillie gave him a kiss on the cheek.

Alfie blushed.

"Hey do you want to hear Today's Special?" Alfie posed with a smile.

"Sure Alfie," Tillie played along.

"Of course. Today is special. How is that?"

Tillie groaned.

"Still got it, Alfie. See you soon."

"Come back anytime, Tillie and bring your sister with you. Off you go, then."

Tillie went to the bathroom to refresh her lipstick, repair her hair, and check that her stocking seams were straight. She couldn't help it – she was feeling excited to see Trevor again.

He greeted her with his big smile and a kiss on the cheek. He was dressed casually in navy corduroy trousers, shirt and tie, and a beige knitted vest. Shaking off the rain from his tan trench coat, he folded it over his arm.

"Well, here we are then. How are you, Tillie? Not too wet?"

They sat at a corner table, the usual Lyons bustle all around them, which they hardly noticed. They were intent only on each other.

"You are as lovely as always, Tillie. You brighten up this dull, rainy, wintry day."

It was true. Tillie's brown eyes were dancing, her cheeks glowed, and her spirit was high.

"Thank you, Trev. I mean Trevor. Sorry, I'm always shortening people's names," she giggled.

"Don't apologize. I don't mind," he replied. He didn't laugh but he did wink.

A smiling Nippy who was probably her mother's age came to take their order. Tillie didn't recognize her, but introduced herself and chatted with her. It was rather disconcerting to be served by a silver-haired woman, but she was charming, if a little slow.

"It's odd to sit at a table here but I know the food is good, and the service is usually fast," she smiled at Trevor.

"I remember you were rather speedy when my mum and I were here," he teased.

A pot of tea and corned beef on toast were drunk and eaten, although Tillie couldn't have described any of it.

"How are your aunt and uncle getting on, then? Settling in? It must be so difficult for them to lose everything," he sympathized.

Tillie couldn't help but compare Trevor to Colin. In this situation, Colin would have brushed off the Fowlers' tragedy, turning the attention to himself. She suddenly felt disloyal and shook herself mentally.

"My aunt is fussing over arranging their room, making it feel homely. She's a bit more cross than usual, but that's to be expected, I should think."

"If you need a hand moving furniture around, I'd be happy to help on my day off," he offered as he took a large bite of a currant bun.

"Thanks Trev," she smiled shyly. "I think we have it in hand now. But there was a lot of shifting about the last few days. I think Pops' back is aching."

They eventually got the message that the table was needed for other customers, so Trevor paid the check and they stood up to leave. Neither wanted their time together to end.

"Could you cope with a rainy walk? It's still too early to report for work," Trevor asked hopefully, as he helped Tillie with her coat.

Tillie didn't hesitate.

"I'd love it," she replied.

They walked the broken streets around Piccadilly, huddled together under Trevor's umbrella. The fog was thicker than ever and the rain poured down, but in the way of two people falling in love, they were oblivious to the outside conditions. They talked of their difficult jobs and their desire to help people.

As they passed the *Café de Paris*, Trevor stopped.

"Perhaps we can go here for dinner one night, Tillie? I hear it's lively."

Tillie had heard of the nightclub, and found it a daring idea. She shivered.

"Yes, if we can find a night off work, Trevor. Is it safe down there with the Blitz on?" They continued walking.

Trevor shrugged.

"As safe as anywhere these days, I suppose. It is underground, so it will offer us some protection. Would you fancy dinner and dancing?"

"I'd adore it, Trev." She hugged him under the umbrella.

Without thinking, he bent to kiss her.

Tillie was so surprised she didn't move. Then, she felt a warmth that spread from her lips down her entire body like liquid heat. Trevor deepened the kiss, and Tillie kissed him back pressing her body closer to his. She felt herself opening up to him, wanting to give more as she wanted more from him.

He broke off the kiss and stared deeply into her eyes.

"I will not apologize for that, Tillie," he said huskily. "I enjoyed it rather too much."

Tillie nodded dumbly as they continued to walk. She had never felt like this before – not even with Colin. As if she was drowning in him and yet hungry for more.

The rain let up as they walked reluctantly towards the nearest underground station.

"Duty calls I'm afraid," Trevor said with genuine regret. "But before we part, I wanted to ask if you'd consider coming for tea with my mum on Saturday? She's been pestering me to have you come by our flat."

Tillie was flustered. Should she go?

"I'd be delighted," she found herself saying. "I'd like to spend more time with your mum."

"Smashing," he replied, blue eyes twinkling. "Mum will be delighted."

He kissed her gently on the lips as they parted to separate trains to get on with the business of war. Somehow, Tillie couldn't stop smiling to herself, hoping she didn't look too much a fool to the other passengers.

* * *

"Come on, Tillie, it's only a few hours. Please come along and help," Alice pleaded with her daughter. "Your aunt is suffering with this dreadful cold that's going around and we are woefully short-staffed."

Tillie sighed over her knitting.

"Oh, alright, I suppose so, Mum. I'm just so tired." And she looked it. Smudges under her eyes spoke of a long night behind the wheel of the ambulance. She'd only snatched a couple of hours of sleep after the all-clear sounded, and knew tonight would only bring more of the same.

"I know, love. You look done in."

"Gee, thanks, Mum," Tillie said gloomily. "Just what every girl wants to hear – that she's looking tired and not her best."

"Sorry, love, I was just trying to sympathize. But thank you. We just can't keep up with all the clothes donations for the bombed-out families, homeless, and refugees. Just a few hours helping sort, and there are always bandages to roll."

Tillie smiled and tried to rally.

"Alright, Mum. After this cuppa."

She got her second wind once they got to the WVS center and

was glad she came. There were mountains of clothes to sort. She was assigned to coats which she carefully piled by size, grateful for the public support of those in need.

A half-dozen other WVS staff and volunteers joked and laughed as they worked through the heaps of shirts, jackets, jumpers, trousers, hats, boots, shoes, and so much more.

After a tea break, they tackled bandage rolling. The women had done this countless times so got right to it. Of course, gossip prevailed. More than once Tillie and her mum shared glances over the bandage table, as stories were told of lazy workers, tardy volunteers, and the general unreliability of the young.

"That's it, then," announced Alice. "We are done for the day. Thanks everyone for making it in. You'd best get on and feed your families before Jerry makes his nightly appearance."

The women slowly dispersed, some wanting to help clear the tea things. Alice shooed them away, reassuring them she and Tillie could manage.

"Whew," she exclaimed when the last WVS volunteer left. "I just couldn't stand another minute of their whingeing. I hope you don't mind me volunteering us to clear away." She loaded teacups and dishes onto a tray.

"Not at all, Mum. I was getting rather fed up myself. Is it always like this?" Tillie picked up another tray and headed down the stairs to the small kitchen to wash up.

"Not always, dear, but it takes their minds off their men away fighting, the endless queues, and this blasted bombing."

"True enough, Mum," she replied, as she took the cups and saucers and dipped them in soapy water.

They made good time washing up. Tillie looked at her watch.

"Mum, look at the time. It's almost four o'clock. We'd best get a move on. We don't want to be caught in the streets."

But it was too late. As they climbed the stairs to collect their coats and purses, the air raid alarm sounded. Both women groaned.

"Oh no, Tillie. Where's the nearest tube station?"

"Parsons Green. But we'll never make it in time. There's a surface shelter just down the street. Come on."

They ran to the front door of the WVS office and bolted in. As Alice fumbled with the key to lock the door, the ground started rumbling. She looked up at the sky, saw a formation of planes, and dropped the key.

"Mum," cried Tillie, as she hastily picked it up and locked the door. She pointed to the shelter halfway down the street. "We can make it." She tucked her mother's arm under her own and the two ran as fast as they could down the street.

They hadn't made it twenty feet when they heard a loud, whistling sound directly overhead. The rumble got louder.

"Mum, get down. Hold on to the street lamp and don't let go." Tillie pushed her mother down to the ground and forced her to clamp her hands around the cold metal of the pole. She threw herself atop her mother, grabbed onto the street lamp, and closed her eyes.

The earth shook like thunder, bright light filled the air, and a thundering explosion threw up glass, bricks, earth, and debris everywhere.

Tillie felt herself being lifted and thrown like a rag doll on the sidewalk ten feet away, on top of a twisted bicycle. Oomph. Red-white flames filled the air and Tillie felt a wall of heat coming her way. Smoke made it almost impossible to see and incendiaries kept dropping, starting small fires all around. Flashes and sparks popped everywhere as red-hot shrapnel dropped down like fiery raindrops. The sky was lit up enough for Tillie to get to her knees, groping around for her mother, heedless of the sharp glass and bricks cutting her hands.

"Mum," she croaked Her throat was filled with dust and smoke and her head throbbed, but she ignored the pain.

"Over here, Tillie," her mother called in a muffled voice.

Tillie didn't dare stand up with incendiaries still dropping. They were bursting into easy targets for the Germans. She crawled towards her mother's voice and found her clear across the road.

"Mum, are you alright?"

She could hardly see with all the smoke, but felt her mother's warm, wet face. Was it blood or tears?

"I'm okay," Alice said, as her voice got a little stronger. "My arm hurts, and I've lost my hat and coat, but I think I'm still here."

Tillie gave her a quick but careful hug.

"Mum, we've got to get off the street." She stood up, trying to spot the shelter. She felt disoriented, having been thrown away with the explosion. Then she realized that the shelter was gone, along with half the stores in the street. Oh no, those poor people caught with hardly a roof over their heads. She heard the faint sound of fire engine sirens coming near, knowing fire crews would soon be there. "We've got to get back to the WVS Center. Our only hope is the basement. Can you run?"

"I think so," Alice said shakily.

The women ran back to the center – or what was left of it. The door and windows had been blown out but the rest of the building seemed to be intact. Tillie grabbed her mother's hand and dragged her down to the basement, where she closed the door and pulled her mother under the long wooden table on which they had spread wet tea towels to dry just a few minutes earlier.

CHAPTER TWENTY-FIVE

Mother and daughter, covered in dust and soot, clung to each other under the table as the world shook all around them.

"Mum, are you alright?" Tillie began a first aid exam, feeling her mother's limbs and chest for blood, breaks, or other injuries. The lights flickered on and off, flashing intermittent light on their ghostly faces.

"Ouch," cried Alice, as Tillie tenderly felt around her left hand and arm.

"I think you've broken your wrist, Mum. Stay still." Tillie scuttled across the floor and pulled a wooden spoon out of the drawer. On the way back, she tugged one of the tea towels from the top of the table and sat cross-legged next to her mum. She used the spoon as a makeshift splint and wrapped the broken wrist with the tea towel around her mum's neck as a sling.

"Don't fret, Mum," Tillie rubbed her shoulders gently, fearing shock. "The ambulance will be here soon and we'll get you to a hospital and fixed up straightaway."

"But they don't know where we are," Alice protested, trembling. "Pops probably thinks we are in a shelter or on the tube coming home."

"Mum, once the firemen and rescue workers see the bomb damage, they'll go from building to building looking for people. Pops knows we were here. They'll find us."

Another series of whistles, booms, shrieks, and crumps sounded all around. Now, they could smell the burning fires, and the smoke. The air was thick with it. They both started coughing. The light flickered again, throwing light on the women's faces.

"Tillie, you're bleeding," cried Alice. She reached forward to touch the cut on the top of her daughter's head.

Tillie winced as she felt the tender area on her forehead. Her mother was right. She was bleeding. Damn. From what she could tell, the bleeding had almost stopped, but it was definitely a gash and probably needed stitches. She snagged another tea towel from the table and pressed it hard against the slice.

"It's just a cut, Mum," she said confidently, not wanting to worry her mother any further. "They'll stitch me up and I'll be right as rain. Luckily, it's not on my face – albeit they may have to cut some of my hair to get at it."

"You saved my life, Tillie," her mum started crying. "You threw yourself on top of me – to save me. How can I ever thank you?"

"Oh, Mum, I'm just so relieved you're okay. And you've done so much for me, it was nothing."

"Oh Tillie, you're such a treasure. I wish you could see that." Alice was still weeping.

Tillie thought fast. Time to change the subject.

"Mum, how long do you think I should grieve Colin?" She asked, a tone of wistfulness creeping into her voice.

This stopped Alice in her tracks.

"Oh love, there is no timetable for grieving. How are you feeling now?"

"I'm so conflicted. I still love Colin, but his memory is fading every day. I can hardly picture his face anymore."

"Tillie, I understand. Sadly, you are not alone. Even wives with children can't conjure up their lost husbands without looking at pictures. This damned war."

"Mum, look at you swearing. Hitler is really getting to you." Tillie tried to joke but it was hard with all the rumbling and booming around them. Now, the ack-ack guns had joined the racket, and Tillie hoped they were taking down at least some of the Luftwaffe.

"This war has changed us all, love." She paused. "You know, you don't have to wait to live your life. It's not betraying Colin to want to move on. You are young, and with a war on, life can be snatched in a moment. Just think of those people who were in that shelter. It's just too sad."

"We don't know yet about the casualties, Mum. Maybe no one was in there."

"Let's hope so, dear. You heard what I said about Colin?"

"Yes, Mum. It's just so hard to think of his life snuffed out. Why should I go on and be happy?" She unconsciously fiddled with her engagement ring.

"Darling, you must. Colin wouldn't want you to be alone and sad your whole life. Without a husband, children, your own life. In fact, he'd be outraged at the thought of you sacrificing your happiness for him. You see that, don't you?"

The flickering lights had stopped and the pair were in total darkness. Somehow, this made it easier to be honest.

"Mum, I have found someone that I really care about. But is it too soon?"

"Is this a certain tall, dark-haired firefighter?" Alice asked with a smile in her voice.

"Mum, how did you know? Did Maggie say something?" Tillie was miffed.

"She hasn't said a word. It's you that's been dropping his name in conversation. Trevor this, and Trevor that. I can tell he means something to you."

"Mum, he's so kind, and helps people all the time. He has such a big heart. And he is so handsome. I just love being around him. I'm so drawn to him."

"And there's nothing wrong with that, love. Absolutely nothing. In fact, I'm happy to hear it. You've always put yourself last. It's time to reach out and grab happiness with both hands – whilst you can." Alice was eager to help her child.

Despite the bombs raining all around them, plaster shaking loose from the roof, and the entire building trembling, Tillie felt relief wash over her. Maybe it was time for her. Maybe Colin would want her to be happy.

"Darling, you believed me when I told you that Kenny's birth was not your fault? Have you really taken that on board?" She held Tillie's hand tightly with her good hand.

"Yes, Mum, I have. It's taken me a while to mull it all over. But I finally believe that it was just an accident. It's just hard to change the habits of a lifetime. Somehow, I seem to always want everyone to be happier than me."

"Mathilda. Hear me now. Look where we are. We're under a table in a basement kitchen. Bombs are dropping all around us. Promise me, promise me that if we get out of here alright, you'll put yourself and your happiness first. Please."

Tillie felt a strange calmness envelop her.

"I will, Mum. I promise."

The fire sirens came closer and Tillie could hear the familiar clang of the ambulance.

"They're coming, Mum. Just hang on a little longer." She wiped a tear from her dirty face.

"Help. We're here. Help," Tillie shouted. Alice joined in.

They heard people stomping on the floor above.

"Is anyone there?" They heard men calling. "Is anyone hurt? Do you need a stretcher?"

"We're here," Tillie shouted back as they scrambled to their feet. "There's two of us, just mild injuries. We don't need a stretcher." They moved cautiously but quickly to the stairs.

"Come on, then, ladies. This building is waving in the wind. Let's get you out of here and into the ambulance." An ARP Warden and two ambulance workers stomped down the stairs in their heavy boots.

When they got to the street, Alice and Tillie saw devastation all around. By then it was dark, and they could see white exploding fires in the sky, along with the BEF searchlights trying to track enemy bombers. Fires burned in some of the upper windows of buildings that were still standing, but most of the incendiaries had been extinguished by the firefighters and ARP workers. Acrid smoke and cordite suffocated them, and the women coughed again, choking on the smoke, throats aching.

They were hurriedly taken to the waiting ambulance, which already had two other patients inside. The attendants were warm and cheery, which was unnerving given the dangerous situation they were in. Tillie recognized this behavior – after all, this was her job too – they were trained to distract patients in shock.

In no time, they were on their way to the hospital where Alice was fixed up with a wrist and arm plaster, and Tillie received five stitches. The gash had been just on the edge of her hairline, so they did not have to cut her hair so the scar would be hidden once it healed.

Walter and Maggie came to collect them and bring them home. Tillie and Maggie embraced tightly – each of them crying and apologizing to the other.

"Darling, I was wrong. Of course, you deserve happiness. I'm sure Trevor is wonderful, and I want you to be with him. I'm so sorry."

"No need to apologize, Mags. I'm sorry for being so cross and stubborn. Let's never be at odds again. I need you more than ever."

Walter and Alice embraced, relieved to see their daughters make up.

They got home safely, and spent the rest of the night in the Anderson, although thankfully the shelling seemed far away.

* * *

Tillie regaled Trevor with her WVS adventure as they hurried to his mother's flat. It was Saturday afternoon, clear but bitingly cold. Trevor put his arm around Tillie to warm her and she rubbed her gloved hands together. When they talked, they could see their breaths floating in the air.

Isla and Trevor Drummond lived in a flat on the first floor in Clare Mews. Walking up the indoor steps, Trevor told Tillie a little more about his family.

"Dad died in the Great War. I never knew him, but he knew me. I was two and a half when he was killed in Passchendaele in 1917. It was ghastly for my mother. She doesn't like to talk about those days but we struggled on her widow's pension. Neighbors watched me, I'm told, whilst she worked in a bank and eventually got her post as a secretary. I'm proper proud of her and all."

They'd reached the top of the stairs and Trevor pushed open the door.

"Ma, we're here."

Isla was a tall woman, so perhaps Trev had gotten some of his height from her. She had long blonde with some grey hair, pinned back, and twinkling blue eyes that matched her son's. She greeted him with a kiss and held Tillie's hands in her own.

"It's lovely to see you again. It seems we are forced into socializing during the daytime now. We're all working at night or cowering in our shelters. It's an ungodly time for tea but what can we do? There's a war on," she shrugged.

"Thank you for having me, Mrs. Drummond. What a lovely flat you have."

And it was. Cozy with lots of bright colors. It wasn't large – just a decent-sized living area, small kitchen, bathroom, and two bedrooms.

"What are these beautiful paintings? Someone is a grand artist."

"Those are mine," Isla blushed. "I enjoy painting watercolors in my spare time." There were several paintings of beaches, mountains, cliffs all overlooking calm blue water.

"Have you been to all these places? You make me want to dip my toes in the ocean," Tillie enthused as she examined one closely.

"A long time ago; water moves me. Especially now. Water is peaceful. I could stare at it for hours." Isla's gaze drifted to a beautiful seascape.

"I'll take you there, Ma, I promise. After the war," Trevor said quietly.

"Did you do these wood carvings as well, Mrs. Drummond? They are exquisite." Tillie carefully stroked a wooden horse.

"Er, no. Those are mine," Trevor owned up a trifle sheepishly. "I can't paint worth a tick, but I love shaping wood into animals. Now, shall I put on the kettle?" He finished quickly.

"Yes, love. I've made Bakewell Tarts. They don't taste a patch on the originals with margarine and tinned cherries, but at least it's a bite of something sweet with our tea."

"Sounds wonderful, Mrs. Drummond. What can I do to help?" Tillie stood up.

"Nothing, dear. You're our guest. Please sit. Trevor is used to being mother."

They had a lovely tea, if a little hurried. Trevor had to get Tillie back to Earl's Court before the inevitable alarm and nightly air attack.

"Thank you so much again, Mrs. Drummond. It was a brilliant afternoon. I hope we can do it again sometime." Tillie shook her hand.

"Me too, Tillie. I trust we'll be seeing a lot more of you. Please take some tart home with you. There's plenty here for us. Be safe, and get on with you. Trevor, I'll see you later. Please be careful," she kissed her son, loathe to see him go.

"Ta ra, Ma. And don't bother about me. I always turn up like a bad penny."

The two young people hurried into the wintry afternoon, hand-in-hand.

* * *

It had been a quiet night in the Anderson. Alice and Shirley spent most of the evening there with Katie who had a night off from fire watching. The men were on ARP duty as usual, both now working almost every night with the Blitz an unceasing nightly hardship. Tillie and Maggie were on ambulance and canteen duties. It was becoming strangely normal, whilst being utterly bizarre.

The all-clear sounded a little early – three a.m. – which gave the family a well-earned breather. They all tromped to bed and fell into deep sleep within seconds, having learned that sleep was such a precious commodity to seize whenever possible.

Tillie and Maggie slipped in within a few minutes of each other. They smiled at each tiredly, washed up, and dropped off. A hush fell over the Kingston house.

The buzzer sounded at 8:01. a.m., waking Walter and Alice. The couple had just got up and were having a quiet moment together over their morning tea before the household woke up.

Walter answered the door in his robe, pajamas, and slippers. The telegram boy stood there, with the dreaded beige envelope in hand.

"Very sorry, Sir," he mumbled.

Walter took the envelope and fished around his pockets for a tip.

"Not necessary, sir." And the boy was gone.

Alice had climbed the stairs from the kitchen and joined her husband in the hall. As one, they walked the few short steps to the dining room, and sank into the nearest chairs.

"Open it, Walter," Alice rasped. "Let's have the news, then."

Walter slowly opened the envelope and read aloud without censoring for his stoic wife:

"The British Royal Navy deeply regrets to inform you that your son, Midshipman Kenneth Walter Kingston, is Missing in Action since February 24, 1941, from the sinking of the *HMS Dainty*. If further details or other information are received, you will be promptly notified." Lt. Commander Henry Dawes.

Walter let the paper slip to the polished table. The couple sat in silence for a moment. A single tear fell down Alice's cheek.

"Well, I suppose it's our turn, then. No family is untouched by this wretched war."

"It is a crumb of comfort that he's not been killed, dear. It said MIA. He may still be found. We mustn't lose hope."

"Yes, of course, you're right, dear. All is not lost."

Alice stood up, felt a little wobbly, and sat back down again. Walter put his hand on hers.

"Steady on, dear. We mustn't give up hope. There are so many means by which he could have been rescued or saved himself. He's a resourceful lad."

"Yes, Walter. Shall I make us a fresh pot, then? Ours is surely gone cold." Alice rose again, slightly firmer on her feet.

The elder Kingstons shuffled down to the kitchen, each lost in their own thoughts. Their shoulders sagged and Alice's hand shook as she made the tea. Walter looked out the back window, unseeing.

And this is where their daughters found them thirty minutes later. They had reveled in their refreshing lie-in and bounced down to the kitchen in search of tea and whatever breakfast Mum had managed to sort.

One look at their parents, and they knew something was terribly wrong.

"Mum, Dad. What is it? You're sitting there like statues."

"Girls, you'd best sit down. It's bad news."

"Is it Kenny?" Katie asked as she knelt in front of her mother, mindful of the cast on her mother's arm.

"Yes," replied Walter, looking up at the twins.

"Is he dead?" Maggie squeaked with her hand to her throat.

"No, he's missing in action off the *HMS Dainty*. So, he may yet be alive. We must be patient and wait for further news. I'm so sorry my dears," Walter continued in a halting voice.

Katie and Maggie gasped. Katie hugged her mother and Maggie turned to her twin.

"We must find out as much as we can about the Dainty," Tillie said urgently. "Kenny is alive. I know it."

But no one heard her. Maggie, Katie and Alice were all sobbing too hard.

CHAPTER TWENTY-SIX

The Fowlers came down for breakfast and the dreadful news was shared.

Each of the family members dealt with the new blow in their own way. Alice and Shirley shut themselves in the morning room for hours, sharing their grief. Despite the cold weather, Walter trudged down to the allotment to work out his frustration on the inhospitable land. Maggie and Tillie talked quietly in their room, then Maggie wrote Micah a letter. Tillie offered her mother and aunt some tea, before taking her turn to wait in long lines at the shops and later on to have dinner with Trevor. Katie bundled up and walked the cold streets of Earl's Court. It was a dark day but the Kingstons would not give up. Ever.

As Tillie stood in the harsh February cold at the greengrocer's, she stamped her feet and blew her gloved hands to generate some warmth.

Kenny. Her impetuous, naughty, smart, and adorable younger brother. She conjured up his image. Tall, blond hair like her own, with the same large brown eyes. When he'd signed up underage, he hardly even had enough fuzz to shave. Funny how she could immediately picture her brother, but Colin's face was fading each day. Was it because she had known Kenny longer? Or because Kenny was still alive and Colin was dead? Somehow, she just knew Kenny wasn't killed. He was coming home to them. He was.

The line inched forward.

"I heard the butcher has kidneys. I hope there's a bit left when I get there," said Mrs. Dobson, shifting her mesh shopping bag to her other arm.

"How am I supposed to feed my husband on a pound of meat a week, two ounces of butter, four ounces of bacon, eight ounces of sugar, and just two measly ounces of tea?" Mrs. Hammersmith grumbled. "There's only so many ways to cook veg."

"Thank goodness fish isn't on the ration," agreed Mrs. Dobson. "That can fill in where meat won't stretch. We're all dead sick of Woolton Pie."

"It's probably offal again for supper tonight," old Miss Plumkin groaned. "Everything else will be gone before we get through this queue and over to the butchers."

"I think I'll freeze to death before I get to the front of the queue," a large woman with a fuzzy brown fringe hanging down to her eyes, complained.

"Me too," Tillie said with a tight smile. "Do you think he'll have any onion left? My mother needs it for stew."

"Chance is a fine thing," replied Mrs. Dobson. "He hasn't had it for weeks."

And so it went. Women of all shapes and sizes stood for hours, most to be disappointed when it was finally their turn, and coveted items were sold out.

Tillie's feet were blocks of ice when she finally got to the front of the line. She handed over the family's ration books, and got the fat, margarine, sugar, and tea needed for the week. And an onion! The greengrocer stamped the appropriate coupons carefully and placed the wrapped groceries in Tillie's basket. After waiting another hour at the butchers, she could only get some dodgy looking sausages and a tiny quantity of kidneys. At least something!

"I don't think I'll ever warm up," Tillie chattered as she clutched her teacup.

"Here, have my coat," Trevor jumped up, shrugged off his tweed jacket, and draped it over Tillie's shoulders. "Your lips are nearly blue."

"Thanks, Trev. I'll take all the help I can get." Tillie shivered. "Those queues are dreadful. There must be a better system."

Trevor poured another cup of tea from the brown pot in the center of the table. The couple had met at a café for dinner.

"The better system is to crush Hitler and the Nazis. Then, we can get back to normal life – not just queuing, but everything."

"Too right. How much longer can we go on like this?" She lifted her mournful brown eyes to his.

"Tillie, I've never seen you like this. What's happened?"

"It's my brother, Kenny. He's missing in action. His ship, the *HMS Dainty* sunk. That's all we know so far."

"Oh bollocks, I'm sorry, Tils. No wonder you're so low. Tell me more." His black brows furrowed in concern as he leaned forward.

Tillie spent the next minutes sharing stories of Kenny as a young, spirited boy. She was filled with pride and love for her younger brother.

"He sounds like a fine young man. I truly hope he will be found safe, and up to mischief and misadventure. Is there anything I can do to help?"

The server deposited soup and fish paste sandwiches, which the couple promptly devoured.

"Can you find out any more about the sinking? Where it was? Were there any survivors? Anything." Two spots of red appeared on Tillie's cheeks, and her eyes brightened slightly.

Trevor nodded.

"Absolutely. I'll try my AFS contacts and if necessary, we can go down to Naval Headquarters and make inquiries."

"Thanks, Trevor," Tillie said simply, reaching out to touch his hand.

"Woah, your hands are still freezing. We've got to get you warmed up."

"I'm feeling a bit better already." She took a sip of her tea and turned to another topic. Dwelling on Kenny's situation was dreadful. "It was a delight to meet your mother. You have the same eyes. She seems quite nice."

"She's the best. A little possessive of me, though." He put a hand through his slicked back hair. "Bothered about me every night I'm putting out fires. It's been the two of us for so long. She relies on me a lot. It's what's kept me from joining up. I don't know how she would do on her own." He turned to look through the taped-up windows out to the street. "She liked you too, Tillie. She's always looking to get me married off to some nice girl. You're the first one I've brought home for tea," he added with a slow grin. Boy, he was so good-looking. Tillie tried not to stare.

"First one? That's a lot of pressure. I hope I passed muster."

"With flying colors, Tillie. And no pressure. I know you are still grieving. I hope you don't think we're moving too fast." He looked a little worried.

"No, not too fast. Just right," she said with a blush. "And thank you for being patient with me. I understand about you and your Mum. Aunt Shirley was like that with my cousin Geoffrey."

Trevor nodded.

"Anytime I get to spend with you is precious to me, Tillie. As long as this war doesn't call one of our numbers, there's no hurry."

It was a sobering thought.

"Tillie, I know you just had a major shock with your brother. Should we postpone our dinner and dancing date at the *Café de Paris?* You might not feel up to going out."

"That's thoughtful of you, Trev, but I still think I'd like to go. As you just said, none of us know if a bomb has our name on it. Of all people, Kenny would want me to have fun. I'd still really love it. Is that alright?"

"Brilliant. It's definitely on. Let's just hope for a quiet night. Once we're at the club, we should be safe enough underground."

Tillie smiled, feeling warmed up already.

* * *

At home, Maggie was re-reading Micah's latest letter. The thin paper was already in tatters, after Maggie had already memorized most of it, but she loved to touch the ink as it brought Micah closer.

"My dearest Maggie,

I can't tell you what a comfort your letters are to me. Truly. I can just picture you hunched over the paper, concentrating on finding just the right words. It makes me smile. I know paper is on ration, but your drawings are so evocative – please send more. The pencil sketch you sent of children playing in a bombed street was extraordinary.

How long are my letters taking to get to you? The post is very slow at my end, but any news from home is most welcome. We are watching what Hitler and the Nazis are doing to our beloved England with horror. My darling, please keep safe. I'm so troubled about you and your family having to go through the nightly bombing. It must be just ghastly. It can't go on much longer, I pray.

We are working quite hard here. Food is hard to come by but having the farm helps. It's strenuous work, Maggie. Up early, working in the fields all day and trying to build our jewelry business by night. My hands are rough and I miss playing the piano dreadfully, but needs must. Grandfather's health is weakening and we watch him closely.

May I leave you with the words of Robbie Burns? They haunt me as I see your fair face in springtime, and long to walk with you again, little one.

O my Luve is like a red, red rose
That's newly sprung in June;
O my Luve is like the melody
That's sweetly played in tune.

So fair art thou, my bonnie lass,
So deep in luve am I;
And I will luve thee still, my dear,
Till a' the seas gang dry.

Till a' the seas gang dry, my dear,
And the rocks melt wi' the sun;
I will love thee still, my dear,
While the sands o' life shall run.

And fare thee weel, my only luve!
And fare thee weel awhile!
And I will come again, my luve,
Though it were ten thousand mile.

All my love, Micah xx"

Maggie's heart hurt with the love swelling inside her, and the longing she had for the serious, tall, lean young man so far away. She also ached for dear Kenny missing but surely still alive. Maggie wept for both of them.

* * *

"Hullo, Jasper. Been busy today?"

Tillie arrived at work mid-afternoon, steeling herself for another savage shift ahead.

"Not so far. But I have some grave news. We lost a team of our own last night – Olive Dobbs and Eunice Baskin. A direct hit outbound on a call last night. The ambulance was destroyed. It would have been sudden."

Tillie gasped. No! Not Olive, her training partner from months ago. Such a young woman to lose her life. She sank into a chair.

"A glass of water," Jasper barked to no one in particular. One swiftly appeared and Tillie took a deep gulp. "Sorry, Kingston, but these things are best out and dealt with straight away. There's no easy way to break this kind of news."

There had already been five station casualties during the Blitz. Each one hit hard. These were comrades in a war zone. They had each other's backs in the worst of circumstances.

Tillie still hadn't spoken. Ernie appeared.

"Come on, Tillie. Let's have a cup 'o tea 'afore our shift."

Tillie nodded. There was no question of not working tonight. If anything, she was needed more with two more staff gone. Seven talented, hard-working ambulance workers. Lucky seven, Tillie thought hysterically.

"Just give me a minute, Ernie please. I'll be alright. I'll meet you back in the lounge."

She went to change into her uniform and sat for a moment on the bench, thinking of Olive. She hadn't known Eunice but she took a few minutes to relive every encounter, every memory she had with Olive. The women deserved at least that.

After a few minutes, she went into the bathroom, splashed some water on her face and repaired her makeup. She looked in the mirror and saw a pinched, drained face with glassy eyes. She fluffed her hair with trembling hands. Get a hold of yourself, girl. You have a job to do. She pulled on her heavy overcoat, tipped on her tin hat, and went to find Ernie. The bastards wouldn't break her.

It turned out to be a heavy shift, with Tillie and Ernie being called out countless times. A steady drizzle began about half-past six. As unpleasant as it was for their working conditions, Tillie and Ernie were grateful that at least it would douse the fires more quickly.

At four a.m., Tillie and Ernie were called out to a street fire on Mansfield Street. They were to pick up a woman and her two children.

As they drove slowly to the site, they tried to ignore the all-too familiar sights, sounds, and smells of droning planes, whooshing whistles, exploding bombs, flying glass and masonry, piles of debris, fire and smoke. Tillie picked carefully around shrapnel – the steel and tin fragments of anti-aircraft shells – some were still red-hot and dangerous.

"It must be almost time for the all-clear," Tillie said anxiously as she peered through the fogged-up windshield into the still-dark streets.

"Steady on, Tillie. With any luck, this will be our last call of the night."

With each nearby explosion, Tillie flinched, thinking of Olive and how terrifying it must have been for her. Come on, Tillie, be brave.

They reached the site where a row of three houses was burning. Two on one side of them were completely demolished, and two more, further down were smoldering in the ongoing rain.

Outside one of the houses, they spotted a young child crying. Tillie saw a slightly older girl running up the steps back into the house where fires still burned on the first floor. She braked and jumped out the ambulance, not noticing the firefighters aiming heavy hoses at the open windows.

"Ernie, look after the little one. I'm going after the girl." She took the short distance in a few big strides and grabbed a hold of the little girl's arm, just as she was about to disappear inside the house. Kneeling down, she turned the little tear-stained girl around. She had a dazed look in her eyes and blood streamed down her cheek.

"What's your name, then? And what's inside?"

"I'm Violet. Mama is there." She pointed into the dark house, glowing with the upstairs fire.

"Is that your sister?" She asked, gesturing to the little girl that Ernie was examining.

"Yes, that's Ivy. She's hurt."

"You look hurt too. My name is Tillie. And that's my friend Ernie. We are going to look after you." She tried to pick up Violet to reunite her with her sister, but she squirmed violently.

"Mama, Mama," she cried.

Ernie was suddenly at her side and took charge of both girls.

"I'm going in, Ernie. Violet, where is your Mama?"

"Mama is cooking. She fell down."

"Well done, you," Tillie praised the little girl, who looked to be about six years old. "I'm going to get your Mama."

"Tillie, no. Wait for heavy rescue or a firefighter. They're just down the street." But it was too late. Tillie had already dashed into the house.

Part of the roof had caved in for which Tillie was thankful. The rain diffused some of the smoke, which made it almost passable to breathe in the open air. It was dark but loud groaning sounds directed Tillie to the kitchen.

"Ma'am, I'm with the ambulance. I'm here to help you."

More moaning answered her.

"Ma'am, where are you?"

"Here. On ter floor. Ahhhh, it's coming."

Tillie found the woman sitting on the lino with her back to the cupboards under the sink.

"I'm Tillie, Ma'am. Where does it hurt? May I examine you?"

"It's the baby," the woman gasped. "Ter baby's coming now. I've lost me waters. I were so fast wit Ivy. Owww."

Panic overcame Tillie. She'd never delivered a baby before. She took a deep breath.

"I'm just going to get my partner with the stretcher. We'll have you out of here on the double and off to the hospital with your daughters."

"No, I can't move. I can feel ter head. Yer must 'elp me."

Tillie knelt down in front of the woman, took out her torch, pointed it down to keep it out of the woman's eyes, and saw a tousled panicked redhead overwhelmed by fear.

"It's going to be alright. I'm going to help you. May I look?"

"Owww, yes, but hurry, Miss."

Tillie felt the swollen belly and carefully lifted the mother's dress. Indeed, an enormous bulge was already protruding below. Oh, my god.

"Tillie, what's going on here?"

She was never so glad in all her life to hear Trevor's voice. Help was here.

"This woman, her name is…"

"I'm Gloria, ohhh me back. I need ter push. Owww."

"Gloria, I'm Trevor, a firefighter and friend of Tillie's. We're going to help you with this baby. Just breathe deep, try to calm your muscles to help push the baby out."

"You've done this before?" Tillie whispered.

She felt rather than saw him nod.

"Tillie, point the torch down so I can see the baby's head. You're doing wonderful, Gloria. You'll have a story to tell when this wee one gets older."

"I have ter push. I can't stop."

"That's alright, Gloria. You can push. Tillie, fetch me a towel, blanket, anything to wrap the baby in. Gloria, I'm going to catch your baby."

Tillie banged drawers until she found one with tea towels and grabbed the lot of them. Trevor laid half of them underneath Gloria's bottom as she groaned loudly again.

As Tillie pointed the torch, she saw the baby's head pulse in and out, then with a giant whoosh, the baby came out face down into Trevor's hands. He gently turned the baby over, wrapped him in the towels, and handed him to his waiting Mama.

"It's a boy, Gloria. You have a son."

CHAPTER TWENTY-SEVEN

"Tillie, go for the stretcher. And blankets. We need to warm them up."

Trevor was rubbing the baby through the tea towel.

"Is he breathing?" Gloria squeaked as she clutched her infant to her chest.

A loud wail went up. All three of them let go of a breath they didn't even know they'd been holding.

Trevor turned from the new mum to Tillie, who was standing there frozen.

"Tillie, now. We have to get them out of here."

Tillie roused to action.

"Righto, not to worry, Gloria. We are going to have you and that noisy young man out of here in two ticks. I'm going to fetch the stretcher, and get you to the hospital in nothing flat." She sprinted from the kitchen, down the smoky hall and out the front door. Even though the air outside was still smoky, she took deep, gulping breaths. She was getting used to that heavy feeling of smoke in her chest, but it was painful nonetheless.

"Ernie," she called out in a raspy voice. "Stretcher."

He came running over with it under his arm.

"Are yer alright? Wot's happening in there? Is she stuck or crushed under a table?"

"No, Ernie, she's had a baby. A boy. Come on, we've got to get them out of there."

"Yer delivered a baby?" He asked astonished, as the pair picked their steps over the surrounding debris, up the stairs and into the house.

"No, Trevor did," she replied. "It happened so fast."

"Over here, Tillie," the firefighter called from the kitchen. The fire was just smoldering now, but the air was filled with a smoky haze and her nostrils were clogged with the wet, soggy smell of soaked furniture and wood and her eyes streamed from the smoke.

Within minutes, they loaded Gloria and her baby son onto the stretcher and the new mum happily greeted her two little girls waiting patiently in the ambulance with makeshift bandages.

"Darlings, look wot I've brought yer. A baby brother. 'E just couldn't wait ter meet yer."

"Tillie, I have to get back. But I'm going to meet you once our shifts are over. I'll collect you and take you home. No arguments," he raised a hand in protest. He gave her a quick, hard kiss and hurried back to join his unit.

Tillie and Ernie rushed their patients to a local hospital and drove back to the station exhausted and somewhat shocked. Crawling at the slowest speed possible, to avoid the harming the tires, it seemed forever before they were back at the Mews.

Tillie double clutched, braked and parked.

"I'm glad that's over, I don't mind saying, Ernie. What with the news of Olive's passing, and then a new baby being born into these frightening times, my head's a bit muzzy."

Ernie patted her hand.

"Yer done well, Tillie. I tink we both need a cuppa."

Tillie sighed and pulled off her tin hat. Her hair was wet, listless, and matted from the evening's exertions. She felt a mess, knew she looked a sight, but didn't have the energy to even pass a comb through her hair or splash water on her face. Sinking into a lounge chair, she took a sip of tea from a cup brought to her by a passing teammate.

She must have dozed off because suddenly someone was gently shaking her shoulder.

"Tillie, wake up. It's time to go home." She saw Trevor's face hovering above her.

"Home?" She murmured dully. "What are you doing here, Trevor?" She tried to shake the muddle in her head. She was so sleep deprived that her little nap had only made everything seem fuzzier.

He looked as if he'd had a turbulent night himself. His hair was tousled and dirty and his clothes were sooty and soggy. The night showed the toll in his weary eyes, but his smile was clear and bright.

"Remember I'm taking you home, Tillie?" He asked her softly, making Tillie's eyes blink unexpectedly.

"Oh. Yes. I forgot. Thank you, Trevor," she smiled wanly and got up slowly. "I'm feeling a bit wobbly actually."

Trevor took her arm, watched her clock out, and helped her with her coat.

"Taxi," he hailed into the early morning gloom. It wasn't yet sunrise, so the murky, too-long night still clung to the sky.

"Heavens no, Trevor. A taxi is too dear. The tube is fine," Tillie protested.

"Nonsense," responded Trevor as he steered her into the back seat of a black cab. "You're asleep on your feet."

Tillie was too tired to argue. She sunk into the seat with Trevor's arm protectively curved around her.

"Trevor, I feel so strange. I can vaguely remember what happened last night, but somehow I just don't feel like myself – like I can't remember what happened when."

"That's perfectly normal, love," soothed Trevor. "You've been dealt blow after blow at home, then you heard about Olive last night. And the trauma of the birth – your brain and your body just can't process what's happened to you – and it's crashing."

Tillie looked at him with teary eyes.

"You're right. I can't think straight. Why is one innocent woman taken in the prime of her life? Then hours later, a new baby is born?" Tears fell down her cheeks, leaving rivers on her dirty face.

"Life will find a way, Tils. But shhh, don't think about it. Just close your eyes and rest. We'll be home soon."

Tillie didn't pause. She slumped onto his shoulder and slipped into oblivion.

She awoke to find herself in Trevor's arms, standing on the doorstep of the townhouse. She struggled to be put down.

"Trevor, please. I'm fine. Set me down." Tillie bristled, smoothing her clothing.

He rang the doorbell.

"Not until we're inside. You're dead on your feet," he insisted.

Walter answered the door, alarm spreading across his face.

"Tillie, are you alright? What's happened?"

Tillie tried to stand up and hugged her father.

"I'm okay, Pops. Trevor just helped me home. It was a long night. We lost someone at the station. I'm just knackered. That's all." She attempted a vivacious tone.

Trevor reached out his hand.

"Sir, I'm Trevor Drummond. London firefighter. Tillie and I are friends. I met her on a call last night. We delivered a baby together. I believe your daughter is suffering from a mild state of shock, along with over-fatigue. I'm sorry to meet you under these circumstances but I just couldn't let your daughter come home via public transit."

Walter shook his hand gravely.

"Please come in, Trevor. I can't thank you enough for your care of my daughter. At least let me offer you a cup of tea."

"Thank you, Sir. I need to get home and check on my mother. She's alone. I hope we can meet again under more agreeable circumstances."

"Count on it, Trevor. In fact, I'd like to invite you to dinner with our family. Let's say Sunday?"

"I'll confirm with my shift, Sir. But I'd be delighted."

"And please bring your mother. We'd be glad to have you both."

"Thank you, Sir. She would love that. Tillie, please get some sleep. And Mr. Kingston, I might suggest Tillie take a night off. She needs to rest."

Walter nodded.

"I'll have her sister nip down to the call box and tell her station manager she won't be in tonight."

Amidst Tillie's loud protests, Walter smiled at Trevor and closed the door.

March 1941

As it happened, lunch at the Kingstons was delayed. It was exceedingly difficult to set up a date with the number of people working different shifts, either regular jobs or with civil defense.

Finally, the night came. Alice and Shirley combined all the ration books to come up with a modest meal. They eventually decided on fish pie, since fish was not on the ration, they could make a decent amount to serve the large group. Katie was scheduled for a WVS shift and Thomas was working late, but everyone else was there.

The doorbell rang at half-past twelve. Tillie rushed to answer the door, dressed in a pale blue cardigan and navy and white striped skirt. She and Maggie had shared their meager supply of makeup to look their best. Maggie wore a dark purple dress with white polka dots. Both girls wore their hair in loose waves. They'd let it grow out a little, so the blonde tresses hung slightly below their collars.

"Mrs. Drummond. Trevor, please come in," Tillie greeted their guests. "It's so nice to see you again, Mrs. Drummond. Coping alright with the Blitz?"

Isla kissed her on the cheek.

"As well as anyone, I expect," she replied with a shrug. "We must get on with it. What else can we do?"

Tillie nodded and Trevor gave her a light kiss. She took their coats as her parents entered the hall. Introductions were made and the little group proceeded to the drawing room.

"Oh my, you two really are identical. Trevor told me, but it's quite remarkable." Isla looked from Tillie to Maggie, and then back again. Two beautiful young women, dressed differently but with the same golden hair, chocolate brown eyes, and engaging smiles.

"I can certainly tell them apart," Trevor grinned as he perched on the arm of the chair next to Tillie. "Right Maggie?" He teased.

Tillie punched his arm.

"Too funny, Trev. I should hope you can tell us apart."

"I'm the quiet one, Mrs. Drummond," added Maggie. "Tillie is the outgoing twin." She winked at her sister.

"Mrs. Drummond, may I interest you in a sherry?" Walter asked, decanter in hand.

"Perhaps she'd prefer a cup of tea?" Alice interjected.

"Tea is lovely, thank you," replied Isla. "Your home is charming. It's a treat to see a house not gaping open with bomb wounds."

There was an awkward silence. Tillie glanced at her aunt who tried to hide her stricken look.

"They bombed us out earlier, but we are grateful daily to be taken in by my sister and her husband," Shirley murmured.

"Oh, my goodness, I'm so sorry," Isla apologized, as her hand flew to her mouth. "I should have known better. So many families have been rendered homeless. How awful for you."

"No need to apologize, Mrs. Drummond. You couldn't have known," Alice jumped in.

"Please call me Isla," she countered. "What kind of war work are you all carrying out?" She asked the group.

The delicate moment passed as everyone shared their daily activities with a few stories thrown in. Isla found she had a lot in common with Alice and Shirley – WVS women bonding in demanding times.

Over dinner, Trevor regaled the group with some of his more daring rescue stories. Tillie shuddered more than once, afraid for her brave firefighter.

"Have you heard about the *Café de Paris*?" Tillie asked no one in particular. "Trevor and I were meant to go for dinner and dancing. It was bombed out just the other night. Terrible casualties – over thirty innocent victims and so many others injured."

She and Trevor exchanged a meaningful look. They both knew of the ghastly devastation of the nightclub after it had been hit with a high explosive bomb. Trevor's unit had been redirected from another fire to help get it under control, so he'd seen firsthand the rows of dead people covered in white dust like ghosts. And the cries of agony from the trapped and wounded survivors calling for help. Identifying the victims had been a gruesome task and many were still unaccounted for.

Tillie had heard about it from her mates at the station. Jasper said the scene had been dreadful – people sitting in their tuxedoes and gowns at tables with drinks in front of them, dead. A haunting memory. They rescued a man with a broken bottle of wine fully embedded in his leg, screaming for help. No one who had witnessed this horrific incident would ever forget it.

"It could have been worse," said Walter soberly. "As I heard tell, an hour later and hundreds more could have been killed. The Café was an exceedingly popular venue."

"You two weren't meant to be there that night?" Shirley asked worriedly.

"No, a few days later. It wasn't our number that night, right Tils?" Trevor gazed at Tillie who shook her head.

"Your fish pie is delicious, Alice," Isla complimented in the lull.

"We are really missing our housekeeper, Faye, I must say. Her cooking was first-rate. Mine is only passable I'm afraid. My sister made the veg. Tasty, Shirl." Alice smiled at her sister.

"You must be a marvelous cook, Mrs. Drummond," offered Maggie. "Tillie says you cook for the WVS."

"Well, I can muster up a meal for two hundred hungry folks. But nothing fancy," Isla replied breezily.

"You can judge for yourself. Mum brought her famous Victoria sponge. It's delicious," said Trevor loyally.

And it was. They all commented on Isla's ability to create a light and fluffy confection with limited rations.

A little while later, Trevor took Isla home. Tillie had accompanied him so they could have a little alone time before reporting for duty.

"I think that went rather well, don't you?" asked Tillie, as they strolled the bombed streets near the flat. It was still cold but the sun peeped out from behind the clouds. "What did you and Pops chat about whilst we did the washing up? I hope he didn't get you onto his pipe smoking."

"Yes, it went alright. I hope my mother didn't offend with her insensitive comments. She does like to speak her mind." Trevor furrowed his brows.

"Don't bother about it, Trev. Everyone's nerves are frayed these days. Even on the tube, any loud noise and several people jump out of their skin. Hitler has got us scared as church mice. And you didn't answer my question, mister. What did you and Pops talk about?"

Trevor grinned, and pulled her close as they walked past shop after shop with broken windows, doors, and missing roofs which they hardly noticed anymore.

"First, I declined his offer of a pipe. I have enough smoke in my body, thanks very much. And as for our conversation young lady," he put a finger to his mouth. "It was between us men. He thanked me again for coming to your aid and protecting you whenever I can. I like him, Tils. He's really a decent man. That's all you need to know."

"You beast," Tillie grimaced. "I guess I'll have to settle for that. But he does like you. That I know. Mum does too. I can tell by the way she looks at you. Somehow, she thinks you're funny."

"I'm chuffed that I pass inspection at the Kingston house, love. But let's talk about something more interesting – you. Seeing you with your family – it's what I want, Tillie. I want to build a family – with you. Not now, I know the timing is all wrong, but when this wretched war is over. Or at least the Blitz."

He stopped in the street and took both her hands in his.

"I'm falling in love with you, Tillie. Hard and for keeps."

He bent and kissed her with all the passion and longing he'd been holding back. And Tillie kissed him back. Her heart swelled and she felt a rush of feelings throb throughout her body.

"I think I'm falling in love with you, too, Trevor," she whispered when she caught her breath. Her liquid brown eyes locked with his cobalt blue ones. "I'm scared, Trev. If I let myself love you and then something happens to you, I couldn't bear it. I really couldn't, Trev." She clutched the lapels of his coat. "What are we going to do?"

He led her to an empty bench where they sat close together.

"We are going to do exactly what we're doing, my darling. Keep getting to know each other, trust each other, and try hard not to get killed," he attempted a small joke.

"I didn't think I could love again after Colin." Tillie shivered in the weak March sunshine. "But somehow, you've crept into my heart, Trevor Drummond. And I want you to stay there. Just think, if we had been at the *Café de Paris* on the wrong night we wouldn't be sitting here today. It really makes me think we need to take hold of whatever this is and not let go. It's such a cliché, Trev, but we just don't know what tomorrow will bring." She waited with bated breath to see what Trevor would say. He'd been listening intently.

"Look at us, Tillie. Two Londoners falling in love during the worst possible bloody time. But we are going to make it, Tillie. I promise you. I won't let you go." He kissed her again, long and sweet.

"Trev, you can't promise that. We're deep into a war. You don't know what might happen at your next call-out. You can't know."

"Tillie, let's just take one day at a time. That's all we can do. I believe in us and our future. Enough for both of us." He checked his watch. "Now I'd best get you to the tube. We're both needed tonight. Hitler will love this clear weather."

The couple hurried to the nearest underground and went their separate ways.

The next morning after her shift, Tillie washed her face, changed into her nightie, and removed her engagement ring. It felt like the right time. A smile flitted across her face as she nodded off.

CHAPTER TWENTY-EIGHT

April 1941

"Let's go for a walk, Mags. It's a beautiful spring day. It makes you think this wretched war might end and life get back to normal someday." Tillie twirled around their small bedroom in a pink and white plaid dress.

"Smashing, Tillie. We've been cooped up or underground I should say, for too long."

Maggie wrapped a pale-yellow kerchief over her hair. It matched the sunny cotton dress with white collar and cuffs she had just put on.

They ran down the stairs. It was a warm April day and the twins couldn't help feeling upbeat. Who couldn't, with the light spring breeze, early daffodils and magnolias weaving desperately needed color in between the grey, grim rubble? They were young, healthy and resilient.

In their matching white coats, the twins drew the usual stares and double takes. Tillie blissfully ignored them, but Maggie was always uncomfortable being the subject of unwanted attention.

"It's been so long since we've had twin time, darling. Tell me everything that's going on." Tillie smiled at her sister.

Maggie laughed.

"Not much is going on, Tillie. WVS work, fire watching, standing in queues at the shops, living halfway underground all night, having nightmares about getting blown up. Same as everyone in London." She shrugged.

"Oh darling. I know. It's been so hard. It must be so difficult serving in bomb zones. Are you getting so sick of pouring tea and handing out buns?"

"No, the men are ever so grateful. When we arrive, they are worn out – pulling people out of ruined houses, putting out huge fires, ambulance drivers like you. It makes me feel useful to do my bit. It just doesn't seem like much compared to what these brave rescue workers are doing." Maggie looked down.

Tillie stopped and grabbed her sister's arm.

"Rubbish, Maggie. You are doing incredibly hard work under dangerous circumstances. Those men and women need the service you are providing. It's vital to the war effort."

"I suppose you're right. I just think I could do more, Tils."

They continued walking.

"Like what? There's no more hours in the day, love," Tillie asked.

"I was thinking perhaps of joining a branch of the service – maybe the WRENS or the ATS?" Maggie stuttered a little. She looked up with liquid brown eyes at her sister. "Do you think Kenny is still alive, Tillie?"

"Absolutely yes," Tillie replied firmly. "You remember what Trevor found out? The *HMS Dainty* patrolled the North African waters in December and January. They were attacked by German fighters and dive-bombers. The ship was hit by a large bomb, which passed through the captain's quarters and ignited the fuel tanks, setting the ship ablaze. How horrible." Tillie recounted.

"There were sixteen crew killed, right? And a number injured? You're convinced that Kenny was one of the wounded?" Maggie asked.

"Yes," said Tillie impatiently. "You have to believe, Maggie. We all do. Kenny is an excellent swimmer. His instincts are amazing. Do you remember the time he ran onto the street and pulled that child on the bicycle away from the tram coming? He knows how to survive, Mags."

Maggie sniffled a little.

"I miss him so, Tillie. Our family isn't the same without him."

"You miss that jokey, rambunctious scoundrel? He was always weaseling out of his chores, remember? And the way he left the bathroom? Disgusting."

Maggie wiped her eyes and punched her sister in the arm.

"Stop trying to joke me out of this, Tillie. I really miss him."

"I do, too, love – so much. That's why I am certain he's still alive.

I would just feel it if he were dead – like Colin. Trust me. Let's promise each other not to give up. Please."

"Alright, Tillie. I promise."

"Now what's this about the Women's Auxiliary Territorial Service or Women's Naval Service? You just tucked that in rather quickly."

"I know the WVS counts as a war occupation, but maybe I could do more – perhaps as a cook? Maybe I'd be posted to France?" Maggie sounded a little unsure.

"Aha. That's it. You want to find Micah in the south of France?" Tillie pounced on the idea.

"I suppose I'm rather down with not knowing what's really going on with him. His letters are vague – I know he doesn't want to frighten me. But it's not good for Jewish people with the Germans overtaking France. I hear stories from refugees at the canteen sometimes. It's harsh for them. Abused on the streets, told they can only shop at certain places. Where will it end? Surely I can help in some way?"

"I don't know, Maggie. You got a letter from him yesterday. What did he say?"

"I live for his letters, Tils. I really do. Each one is proof that he is still alive. He hates working on the farm. He's a gentle soul but loyal to the core."

"How is the grandfather?" Tillie asked, as they slowed to a gentle stroll.

"Failing. I don't know how much longer he can hang on."

"What will happen when he passes? Is it awful of me to ask?"

"No, of course not, darling. I think of it too. I'm not quite sure, but I think Micah wants to escape back to England."

Tillie gasped.

"But is it safe, darling? How can they possibly come home?"

"I'm not sure of his plan yet," Maggie said, her breath coming a little faster. "I understand boats leave from the coast all the time. Many turn back, some are…some are attacked."

Tillie turned and hugged her sister tightly.

"Why didn't you tell me, you ninny? I'm here for you. To listen to you always." She let go and looked deep into her twin's troubled eyes. "What happens next?"

"I don't know," Maggie wiped her eyes. "Like everything else with this bloody war, we wait. We bide our time, we keep busy, and we just keep on waiting. And hoping."

"Is there nothing that the British Embassy can do? Aren't they English citizens?"

"Only Micah and his sister," Maggie replied miserably. "His parents were born in France. Hannah could probably be sent back here. But how could she come safely on her own? I don't see how any of them could be evacuated."

"Let's talk to Uncle Thomas about this. Surely, with his contacts in the government, something could be done? Even to help Hannah get here. Micah, I don't know if he would leave his parents, but Hannah is a young girl. She belongs here. I'm certain Mum and Pops would take her in."

Tillie saw a glimmer of hope on her sister's face.

"It can't hurt to be sure. Thanks sis."

Tillie hooked her arm through her twin's.

"Let's have no more talk of you joining up with the women's services. You'll talk to me before you doing anything foolish like Kenny and signing on in haste?"

Maggie nodded and sighed.

"Good. That's sorted. How about an ice cream on the way home? I can tell you all about my dishy fireman."

Maggie giggled. It was a small one, but a giggle nonetheless.

"Let's get on, then. Your treat, Tils."

* * *

It was ten past four in the morning when the explosion sounded. Only Alice, Shirley, and Katie were in the Anderson shelter behind the Kingstons' home. The men were out on ARP duty and the twins were on night shift. The women in the shelter had heard continuous waves of aeroplanes buzzing overhead since nine p.m. They could hear the ack-ack guns blasting all night long. The Anderson shuddered from time to time with the force of explosives raining down what seemed like next door. Whistles, whooshes, cracks, crashes, and splinters sounded from all directions.

Inside the shelter, the women pretended to be brave, which meant they were. Early spring rainstorms had seeped into the shelter, creating a small pool of water making the small, dark shed damp and chilly. The women crowded together, feet off the floor, knitting and chattering. Katie tried to sleep, knowing that morning and her early WVS shift would come in no time. The tea flask was long since empty.

"Jerry sounds like he's dropping every bomb ever made in every German factory on London tonight," Shirley complained bitterly.

"I'm afraid of what we'll see when the all-clear sounds," Alice said fearfully, clutching one of her sister's icy hands.

When the ear-splitting explosion came, all three women jumped in fright. They closed their eyes, expecting the Anderson to lift up in the air, burst into flame, and kill them all.

Katie was the first to open her eyes. Like the others, she was shocked to find she was still alive.

"Are we still here?" Alice whispered. "That sounded like a direct hit." Incredibly, the shelter was still standing. Another crash hit the side of the shelter, making them all flinch.

"I was sure we were struck," Shirley added. "Whatever could that have been?"

"We'll have to wait to find out. We can't chance leaving the shelter whilst the air raid is still in effect. Not with that racket going on," Katie said grimly as the whistles and booms continued unabated.

"I can smell smoke and cordite. I can hear flames crackling and burning. What if the house is on fire? It could catch us up too." Shirley was petrified.

"I thought I heard glass crashing. Whatever is happening out there?"

The sound of approaching bells signaled a fire crew was getting near which was terrifying and reassuring at the same time. Whose house was on fire?

The barrage continued its relentless assault until the all-clear rang out at five a.m. The women trudged through the freezing water and wrenched the door open. One by one, they cautiously stepped out and up the dirt wall to level ground. And gaped at the back of the house, barely seen in the eerie in-between of night and day.

"It's still standing, thank goodness," Alice uttered with relief. Katie propped her up on her good side, the other still in a plaster cast.

"But the windows. Look, Alice. All the windows and doors are blown off! There's glass everywhere. Look, I can just about make out the hanging light in the library from here." Shirley pointed at the first floor. Some of the window frames still hung brokenly and tape remnants fluttered dejectedly in the early morning breeze. The back door had blown all the way to the back of the garden.

"That's what must have hit the Andy – the back door as it flew to the back," Katie said. "Bloody hell."

Alice shrieked as the morning light brightened enough to show the damage to the other houses in the block. Like a macabre game of checkers, every other townhouse stood, whilst the alternate ones were on fire or demolished into a massive pile of bricks and glass.

The next sound they heard was wailing, as weary neighbors crawled out from shelters to discover their homes were destroyed or seriously damaged.

Mrs. Stonebridge from Number 46 dropped to her knees, and was crawling through three-foot high piles of bricks, wood, and glass fragments for any belongings that hadn't burned or blown up. Her husband rushed to her side, pulling her up with her knees already scraped and bloody.

The Kingston women stepped warily from the back of the house to the front, wary of what they might find, or not find. Holding hands, they slipped a few times on the wet rubble, but made it safely to the street.

Alice gulped as she surveyed her home of almost twenty years. The roof held and the structure seemed to be sound. As in the back, all the windows had blown out, and the front door was nowhere to be seen. It looked as if some of the furniture on the main floor was damaged, but still there. Her house was pretty much intact. She stifled a sob, knowing they were the lucky ones.

City workers had already started to arrive.

"Is this yer 'ouse, ma'am?" asked a burly, heavy rescue worker with red cheeks and a dark red beard.

"Yes, it is. Oh my God, yes, it is," she replied swiftly.

"Any chance of anyone trapped inside? I'll go and 'ave a look."

"No, I don't think so," Alice replied. "Everyone else is on duty."

"Good show. It ain't safe to go in yet. I know yer wanting to see ter yer things, love, but yer has to wait till the engineers give it a safe pass. Fer now, yer can guard it from looting. Any men comin soon?"

"Yes," answered Shirley for both of them. "Our husbands should be home from ARP duties any moment."

"Good. Once yer get the ok, yer'll have a busy day of cleanin. That dust goes everywhere." He tipped his hat and moved on to the next house.

Trucks appeared, driving slowly down the littered street. The men began to remove bricks and rubbish. It would take a few hours but the street would be mostly cleared before the next dreaded sound of Moaning Minnie cut through the evening ahead.

"Mum, Aunt Shirley, Katie. Are you alright?" Maggie ran as fast as she could to the women standing in front of the house. She hugged them all, and gaped at her lifelong home.

"We're fine, dear. In shock, but look – our house is still standing. It looks like just the windows and doors. It could have been so much worse." They all looked around at their neighbors – some crying, some standing frozen, others angry. All of them began the painful process of looking through rough and sharp brick heaps, trying to locate any personal belongings.

An ambulance made its way slowly down the street and as it stopped, a driver and attendant rushed into the building with a stretcher. They returned minutes later with a body covered in a blanket.

"Oh no, Mr. Milner," Alice cried as her hand flew to her mouth. "He lost his wife last year in an air raid explosion. Since then, he's refused to go into his shelter at night. He said he's just been waiting for his turn. Oh no, I can't believe it." She watched him being quietly placed in the ambulance and driven away.

Tillie and Walter arrived together and were reunited with the rest of the family. Thomas joined them soon after and Shirley broke down in his arms.

A mobile WVS canteen van rumbled down the street and parked in front of Number 40. The driver beeped the horn and two WVS women in green emerged, and efficiently opened the side window and started serving the small line that had already started forming.

"Maggie, are yer and yer family alright, then?" Trudy called. "We knew yer lived in Earl's Court, but didn't know this here were yer place. It's yer turn to be served. Fancy a cuppa?"

"Trudy, I am so glad to see you. Is that you, May?" Maggie hugged her work chums. "What a huge relief."

Exhausted from tense nights in the shelter or on duty, followed by discovering the devastation of their homes, left the residents of Longridge Road confused and near collapse. A cup of tea and a biscuit or sandwich restored a small sense of the ordinary to a grotesque situation.

Tillie insisted on examining everyone in the Kingston family, and was relieved to find no physical injuries.

No one got any sleep that day. Once the engineers had given the all clear for the Kingstons to safely enter their home, the family worked all day to clear the smashed window shards from the inside of house. Dust was everywhere so the women wrapped kerchiefs on their heads and cleaned from top to bottom once the repairs to the water system were completed. The men inspected the furniture and repositioned pieces that had been flung everywhere and broken items were collected for later repair. Trevor came by after his shift, rolled up his sleeves, and got to work nailing wooden boards on as many windows as possible, particularly at street level, to discourage theft.

"Mum, look at this," Tillie cried pointing at a dining room chair embedded upside down into the wall by the doorway.

"Bloody hell," Katie murmured. They found other oddities throughout the day. How the coatrack from the front hall had made its way downstairs to land underneath the wash table in the pantry was a mystery to all of them.

Stopping only for brief meals, the team worked all day. By nightfall, the house was reasonably habitable and the Kingstons turned to help their neighbors. Mr. and Mrs. Ogilvy from next door had spent most of the day at a rest center, registering their new identity and ration cards.

Walter had offered them a bed as long as needed, which was gratefully accepted.

They found out later that the attack had been one of the fiercest of the Blitz so far. Over five hundred bombers flew over London, dropping about four hundred tons of explosives, killing over a thousand people, and leaving widespread destruction and ruin.

CHAPTER TWENTY-NINE

"Who's for fish and chips, then?" Maggie offered the next day. With a pale face and blue-grey smudges under her hollow eyes, she was the emblem of the Kingston family fatigue.

"Sounds about right, Maggie. I'll go with you," Katie offered, a shadow of her bouncy self.

"I'd say no but I'm afraid I'll fall over or not find my way home, so I'll gladly take the help, sis," Maggie managed a ghost of a smile.

There had been little sleep in the Kingston house. The house was cleaned up, at least the first round, as the dust was settling again and would need to be mopped a few more times, and the windows and doors boarded temporarily.

"At least we don't have to bother about the blackout," Tillie had joked half-heartedly last night. No one had laughed.

The house was very dark and gloomy. It would be weeks before replacement glass could be ordered and the windows replaced. Most of London desperately needed building materials which were in short supply, as they were needed for war production. Trevor had retrieved the back door from the garden and re-attached it. He'd also located the front door, two streets away, and with his carpentry skills easily mounted it so that it looked almost as good as new, with a few dents and scrapes, of course.

Mr. and Mrs. Ogilvy made arrangements to stay with their daughter in Basingstoke and were about to take the train later today.

After the cleanup, they all departed to their assorted night shifts. After another night of air attacks and shelling, they stumbled home and dropped into their beds, snatching a few prized hours of sleep.

It was now dinnertime and no one had the energy to cook, nor was there much food in the house. Someone would have to stand in line tomorrow for the weekly rations. But that was tomorrow. Today was about survival, putting one foot in front of the other, and getting through the day.

"Extra chips for me, please, ducks," Tillie asked, slumped in a chair in the dark drawing room. "I'm floating on tea, and need something solid in my stomach."

A short while later, Maggie and Katie returned with newspaper-wrapped bundles. The family devoured the tasty fried fish and chips in silence.

"I'm proud of each and every one of you," Walter spoke softly as he gazed around the table at his bone-weary family. "These times are more trying than we could ever have imagined and you have all risen to the challenge. Your spirit is unbeatable and I know that no matter how long this may last, we can carry on. We are all fighting this war against Hitler and his evil. He won't breach our shores with the Kingston family defending Britain," he beamed.

"Thanks, Pops," Tillie spoke up first. "The alternative doesn't bear thinking about, does it?" She popped a vinegar-laden chip into her mouth.

"Quite right, Tillie. And it seems the fitting moment to thank you properly for taking us in after our own home was destroyed," Thomas glanced at his wife and gave her a reassuring smile. "You have been a godsend for us."

"We are more than grateful," Shirley echoed. "And you've been such a comfort to us – all of you," she sniffled.

"Now, Shirley, no tears," Thomas admonished. "We must stay strong." She nodded.

"I spoke to Mr. Sharpton this morning at Number 12. His house is largely intact but his wife doesn't want to spend another night in the shelter. She's rather disheartened and just can't take it. They are going to her brother in Wales who has been urging them to come, and this has just brought it to a head. He's going to stay in London for a few weeks to settle his job before taking up a new life in the country." Thomas paused. "I've fixed it up with him. We'll let the house with furniture until such time as they come back. Or if they sell up, they'll give us first right of refusal."

"Oh, that's wonderful," Katie clapped. "And you'll be just down the street. Marvelous. I'll miss your cooking, though, Aunt Shirley," she added with a twinkle in her brown eyes.

"I am relieved to stay so close," Shirley replied. "Maybe we can even share a supper or two, Katie. I find I still want to be close to my sister." She and Alice exchanged warm smiles.

"That's sorted, then," Walter replied, satisfied. "And you're to stay here until Number 12 is ready, no rush whatsoever for you to leave."

"Thank you again, Walter. We won't forget this."

"Uncle Thomas, whilst you're here, may I ask you a question about refugees?" Maggie turned to her uncle.

"My, that's a turnabout in the conversation," Katie laughed. "Whatever are you on about?"

"I received a letter from Micah," Maggie began slowly. "His grandfather has died. In his sleep, thank goodness, so he didn't suffer."

A chorus of compassion greeted the news.

"I'm so sorry, Maggie. How awful for Micah and his family," Alice spoke for them all.

"Thank you. They are grieving but also relieved that the grandfather is out of pain and not having to deal with the everyday hardships."

"How can I help, Maggie?" Thomas asked seriously.

"It's Hannah, Micah's sister. Both of them were born in England but the parents are French, so they are not allowed to leave the country under the German occupation in the north. Micah won't leave his parents but surely there is a way to evacuate Hannah back to London?"

"So, let me understand this," Thomas took it all on board. "She's English, but her parents are French. How old is she now?"

"She's eleven. Very smart. I don't know her well, but indeed, she belongs here."

"I'm not sure what can be done, Maggie, but I'll make inquiries. There are really two essentials here – one is finding safe transport for her across the Channel, which is no small task. The second is a home for her in England. Does she have any other family here?"

"No. She has no one here," admitted Maggie slowly.

"We were hoping she could stay with us," Tillie interjected quickly. "We have space, and how could we not take her in? It's very dangerous in France."

"By all means, she's welcome in our home," Alice spoke without even thinking. "We've known the Goldbachs for years. They are like family to us." She belated turned to her husband, who swiftly nodded.

"I told you it would be alright," Tillie grinned.

"Thank you so much – both of you," Maggie turned to her uncle.

"And thank you for anything you can find out to help Hannah."

"I can't promise anything but I'll see what I can do. Are all her documents in order?" Thomas asked.

"As far as I know," Maggie replied.

"Good enough, then. It will take some time," he warned. "It's rather a shambles getting communications between the two countries. So, it won't be overnight."

"I understand. Whatever you can do, we're grateful – Micah, his parents, and me."

"Is it serious, then, with your young man?" Thomas asked curiously.

Maggie blanched a bit, then cleared her throat.

"He's not my young man, leastways not officially," she smiled awkwardly. This line of questioning made her uncomfortable. "But I do care for him and I hope we can make something of it after the war. It's distressing thinking of what he and his family are going through." She held the packet of chips aloft. "Anyone for more? You lot have fair devoured most of the fish."

"Anything about for pudding?" asked Katie hopefully, tacitly changing the subject on Maggie's behalf.

"Not much, I'm afraid. Some stale bickies, and half of a bread pudding but I fear it's on the dodgy side."

"I'll have whatever's going and be grateful for it, dear," chimed in Walter. He had to have his.

"None for me, ta," said Tillie, as she stood up. "I'm meant to call in at Mr. and Mrs. Redwood's. I haven't seen them for a piece, and I want to make sure their house is alright before my ambulance shift. Thanks for dinner. It was just what I needed."

"Goodbye, love, and give our regards to Colin's parents. See you early tomorrow morning. And be careful."

Tillie couldn't get used to seeing the destruction on Longridge Road. Neighbors continued to comb through debris, and repair whatever they could of their broken homes.

As she exited from the underground, her heart started racing. She was overdue calling on her late fiancé's parents and felt guilty about it. The truth was she'd been avoiding it. They had little to talk about so conversation was stilted, and she didn't quite know how to tell them, or should, about Trevor. Would they think she was disloyal to their dead son? Rushing too fast? Dishonoring Colin's memory? Still, she had to face them. She knew they missed her and her link to their lost son.

She turned the corner to their street, and let out a sigh of relief to see their house sitting there in the bright sun unharmed. Pasting a smile on her face, she rang the doorbell. Mrs. Redwood answered almost immediately.

"Tillie. How wonderful to see you. Please come through," Mrs. Redwood kissed her on the cheek. Mr. Redwood shuffled in from the hall and did the same. They seemed pathetically happy to see her, which made Tillie's heart sink even further.

"I'm sorry I couldn't come last week as I'd planned. Our house was bombed." Mrs. Redwood gasped, and Tillie held up a hand. "It's alright, the house wasn't ruined but all the windows and doors were blown out and it's been a jolly mess to clean up. But we are all safe and grateful. Some of our neighbors weren't so lucky."

"Oh my, you poor dear. Your mother must be beside herself. What a dreadful experience to go through. Who could have imagined what our battered London has endured? And it's far from over, isn't it?"

They spent the next few minutes discussing the latest war news, how Tillie was getting on with her job, and updates on both families. Tillie sipped her tea and looked around the familiar sitting room with sadness.

"How are you coping, then?" She asked Colin's parents finally. "I can feel Colin's presence in this room, this house."

"We miss him every day," Mrs. Redwood answered instantly. "It's hard to go on some days but needs must." The light had gone out of her eyes and Tillie hoped it would someday return. Mr. Redwood had new lines on his forehead and around his mouth that reminded her so achingly of Colin's.

"I miss him too," she replied simply.

"I see you're not wearing his engagement ring any longer," said Mrs. Redwood calmly. Tillie's gaze immediately dropped to her left hand. She looked up guiltily.

"It's alright, dear. You're young. I know how much you loved our son. And how much he adored you." Her voice broke but she regained her composure. "But you must live your life – especially now when each day is so fragile, like the shards of glass littering our beautiful London. Colin wouldn't want you to watch your life go by, but to live it to the fullest."

Tillie's eyes filled with tears.

"That means the world to me, Mrs. Redwood. I loved your son very much. And I have so much regret for the life together that was taken from us. Being totally honest with you both, I am seeing someone. I don't know where it's going yet but he's a wonderful man. Please don't be too disappointed in me," Tillie caught herself. That was the old Tillie. She had done nothing wrong or betrayed Colin. She deserved happiness. She sat up a little straighter.

Mrs. Redwood patted her hand.

"I'm not disappointed at all, love. Neither of us is. Even though you never married Colin, we still consider you a daughter-in-law, a daughter even. We support you moving on. You need have no fear on that score."

"Thank you both. I'll always feel close to you. I hope I can still come to see you from time to time."

"Of course, Tillie. Albeit we are considering moving from London. There doesn't seem to be anything left for us anymore. We can make a fresh start in a smaller town. We have decided nothing yet but we'll certainly let you know if we resolve to go."

There wasn't much more to say after this. Tillie said her goodbyes, and left the Redwood's house feeling sad but peaceful, lighter than she had in weeks.

As she walked up to the ambulance station, she saw Trevor leaning tiredly against the door. She hurried to greet him with a hug and quick kiss.

"Is everything alright, Trevor? You look like death warmed over." And he did. He had just finished a day shift, as Tillie was about to start her evening's duties. He was covered in soot and dirt, and his hair was wet. Grey with weariness, he didn't flash his typical charming smile.

"We lost three men last night, Tillie. Three hardworking, splendid chaps. I was proud to work alongside them. One of them, Fred was a good mate. We signed on at the same time. His wife is expecting a baby in just a few weeks."

He ran a hand through his hair and hugged her tightly.

"Do you have time for a cuppa before your shift?"

Tillie didn't hesitate.

"Absolutely, although I think you need something stronger. There's a pub around the corner. Let's brace you up with a whiskey if we can find one." She took his arm and marched him into the nearest pub.

They were in luck, there was whiskey. Trevor took a big gulp whilst Tillie sipped on her lemonade.

"Tell me everything, Trev. Start at the beginning," she held his gaze with sympathetic big brown eyes.

"We were called out to help with a huge bank of fires near Piccadilly Circus. It was rows of office buildings facing each other. A bank of fire and smoke. A full shift of three fire brigades hadn't been able to control the raging flames. It was such a visible target for the Germans that they just kept hitting us again and again. Incendiaries, high explosives, and parachute bombs just kept crashing and setting off more fires." He stopped and took another deep swallow. He was getting some color back in his cheeks for which Tillie was grateful. She'd never seen him so shaken in all the time she'd known him.

"There was a large building – I think it was a factory built before the first war. From what I could see, there were four floors, each with a row of a dozen symmetrical windows. They were arched. It was a beautiful building." He stopped and looked down at his drink.

"I was on the street on hose duty with two other blokes. It was tough going – the bloody Hun have figured the ebbs and flows of the Thames – they prey upon us when the tides are low so once the water mains burst on any given night, our supply from the river is compromised. The bloody bastards. Our water reserve just wasn't cutting it. Suddenly, we heard a scream. We couldn't believe someone was still trapped inside. I reckon the woman had lost consciousness whilst the other rescues were going on, and came to in the middle of a frightening inferno. Fred and another chap, Edmund were nearest so they ran in to find her. The building started to sway and we heard some cracking noises. I was relieved to see Fred come through one of the archways carrying a young woman. At that exact moment, the whole facade of the building fell forward almost in one piece. It was like a child's tower Tillie, knocked over by some giant hand."

"Oh Trev, how awful." She placed a hand on his. To her surprise, his hand was shaking.

"The way it fell forward, it looked for a moment as if Fred and the woman were okay – they were framed in the archway and I thought it had collapsed around them. But after the billows of smoke cleared slightly, we could see that it had crushed them both. Not only them but two other firemen just in front of me. If I'm honest Tils, it barely missed me."

And it had. As soon as Trevor had seen it start to fall, he and his mate had instinctively retreated and narrowly missed being buried under the wall.

"Darling, no," Tillie couldn't help crying out. The patrons at the next table stared but the couple ignored them.

"We spent the next hour digging them out hoping against hope that any of them would still be alive. But they weren't. We lost them all. We lost them all, Tillie." he put his head in his hands, and tried desperately to control himself.

"Why, Tillie? Why them and not me? Why was Fred's number called?"

"Trevor, stop. You and I both know there is no rhyme or reason why some people are killed, and others aren't. How many times have we seen with our own eyes one man get blown up whilst the person next to him walks away unscathed? It's not predictable, and it's no one's fault. Except Hitler's," she finished bitterly.

"He told me on break how he's hoping for a son. Fred Junior, he wanted to call him. Now Nancy will have to raise him on her own. I'm going to be the one that has to tell her. He was such a decent lad."

"I'll go with you, if you like, Trev," she offered quietly.

He nodded, finished his whiskey in one gulp, and stared out the window.

There was no way to make sense of it. None whatsoever.

CHAPTER THIRTY

May 1941

"Do you think it's really over, Pops?" Maggie asked.

"I fervently hope so, love. The last big air attacks were May 10th and 11th. We haven't had an alarm or a night strike since. That's a fortnight now."

"But what an attack that was. The worst yet. How many hundreds of planes? Over five hundred. As usual, the papers were vague about the damage but Thomas told me near a thousand bombs were dropped. The casualties numbered fifteen hundred. Do you know that 11,000 more homes were destroyed, love? How many lives ruined or shattered?" Walter had seen enough death and destruction to last him a lifetime. Ten lifetimes.

Maggie shook her head. It had been a terrifying night at the mobile canteen. She blotted out some of the horrors she'd seen, like she did most nights. Please let the Blitz be over.

"And there was heavy damage done to The House of Commons, Westminster Abbey, and even the British Museum. Our city's important landmarks are being ravaged one by one, Pops." Maggie's tone was glum.

Walter and Maggie sat in the dim morning room. Though the May sun was shining it was dark inside. The new windows had been ordered but would take weeks or months to arrive. Everyone else in the family was out so it was a rare quiet time.

"Maggie, I know everything looks bleak right now. We don't know when the war will end. Rationing will carry on and that's hard for everyone."

"And now cheese is on the ration. So many of our simple pleasures are gone for us. What will be next? That's the worst part, Pops. This just going on and on with no end in sight."

"I understand, love. I won't try to cheer you up with a pep talk. Sometimes we just need to wallow and feel wretched for a while. But let's also take heart that it seems Hitler has called off the lightning strike – at least for now – so that he can move the Luftwaffe towards his next target – Russia."

Maggie started laughing. A giggle that turned into a chuckle and all of a sudden, she was clutching her belly as laughter rumbled out of her.

"What's so funny, Mags? Are you alright?" Walter eyed his almost-hysterical daughter with concern.

"You just said it was alright to feel wretched. In the next breath, you're telling me to look at the bright side. You're just too much, Pops." Maggie wiped the tears from her eyes.

A smile spread across her father's face.

"Well, if I got you to laugh like that, I suppose I don't mind the means."

They both giggled as Maggie turned up the heat under the gas ring for tea.

* * *

"Well, that's sorted for today. The queues seem to go faster when you have someone to natter with." Alice smiled at her sister.

"Too right, love. And Thomas will be right chuffed that we're not having spam again for our supper tonight."

The sisters walked arm in arm and stopped at the rented house.

"Do you fancy stopping for a cuppa? You don't need to rush off home yet, do you?"

"I'd love to, Shirley. It's a treat not to live with the nightly attacks, at least for now. I pray that's over. How are you getting on in the new place?"

The women climbed the stairs, took off their coats, and entered the downstairs kitchen with their shopping baskets.

Thomas and Shirley had moved into the rented home a week ago and were settling in. The sisters still loved being close to each other.

"We love it. Not that we didn't appreciate being at yours," Shirley grinned. "But a woman likes a kitchen of her own and a place for all her bits and bobs, doesn't she?"

The two settled into the sunny kitchen for a good long chat, with no imminent rush for the shelter.

* * *

The family slowly gathered around the wireless for their renewed routine of the six o'clock news. Alice was happy to see her family looking slightly better after the long Blitz ordeal. Thinner – well, rations will do that to you – but otherwise healthy.

"This is London. Tonight, we are broadcasting live from 10 Downing Street. Prime Minister Winston Churchill."

"These cruel, wanton indiscriminate bombings of London are, of course, a part of Hitler's invasion plan. He hopes by killing large numbers of civilians, and women and children, that he will terrorize and cow the people of this mighty imperial city...and thus distract our attention unduly from the ferocious onslaught he is preparing. Little does he know the spirit of the British nation, or the tough fiber of the Londoners...have been bred to value freedom far above their lives.

This wicked man, the repository and embodiment of many forms of soul-destroying hatreds... has now resolved to try to break our famous island race by a process of indiscriminate slaughter and destruction...

He has lighted a fire, which will burn with a steady and consuming flame until the last vestiges of Nazi Germany have been burnt out of Europe...

This is a time for everyone to stand together and hold firm as they are doing. I express my admiration for the exemplary manner in which all the ARP services of London are being discharged, especially the fire brigades, whose work has been so heavy and also dangerous.

All the world that is still free marvels at the composure and fortitude with which the citizens of London are facing and surmounting the great ordeal to which they are subjected, the end of which or the severity of which cannot be foreseen.

It is a message of good cheer to our fighting forces on the seas, in the air, and in our waiting armies in all their posts and stations, that we send them from this capital city. They know that they have behind them a people who will not flinch or weary of the struggle hard and protracted though it will be, but that we shall rather draw from the suffering itself – the means of inspiration and survival."

Walter switched off the wireless and looked at his family around him. They had all suffered so much and yet continued to persevere. They were thinking of those lost or in parts unknown – Geoffrey, Colin, Micah, and Kenny, and of the uncertainty still ahead.

"That was moving, wasn't it?" asked Tillie. "His speeches are always so rousing."

"It does make one feel patriotic. And like we can carry on despite the trials and tribulations," agreed Maggie.

"What choice do we have?" Katie asked.

"After all...," Tillie started.

"There's a war on," Katie and Maggie said in unison with their sister. They all laughed.

"Too right, love," answered Alice. They had all become rather fatalistic over the last eighteen months. "Who is home for supper?"

"Not me," replied Tillie promptly. "Trev is taking me to a posh restaurant – to make up for our doomed *Café de Paris* dinner and dancing evening. Mags, can you help me get ready?"

"Brilliant, Tils. Mum, I'll be back to help with the supper." Maggie and Tillie jumped up, on to the next thing.

"Katie will help me," Alice offered her other daughter without asking. "It won't take much to put marrow pie on the table tonight. Soon enough, Walter, you'll be bringing me some spring veg from the allotment." Alice smiled. They were all anxious for normalcy to resume.

Tillie was eagerly looking forward to her date with Trevor tonight. He'd been down after losing his mate, Fred, but had since bounced back to his cheerful self. Almost but not quite. These war traumas left scars on everyone's hearts.

"It's May, but there still might be a chill in the air tonight. Do you think the burgundy will be too cold?" Tillie asked her twin.

"No, you must wear it. It looks so fetching on you. A little daring perhaps but you can carry it off."

Tillie put on her dress. It was satin with a tight bodice and sweetheart neckline. Black lace straps matched a black lace bow across the breast and trimmed the bottom. The gown fell in waves down to below her knees. It fit her like a glove, and accentuated her small waist and creamy skin.

"Do you think you could help me put my hair into a victory roll? It's the latest style."

Maggie helped her sister comb her hair back and pin it up on top of her head. The rest of her blonde curls fell softly.

"Nice work, sis. I hope I can make this lipstick last." Tillie put on a little over her lips.

The doorbell rang.

"Blimey, Trevor is always on time. Where's my camel coat and hat?" Tillie rushed around, collecting her bits and pieces for the night ahead.

As she left the twins' bedroom, Maggie put out a hand to stop her.

"Have a smashing time, Tils. You deserve it. Trevor is a fine young man. Open your heart to him." She smiled.

"You're tops, Maggie. I plan on having a brilliant time." And with a whiff of perfume, she was out of the room. In no time Trevor had picked her up and they entered the stylish *Goring Hotel* in Belgravia.

A maître d' took Tillie and Trevor's coats and showed them to a corner table in the Dining Room.

"Trevor, this is ever so posh," Tillie stared around in wonder. "It's beautiful."

"You are beautiful, Tillie. I'm the luckiest man in the room to have you on my arm." Trevor admired his stunning date.

"Oh my, you'll make me blush, Trev." And sure enough, a telltale red flush crept up her neck, matching her dress. "But thank you. I am lucky too. Every woman in the room is admiring my handsome firefighter," she teased with a broad smile.

And he was gorgeous. In a dark grey wool suit with a pristine white shirt and grey and navy striped tie, his shoulders were broad. His black hair shone and his blue eyes twinkled. As always, his devilish smile and dimple made her shiver.

"Shall we start with caviar? They are famous for it here."

"Trevor, so extravagant. Aren't they fish eggs? I wonder if I shall like it?"

"Let's do give it a try. I need to make up for our botched evening of dinner and dancing. I can't promise you any dancing tonight, but I want it to be special – a night to remember."

"Trevor, that wasn't your fault. *Café de Paris* was bombed. What a horrible tragedy. Like so many – on every street corner in London."

"Tillie, stop. We can be grey and gloomy every day. Tonight, let's celebrate."

A waiter appeared.

"Champagne please and caviar," he ordered with authority.

The waiter bowed.

"Very good, sir."

The evening passed in a dream. Music played in the background and the room hummed with conversation. Delicious smells filled the air and the food was heavenly.

"I'm not sure I loved the caviar Trev, but the dover sole was so tender. How did they ever produce such a sauce on the ration? And the soup. Everything tastes so airy and delightful. Not like the stodgy meals we have at home."

"I'm sure your mother does her best, Tillie," Trev defended Alice. "It's hard for all of us."

"I know. I couldn't eat like this every day, in the event. It wouldn't be good for the digestion." She took a sip of her champagne. "This I love, Trev. Although I think the bubbles are going to my head." Tillie giggled.

She was getting tipsy and glowed with happiness.

"Mathilda Kingston, I do believe you are flying a little high. But it suits you."

Tillie giggled then frowned.

"It feels somehow wrong to be having so much fun when there's so much death and destruction out there. I'm so conflicted, Trevor. On one hand, so many have lost so much. Yet, we're still here. We're young, we're healthy, and most importantly – we're alive." She waved her champagne glass in the air.

"And we're in love," Trev added quietly.

Tillie paused as she brought the glass to her lips.

"We are what?" She asked, confusion clouding her eyes.

"Well, I hope we are. I know I'm in love with you, Tillie. Your bravery, your kindness, your beauty, your spirit. I am more alive when I'm with you." Trevor beamed at her with a question in his eyes.

Tillie shook her head in disbelief. Trevor was in love with her. Her heart fluttered wildly, and her hands felt clammy.

"Really, Trevor?" She asked.

"Really," he replied fervently. He put his large hand over her small one. "Permanently, lustily, crazily in love with you."

A rush swept over Tillie as memories of Trevor flooded her mind. Meeting at the royal garden party, dinner with his mother at Lyons Corner House, walks in the park, rushing into a burning building to deliver Gloria's baby, his care and concern for his mum, their first kiss in the pouring rain, helping her family boarding up their blown-out windows, and so much more. Somehow, he had become a fixture in her life. Steady, reassuring, kind, never judging or pushing her, or finding her wanting. She gazed deeply into his cobalt blue eyes.

"I love you, too, Trev. I must have done for a while, but I just realized it. Or discovered it. Or something," she blabbered.

He reached across and kissed her in full view of the other patrons. Tillie felt the familiar hum and thrill of his lips on hers.

"Excuse-moi, monsieur. The dessert and café au lait?"

The waiter had returned bearing a silver tray with two coffees and crème brûlée.

"But we didn't order pudding, Trev," protested Tillie.

"I took the liberty of bringing something for you," the waiter smiled. "You seemed deep in thought."

Tillie sat back in her chair, basking in the glow of their shared love. Nothing could be wrong tonight.

She took a sip of her coffee.

"Oh, that's yummy, Trev. Real cream and sugar. Heaven." She crunched down on the hard topping of the brûlée and brought a spoonful to her mouth. "Oh my, that's brilliant. So light. I didn't think I could eat another bite, but here I am, practically licking the dish." She beamed at him, her smile a little crooked.

"Well, why don't we stretch our legs and walk it off darling? It's a beautiful night." Trevor polished off his own brûlée and sat back in the plush chair.

They leisurely finished their coffees and Trevor paid the check. He helped her with her coat and they strolled towards Lower Grosvenor Place.

"Trev, it is a lovely spring evening. We can finally take a breath without the nightly Blitz attacks. Could the war be over soon?" She furrowed her brow as Trevor took her arm.

He shook his head.

"I fear not, dear Tillie. Our boys still have a long road ahead. But we will beat Hitler. As Churchill said: 'We shall not fail or falter; we shall not weaken or tire.'"

They walked in silence, the May night enveloping them in a warm embrace.

"Trevor, look – Buckingham Palace. I wonder if the King and Queen are at home. Do you think Her Majesty remembers us?" Tillie skipped along the famous black and gold gates, peering into the

courtyard as the evening turned to dusk.

"Tillie, this is where we first met." Trevor's voice was suddenly serious.

She spun around to face him and clapped her hands.

"Yes. At the garden party. Oh my, that was already two years ago. I thought you were proper handsome," she admitted shyly.

"And I thought you were a beauty – even covered in that horrid woman's blood," he smiled in the darkness. "I wanted to bring you back here where it all started. And to ask you something."

Trevor reached into his pocket, and knelt down!

She gasped.

"My darling. These hard times just make me know that our time is now. We can't know the future. But I am certain of our love. Will you marry me, darling Tillie?"

Tillie looked at the sparkling ring and Trevor's smiling face looking up at her. She had no doubts, not one.

"Yes, Trev. I will. I will," she answered with assurance and joy.

He stood up, pulled her close, and placed the solitaire ring on her finger. He took her into his arms and kissed her deeply. A nearby cabbie whistled in approval. Tillie felt herself blushing.

"Trevor, you clever man. You planned this whole thing, didn't you? I never had a clue what you were up to."

She gazed at the lovely ring. She couldn't help thinking of Colin and the flower engagement diamond he'd given her. But that was then. As Trevor said, their time was now.

"This just felt like the right place for us to take the next step," he replied.

"Trevor, you've taken my breath away." Tillie tried to take it all in.

"I know I've sprung this on you, but I just couldn't wait any longer, darling. We don't need to get married straightaway – we can talk about that later. I just want to marry you."

"I do want to marry you, darling. I'm not sure when either, but I know we'll sort it together."

"Tils, this war is far from over. I mentioned before, but now that the Blitz is over, I must do my bit to save England. I know my work as a London firefighter is important, but young men are desperately needed in all branches of the military. Now that I know Mum is safe for now, and you and I have a future together, I'll be signing up." He looked serious, pleading for her support.

"I understand, Trevor. And please know that I'll always look after your mum if you're away. After all, she's going to be my mother-in-law, isn't she?'

Trevor beamed.

"I knew you'd understand, my love."

She hugged him and lifted her face for a passionate kiss.

"Let's go home and tell Maggie our big news. She's going to be my maid of honor, after all." Tillie glowed.

"Of course, darling. I'm ready when you are."

ACKNOWLEDGEMENTS

Writing about brave and courageous women in World War II England has always been a secret passion of mine. I have such admiration for the women who sent their husbands, fiancés, sons, and friends to fight in a deadly war against Hitler and the Nazis.

They did this while trying to cope with more work at home, taking care of children, rationing, huge shopping lines, taking on jobs to support their families, and so much more. Add the London Blitz and these brave females suffered nightly bombing and uncomfortable sheltering for seventy-two nights straight. Many of them accepted the call to action, and signed up for civil defense volunteer positions, factory work, and different branches of the military service. I believe each and every one of them was remarkable.

World War II resources are vast and honestly overwhelming at times. As always, I am determined to be as factually accurate as possible, while giving you a taste for a *day in the life* of these incredible women.

I'd like to acknowledge two wonderful people who provided a vast amount of help to me. First, Jeremy Clinch is a first-rate London cabby who is also a dear friend. He cheerfully helped me with so many details about London streets and regions, pictures of specific locations, and was a terrific fact-checker to keep me up on all details of English life.

Second, I was lucky to have the insights and fascinating stories of Roy Williamson, a Londoner who immigrated to Canada many decades ago. He was a child in WWII London, and helped shape Tillie's story with advice on the practical fine points of daily life, British terms, and overall common sense. I owe an enormous debt of gratitude to both amazing men!

It's impossible to name all the resources I researched to tell Tillie and Maggie's story, but here are the main ones I mined to make *The War Twins of London* as compellingly realistic as possible:

Broad, Richard and Fleming, Suzie. *Nella Last's War, The Second World WR Diaries of Housewife, 49.* Profile Books Limited, 2006.

Brown, Gordon. *Wartime Courage, Studies of Extraordinary Courage by Exceptional Men and Women in World War Two.* Bloomsbury Publishing, 2008.

Brown, Mike and Harris, Carol. *The Wartime House, Home Life in Wartime Britain 1939-1945.* The History Press, 2011.

Burrows, Deborah, *Ambulance Girls.* Ebury Press, 2016.

Burrows, Deborah, *Ambulance Girls At War.* Ebury Press, 2019.

Gray, Andrew & Timereel Studios. *London's War During WWII.* BFS, 2012. (DVD)

Harry, Lilian. *Corner House Girls.* Orion Books, 2001.

Jeffreys, Alan. *London at War, 1939-1945, A Nation's Capital Survives.* Imperial War Museum, 2018.

Knight, Katherine. *Spuds, Spam and Eating for Victory, Rationing in the Second World War.* The History Press, 2011.

Malcolmson, Patricia and Robert. *Women at the Ready, The Remarkable Story of the Women's Voluntary Services on the Home Front.* Abacus, 2013.

Miles, Constance. *Mrs. Miles's Diary, The Wartime Journal of a Housewife on the Home Front.* Simon & Schuster UK, 2013.

National Fire Services Anthology. *Fire and Water, The London Firefighters' Blitz 1940-42 Remembered.* Firestorm Publications, 1992 (original edition 1942).

Nicholson, Virginia. *Millions Like Us, Women's Lives During the Second World War.* Penguin Books, 2012.

Raby, Angela. *The Forgotten Service: Auxiliary Ambulance Station 39.* Battle of Britain International Limited, 1999.

Waller, Maureen. *A Family in Wartime, How the Second World War Shaped the Lives of a Generation.* Imperial War Museum, Conway, 2012.

Wynn, Stephen. *City of London at War, 1939-1945.* Pen & Sword Military, 2020.

I'm also grateful for all the online resources, videos, first-hand accounts, podcasts, and so much more at the Imperial War Museum and BBC archives. What amazing resources.

Printed in Great Britain
by Amazon

30883095R00158